LISA HELEN GRAY

MYLES

A CARTER BROTHERS SERIES: BOOK THREE

Donna Mansell
July 1983 – July 2010
When someone you love becomes a memory
The memory becomes a treasure.

R.I.P

CONTENTS

PROLOGUE

KAYLA

I grew up believing my life would be forever what it was: easy, straight forward. I lived a life that was incredibly dull and boring.

Nothing exciting ever happened to people like me.

I was also naïve. I walked through life thinking nothing bad could ever happen to me. My biggest challenge had always been my mum, but once I turned five and began attending an all-girls school in Dartmouth, I was safe from her.

That changed when Miss Niles, the woman who raised me, died of cancer. I was only thirteen, so I was sent back home to live with the woman I barely knew and didn't like all that much. I hated my time with her during the school holidays, but with Miss Niles visiting family, I didn't have a choice. I wasn't the only one who disliked it. My mother was never happy about my return either. But there was no way they could replace Miss Niles, which is why I made the decision to come home. My dad happily agreed with the choice.

Things got worse when my mum sent me to Grayson High as a punishment, instead of letting me go back to boarding school. My entire life changed that day, and it wasn't because I had moved back home, or lost the woman who was like a mother to me, or because I had to leave people I had come to care for behind.

From the very first day, my life became filled with anguish and misery. It was an endless nightmare.

It changed me.

I was bullied, torn apart, humiliated, and brutally victimised. It wasn't your average high school bullying; I'm talking about being cornered and beaten, stripped of my dignity, and left feeling afraid every night I went to sleep and again each morning I woke up.

I was in two nightmares. There were days when I dreaded going to school, but then there were others when it was safer to be there than at home.

Like people say, evil isn't just in those unknown around you; it can be in those who are the closest to you.

And the one day I was at my lowest, my day went from bad to worse. I was at a point where I had given up.

It was how *he* found me.

Craig Davis had been one of my worst tormentors. The lad thought he was untouchable. And back then, he was; at least to me.

He raped me. He dragged me into the forest near the back of my house, stripped me bare and beat me, before he used my body, performing the most heinous act.

I felt ashamed, scared, and dirty. I couldn't see a way out of the endless loop of a nightmare he had forced me into. I no longer saw colour in the flowers, or felt the warmth of laughter, nor the sadness in 'save the animals' adverts. I disconnected from the world and from myself. I no longer trusted those around me or had faith that things would get better.

The hurt from what was done to me, the pain I felt deep inside, consumed me. He marked me that day, and I couldn't erase it no matter what I tried.

I became a shell of the person I once was and started fearing my own shadow, even my father.

I had no one to protect me after he raped me. My own mother

didn't help me. So after leaving with my father, I thought I'd be able to escape my nightmare.

I was wrong.

For two and a half years, I lived an isolated life, letting no one in. I pushed away those who tried.

When my father said he was opening another office in Coldenshire, I was in two minds about what to do.

I didn't need to decide. When a friend of mine, Charlie, emailed me and informed me of what had happened with Craig Davis and another female, I knew I had to come back. I had to take a stand, just like she had done. I came clean about it all, leaving no detail out, including the part my mum played. The day he got sentenced, something inside of me healed. It clicked on a switch inside of me that I could no longer ignore.

My story isn't pretty, but it also isn't over. I still have demons to face, and a path to walk to find out who I am now.

I'm Kayla Martin, and this is my story.

CHAPTER
ONE

KAYLA

I glance up at the school that started the nightmare of my life. It's a place that holds so much pain for me, but it's something I have to face. It's another step towards healing.

After being home-schooled for so many years, it's going to be hard to adjust. My councillor and dad said it would be easier to finish my final year of sixth form here.

They were wrong.

It's my first day back at Grayson High, and I can't even move from the passenger seat of my dad's BMW. I've tried to find the courage, but each time, my fingers only gripped the door handle tighter, turning my knuckles white.

I close my eyes as a wave of nausea hits me. Will I have more abuse shouted at me when I walk down those halls? Will they call me the girl who cried wolf? Will I still be the liar, the whore, the bitch they once labelled me?

My dad's voice cuts through my thoughts, making me jump. "Darling, you're going to have to actually leave the car if you want to complete school."

I force a smile and steel my shoulders. If he knew how terrified I am about going, about my fears of what will be said, he might force me to stay home. And as much as that appeals to me, I know it isn't the right choice to make. I want to be normal again, to find who I am. And I can't do that isolated and alone.

"I know. Sorry."

"Don't be. I'm here if you need me," he assures me.

Inhaling, I finally find the courage to open the door. I push it open, placing one leg on the ground before turning back to my dad. "Have a good meeting, Dad."

"Enjoy your first day," he calls back as I step out of the car, closing the door behind me.

I wave goodbye, inwardly moaning at the spring air cooling my clammy skin. My anxiety spikes as I listen to the rumble of the car pulling away from the curb.

Immediately, I reach for my pocket, my fingers closing around the mobile phone he bought me. I relax, knowing that if there is an emergency, I won't be alone. I just have to call him. It doesn't matter when either. Dad has spoken to the school principal to make sure it wasn't confiscated during class, and assured her it wouldn't be used unless necessary. She agreed, but then I know people find it hard to say no to my dad. His job is to negotiate deals, after all.

The smell of cut grass fills the air as I walk across the field to the school entrance. One good thing about coming back to Grayson High: I already know all the exit routes and where to go for some peace and quiet. The worst thing about coming back, apart from my fears, is that everyone here will know my business, and the ones who don't will no doubt know by the end of the day.

I hate that I will have to face those who bullied me all those years ago.

"You made it?"

The deep, husky voice startles me, and I jump, clenching my fists. When I face the person who spoke, my breath stills. He's taller than I remembered, more muscular.

"Myles," I breathe out, my cheeks immediately heating.

Myles Carter was someone I talked to after everything happened. I wasn't even sure why I opened up to someone I barely knew; I just felt like I could. He was the only person who didn't look at me with disgust or judgment.

He used to be one of the few people I got excited about seeing, but when I went to visit Denny, to apologise for my part in what happened to her and her friend, Harlow, he didn't seem so happy to see me. At first, I thought it was shock—it had been a long time—but he seemed tortured by my presence.

"Hey," he greets, smiling wide.

There's a slight dimple in his left cheek that makes me inwardly sigh. There's something about him that makes my stomach flutter and causes my nerves to skyrocket. It never happened with his brothers, and all the Carter siblings are hot.

It isn't just his looks that pull me to him. It's his personality; his kindness and loyalty. I also think he got the brains between him and his twin brother, Max. They are polar opposites.

Those aren't the only reasons I'm drawn to him. I crave his gentleness as well as his caring nature. He cares about those around him, and not only his family.

He comforted me during a time when I was ready to give up. He found me sitting in the library, contemplating how many of my mum's anti-depressants and my dad's painkillers it would take to end the suffering.

Then he came and sat down next to me. At first, he didn't say anything, but even his presence was a relief from the hurt I was going through. It eased. And for the first time since being attacked, I felt clean.

Once he sensed I had relaxed, he spoke. For twenty or thirty minutes, he talked, and sometimes, I replied.

He saved me that day.

"Hey," I breathe out, then blink, shaking my head.

I duck my head, realising he caught me staring at him.

"Mrs Collins sent me. *I'm to accompany you to your classes,*" he explains, trying to mimic her voice at the end. Mrs Collins is posh, and he didn't pull it off.

"Ahh, well, I hope she's paying you well to babysit me," I mutter dryly, my hopes of him coming to see me voluntarily dying in an instant.

I begin to walk away but he jogs past me, stopping in front of me to block my path.

"Okay, I lied. *I* wanted to accompany you to your classes."

I tilt my head up, giving him a sharp glance. "How do you even know we have the same classes?"

My stomach flutters when he steps closer, my heart racing with something other than fear.

"I got a copy of your timetable from the head teacher?"

"Are you asking me or telling me?" I ask, fighting back a smirk. I can't help it. Whenever I'm around him I either get lost for words or end up having a permanent smile on my face.

"Both?" he answers.

I arch an eyebrow, not believing him. He throws his hands up in surrender, and the action causes me to flinch. I take a step back, the movement quick, and I end up catching my foot on something.

I begin to fall, and just as I close my eyes, prepared for a day of humiliation, strong arms wrap around me. I'm saved mid-air, and when I open my eyes, Myles is looming above me, his warm hands around my back.

His forehead creases with worry, and the back of my eyes begin to burn. He probably thinks I'm a freak for flinching away, and I can't help but feel humiliated over the fact.

Why can't I react like a normal girl?

I want to be the girl who flirts when a guy flirts with her. I want to be the girl who can laugh and have fun with a group of friends. I don't want to be this scared girl who's frightened by the slightest movements or noise. I want to be free. Free to be who I want to be and not who I have been moulded to be.

I can wish.

"You steady?" he teases, making light of the situation.

"Yeah," I whisper, unable to look him in the eye as he straightens, pulling me with him.

I run a hand down my side, my palms feeling clammy.

"Come on, we have English after Registration."

I nod and follow him into the main building. The halls are crowded with other students, and with each step, I can feel panic crawling up the back of my throat. Sweat trickles down my spine as I glance around.

A few people I recognise stop what they're doing and send me curious glances. Once I walk past them, I hear the whispers, and I know it won't be long until the rumours begin. It was like this before. Now, they have platforms to do it. I wouldn't be surprised if someone hasn't already announced it on Facebook or Twitter.

I jerk to a stop when I see a group of Davis' friends up ahead. When I was here last, some were in the year below us and would make more of an effort to prove they were cool enough to be in his group. They did everything he asked. They were his lap-dogs, pure and simple.

I feel the blood drain from my face as I remember the cruel words they threw at me.

For the millionth time today, my palms become clammy and I wonder what the hell I am doing here. I want to complete sixth form. I have to. My last marks were below average, and if I ever want to get a job that doesn't involve doing something I dislike, I need to get good grades.

"Are you okay? You're looking rather pale," Myles asks, coming to a stop beside me.

My mouth opens to reply, yet only a gush of air escapes. I shake my head, fighting back tears.

He steps forward, his face a mask of concern, when suddenly, fingers dig into my side.

"Good morning," a voice booms.

I scream, falling into Myles and clutching his shirt. I clench my eyes closed, ignoring the ringing in my ears as I try to stop myself from shaking.

He wraps his arms around me, and surprisingly, I don't shy away from his touch. It's been two years since I let another male touch me—or anyone, for that matter.

Myles tenses against me. "You fucking dickhead."

"Shit, I didn't think. I just got overexcited when I saw you and Kayla. I didn't think," Max swears, sounding apologetic.

"You only saw me twenty minutes ago, you jackass," Myles snaps.

His hand runs up and down my back in a soothing gesture, and although my heart is still racing, his comfort oddly works, and I begin to relax a little.

"I know, but we're connected and shit. When you're not around, I miss you, bro," Max whines dramatically.

"How so?" Myles asks dryly.

"Well, you know; you cry, I cry. You smile, I smile and all that bollocks. So when you're not around for me to know what I should be doing, I get jittery and nervous and shit. Then I got excited when I saw you—well, sensed you with my twin power—"

"Jesus, cut to the chase, Max," Myles barks, and I feel him bring his hand up to his face. Most likely to pinch the bridge of his nose.

"See? Now I've got to go to registration cranky," he tells him, sounding put out. "Oh, look, Jessica Seymour."

Once he's left, Myles gently prises my fingers from his shirt, glancing down at me. "I'm sorry. He can be a bit much."

I take another step back, rubbing my arms to ward off the chill. I feel cold now he's no longer embracing me. "It's okay. I overreacted," I tell him.

I still can't believe I let him hold me without having a panic attack or freaking out. My dad only has to reach for me and it sends me into a meltdown.

I sneak a glance at him, hoping he doesn't realise how badly I'm freaking out inside. It might seem minor to most people, but for me, this is huge. I need to be in control of who touches me. It's about getting my power back. And yet, having him hold me, it relaxed me.

"You sure? He can be a bit aggressive when it comes to being around people. He acts like a kid on Christmas morning every day," he declares, grinning.

I tilt my head up and smile before glancing over his shoulder to where Max has a girl against a locker, his tongue playing tonsil tennis. I vaguely remember the girl, but my view is obstructed so I can't see her fully.

"And he looks like he got his present early today," I blurt out, before turning bright red.

I slap my palm over my face once I realise what I just said. When I peek through my fingers, Myles' shoulders are shaking, and his lips are turned up in a smile as he watches me.

When he turns around, he bursts out laughing. "As long as he makes it to first class, I don't care."

He ushers me away, and together, we head into Registration. Myles explained a new teacher was starting today, so I'm glad I won't be the only newbie.

My dad made sure to get a detailed timetable for me so I could prepare myself for each lesson, and who would be in what class. It's the only way for me to handle my anxiety. The unknown and being cornered scares me. Plus, I needed to make sure I wasn't going to be in any of the other boys' classes who played a hand in bullying me.

Walking into the classroom, the first thing I notice is the tables are set out differently than before. Instead of being seated in pairs, the tables now hold three. This wasn't on the detailed plan they made for me.

I turn to Myles, my eyes widening as I fiddle with the strap of my bag.

He takes pity on me. "Come on. We'll sit at the back in the corner."

"Yo, wait up," I hear Max call out, but I don't turn around to look. I keep up with Myles, following him to the table, ignoring the curious stares.

"Katie, Katie, Katie, do you need a picture, babe? Because I'm gonna have to disappoint you. I just gave the last one away to Mr

Hawks," he explains, and when I turn, I find him smirking down at the girl in question.

When her gaze meets mine, I jerk my attention in front of me, wondering when he got so cocky.

"What? Huh? What are you going on about, Max?" she replies, sounding bewildered.

"You were staring," he tells her, amusement gone. "Stop it. Didn't your mother ever teach you not to stare?"

I shiver at the warning in his voice. He doesn't wait for a reply, just continues up the aisle behind me.

"Shotgun the window," he calls out, sounding close to my ear.

I wince, rubbing my ear, and tilt my head away. I glare down at the floor, too scared to say anything. I desperately want to glare at him, but as always, I'm afraid of the consequences. Although my confidence is growing each day, I still have a long way to go.

Max barges past me when we reach the back of the room, nearly knocking the bag off my shoulder as he does. Myles, who notices, punches Max in the shoulder, glaring at him in warning.

My heart warms at his protective gesture. He was always like this. Half the time, I don't think he realises he does it. He looks out for people, and not because of an agenda. It's in his nature.

His presence is already making today bearable. I don't think I could have walked through those doors had he not been walking alongside me.

He pulls out the middle seat. "Here you go."

Jesus! A Kayla-Carter sandwich.

I look from Myles to Max, biting my bottom lip. If I sit there, I'll be blocked in. There will be no way I can escape without Myles having to move. And although I trust him, I'm not sure if I can do it.

I reach for a strand of my flaming red hair that has fallen from the messy bun on top of my head and twirl it around my finger as I lower myself into the seat, trying my hardest not to cry. I don't want to be weak, not in front of them.

Once seated, I begin to wish I had kept my hair down. At least then

I would have something to shield me from prying eyes and the two boys sitting beside me.

Myles' leg brushes against mine, but instead of the normal anxiety and fear that usually creeps in, all I feel is a blush rise in my cheeks and butterflies flutter in my stomach.

What is he doing to me?

"Sorry," he whispers, his gaze darting to mine.

"It's okay," I whisper, staring at my bag on the table.

"You two are just too talkative," Max whines like we're getting on his nerves. "The conversation is so stimulating, I might need to cool off outside."

His sarcasm isn't lost on me, and my lips pull up at the corners. I tilt my head a little to the side, getting a look at him.

Max has this easy-going charm and banter going on. His easy, carefree attitude and his sociable personality could quite easily make him friends in an empty room. There is just something about him that draws you in. He's sharp, sarcastic, and the biggest flirt you could meet.

His hair is darker than Myles', and his eyes are a shade lighter than Myles' chocolate brown ones. They're the only differences someone could point out if they knew the twins. Because their facial features are the same. At first glance, there is no way you could tell them apart. Although, Max has a slightly bigger build, more defined due to his love of sports.

Myles isn't a slouch though. His body has more of a natural look than his brother's. He's more mature and plans for the future, including what job he wants when he leaves school.

Max, however, only worries about what he's going to have for dinner that day. I guess it's why everyone worries for him.

"Do you have a game this weekend?" Myles asks Max.

I listen to them talk back and forth, relaxing when they don't force me into the conversation.

When they start talking about a football game they had watched on the weekend, my heart clenches. I want a weekend like that. I want to be able to say how much fun I had, but instead, all I have to think about is the nightmare I endured.

When Registration is over, I jump from my seat, thankful my next class is only next door. I wait for Myles to leave, following him with Max behind me.

As we reach the door, Max jerks to a stop. He peeks his head around the doorway, looking left, then right up the corridors.

"Who are you looking for?" Myles asks.

"Oh, Maddie. She's turned into some kind of stalker and the police won't put a restraining order on her."

"You actually asked the police to do that?" I ask, horrified.

Max has a reputation. He has since the age of twelve. So the chances of a girl stalking him is pretty realistic, but it might not be for the reasons he thinks.

He really shouldn't sleep with them if he doesn't want anything more.

"Um, yeah. She tried asking for my number, and after we fuc— made love, she tried to take my T-shirt home," he explains, curling his lip. "Who does that crap?"

My cheeks heat as I nod like I understand. I don't. In fact, I'm wondering what the issue was. When I turn to leave, Myles follows. He grins down at me, winking.

"Clearly I got the brains," Myles declares as Max steps up beside us.

"Yeah, up there maybe," Max comments, poking Myles in the head. "But clearly, I got the brains down there."

I gape when he points to his junk.

"Could you please refrain from touching your junk in the hallway, Mr Carter," a teacher snaps.

"Oh, Miss French, you love my junk," he teases, winking at her.

My eyes widen and my lips part as I watch the teacher's reaction. I was waiting for her to blow a fuse, but instead, she just lets out a sigh before walking down the hall.

"She totally wants my cock," Max gloats, puffing his chest out.

Myles and I both snap our heads in his direction at the same time.

"Seriously, bro. Do you have any kind of filter? I'm pretty sure she's in her forties."

"More experienced," he announces, wiggling his eyebrows. When he sees my expression, he laughs. "I'm off to maths before Mr Hugh has my arse."

Myles opens his mouth to say something back, but he just shakes his head at Max's retreating form.

He turns to me as he holds the door open to English. "After you."

Most of the students are already seated and listening to the teacher, Mrs Perry. She worked here when I first attended, and I liked her. She was nice, unlike our other English teacher, Mr Roberts. He was a complete arsehole.

"Kayla, Myles, how lovely for you to join us. Come in and take a seat," she greets, marking us down on her register.

Following Myles' lead, I walk behind him to the back of the class, where he takes a seat at a table in the middle row.

I can feel stares as I take a seat, placing my bag on the floor next to my feet. I duck my head when I notice a few people glaring my way, whilst others just stare in curiosity.

Once Mrs Perry begins the class, I ignore their stares and concentrate on what she's saying, since my education relies on it. I'm already behind because of being home-schooled and then the court case. Once I knew I had to testify, I couldn't continue with schoolwork. Everyone else in here has already had months of teaching. The only advantage I have is some of it, I have already learned.

When Myles' knee knocks into mine, I slowly, without being obvious, move my leg away. It isn't that I'm repulsed by his touch, I just don't want to risk a panic attack coming out of nowhere.

I also can't handle spending the lesson with my stomach fluttering.

Myles leans in, whispering, "You okay?"

I nod, clearing my throat. "Yes."

When he doesn't say anything, I catch a glance of him. He's watching me, a knowing smirk on his face. I drop my gaze down to the table, feeling my cheeks heat.

"Good," he murmurs.

I spend the rest of the lesson trying not to look at him or think about how close he is and how good he smells.

I also can't help but get distracted by my own thoughts. I've never reacted to a guy like this. Not even before I was attacked.

The connection I feel between us scares me. But it also excites me at the same time.

CHAPTER
TWO

KAYLA

I fiddle with the strap of my bag as I sit on the bench, waiting for my dad. I think back on the day, and I'm grateful Myles took it upon himself to stay with me. He walked me to each of my classes, even the ones we didn't share.

I don't think I would have made it to Registration, let alone through the rest of the day, had it not been for him. He seemed to know what I needed and when I needed it.

Dad pulls me from my thoughts as he honks his horn. I force a smile and shove my bag over my shoulder.

He smiles as I get into the car. "How did your day go?" he asks.

"It went fine. I spoke to a few people, but other than that, I just concentrated on work," I tell him, leaving out Myles and his involvement. I know he wouldn't approve.

He beams. "That's great news, darling."

"Yeah," I whisper, pulling at the small piece of cotton that has come loose from my jeans. I don't want to lie to him, but if I don't, he will send me to an all-girls school or make me home school again, and I don't want either.

If I want to get a handle on my anxiety, I need to do it while being surrounded by people.

"Did you get any homework?" he asks as he manoeuvres the car through the busy streets.

"I only got a little light reading," I admit, staring at the houses that pass by in a blur.

He clears his throat. "Sweetie, your mother called this morning on the way to work. She said she wants to have you for the Easter holidays. Is that okay?"

My heart begins to race. "For the whole two weeks?"

"Yes. I'll be working a lot and you'll be at home alone all day and night; that's not good for you," he explains.

"Dad," I groan. "I'm eighteen. I'll be fine on my own. I'll go to hers during weekends like I usually do." I can't go for the two weeks. I just can't. I also can't tell him why.

"That's fine. I'll call her back later to tell her."

My mind races for an excuse for him not to do that. It's the same every time. She'll make up some sob story and then he'll force me to go. "Maybe you should tell her I have schoolwork to catch up on and that I'll be doing some odd jobs around the house. We don't want to hurt her feelings, do we?"

He pulls his attention away from the road for a second, smiling. "Good idea."

Once his attention is back on the road, I sag back against the seat, letting out a breath. She has a way of manipulating everyone around her, including my dad.

When he first found out about the rape, he filed for a divorce because she had kept it quiet. He was angry for so long, and he took me away. I thought it was the last I'd ever have to see of her, but then she turned up one day putting on an act. She cried and told him how she was worried for my safety and that's why she couldn't tell anyone. Just as the divorce was finalizing, she won custody for weekends, like I wasn't old enough to make my own decisions.

I tried to decline going, but it only made things ten times worse, and my mum on a normal day was terrifying. So I went. And I knew it made my dad happy. He never said anything, but some-times I wonder if he did it because he knew how dramatic she could get.

"Want me to make spag bol for dinner?" I ask, changing the subject as we turn onto our street.

"That sounds delicious. I'm going to be in my office so shout me when it's ready," he announces as he puts the car into park.

"Got ya," I tell him.

It's another reason why I love living with my dad. He doesn't get in my space or breathe down my neck every two seconds. He leaves me to do my thing. Then again, I could have a party while he was in the house and he wouldn't notice or hear a thing. But being alone gives me peace. Still, I know the minute I can, I'm moving out and getting my own place.

———

A fter helping me clean away the dirty dishes, Dad heads back to his office. I won't see him now until the morning, when he drops me off at school.

The doorbell rings and I jump, my body shaking as I stare at the door. My feet itch to move, to escape upstairs. No one ever comes here but my mum.

"Can you get that, darling?" Dad calls, sounding like he's in the bar room.

I sigh. I can't ignore it now he's heard. Straightening my shoulders, I lean up on my toes, peeking through the peephole.

Harlow and Denny are there, a pushchair between them. I pull open the door, hoping I can hide my surprise at seeing them.

"Hey, guys, what are you doing here?"

"We brought a chocolate cake to celebrate your first day of school," Denny announces.

Harlow grins. "We know it must have been a trying day."

I run the tip of my toe along the carpet, feeling my nose begin to sting. "Thank you," I whisper.

"Don't thank us just yet," Harlow warns. "Denny still hasn't lost her appetite after having Hope, so I'd hurry if you want some cake."

I smile back. I like Harlow. She's one of the nicest people I have ever met, right alongside Denny and Charlie, my other best friend. They are the only girls I have met who aren't bitches to everyone. I was grateful to have Charlie and Denny when I first started school.

Harlow's brown hair blows into her face, and it snaps me to attention. "Sorry," I rush out. "Come in. Come in."

I pull the door open wider, letting them in. Harlow walks in first, carrying one side of the pushchair, while Denny gets the other.

I peek into the car seat attached to the pushchair, smiling down at Hope, who is awake and sucking on her thumb. She's so adorable and is the spitting image of her father. The only trait she has gotten from Denny is her blonde hair. It has gotten even lighter since the last time I saw her.

"Come through to the kitchen. My dad's in his office down the hall so he won't hear us in there," I explain.

"Where are the plates?" Denny asks when we enter, clearly eager for chocolate.

I point to the cupboard where they're stored as I pull open a drawer and grab some forks and a knife to cut the cake.

I pass her the knife, and my eyes widen as she cuts the cake into large slices.

"I can't eat that much," I declare, my lips parted.

"Oh, that piece is for me," she admits.

She cuts off another piece, this one half the size, and I let out a chuckle.

"You're lucky we got the cake out of the house. Max walked in from school to see Hope and nearly took the whole thing home with him," Harlow states, shoving her fork into the cake.

My lips twitch in amusement, especially when Denny begins to demolish the cake in front of her. "Thank you. This is really kind of you."

"Don't thank us yet. We have another motive for coming round," Denny admits.

When her grin turns mischievous, my stomach swirls. They share a look, and I gulp. "What?"

"We want you to come round mine over the weekend for a girls' night in."

I relax. I thought they were going to bring up something else. A grin creases my face. I've missed this so much. For years, I have suffered with my depression, isolating myself from everyone, but I want it back. I want to be normal again and do things that girls do. I've already missed out on so much.

Just as I open my mouth to say yes, my smile falls. I remember where I have to be this weekend. "I'm sorry, I can't. My mum has me on weekends," I explain, glancing down at my plate.

Denny hesitates a second before replying. "Tell her you've been invited to mine. I'm sure she won't mind."

I can tell she doesn't believe her own words. Denny met my mum a few times, and each time, my mum was rude and condescending. Like Denny's mum, she wears a mask in front of others, but behind closed doors, it comes off.

"I'll ask and let you know," I offer, lying my arse off. I already know what the answer is going to be—and what the repercussions will be if I even attempt to ask.

Once the cake has been demolished, I invite the girls to watch a movie in my room, not knowing what else to say or do. It's evident I'm nervous. This is all new to me.

"Sure," Denny agrees, and reaches for Hope's car seat, where she's sleeping soundly. Harlow grabs the changing bag, and I gape at how much it bulges. It's like she packed for a week's holiday, not a visit.

"What would you like to watch?" I ask once we're in my room. I head over to my DVD shelf, scanning through the options.

"I don't mind," Harlow replies absently as she takes in the room. "God, this room is amazing."

I beam with pride. I love my room. It's the one room in the house that has any kind of homey stamp on it. It's where I spend the majority of my time, so I make sure I take care of it.

The walls are painted purple, and above my bed there's a huge star that has little twinkle lights shining down. It was the first thing to be fitted when we moved in.

My next favourite thing is my bed. It looks more like one large sofa. It's huge. I've always loved the blackbirds printed on the wall behind it. They look like they're flying toward the window.

In the corner of the room are my white shelves that have lights behind each one. They have a soft glow to them, which are perfect during the night, when I have nightmares. They erase the shadows in the room but aren't bright enough to keep me awake. My DVD shelf is different. Instead of lights behind them, they have twinkle lights beneath each shelf that light up what's below.

My desk matches the white shelves. It's simple, with a white chair that has a purple soft cushion attached.

My wardrobe, however, takes up an entire wall. Originally it was an alcove, so my dad had some builders come in and make a wardrobe out of the space. One side has two poles fitted from the wall to the centre, where my cube boxes are, each a different shade of purple. The other side is cubed, but instead of using boxes for storage, I have a door. It's where I keep my jeans and stuff. The last part, which is a smaller section, has star-shaped hooks to hang coats, scarves and bags.

"Thank you," I reply, glad they don't think it's too girly.

When Dad brought Mum around to see the house, she made her opinion clear when she said it looked like a two-year-old's bedroom. She was wrong. It's sophisticated and elegant, and yet it has personality. I couldn't have asked for a better space.

Denny kicks off her shoes before dropping down onto my bed. Her phone rings, and she groans, rolling to the side to grab it out of her bag.

"Hello?" she greets. Her skin creases between her eyes as she listens to whoever is on the other side. She rolls her eyes, letting out a sigh. "She's fine. For heaven's sake, we've been gone half an hour, an hour at most. No. We're watching a film. What? No. We're with Kayla. Go away. No. She's fine where she is," she snaps, quickly ending the call.

"Mason?" I question, my lips twitching.

It's nice to see her so happy. Denny had a crush on him for so long. When we used to hang out, she'd tell me her plans to marry him. Now she's engaged and has a baby with him. I guess dreams do come true.

"No, worse... It was Max."

"Max?" I ask, my eyebrows pulling together.

"Yeah. Since Hope was born, he hasn't left her alone. He's constantly around," she explains, chuckling to herself. I can't help but chuckle myself. I can't picture him being a children person at all. He seems too... childish. Immature.

Still... "That's kind of cute," I state.

"No. Trust me, it's not," Denny admits, and Harlow nods in agreement.

"He can be a little much at times," Harlow explains as she walks toward me, scanning the DVD shelf.

"Oh my god, *Labyrinth*. I love this movie. Can we watch this?" she asks.

"Sure," I agree, since it's one of my favourite films.

Hope stirs in her car seat, and I freeze mid-step, worried I'll wake her up, but Denny doesn't seem to mind as she talks normally to me, so I carry on.

"So then, how was your first day of school?" she asks, while Harlow busies herself putting the DVD in the DVD player like she's done it a million times before.

I relax a little more knowing they feel comfortable and it's just me making the situation awkward. It's then that I realise I've been in my own mind and I forgot to answer Denny.

"Oh, um, it was okay. It went well."

I take a seat closest to where Hope is in her car seat. When I glance down, she's staring up at me, sucking her tiny fist into her mouth.

My fingers twitch to get her out. She is so cute.

Exhaling, I pull my gaze away and turn to find Denny watching me, a smile on her lips. "Do you want to hold her?"

My lips part and I shake my head vehemently. "Oh, no. I-I don't know. I've never held a baby before."

"It's easy. Don't worry," she tells me as she gets off the bed. She kneels down, unstrapping Hope from her car seat. Hope begins to wiggle in excitement, and I smile at her enthusiasm. She is damn adorable.

When Denny lowers her into my arms, I stiffen for a second, scared I'll hurt or drop her. But when she starts cooing up at me, I relax and smile down at her.

"She's so tiny," I whisper, then jump when the doorbell rings. "Oh shoot, I should get that."

I shake a little, not knowing who it could be. If Charlie was going to turn up, she would have text me to let me know. She knows about my anxiety.

"You stay there. I can get it if you'd like?" Denny offers.

I bite my lip, hesitating for a second in case it's my mum. But she wouldn't cause a scene if she knew my friends were here, so I nod. "Thank you."

Denny leaves, the door shutting quietly behind her, and Harlow comes to sit down next to me. "You don't have to be shy around us, Kayla, or embarrassed. We understand, you know. We may not know exactly what you're going through, but you're not alone anymore. I promise. I'm glad you've moved back too. Denny missed you a lot."

"Denny spoke about me?" I ask, stunned.

I didn't think I made that kind of impact on her life. It wasn't like I was a memorable person, not unless you count the rumours everyone spread around the school about me.

She smiles. "She missed you."

I'm struck speechless. It's overwhelming for me. There was a time in my life when I assumed no one would notice if I died. I thought for sure I'd be forgotten once I left town. To know I was wrong is something else. I don't think I've ever felt like I mattered to anyone before.

I open my mouth to reply, when the door to my bedroom flies open. Denny storms in. I'm so surprised by her hasty entrance that it takes me a few seconds to see who has followed in behind her. I look to Denny first for answers, but then my eyes flash back to Max when he storms over to me.

"Please don't," I shout, shuffling back on the bed until my back hits the bars. I go to curl into a ball, when I remember I have Hope in my arms. He pauses, looking at me like I've lost my mind. "I'm so sorry."

His gaze softens on me before his eyes land on Hope. "I just came to see if my niece was okay," he explains, his voice low.

My hands shake as I hand Hope to him. He eagerly takes her, unaware of the turmoil going through me. My heart races and my skin begins to burn as I shakily get to my feet. I feel like I'm seconds away from passing out, and I don't want to do it with an audience.

"I'll be right back," I mumble, racing to the door. I pass Myles, seeing him for the first time, and my stomach sinks.

Tears gather in my eyes when I feel his stare burning into my back. I rush down the hall to the bathroom, trying to control my breathing as I go.

This is mortifying. And I've reacted the same in similar situations. I did when I first came close to Malik during the time I went to Denny's to speak to her and Harlow.

I make it to the door, when a hand reaches out, snagging me around my elbow. A squeal escapes me. I clench my eyes shut as a wave of dizziness hits me.

"It's me," Myles whispers, pulling me a little closer. I take in a deep breath and exhale, before repeating the process. "Hey, it's okay. It's just me. Don't panic."

I relax against him, confused over my body's reaction to him. I can't relax around my own dad, and yet a few words from Myles, one simple touch, and already I'm calming from what would have been a full meltdown.

I open my eyes, my attention going to my bedroom door and then to him. "I didn't mean to react like that. I didn't mean anything by it. I can't control it," I explain, feeling my cheeks heat.

I wouldn't be surprised if he looked at me like Max first did, or if they hightailed it out of here before I got back. And I wouldn't blame them for it either. I have a lot of baggage.

"Stop worrying about what we all think. We understand. You don't need to be sorry, or worry about your actions around us. Just be yourself, even if it means you lash out at one of us. None of us are judging you, Kayla."

"What if I'm always like this?" I find myself asking. Shocked isn't the word I'd use right now. I've never even asked my therapist that question.

He runs a hand down my arm, causing me to shiver. "Once you trust us, trust in the people around you, I don't think you'll need to ask that question again. We'll all help you through it, even if it means getting in your space." He grimaces as he glances at the bedroom door, his face twisting up in guilt. "I knew I should have stopped him."

I tilt my head to the side. "What do you mean?"

"Max," he sighs, his cheeks flushing a shade of pink. "He went back round to Denny's after dinner and found she had gone out. As soon as she let slip where she was over the phone, he was rushing over here. I caught on to the end part of the conversation, so I knew he was coming. Before I could stop him, he was already on his way, so I tagged along as backup in case he got too much."

"Oh, you mean like charging into my bedroom?" I tease, a genuine smile lighting up my face.

"Yeah, that," he replies, chuckling. "Are you okay now? We can go, if you'd like?"

"NO! I mean, no. It's fine. He took me by surprise is all. I hope you guys don't mind watching *Labyrinth*?"

"Ha! I love that film, but Max will probably have nightmares," he admits.

I relax once more, feeling a million times lighter now I have talked to him. When he gestures for me to go ahead, I easily listen, no longer anxious about their reaction. Because I know he's right. They are my friends, and they are here for me.

Walking in, I find everyone is sitting on my bed. I stumble to a stop when I realise we've walked in on an argument.

"She shouldn't be watching this, Denny. Does Mason know you coerce your child into watching this?"

"It's a freaking kid's film, Max. One she is far too young to understand," Denny snaps.

"It's not good for her. They kidnap a baby, for Christ's sake, and you want her to watch this?" he demands, glaring down at her. He gives the TV a brief glance before quickly looking away.

"Yes, because she's going to wake up in the middle of the night and panic about a hot, bad Goblin King coming to kidnap her, Max. Seriously, grow up," she argues, her lips twitching in amusement.

He clutches Hope tighter, turning her away from the television. It's cute that he's so protective of her. I never thought I'd see the day when Coldenshire's big-time footy player and man-whore became whipped by a baby. Normally, guys like him run a mile in the other direction if the word 'baby' is mentioned.

Harlow spots us and beams. "Oh, hey. Sorry, we're hogging all the bed," Harlow says, going to stand up, but I wave her off.

"It's fine. I'll go get the beanie," I tell her, and head over to my wardrobe, grabbing the beanie shoved in the corner.

I drop it down next to the bed where I can still see the television, but then hesitate when I realise Myles doesn't have one. I glance back down at the beanie. It's big enough for the both of us, but I'm not sure if I can sit that close to him.

"It's okay, sit down," he tells me, reading my mind.

I do as he says, not wanting everyone's prying eyes. My palms begin to sweat as he walks over to me. My heart races as he sits down next to me, but I relax when his arse hits the floor and not the beanie. He kicks his legs out, leaning against the bed.

He gives me that half dimpled smile when he notices me staring. I jerk my attention back to the movie, my cheeks burning.

The film turned into two, and just as the second one is ending, my dad pops his head through, jerking to a stop when he sees my room filled with people. His eyes widen when they land on Max bottle feeding Hope.

"I'm sorry. I didn't know Kayla was having any friends over," he explains, before turning to me with a questioning look.

"Sorry, Dad. It was a last-minute thing. You remember Denny, right?"

"Denny Smith?" he asks, smiling. "How's your mother and father?"

"Hopefully, my mother is still in the place the police put her," she answers, before smiling. "My father is wonderful though, thank you. How are you?"

He opens and closes his mouth like a goldfish. "Um, good."

I clear my throat. "The baby is Hope; she's Denny's daughter. Mason, her fiancé, isn't here. He's at work. These are his twin brothers, Myles and Max. They go to school with me. And this is Harlow. She's, um…"

"I'm a recent friend of Kayla's. We met through Denny," she explains, getting up to shake his hand. "You have a lovely home."

"Thank you. By any chance, are you Miss Dean's daughter?"

Her eyebrows pull together, although she continues to smile. "Yes, sir, I am."

'Sir?' Max mouths to Myles, and I try hard not to giggle.

Dad turns to me. "Sweetie, it's getting late. I was just coming to say goodnight."

"We should be going anyway, Mr Martin. I need to get Hope to bed," Denny cheerfully interrupts.

My shoulders drop a little. I was having a good time, and I was finally beginning to relax, even with Max's outbursts.

Harlow gives me a knowing smile. "Maybe we can do this again sometime?"

"I'd love that," I answer, briefly turning to Myles.

I don't want him to leave. I'm so used to his comfort. Each time his leg brushed mine, or he'd move closer to ask a question, it would make my stomach flutter.

It was exhilarating to feel something other than fear. And I long for a touch that doesn't repulse me or make me want to run and hide.

Harlow claps her hands together. "Come on then, guys. Let's leave Kayla to get some sleep."

Max hovers over Denny as she puts Hope's coat on. A few times during her putting Hope's arms through the sleeves, I see his fingers twitch to help her.

When she's all strapped in, I chuckle. Max takes her off Denny, smiling down at her. "Bagsy pushing the pram home."

Denny rolls her eyes, not fazed by his outbursts. When I glance back over to my dad, his gaze is on me and Myles. His smile falls when he sees how close we are sitting and concern washes over his face.

It's weird seeing this side of my dad. He has never been overly protective before, but I find I kind of like it. I just wish he would open his eyes to the other things going on under his nose and in my life. But I guess ignorance is bliss.

Myles clears his throat as he moves to stand. I follow, and when I stand, the others are standing in the doorway, looking smug for some reason.

"Need a minute or two, bro?" Max coughs, glancing down toward Myles' crotch.

Myles glares at his brother, who only chuckles in response. "Yeah, actually. I want to talk to Kayla alone. Can you wait outside for me?"

Dad steps further into the room. "Son, I don't—"

I hold my hand up, stopping him before he can embarrass me. "Dad, it's fine. Go on off to bed. I'll lock up downstairs," I tell him, which is something I do every night anyway.

It's something I've become accustomed to since the attack. I never felt safe, and I didn't believe my parents could keep me safe, so even if they had locked up, I would double check everything before coming to bed myself.

And if he's worried about me being freaked out over being alone with Myles, he doesn't need to. I'm not scared of him, not in that way, because I know he'll never hurt me.

For a minute, I don't think he'll leave, but when he does, I relax a little, until I hear him follow the others downstairs instead of going to bed.

Whatever.

"So…" I murmur, starting the conversation.

"Yeah, so, I was wondering if, um, you wanted to be my partner in Childcare tomorrow? Last week, the teacher warned us that we'd be picking partners for our essay and presentation, so we needed to pick wisely. The marks go toward most of our grades."

Okay, I hadn't expected that. "Oh, um, sure. I'd love to. I'll warn you, though, I'm not good with vocal presentations."

He grins, winking. "That's fine, I'll do most of the talking." He heads toward the door and grabs the handle, before he turns back to me, his cheeks turning pink. "Did you want to walk to school together?"

My nails dig into the palms of my hands at his question, and my pulse races. I have butterflies in my stomach over it, and all he's going to do is walk me to school.

I frown when I realise I can't. "I'd love to, but my dad, he, um, he drives me. Maybe another time?" I offer, not wanting him to think I'm brushing him off.

"Sure," he answers, his smile dropping a little. "I'll, um, go."

I'd say he's disappointed by my answer, but my eyes could be deceiving me. I am tired.

I follow him downstairs, groaning at the sight of my dad talking to my friends.

Friends.

It feels so weird calling them that. Well, mostly having someone *to* call that. They all turn their heads our way when they hear us approach, and another blush rushes up my neck. Max grins when he notices. I go to narrow my eyes, but I stop myself and widen them instead. *I know all too well what happens if I show defiance.* Max see's my knee-jerk reaction, and his eyebrows pull together.

"See you tomorrow," Max calls out.

"We'll do this again soon," Harlow promises.

"Definitely," Denny replies.

I wave goodbye, watching their retreating forms walk down the driveway. Well, mostly *one* retreating form. He really does have a nice figure. His jeans fit him snugly in all the right places.

"Are you sure those boys are just friends?" Dad asks as I lock up behind them.

My lips part. "What?"

"I just don't think hanging out with those boys will do you any good, sweetie. You need to make girl friends too."

"Dad, as much as I love your concern, it's fine. Plus, I'm pretty sure Harlow and Denny are girls, Dad. I think baby Hope proves that," I tell him, giggling at his expression.

"I guess. I just don't want to see you getting hurt."

"I know, Dad, but I'll be fine. I promise. They're good people," I assure him.

And they are. The boys were raised by their grandfather, and he's a good man. Their parents are a mystery to people, as they never speak about them.

But even with that, you can tell by just one interaction with them that they are good people. It's all in the eyes. And Myles' hold nothing but kindness.

"I hope so," he replies, exhaling. "Let me know when you have guests over next time."

"I will," I promise.

"Goodnight, sweetheart."

"Goodnight, Dad."

Once he's gone, I do my nightly ritual and check the doors and windows, making sure they are all locked. My mind drifts back to Myles and the flutters I encounter whenever he's around. I like him. I did back then too, but this time it's different. It feels different.

However, it doesn't matter how much I like him. I can't have a relationship. Can I? I shake those ludicrous thoughts away. There isn't a chance. I'm dirty, unclean, and tainted. Even if I do somehow move past what happened to me, Myles deserves someone pure, someone who isn't tainted with the sins of others.

As I finish with the last window, tears gather in my eyes. I make a vow right there to keep my distance. I want to protect my heart. I just hope my heart gets the memo before I next see him at school tomorrow.

CHAPTER
THREE

MYLES

I scan the crowd for bright red hair as I walk into school. My shoulders slump when I don't spot her anywhere. I had hoped I would catch her on the field again, but she isn't there. When I went back to wait near the gates, I didn't spot her arriving with her father either, and I have been here twenty minutes.

You're acting like a pussy.

I inwardly groan. I wish I could get her out of my head, but since she returned to Coldenshire, I haven't been able to get her out of my mind.

With a sigh, I head inside and strut through the halls, over to my building. Registration is going to start any second. It's the one place I haven't looked for her, so maybe she got dropped off early and is already waiting inside.

Before I left hers last night, I should have asked her to meet me. She isn't the type of girl to seek someone out. Not because she's a snob, but because she is afraid to. She is afraid of everything, and it tears me apart to witness it. It's one of the reasons why I want to be around her. I feel this urge to protect her.

I also missed her when she left, which is weird because we barely knew each other. We hadn't even dated and yet I was drawn to her in a way I'd never felt toward anyone else. Still, with those few interactions, she made an everlasting impression.

When I first heard the rumours about what Davis had done to her, I went crazy. I cornered him in the boys' toilets and beat the crap out of him. It didn't end well for me. That same day, he got a group of friends together after school and battered me. It didn't matter to me. I still managed to do damage earlier in the day, so the bruises I ended up with were worth it.

My brothers pestered me for weeks after they attacked me, but I didn't tell them. I couldn't. They would have wanted to know why I did it, and I wasn't sure I could explain it to them. I also didn't do it to be praised. I just wanted her to get some kind of justice.

Having her back within touching distance is killing me. It's giving me blue balls too. Her floral scent, the colour of her hair and the way it looks when light touches it in a certain way, her eyes... it's all driving me wild. She's a drug to me, and I am addicted.

It's her personality I admire the most. She's strong. The strongest person I know. She is a shell of the person she used to be, but there are times when I catch glimpses of the old her.

She hasn't always been shy or scared. In fact, she used to be a little fiery. When she first started at Grayson High, everyone took the piss out of the red glasses she wore. She didn't care. She wore them anyway. Her retorts were humorous and sassy.

I want to help her find her confidence again. Her trust in life.

Walking into Registration, I find her already sitting down next to Max. My gaze narrows on Abigail, the girl who normally sits in front of us. She's sitting on the desk. Kayla shifts her chair away, her lips turned down, and frowns down at the table.

I glance to the front of the room, noticing the teacher hasn't arrived yet. I'm not surprised since it's becoming a common occurrence.

I rub at the ache at seeing such despair on her face as I walk up the aisle towards her. Once I'm close, I notice more than her sadness. She has dark circles under her eyes that look slightly puffy from crying.

I open my mouth to demand what is wrong, when her gaze flicks back to Abigail on the desk. She flinches slightly.

Fuck! I'm getting tired of Max and his fuck buddies.

She tilts her head up when she feels me approach. Our gazes lock, and her eyes burn into mine, captivating me. Her ruby red lips part, and I inhale sharply. She is the most beautiful girl I have ever seen. And one of a kind. With her fiery red hair, emerald green eyes and gorgeous tan, she is every guy's dream. It's still a wonder someone with red hair can even tan, but it's just another thing that makes her unique to me.

"Hey," I greet, pulling out the chair beside her, boxing her in the middle of me and Max.

"Hey," she whispers, tucking a strand of hair behind her ear. She bites her lip, her gaze flicking back to Abigail.

"Myles," Abigail squeals, and I wince at the sound. Her voice is like nails on a chalkboard.

I grit my teeth as she leans in a little, giving me crazy eyes. At first, I think she's about to be sick, but when she widens her lips, I realise she's trying to smile.

I give her a chin lift, not wanting to engage in any conversation. I turn my attention back to Kayla and smile. She returns it with a small one of her own, but then flinches, leaning back as Abigail slides her arse across the table.

I arch an eyebrow when she comes to a stop in front of me, running her finger along the desk.

"Can I help you?" I don't want to be rude. It isn't that she's a bad person, but Abigail has always been persistent. Most of the guys love her for the easy lay, but the others stay clear. I'm one of them. She knows that, since I made it clear I wasn't interested. Everyone knows Max is the easiest Carter to get into bed. So unless Max put her up to this, she's wasting her time.

"Oh, you most certainly can. I heard you're a legend at chemistry, and I was wondering if you'd tutor me after school," she asks, leaning forward.

When her fingers begin to run down my shirt, I scrape my chair back, glaring over at my brother. His expression stops me from chewing him out. He stares between us, looking dumbfounded by the whole ordeal.

I should have known he wouldn't do anything like this. He knows what Kayla means to me, and with her sitting right next to us, he wouldn't fuck that up. So it begs the question: who has put Abigail up to this? It wasn't just her I brushed off. Everyone knows I'm unapproachable. I don't do the whole 'bag 'em and sack 'em' bullshit.

"Sorry, but you heard wrong. I'm not that good. You should ask George. He gets straight A's."

Her eyebrows pull together. "George? But I want you."

I roll my eyes. I hate being rude, but she isn't going to give me a choice. With Abigail, you have to tell her straight, and even then, it can sometimes go over her head.

"Yeah, George. He sits over there," I tell her, pointing to the pimple-nosed kid at the front. Hearing his name, he turns in his chair whilst pushing his glasses further up his nose. His gaze locks on ours when he sees us watching. He waves, smiling, before turning back to his notes.

"No thanks," she mutters, her lip curling. "I want you to teach me."

"Sorry, but no can do." I try to smile but it probably looks like a grimace. "Plus, my girlfriend wouldn't like it," I blurt out, resting my arm along the back of Kayla's chair.

"Oh, I didn't know you two were dating," she tells me, giving Kayla the side eye. The girl must really be clueless because she blushes and jumps off the desk. She gives one last wink to Max before sauntering off back to her seat.

Max laughs once she's out of earshot. "Wow, bro, talk about subtleties."

"Girlfriend?" Kayla chokes out.

Shit.

"Yeah, about that. I'm sorry. It slipped out," I explain, wincing. "I can't stand girls like her. They get my back up and they don't leave you alone. I'm sorry."

She ducks her head, a blush rising on her cheeks as she grabs her pen. "No, it's fine."

I don't get a chance to start up a conversation because the teacher chooses that moment to walk in. Ten minutes late.

I grit my teeth when she doesn't even apologise. If that had been any of us, we would be in detention or getting a warning. Yet she gets a free pass to do whatever she wants.

I run a hand through my hair. I'm sounding more like Max every day. He's rubbing off on me and that isn't a good thing. We may be twins, but that's where our similarities end. He's more easy-going, and although he is a genius, he acts like a dumb kid who doesn't know his left from his right. I want to be a social worker, whereas he's happy to run V.I.P with Maverick. But even that occupation may change.

And whereas I want a family when I grow up, he's looking forward to lads' holidays, getting rat-arsed, and living for the day.

I want to make something of myself, be a better person than my parents were. I don't want to go hungry to the point I can't move. I want a better life. I want to help support my brothers and pay them back for everything they did for us growing up.

Max, however, isn't interested in any of that. But I know there will come a day when he's going to meet someone he wants for more than a quick fuck. And when that day comes, I don't think she'll be interested in someone who didn't take at least some of life seriously. He is a manwhore, and if he doesn't slow down, no girl will want him for more than a fuck.

Max's phone goes off, and I watch his fingers fly over the screen, typing back a response.

"Max, turn your phone off and put it away before I confiscate it," the teacher snaps, glaring at him.

From the corner of my eye, I watch as Kayla's cheeks flame bright red. She bites her bottom lip, trying not to look at Max. Fuck, she's beautiful.

"Sorry, Miss. Two more minutes, I'm just checking to see how my baby girl, Hope, is," he explains, not looking up from his phone as he continues to message.

"Max," I warn, narrowing my gaze on him.

Mason already warned him to stop texting Denny through the day in case she's taking a nap. Hope hasn't been sleeping through the night, and with Mason working all day, and most nights, Denny is the one staying up and doing the night feeds.

Kayla tilts her head toward me, her lips pulled up into an amused smile. I feel like the wind has been knocked out of me. It happens each time she directs a smile like that at me.

"No, Max, I will not wait two minutes. Either you turn your phone off and put it away, or I'll take the phone away from you, and you won't have it back till the end of the day. You should be able to refrain from texting your girlfriends in the day by now," she snaps and the whole class erupts with laughter.

Max's eyebrows pull together as his lip curls. "One, eww. She's my niece, Miss! And two, she likes it when I check on her. When she doesn't hear from me, she doesn't settle for her mum," he brags. My eyes flick back to the teacher, and I watch her give Max a 'how naive do you think I am' look. I have to grin. The teacher hasn't been here long, but already she has Max pegged out.

"What?" he shouts, offended by her expression.

Kayla jumps, pushing her chair toward mine. I watch as she closes her eyes, taking long, deep breaths.

When her gaze meets mine, her eyes glisten with tears. "Sorry," she whispers.

"It's okay," I assure her, rubbing her back.

Her tongue snakes out, licking her bottom lip, and my groin tightens. God, how am I supposed to be friends with the girl if all she has to do is lick her lips and I'm hard?

Max's voice cuts in and I snap my attention back to him, my hard-on disappearing.

"It's a true story, Miss; I made it up myself," he whines, shoving his phone into his blazer. The other classmates chuckle at him.

"Max, you have detention after school Friday." The teacher

dismisses him on a snap, and he throws his hands up in the air, frustrated.

"Honesty is the best policy, Miss. You can't give me detention for being honest," he whines, sounding like a girl. I'm thankful when the bell rings because I can't take any more of their arguing back and forth. I have to listen to enough arguing involving him at home.

"Max, you can have detention for lunch today too," she snaps, sending him a glare.

"Jesus, if I give you a straw will you suck the joy out of someone else's day instead?"

A few snickers erupt in the room, but I tune them out, shaking my head. My brother never learns when to keep his trap shut.

"We have Childcare now, don't we?" Kayla asks, keeping her voice low.

"No, we have History first, then Childcare," I explain, gesturing for her to go ahead first. "I'm not sure what you have for the rest of the day. I have P.E. after lunch and then Biology."

I was gutted when I found out she wasn't in more lessons with me. I even tried to ask the principle to arrange it so we were. I guess it worked out for the best. I think being with her twenty-four-seven will make me look like a stalker.

She comes to a stop outside the class, moving aside to let people past. She frowns, fiddling with the band on her wrist. "Oh. I have Chemistry third and P.E. for last period, but I don't think I'll be going to P.E. I'm hoping my dad remembered to get me excused," she tells me, a blush rising in her cheeks.

Her hand shakes as she tucks another loose strand behind her ear. My brows pull together. Is she worried about going because she heard about what happened to Harlow? If that's the case, she doesn't need to worry. I'd never let anything like that happen to her.

We begin to make our way through the halls, heading to our next class. "Why are you excused?" I ask, hoping I don't sound too interested.

She gives me a quick glance. "It's nothing," she mumbles.

"Tell me," I tease lightly, hoping she trusts me. Something about needing her to trust me burns deep down inside me.

She steps closer, her arm brushing mine. "I have some scars," she whispers, though I can barely hear her over the chatter from other students.

I pull her to the side, positioning her against the wall. Her lips part and her chest rises and falls with each breath she takes. Slowly, so as not to scare her, I lift my hand, tucking another strand of her hair behind her ear.

"Scars?" I croak out, emotion clogging my throat.

She tilts her head up, startled, and fear clouds her expression. I take a little step back, not enough for her to escape, but enough for her to try and relax around me to talk.

"Can we go? We're going to be late." She tries to sidestep me, but I put a hand firmly on her hip, the movement causing her to jump.

"Tell me," I order gently, pleading with not only my words but my eyes.

She lets out a breath. "It's from when... From when Davis..." Her eyes begin to water, and her body shakes.

I inwardly groan, feeling like a complete prick for pushing her. I should have known it had something to do with that wanker. I pull her in for a hug, and her body stiffens. I run my fingers up and down her back until she begins to relax into me, her body softening with each second that passes.

"I'm so fucking sorry. If I'd known—"

"You couldn't have known. It's okay," she assures me, her body shuddering beneath me.

It kills me that she has to live with this day in, day out.

"I shouldn't have pushed. I'm sorry," I tell her honestly, wishing there was something I could do to fix this.

"I'm being stupid," she declares, pulling away. She wipes the tears from under her eyes, unable to look at me.

I feel the coldness seep in with the distance between us, and I want to pull her back.

"No, you're not. Come on, let's get to class before *I'm* the one getting detention," I tease.

I force a grin, not letting her see how much her words have affected me. I need to make it up to her somehow, or at least try to help her.

———

A rriving in Childcare, Kayla and I take the seats at the front, nearest the door. We both have lunch after this, so we want to be the first ones out.

I like our Childcare teacher. She's pretty cool for an old chick, and she's pretty lenient with things other teachers give out detentions for.

"Hey, class. I come bearing gifts," she cheers, holding out envelopes with our assignments in them. Each will have a different subject and topic to discuss, and we will write a twenty-thousand-word essay, along with a five-minute presentation.

Students groan, but not heatedly. You can tell they enjoy this lesson just as much as any of the others. I'm not the only male in the class; a few other kids picked it too, thinking it would be an easy grade, but the joke is on them. Now they're stuck with it until we finish up with school.

The teacher walks around handing everyone their assignments. When she gets to our table, she gives us a big grin.

"Hey, you must be Kayla?" she greets.

"Yes," Kayla answers, biting her bottom lip.

"I'm Miss Watson. I teach Childcare and Health and Social Care. Myles told me you were transferring so he paired himself with you, but if you'd like to change, I can try moving some people around," she offers, pulling out a chair in front of us.

"No, I'm okay working with Myles," Kayla replies quietly. She scoots her chair closer to mine, as if the teacher is going to send her away.

I'm confused with her nervousness. I assumed it would be men she was scared of, but I've noticed it's females too, like she can't trust them.

It's probably because she's never met Miss Watson, dickhead.

I scold myself for not thinking of it sooner. "You've not met Miss Watson yet, have you?" I ask, looking to Kayla.

The teacher looks between us, seeming deep in thought, as if she's trying to get a read on us. She's probably wondering about Kayla's reaction. She wasn't here when everything went down, and I don't think the school had a meeting over it either.

"No. It was Mrs Deer who taught me."

"I only got to meet her a few times. She was a lovely lady," Miss Watson admits, and then opens the envelope with our papers in them. "Here is your assignment. Most of the class already know how they're going to work on their projects, but I wanted to come by and check in with you both before I leave you to do it. Do you have any idea how you'll work on it?"

Kayla looks at me, and from the corner of my eye, I can tell she is panicked, but I give Miss Watson a nod and smile.

"Yeah. If it's okay with Kayla, she can come around mine to study. I haven't thought much about it, but we did discuss the presentation and we were wondering if I can do all the speaking?"

It's worth a mention while we have the teacher's main focus. I know Kayla isn't going to like being in the spotlight, so we may as well get this over with just in case the teacher is grading us on our speeches. It will give Kayla more time to prepare herself.

"Not big on speaking in front of the class?" she asks, giving her an understanding smile.

Kayla shakes her head in reply, and Miss Watson looks on in concern.

"That's fine. As long as you contribute somehow, like stand with him, hold up cards, or even press a button on a computer if you're using Power Point, then it's fine. Your topic is a difficult one. You'll need to do a lot of research, and if you can get some interviews and back up your research that would be even better."

"What's our topic?" Kayla asks, seeming more interested, but I can feel her leg bouncing up and down beneath the table.

"Well, you'll be writing a presentation and an essay on the effects and after effects of an abusive home. You'll be finding out how it affects kids' long term, like in relationships, jobs, having their own kids, and school and such. You can use your own experiences, or others, as long as it's kept confidential."

"What makes you think I have experience?" Kayla blurts out, eyes wide.

"Oh, I worded that wrong. I apologise," she quickly interjects. "I know a little about Myles' background, and he explained he can give input from his perspective."

"Oh," Kayla breathes out, slumping back into the chair.

"It's whatever you are comfortable with," she adds. "Let me know your schedules when you work them out. I'll need some idea of how much time you'll spend on it. It won't need to be finished until three weeks before the school year ends. I know that's a long time, but don't leave it until the last minute. The more preparation you do, the better."

"We will," I assure her, taking the worksheets off her and placing them between us. Once she leaves, I turn to Kayla, grinning wide. I'm glad to be working with her on this. One, because I know she will do the work, but mostly because I get to spend time with her. "So, when did you want to get started?"

CHAPTER
FOUR

KAYLA

It's a new week, and I'm glad to be back at school. Last week seemed to pass by so quickly, and I think that was partially because I didn't want the weekend to come. I was having such a good time hanging out with Myles.

I haven't made any friends yet, like I was told to work towards, but I can't do it. I like the bubble I'm in, even if sometimes I wonder if I'm getting in the way or crowding him.

Whenever I've tried to give him space though, he's always sought me out, so if I am getting on his nerves, he isn't showing it.

I'm hoping that being here today will keep my mind off everything else. I wince as I take a seat, biting my lip to stop the whimper from escaping. My back is sore, stiff, and school has only just begun. I still have the rest of the day to get through. I'm glad I got Dad to drop me off earlier because I don't want people asking questions.

The bell rings, alerting everyone to the fact it's time for Registration, and my head begins to throb with a headache. I'm glad I won't have to sit down in front of people or dodge the girls that fawn all over Max, but I had forgotten about the bell.

I shift in my seat, wincing as pain throbs and burns in my sides. All I want to do is spend the day soaking in a hot bath or standing under a hot shower spray. It's how I spent most of my night. When I tried to fake sickness, Dad saw right through it and sent me anyway. He didn't know why I wanted the time off and I couldn't tell him.

My gaze flickers toward the classroom door, and I hate that it's because I'm searching for him. I'm always searching for him.

I pull out my English homework, trying to focus on that, when a commotion near the entrance startles me. I tilt my head up, finding Max walking through the doorway with his arms wrapped around a girl's shoulders.

I glance back down, having seen it all before. I don't think I've ever seen him with the same girl twice.

The hairs on the back of my neck stand on end, which can only mean one thing.

Myles.

I glance back up, my nerves going haywire when I see him. He's handsome, and when he smiles, I get this funny feeling in my stomach. It's like being on a rollercoaster ride each time I see him or he's near.

My stomach drops when a girl walks over to him and rises to the balls of her feet to kiss him. My breath hitches, and I glance back down at the table. Tears gather in the back of my eyes and my chest begins to ache.

I have no right to feel any of this. I'm not his girlfriend. I'm not really anything. I have no right to be jealous of who he does or doesn't see.

And yet it hurts inside to think of him with another girl.

I close my eyes when it hits me. I'm jealous. I am so jealous I feel sick to my stomach. I saw her though, so there isn't any question as to why he chose someone like her. I'm clueless, scared of my own shadow, and have baggage. She is gorgeous. Perfect bone structure, perfect figure, and she makes the school uniform look stylish.

My heart races when he pulls out the chair beside me. I try to ignore him, to focus on the work in front of me, but all the words blur together. It's hard to concentrate on anything other than him.

I squirm in the chair, trying to act like I haven't noticed him yet.

"Think she's ignoring you, bro?" Max asks, sounding close.

I jump, glancing to the side where Max is seated. I didn't even feel or hear him take a seat.

When the hell did he get there?

He gives me his signature smirk and knowing eyes, which only has my cheeks burning. *Did he see me looking at that girl kissing Myles?*

I inwardly groan, hoping like hell he didn't notice my reaction, or if he did, that he doesn't read into it. I don't want him telling Myles.

What if he does and Myles doesn't want to hang out with you?

"Calm down, Little K, your secret's safe with me," he whispers, just as Myles interrupts him, causing me to jump again.

It's official. I'm getting them both bells. I'm going to have a heart attack if they keep sneaking up on me.

"Who's ignoring who?" Myles asks, his brows pulling together.

I tighten my lips, scared that if I speak, he'll hear the turmoil going on inside of me right now.

"I was being sarcastic." Max scoots his chair forward, smirking. "What was that about with *Layla*?" he asks, emphasising her name. Layla! Even her name is pretty.

"No idea. Did you see her nearly kiss me? I swear, some of the chicks in this school have no boundaries," he grumbles, and my heart skips a beat. He didn't kiss her back.

I don't even care that it makes me a weirdo. I'm grateful and that's that.

"Just the way I like 'em," Max cheers, and a few classmates turn around to see what all the excitement is about. I bury my head into my book, nearly screaming out in pain when I do. I bite my tongue so hard I can taste metal in my mouth.

"Hey, Kayla," Myles greets, sitting down in his chair next to me. "What you reading?"

"Nothing," I whisper, my voice laced with pain.

"You okay?"

I fold my arms underneath me, resting my head on them, and turn to look at him. "Just tired," I explain.

I'm afraid to move. The muscles in my back are already throbbing, and I know the second I sit up, it's going to get worse.

I'm scared. Scared of them finding out. I don't want to be the talk of the school again.

When the teacher walks in, my hope of staying in this position dies. I slowly raise myself up, cursing under my breath as I grip the edge of the table.

I hate my dad for bullying me into coming. What gets me the most is his lack of attention. I get like this every Monday, sometimes for longer, and not once has he picked up on it, read into it. He just goes on with his jolly day believing everything is okay in the world. And it isn't. Sometimes I want to scream at him so badly to look. Really look at what's in front of him.

I take slow, steady breaths, trying to block out the pain coursing through me.

"Are you sure you're okay?" Myles asks, his eyes scrunched up with worry.

I shrug, wincing at the movement. I have to come up with a lie, since we share nearly every class together. But he's bound to know I'm lying.

I force a smile. "Yeah, I must have slept on my side funny."

He watches me for a minute, and I begin to get nervous that he can read my mind. I can feel him gauging my reaction too, so I try to keep my expression passive.

I glance away when he doesn't say anything, not one for confrontations. He doesn't need to though. It's written all over his face that he doesn't believe me.

"What are you doing at the weekend?" Max asks. "Kayla?"

I jerk in response, shocked that he's talking to me. "Um, I go to my mum's on weekends," I whisper, glancing up at the teacher to make sure they haven't heard me.

"Want to come round Denny's?"

My eyebrows pull together. "I'm at my mum's," I repeat, wondering if he didn't hear me the first time.

He smirks and shakes his head as if he finds something amusing. "Yeah, but you can ditch the rent and come have some fun with us."

I wish. "Yeah, I can't. Since they broke up, I only get to visit Mum on weekends. She'll be pissed and will probably take my dad to court if I miss a weekend," I half lie. I really do go on weekends, but I don't think my mum could afford to go to court again. I hope! Or have the motivation to go to so much trouble to see me. And because of my mental health, being eighteen means shit. Dad has a say over my care.

Max grimaces. "That's shit. So you don't get a weekend off?"

"Yeah, I get the last weekend of every month to do what I please with. It's why she gets upset if I don't make it on her weekends."

"So that's in what, two weeks?" Myles asks, and I lock eyes with him, feeling an intense pressure in my chest.

"Yeah," I agree. My heart skips a beat like it always does when I look at him. The teacher calls out our names, breaking the spell we're under.

"We'll make plans for then," Myles declares, keeping his voice low. A shiver runs down my spine and I mutely nod, unable to form words.

I don't get it. I don't get my reaction to him and only him. And I wish I had the courage to ask someone about it. It feels wrong to like him so much, not when I have been through what I have. He deserves better.

"So, are you okay to start our project after school?" Myles asks during lunch. We're sitting at a table with a group of his friends. I'm tucked into my normal corner away from everyone else. I struggled sitting here when he first invited me to eat with him, but then when I realised no one could approach me, or sit anywhere near me, I started to relax. I think the fact no one can sneak up behind me from this position helps to ease my apprehension too.

"Yeah, I am. What time were you thinking?" I try to remember if my dad will be home or not. He didn't get back from work until way past midnight last night, and I'm pretty sure he said it would most likely be the same tonight.

"About half four? I need to go back home to change and take a shower."

"Where do you want to meet up?" I question nervously, not really wanting to go out in public somewhere, especially at that time.

"Is your place okay? Or do you want to come to mine?"

The cafeteria is bustling with noise, but I'm so nervous the only sound I can concentrate on is the thumping in my ears. "Cool." I smile, wringing my hands in my lap nervously.

The bell rings when lunch is over, and I get up, grabbing my bag from under my chair. Myles stops me just before I go to step past him.

"I'll see you later then?" He smiles, and it's so warm and genuine my heart stops for a few seconds, basking in his beauty.

I shake my head and give him a smile in return, hoping it looks genuine. "Yeah, sounds good. Oh, I'm cooking pasta bake for my dad, so there will be tons left over if you fancy some."

"I'll look forward to it. I haven't had a cooked meal all week." He opens his mouth to say something else, but then his friend, Liam, who I've seen him hang out with, pats him on the back, getting his attention.

"Hey, Myles, a few of us are heading over to the skate rink after school. Do you want to come?"

I can feel myself stiffen, and as much as I try to relax, I can't. I'm waiting for Myles' reaction, but he doesn't give anything away in his expression. I don't even know why I'm reacting this way. It feels foreign, and I start to squirm, feeling uncomfortable.

"I've got plans, mate. Maybe another time." He smiles down at me and my body instantly relaxes. He's blown off a night out with the lads to come and study with me at mine. I want to interrupt, to tell him we can rearrange it for another night, but something inside me stops me from opening my mouth. It's selfish of me to keep my mouth shut, but I like Myles. I like spending time with him. I like the way I feel when I'm around him, the safeness he cocoons me in. It's refreshing from the normal fear that clouds my mind. Even with my dad, I don't feel the same safeness I do with Myles, which is weird because I've known him my whole life, whereas Myles I've only known for a short amount of time, yet I feel the safest when I'm around him.

"See ya later," Liam shouts as he rushes off to class.

I wave timidly at Myles, who just gives me a cheeky smirk in return. My cheeks flush red, but once I've turned and I'm out of sight, I grin from ear to ear.

———

A t the end of school, I hurry home, rushing through the door and up the stairs, straight into the shower. Once showered and dry, I quickly look through my choice of clothes and groan. Most of my clothes are baggy, boyish, or just boring. I want to look nice—not that I want to do anything, or for him to try something, but I want to make a good impression for the first time in my life.

"Why are you even bothered?" I mutter to myself, knowing I'll never be able to have a relationship with him. I'm damaged. I'm broken and I'm completely messed up. Just the thought of letting someone be intimate with me after what *he* did makes me want to vomit. I couldn't do that to someone.

So instead of going for a girly, nice look, I just grab my normal casual wear. I grab a Guns and Roses T-shirt with a pair of faded, washed-out jeans and put them on. I continue to move at a fast pace, wanting to get dinner started before he comes over. I'm in the middle of blow drying my hair when my phone message alert goes off. I quickly grab my phone, my heart pounding at the thought of Myles texting to cancel tonight. But when I see my dad's name on the screen, my body relaxes.

Dad: I don't know when I'll be back tonight so don't wait up. I'll grab something to eat at work. Dad x

I grunt at the phone. I'm still planning on leaving him some leftovers. He will only moan come morning that he hasn't got anything ready for lunch. I'll box it up for him to take to work. I fire off a quick text, telling him I'll leave it boxed up in the fridge, and quickly carry on drying my hair.

Once it's done, I decide to run some product through it, before leaving it wavy down my back. It's redder than it normally is due to the sun being out. You'd think with my red hair, I'd have extremely pale skin, but I don't. I'm actually quite tanned, and I don't burn easily like my mother does in the sun. I opt for some lip gloss and a thin layer of mascara before making my way downstairs.

It doesn't take me long to prep dinner and get it cooked. I'm just putting it in the oven to keep warm when the doorbell rings, startling me. Wiping my sweaty palms down my arms, I walk toward the door, standing there for a few seconds to gain my composure.

Shit! What if it's not him?

Cursing myself, I quickly move to the peephole to find it is indeed Myles. He's standing there with his hands in his front pockets, his bag dangling off one shoulder, rocking back and forth on his heels. He looks like a magazine model. He's lean, muscular, and is taller than most boys I've seen my own age. It's not as intimidating, though, as it should be for me. In fact, little Tim in my cooking class, who is shorter than me, intimidates me more than Myles. There's just something about him that doesn't make me crouch back into myself, or jump when I'm around him, even though whenever his presence is around me it's like he's dominating my thoughts.

The doorbell rings again, and I realise I've been peeping through the peephole, ogling Myles. What the hell is wrong with me lately? I need to give myself a good talking to because I'm only setting myself up for heartbreak and I've had enough of that to last me a lifetime.

Rushing over to the door, I open it and quickly jump back when I nearly swing the door in my face.

"Shit." I jump back, my face flaming red from embarrassment.

Way to go, Kayla.

"Hey," Myles chuckles. "Excited to see me?" he teases, and my shoulders relax.

"Yeah, I nearly knocked myself out from not being able to contain myself," I tell him. Then my eyes widen when I realise I just flirted with him. Or is he just teasing? I don't know. God, I'm such a loser when it comes to things like this. I don't know what to do. And now I'm standing in the doorway staring at him like an idiot, and I realise he's trying to talk to me.

"What? Sorry."

"I said, something smells good," he repeats, not commenting on my flabbergasted state.

"Oh, yeah, crap, come in. Dinner is done if you want something to eat now?"

"That'd be good, if that's okay with you?"

"Yeah, I didn't really eat much earlier," I tell him, not wanting to admit it's because of my bruised side. I lost my appetite Friday night, but I'm actually hungry now I've had a warm shower, although the dull ache from rushing around when I got back is still there, pounding away. It's like a constant reminder of what a failure I am.

"Take a seat. I'll just dish this up," I tell him, gesturing to the chair at the table. He walks over to the chair and plonks himself down gracefully, and I can't help but stop and stare at how good he looks doing it.

"Where's your dad?" he questions, and for the first time while in Myles' presence, I freeze. Should I tell him the truth, that my dad won't be back tonight, or should I lie and tell him he's in his office upstairs? Knowing I won't be able to lie, I look over to Myles with a sheepish smile, hoping he understands how much trust I'm putting in him by telling him this.

"He's at work and won't be back until later," I tell him, opting at the last minute not to mention the time. It's not like he asked me what time he's coming back or anything. I've not lied. *Jesus, Kayla, get a grip of yourself.*

I busy myself getting the plates out, before dishing out our food and bringing them over to the table. Having forgotten to offer him a drink, I ask him what he would like.

"Just a coke or something, if you've got it." He smiles, then scoops up a forkful of food before shovelling it into his mouth, moaning when he does. "God, this is so good," he mumbles around his food, and I smile wide before getting up to make us some drinks. My nerves are slowly evaporating, which I'm thankful for. I don't want the entire night to be stiff and awkward on my part. I'd never live it down.

We eat the rest of the dinner in silence, and after we've finished, Myles helps me clean up before he gets his books out. I look at him, confused for a second, and it takes me a few minutes to decide what to say.

"Um, Myles? We, uh, can we go to my room?" I shake my head, embarrassed. "I just... My work is up there and I feel more, um, comfortable. Forget it, I'll go get my books," I stammer, my voice low and unsure.

"No, wait, it's fine. If you want to study in your room then we can. Lead the way." He smiles and I relax. Then I begin to panic. I never thought about it being just the two of us alone in my room. I turn on the stairs, my eyes wide and probably full of fear. Myles nearly bumps into me, and when he looks up, his eyes soften.

"We can study down here if you'd like. I'm not going to hurt you," he says softly, and I scrunch my face up. Am I that transparent? Does he really believe I think he'd hurt me? But that was what I was thinking, even though deep down inside my heart, I know he wouldn't hurt me. God, my head hurts with all this backward and forward shit going on. It's confusing the hell out of me.

"No, no, it's fine. I, um, I was just going to ask if you want another drink and some snacks?" I lie, hoping he believes me.

He smiles back, and I relax. "I could use another drink if you've got one. I'm not fussed about snacks. Maybe something for later?"

I nod, grateful to have a few minutes alone to gather my thoughts. "I'll just go get them. You head on up." I smile before rushing past him down the stairs.

It's late when I roll onto my back and groan. We've been going over our project for hours and my back is beginning to hurt. Myles chuckles, and I lazily turn my head to watch him. He's leaning against my bed, his legs stretched out in front of him and crossed at the ankles.

"So we've done the outline of what we can do, now all we have to do is research and stuff. It's a pretty sore subject to bring up to other kids at school, so I might just use an anonymous source."

"What do you mean?" I ask, sitting up and leaning back against the bed the same way Myles has.

"You know my brothers and I come from a broken home, right?" he asks softly, and I can hear in his voice that the subject is hard for him to talk about. I nod, opting to keep quiet as he talks, wanting to know everything about him. "Well, I don't remember our mum, but our dad... our dad was a sick son of a bitch. He beat us, mostly Maverick and Malik, though. They think we never knew or heard him, but we did. Max and I, we had trouble sleeping because of the noise, so we would hear things." He shudders, and I reach out on instinct for his hand, covering it with my own. Tingles shoot up my spine from the touch and a nervousness that I've never felt before seeps into my body. Our eyes lock and my palms begin to sweat.

"Go on," I croak, my voice not sounding like my own.

"I think it affected us all in different ways. Max and I got less of the brunt because of how young we were, or because Maverick protected us. I'm not sure. Either way you look at it, Max and I got off lightly compared to the others."

"How did it affect you?" I whisper, the conversation hitting close to home. I'm interested in his answer though, which surprises even me.

"We all came away with something different from our time with him. I want to help other kids that go through what we did. None of us spoke up to an adult because we didn't think they'd care or take us seriously, but most of all, we didn't speak up because we didn't want to be separated. I don't remember a lot, but I remember our dad telling us our granddad didn't care, that he saw us as worthless brats just like he did. I think it was the main reason none of us spoke. We didn't have any other family who would take in five boys.

"I guess if I could just help one kid in my life, it will make everything worthwhile. I don't know."

His demeanour changes to sad and helpless, and I wish I could take some of his pain away. I know all too well what he's going through. I just wish I had a quarter of his courage.

"You'll be a great social worker, Myles. Tell me the rest, about your brothers," I encourage, then realise I'm sticking my nose into his business. "Only if you feel like it. I'm sorry, I'm being nosey."

He gives me a soft smile before moving his writing pad onto the floor next to him. "Max, well, he doesn't do commitment or even love. It's why he sleeps around, I think. He doesn't want to get attached to anyone because he thinks in the end, they will leave or hurt him. He doesn't talk about our mum, so I'm guessing he has what people may call 'mummy issues'. Malik is angry all the time. Well, he was until he met Harlow. He changed when he met her."

"She's a great girl," I agree.

"She is." He smiles. "He was just angry all the time before her, always getting into fights and brooding all the time. He was angry at everyone for a long time. Then Mason, well… Mason slept around a lot. I don't think he knows it, but I think he used sex as a coping mechanism. He'd also leave them hanging high and dry before they could do the same to him." He shrugs.

"What about Maverick? He's the eldest of you lot, isn't he?" I ask, not knowing much about the guy.

"Yeah, he's been like a dad to us, always getting us to school on time, keeping us fed and clothed and shit. I think when we moved into Granddad's, he lost a part of himself not being our full-time carer. He still bosses us about and hands us our arses—well, Max's—if we don't go to school and shit. I don't know what our mum and dad put him through, but you can see it's affected him. He's never said anything, but I've heard things at night. I don't think I'll ever be able to work him out."

"Maybe his need to look after you guys is how it affected him. It could be that he feels like he failed you all somehow and that's why he's so protective of you. I don't know." I shrug, my heart hurting. They all had each other growing up, someone to talk to when things got bad. I, on the other hand, have no one to confide in, no one to talk to or ask for advice. It's hard, and I hate it. It's like I'll be forever stuck in some sort of nightmare, one I'll never get out of.

"What about you?" he asks lazily. I can feel the heat of his stare on the side of my face.

"What about me?" I squeak out nervously.

"Do you have a good relationship with your parents? Abuse isn't just physical, it's mental as well. Abuse can come in all sorts of ways."

"Um...why are you asking me this?"

"It's our project," he reminds me, looking at me in confusion.

"My dad and I get along fine," I rush out, my cheeks burning.

"What about your mum?" he asks, and I know he already knows the answer to the question by the look in his eyes. I start to feel cornered, like he can read my mind, and I wipe my palms down my jeans in a nervous habit.

"We clash I guess," I whisper. "I'm tired. Do you want to watch a film or do you need to go?" I blurt out, hoping he doesn't question my quick subject change.

"I wouldn't mind watching a film. My back and arse are killing me though, so can we move to the bed?" he questions, and my heart rate picks up again. I swallow the lump in my throat and nod my head in a quick, jerking movement.

We both pack our books away together. When Myles takes a seat on my bed, I pause to watch him there. You'd think having him on my bed with just the two of us in the house, alone, would cause me to have a major panic attack, but looking at him getting comfortable, fluffing up all my pillows, it causes something else to constrict inside my chest.

Blushing, I turn away quickly to look at my collection of DVDs. There are a few I haven't seen yet, so I grab a pile and turn back to Myles.

"So, I have, *The Voices, The Boy Next Door, Two Night Stand,* or *X-Men: Futures Past.*" I read them off slowly, flicking from one DVD to the next.

"*X-Men: Futures Past,* if that's okay? I've not seen it yet."

"Me neither." I smile, excited to finally be watching it.

CHAPTER
FIVE

KAYLA

I whimper at the sound of his footsteps getting closer.

"Where the fuck do you think you're going?" he roars.

I try to pump my feet faster. Why can't I run faster? My feet feel weighted to the ground, and I can't get them to move as quickly as I'd like. My pulse thunders in my ears. Adrenaline is spiking through my veins, overriding the fear looming there.

The edge of the forest is getting closer. I can see it. But then it moves further away in the blink of an eye. I scream out in frustration, but the sound is muted. I try harder and louder, but nothing comes out.

The sound of his feet on the ground grows closer, and a shiver runs down my spine.

His hand reaches the back of my blazer, and I cry out, flying forward to the dirty ground. Mud and dried leaves blow up in my face and into my mouth. I cough as I roll over, kicking out and trying to fight him off, but my fists and feet kick out at thin air.

It hurts.

Everything hurts.

His hands are everywhere, touching, slapping, grabbing, and I can't *wiggle myself free. The sound of a belt undoing has another scream tearing from my mouth, until his hand clamps over it, muffling the sound. I try to break free, to scream harder for help, but nothing works.*

Another sharp pain, another muffled scream. My voice is hoarse, broken and filled with anguish. Then I hear voices, and my eyes flicker open to find my mother standing above us. She's watching him with sickening delight, laughing that laugh that sends chills down my spine.

"Help me, Mum!" I cry, but she looks through me, not an ounce of sympathy or remorse on her features.

I'm thrown onto my stomach, the cruel sound of them laughing echoing into the trees. I try to crawl away, the pain unbearable, but I fight it. I fight him. A sickening whistle sounds through the air, and for a split second as time freezes, the pain stops. Until an excruciating, red-hot burn slices through my back. The thick leather belt and buckle cuts through my flesh. My entire body is screaming at me to stop, but my mind won't let me, and I continue to fight. It does nothing to stop him, and only aids him in removing my knickers. The cold air hits me below and vomit rises in my throat.

My face is shoved into the dirt.

Please no! Please, don't do this. Please don't let this happen.

"You deserve this, you little bitch. Enjoy it while you've got it," my mother's voice rings out sweetly from somewhere nearby.

"You'll enjoy it, I promise," my rapist laughs, no compassion or remorse in his voice.

"Stop! Please don't do this!"

Then he thrusts inside of me, punishing and unforgiving, and I feel like my insides are splitting apart.

"No! No! No! No! Get off me, get off me," I scream, shoving a large body off me.

"Hey, it's me, Kayla. It's me, Myles. It's okay. You're safe," he tells me through my terror.

"Please don't touch me," I heave out through my tears before rushing off the bed and out into the hallway towards the bathroom. As soon as I enter, I turn on the shower, taking deep, steady breaths. It doesn't help, and seconds later, I'm spinning around to the toilet and emptying the entire contents of my stomach.

Once I'm sure I'm not going to be sick again, I strip out of my sweat-coated clothes.

I notice the time on my watch when I take it off, and gasp. It's half two in the morning. Oh my god, did we... did we fall asleep together? I nearly rush back over to the toilet to be sick again, but the need to get *his* touch off me is overwhelming.

The temperature of the water is scalding hot when I step into the shower. I begin to scrub my body raw, making sure to pay extra attention between my legs. It's moments like this that I do feel clean, but I know the second I step out of the shower, I will feel *his* dirty hands on me all over again.

I don't know how long I've stayed in the shower for, but when I begin to feel lightheaded from the heat, I shut the shower off. I grab a towel off the rack to wrap around my body before stepping out.

I listen to the sounds in the house, not hearing any movement, which I'm hoping means Myles has left. He probably ran as fast as he could after I freaked out on him like that. I don't blame him after that performance. He probably thinks I'm crazy.

I don't even want to think about what I might have cried out in my sleep. Mortified, I grab my dressing gown off the back of the bathroom door and tie it securely around me before walking back down the hall to my bedroom.

I'm surprised to find my bedsheets have been changed and the old ones are in a pile by the door, but what surprises me the most is Myles is sat on the edge of the bed, his shirt forgone and his head in his hands. He looks like a dark angel sat there, the muscles in his shoulders tensing and the muscles in his arms bulging from where he's leaning them on his knees.

"Hey," I whisper. He must not have heard me walk in because as soon as he hears my voice, his head snaps up. There's a tortured look in his eyes when his gaze meets mine. I can't take that look, so I lower my head.

"That was about *him,* wasn't it?" he questions, but it sounds more like a statement.

"Yes," I whisper, still unable to look at him. "We must have fallen asleep."

"Yeah, I... um, here, put this on," he tells me, walking over with his lost shirt. I take in a huge gasp of air when I see the outline of his abdominal muscles. They're cut to perfection, and he has that V thing going on that I read about in my books. He has a faint line of hair trailing down to his nether region too, and it looks sexy as hell. I swallow the lump forming in my dry throat. The sudden need for water feels almost painful.

He lifts his arms with his T-shirt scrunched up and moves closer towards me, pulling the T-shirt over my head. I breathe him in, feeling dizzy from it.

"Um, you should do the rest." He clears his throat before turning around.

I slip my arms out of my dressing gown and push them through the T-shirt before pulling it down over the towel.

"Stay turned," I whisper, my voice hoarse from the dryness and from the crying I've done. With shaky fingers, I walk over to my chest of drawers and find a pair of knickers and shorts. I slip them on under the towel. Once I've done that, I remove the towel and throw it over the chair.

His shirt smells like him, and I find it oddly comforting. I inhale the smell, loving his intoxicating scent, before dropping it back down. It falls loosely just above my knees. "You can turn around now."

I move over to the bed to sit down, embarrassed, not knowing what I should say. It's late, I'm tired, and I just want to curl up in a ball and forget about my nightmare.

"You should probably go," I choke out, then startle when I feel him sit on the bed next to me.

"I'm not going anywhere," he starts, and when I go to protest, he holds his hand up, stopping me. "I'm not leaving you here alone when you've just had a nightmare. Your dad isn't even back yet, so I'm not leaving. Come on, get into bed. I'll lie on top of the covers."

He opens up the duvet, and I get in and lie down facing him. I watch as he tucks me in before he gets comfortable, mirroring my position.

His fingers brush a strand of wayward hair from my face. "Do you want to talk about it?"

"Not really. I have a nightmare or two every night. Sometimes it's about what happened, sometimes it's different, and my mum or someone will be there, taunting me." I shrug, feeling another tear slide down my cheek. Before I can wipe it away, Myles reaches out, rubbing the pad of his thumb under my eye.

"What does your mum say?" he asks.

Dread fills my stomach at the question, but not because he asked. It's because for the first time, I want to talk. I want to tell him all of it. And it scares me.

As soon as I begin, the words flow out of me. I tell him how my mother taunts me in my nightmares, laughs at me, and encourages Davis to hurt me. I tell him about the other voices I can't place a face to. I tell him my regrets about that day. How if I didn't take the shortcut home, it might not have happened.

"I'm sorry that happened to you," he whispers softly, but his jaw is hard and his eyes look distant and lost.

"Life happens," I mumble, not believing a word of what I say. Life is cruel and unfair. Sometimes I feel selfish because there are people all around the world with a harder life than mine. "There are people far worse off."

"That may be true, Kayla, but it doesn't excuse what happened to you. Just because someone out there has it worse, that doesn't make your pain any less significant. It happened to you, not them. It's your pain that you suffer with. You're a brave, strong woman, and I don't think you should blow off your pain just because someone else has it bad."

My mind runs over what he said, and I can understand what he's trying to tell me. It still doesn't excuse the fact that life keeps fucking me over. I must have been a worldwide known serial killer in my previous life, because I know I've done nothing in this life to deserve what I'm going through. Or maybe my mother is right and I deserve everything that happens to me.

My eyes flick to Myles' deep, dark brown ones. We stare for what feels like hours, neither of us talking, and before I know it, I'm drifting off to sleep.

———

My body is warm and the bed is comfortably hard beneath me. I groan when the stiffness in my neck cricks. The bed shifts beneath me, and I freeze when I hear a male groan. My body is curled around Myles' like a blanket. My leg is thrown over both of his, my girly parts shoved against his hip, and I can feel his... I can feel his morning wood against my thigh.

Nervously, I lift my head off his shoulder and lean up to look down at his sleeping form. Asleep, he looks relaxed, peaceful, and much younger than he does when he's awake. With a mind of its own, my hand reaches up and I lightly run my finger along his eyebrow. His eyebrows pinch together, and I find myself smiling at how adorable he looks. I trace my finger down his beautiful, straight nose to his full, plump lips. His bottom lip is fuller than his top one; it's sexy, and I run my finger along them, loving how soft they feel under my touch. His lips pucker, kissing my fingertips, and a delicious shiver I've never felt before runs through my body.

"Was I drooling?" he asks, his hard body rumbling against me, and I fall back, squeaking.

"I'm sorry. I'm... Oh God, I'm so sorry," I blurt out, my face heating like an oven.

He chuckles, and I notice my leg is still over his. When I try to move it slowly, hoping he doesn't notice, my knee grazes against his morning wood.

Oh crap, now what do I do?

It's taken out of my hands when Myles reaches down and grabs my knee, lifting it off him as he follows, rolling onto his side to face me.

"Morning," he breathes huskily. His eyes are half mast, still full with sleep.

"Morning." I blush.

"Did you sleep okay?"

"Better than I have in a long time," I tell him honestly. There's no point in lying. We both know he would have heard me if I'd had another nightmare.

"Sweetie, it's half seven. You're going to be late," my dad calls. I jump back from Myles, banging my head against the bedframe.

"Yeah, Dad. I'm up," I yell back. I'm so glad he isn't one of those fathers who walk in to wake their kids up.

"I'm going to bed, kid," he shouts.

My brows pinch together at his comment, and I race up to question him. Which means I straddle Myles to get out. His erection presses against my core, and I squeak, rolling the rest of the way off.

Ignoring my inner freak out, I crawl on the floor. "Hold up, Dad," I call out, out of breath as I get to my feet.

Too scared to look back at Myles, I continue to the door. I can't believe I just got out of bed like that, pressing myself unintentionally against his erection. Jesus, it was hard. And long. And, my god, something else.

I rush to open the bedroom door, before slamming it shut behind me. Dad isn't there, so I race down the hallway to his room. His bedroom is at the back of the house, his room the farthest away from any of the others.

"Have you only just got in?" I question worriedly when I enter. He's been working a hell of a lot lately, and it seems to be since we moved back to town. I feel like he's not telling me something, but then, he's never really discussed his business with me before, so I don't expect him to start now.

"Yeah, darling. We've had a lot going on opening up the new branch. I'm hoping my hours will die down once it's all settled."

"Are you sure everything's okay?" I can tell when he's hiding something or lying. His eyes always flicker to the left before landing back on me.

"Yeah. Get to school and I'll speak to you later. I probably won't be back until ten tonight, but I promise to call the next time if I'm going to be out all night. I should have called your mother or something," he tells me.

"No. No, that's totally fine. I'm a big girl, Dad; I'm eighteen, nearly nineteen. I'm old enough to look after myself. You know this."

"I know, sweetie, but until you turn twenty-one, you know the rules." He smiles, and I groan. Because of everything that happened, I have to wait until I'm twenty-one to legally become an adult as such. While most kids my age are attending college or university and out drinking in nightclubs, I'm stuck living with the rents like a sixteen-year-old child. All because of the state my mental health was in when everything happened. I'm classed as unstable until they do another consultation at the end of the month.

It's one of the reasons I see my mother on weekends. You see, the real reason isn't because we're mother and daughter and we're legally bound; it's because she's blackmailing me. She's pretty much done it since I gave in my statement a few months back. She said if I didn't keep up appearances, she would make sure a court sees me as an unfit person and I'll never be free of parental supervision. I truly believe she will do this, especially since she wants legal rights to my trust fund, and the fact my father pays for her house and bills. And the only reason he does this is so I have somewhere safe to stay when I'm with her.

I was supposed to inherit my trust fund when I turned eighteen, but because of my mental health at the time, they decided against it, so now I have to wait until I'm twenty-one. Which I'm not really bothered about. I never earned the money in the first place, but it's the fact that I could use that money to get away from her. So one wrong move on my end and she will make my life a living hell more than she already does.

"I know, Dad," I say, rolling my eyes. "When I have my examination at the end of the month, you'll see I'm better. I'm not bothered about what I get or don't get, I just want my independence back."

"You are independent, and I can see a massive change in you since we've moved back here. To be honest, I was worried at first about coming back, but I think facing your fears has helped in some way. I know I can trust you, but after... after last time, honey—"

"I know, Dad," I tell him, forcing a smile. I don't need to hear about the mistakes I've made in the past, but if only he knew what it was like to feel that worthless, to be that dirty; maybe then he could somehow understand the reasons why I did what I did.

"Go get ready for school," he orders gently, his eyes worn and tired.

I nod, bidding him a goodnight, and head back to my bedroom. My mind is so busy running through all those bad memories that I forgot Myles is still in my room, so when I find him standing there, shirtless and looking hot as hell, I jump, a scream nearly escaping my mouth.

"Jesus, I really need to buy you some bells," I mutter.

He grins with a shrug. "I'm going to get going so I can get a shower in before school. Do you need us to come and get you? Mason is taking us today because he's heading that way for work."

I'm about to decline, but then the conversation with my dad runs through my mind again and I find myself nodding. I need this. I need to move forward, to prove to my parents that I can do this; I can go off to college without them having to worry. Not that I think that's the part my mother cares about. I just feel like I'll have more freedom once I've proven myself.

"I'll be back here just before half eight. Make sure you're ready," he demands teasingly, as he steps forward.

At first, I think he's going to kiss me, but he stops, looking away with wide eyes. "See you," he rushes out, grabbing his backpack.

He hightails it out of the room, and sadness fills me. I don't know why I'm hurt he didn't kiss me when I know I would have freaked out. But I do know I can't let him inside my heart or give him mixed signals. It will only hurt me when it's over. And I know I'll never recover from him.

CHAPTER
SIX

KAYLA

The rest of the school week is really slow, and come Friday I just want to go to bed and sleep the whole weekend away.

Myles and I haven't seen each other out of school again this week. He's been busy studying and doing other things, but something inside me can't help but feel like he's avoiding me. After the night we spent together, Myles hasn't been back. He texted me that morning to meet him at the end of my street and that was that. We still hang out all the time at school, but something feels different between us now. I could just be imagining it and blowing this up out of proportion.

"Good, you're here. It's about damn time," my mother snaps.

I want to roll my eyes and tell her to fuck off, but I keep my mouth shut and my eyes focused on her mouth. Heaven forbid I don't pay attention when she's talking.

"The bus was running late," I tell her, but I already know there's no point in explaining. She will only see it as an excuse.

She clicks her tongue, looking at me with so much disgust. I squirm where I'm standing, waiting for her to blow. "Go put your stuff in your room and get started. I have a *'friend'* coming over for dinner and I want the place looking sparkling."

I nod, my shoulders dropping at the news. It's not a friend coming over. It's her way of telling me she's dating an obscenely rich man, and to get her claws into him, she wants to look good in front of him. She's desperate too because she knows my father will cut her off soon. My mother didn't get anything from the divorce because of the circumstances, so she's now on the hunt for another male she can manipulate, just like she did my dad.

"Speak when you're spoken to," she snaps, and quick for her, she swings her hand out, slapping me in the face. The force whips my head to the side.

My hand covers my stinging cheek, tears welling in my eyes as I look at her. I hate her. I've never hated anyone as much as I hate her.

"Do you understand, or do you need to be taught a lesson?" she snaps, her voice grating on my nerves.

"No. I understand. I'll get it done," I politely confirm, my voice high and clear so she doesn't find another excuse to lash out at me.

"So why are you just standing there?" she roars, her face murderous, vein lines pumping in her forehead.

I don't reply, and instead rush off upstairs. My room is the small storage closet that should be used to store the hoover and stuff.

It's actually pretty cool in here. It fits a bed and a chest of drawers, and there's enough room in between the two to walk down to get out. I'm just lucky she didn't have a cellar, since she would find joy in making me sleep down there.

I quickly chuck my bag on the bed and change out of my school clothes. Once I'm changed, I quickly rush down to the kitchen and get to work. The place isn't a dump, but she's not used to doing things herself. She's lazy. I'm pretty sure she's never worked a day in her life. It's another reason I hate her. She expects everything handed to her on a silver plate. I wish I could walk into the front room, where she's watching some snooty show about housewives, and tell her where she can shove her goddamn broom and mop, but I know the consequences of speaking out of turn when it comes to that woman.

A few hours later, I'm putting away the last of the cutlery, when there's a loud knock on the front door. The blood drains from my face. I wanted to escape before her friend arrived, but instead, I rush to the front door.

My mother stands near the fireplace, glaring at me like I took too long to answer it. When my hand reaches the lock, she loses anger and smiles.

An overweight man wearing a suit is waiting on the other side of the door. His receding hairline makes his forehead look double the normal size. He's wearing silver-rimmed glasses that make his eyes look magnified. He leers at me, and a shiver crawls along my flesh. I would normally shower after feeling like this, but Mother doesn't let me shower here.

His gaze runs up and down my body, and I inwardly gag at the desire shining back at me. He runs his tongue along his lower lip as he stares at my chest, and I have to swallow back vomit. I try not to react, knowing it will fuel my mother's anger, but I must not have done a good job, because when I meet her gaze, there's a promise of retribution. I duck my head, holding back the tears threatening to fall. She'll never be the mother who protects me.

"Good evening, you must be Kayla, Jessica's daughter?"

"Yes, sir," I mutter tightly, before moving away.

The minute she starts flirting, I escape to the kitchen, where I retch into the sink. I'm swilling my mouth out with water, when she calls my name.

"Get our drinks," she demands.

I slowly head back into the room. "What would you both like to drink?" I ask, forcing my voice to be soft.

"Well, champagne of course," she declares, irritated.

Once in the kitchen, I pour both of them a glass of champagne before putting the bottle back into the fridge to cool. The last time I tried to put it in the ice bucket, she beat me with a broomstick. She said it looked tacky, so I learned my lesson quickly.

The glasses shake in my hands as I enter the dining room. I place the drinks down in front of them, careful not to spill.

"Oh, Harold, you are so funny," she giggles flirtatiously, and I have to bite back a groan.

"Thank you," Harold says, leering at me with a sneer, which I'm sure he thinks is a smile.

"We will eat now," Mum demands.

I head back into the kitchen and it takes minutes to dish out the food onto their plates. They are still flirting when I enter, and place their food in front of them.

I'm about to retreat to my room, when a hand reaches out, touching the back of my thigh, near the globe of my arse. I step back, a black haze clouding my vision. I knock Mum's chair, which jolts her drink, spilling a little over her hand.

My throat tightens and sweat begins to coat my skin.

I know this feeling all too well.

God, please don't have a panic attack now. Not here.

"You stupid little—urgh, get to your room now," my mother scolds. Not needing to be told twice, I race out of the room. "If you even think of helping yourself to food after what you just pulled, young lady, then you've got another thing coming."

It doesn't even bother me. I don't think I could stomach food anyway, but I don't let her know that because she'll probably force feed me.

"I'm so sorry, Harold. She's such a clumsy young girl. We tried to raise her the best we could, but there's only so much you can do, right?" I hear her explain.

Tears sting my eyes. Why can't I just have a normal mother, one who is proud to call me her daughter, and one who will stand in front of a loaded gun for me? I'd be lucky to get my mother to stand in front of me in a queue.

"Kids nowadays need discipline; a firm hand and a voice of reason. I'm a firm believer in kids should be seen and not heard," I hear him tease, which earns him a chuckle.

My skin prickles from his choice of words as I climb the stairs, and I wonder if he has kids of his own.

"I couldn't have said it better myself, Harold. She will be getting punished, don't you worry," she promises, before her voice lowers into a seductive plea. "But we shouldn't let the girl stand in the way of what is turning out to be a delightful night."

She's sick. She's getting off on someone who feels the same way she does about me.

I decide to get into bed and don't bother with my pyjamas. I feel safer with as much clothing as I can wear when I'm in this house. And with a complete stranger who just happens to be as cruel as she is in the house, I decide to keep my mobile phone under my pillow too. I don't usually leave it where my mother will find it. She will only break it like she did the last five mobiles I had, so it's best to keep it out of sight. If I'm honest, I believe she breaks them because she thinks I'm recording her or some shit, and believe me, I've tried. It was just when it got to the blackmailing part that I chickened out and ended up having a panic attack. I'm not strong enough to hold my own. At least, I wasn't back then, but maybe I'm stronger now. Like Dad said, he can see how much I've changed since moving here.

My eyelids lower as I concentrate on Myles and what he would do or say. And before I know it, I'm falling asleep and dreaming of him.

———

A sharp tug on my hair has me falling out of bed with a loud thud. I cry out in pain when I knock my previous injuries.

"Get up," Mum screams, like a banshee. Before I can get my bearings, she's grabbing my hair again and lifting me up.

In the small room, I use the bed as leverage to get up faster. When we're face to face, her eyes are bloodshot and I can smell the alcohol on her breath. From the corner of my eye, I look at the clock out in the hall, shocked when it reads three-thirty in the morning. *How long has she been drinking? Is Harold still here? Oh my god, what if he is?*

"Please, Mum, stop," I cry out, her grip on my hair tightening.

"Did you deliberately try to make a fool out of me tonight? Do you think it's a joke?" she demands, her hand rearing back before coming down hard across my cheek.

My hand reaches up to cover the sharp sting and more tears fall from my eyes. I don't argue back with her. There's no point. She doesn't really want an answer. She wants control. "I should have given you up at birth. You're a useless, selfish brat."

This time, instead of a slap, she lands a solid punch to my already sore ribs. A loud cry leaves my mouth as the resulting ripple of pain feels like each rib is shattering. I cower back, my arse hitting the bed, and I move backwards to try and get as far as I can as I watch and listen to her shout expletives at me.

She leans over the bed, her nails digging into my thigh. I'm thankful I left my normal clothes on because if I hadn't, I'd have more than a bruise on my thigh right now. I'd have cuts from her nails that are sharply digging in. I'd actually be surprised if she isn't already drawing blood.

"You're going to regret what you did tonight. Why can't you be a good daughter, one who listens? Instead, I get a whiny, snivelling, ugly, useless, thickhead for a daughter. No one will ever love you. No one. Because you're not fucking worth it," she spits out.

Her words cut deep, hurting more than her physical blows, and I bow my head in shame, which only makes her snicker. I don't look up. I already know what expression her face will be masked in, one of pure enjoyment and evil as she continues to throw insults at me.

I was born to a cruel woman who should never have become a mother. She doesn't have a caring bone in her body. If I was ever going to be a mum, I know I'd never treat my son or daughter with an ounce of how she treats me. They'll be raised knowing they can come to me and I'll be on their side, always. I'll make sure no other breathing soul will ever touch them.

Because I'd never want another human being to feel how I feel right now.

Like the world is too much, and it would be easier to slip away.

It's reaching five in the morning when she finally leaves my room. My face is throbbing, but thankfully, she hasn't drawn any blood. I'm pretty certain the only bruise forming that will be visible to other people will be the one on my forehead, where she whacked it against the chest of drawers. With the room being so small, it's hard to avoid hitting something.

I groan and roll over, reaching down to grab my small bag that contains a change of clothes. I quietly grab my stuff before heading down the hall an hour later. I check in on her room and find her snoring, fully clothed on top of her covers. Happy she's out cold, I gently close the door and make my way back down the hall to the bathroom. Luckily, her room and the bathroom aren't close together. I wouldn't normally risk taking a shower, but if I want to soothe any of these new bruises, I need to.

I shove the window open, letting the steam out of the small window before peeling the clothes off my aching body. Tears fall as I enter the shower, but once the scolding, hot water hits my flesh, those tears turn into sobs.

I grab my sponge and begin to clean myself up, not letting myself really look at the marks she's inflicted. It won't do me any good to look at them. Once I'm done, I get dressed and clean up any traces of me being in here. It also helps pass the time since I have to be at the church shelter in just over an hour. It's the only thing my mum gives me permission to do when I stay with her. She thought it would be a punishment, but what she never bothered to see is that it's a holiday for me. I get time away from her, and I like the work I do there.

Back in my room, I pull out the small compact mirror and inwardly groan at the dark bags under my eyes. I dab on some concealer, knowing it's the best I can do to hide them. I don't bother to hang around, and quietly tip-toe downstairs.

A half-naked Harold is snoring on the sofa, and I nearly trip at the sight of him. I thought he would have gone by now, but it looks like Mum has her claws in him. Literally, if the scratches on his chest are anything to go by.

I avert my eyes away from the large man and open the front door, whimpering when it causes the hinges to creak. I freeze when the snoring stops, and glance at the man on the sofa. He rolls, baring his arse to the room. I slide through the small gap, not wanting to risk waking them up, and slowly close it behind me. I don't take a breath until I hear the click of the door shutting. One day, I'll stand up to her. Or I hope I do.

My walk to the church is calming, and I use the time to gather myself. I picture my happy place, and I'm startled when a world in a book I read isn't what I picture. No. It's Myles.

"You're early," a soft voice announces when I arrive, pulling me from my thoughts.

I turn to the sweet lady who I've come to adore. Joan is Harlow's nan, and she may be old in age, but in spirit, she's as young as the people in my school. "Hey, Joan. I thought I'd get an early start on the food boxes that are being delivered."

She frowns. "You didn't need to come in early, sweetheart. I have it covered. You should go out and enjoy life."

"I wanted to," I explain without going into detail.

She stares unnervingly at me, before finally giving me a sharp nod. "Well, I really appreciate it. They've already been delivered, and I got the nice, fit men to put them in the back room for me."

"You weren't flirting with the nice, young men again, were you?" I tease.

She cackles. "You only live once, young lady. If I want to watch some flexing muscles and an arse or two, I will. Keeps me honest. Keeps me young," she sings.

I laugh with her. I've seen her in action, and she puts the fear of God into some of them. It's all fun and games, and personally, I think she loves that she can make them blush. She's a hoot.

I give her a bright smile. "I'll go and get started." I leave, but don't get far when she inhales sharply.

"Jesus Christ. What on earth has happened to you, Kayla? Are you okay? We should go get you checked out," she orders hysterically.

The blood drains from my face as I spin to face her. I wince at the pain in my neck, but it's nothing compared to the turmoil going on inside me. I know my clothes are covering the bruises on my body. There is no way she can see them.

"W-what?" I ask shakily.

"Your neck has bruises," she reveals, focusing sharply on me. Her gaze falls to my wrist, and I inwardly curse myself for not covering them better. I tug down my sleeve and paste on a smile.

"Oh, I fell down the attic stairs while getting some boxes down for my mum," I lie, hoping she'll buy it.

She doesn't look like she believes me, but she nods anyway. "You should have messaged me. You should go on home and get some rest. Maybe ice those bruises on your neck."

Panicking that she'll send me home—to *her*—I rush to plead my case, hoping I can stay. "No! No, it's fine. *I'm* fine. Honestly, it's not as bad as it looks. I promise. Can I stay?" I plead, feeling my eyes begin to water.

I know what will happen if I go back there now. Mother will wake up around eleven and will take her hangover out on me. The day will only get worse from there. I have one more night to suffer through, and then I'm safe for a whole five days.

Her brows pinch together. "Of course, if that's what you want, honey. If it gets too much, though, you come find me, okay?"

"Okay," I answer quietly, before quickly rushing off to the back room, furiously wiping away the tears that have spilled over.

An hour later, a girl around my age walks in looking like she's hardly had any sleep. I know that feeling all too well, but there's also a sadness in her eyes that I can relate to. I've seen her once before when I've helped out with the food bank, but I've never actually approached her or spoken to her. She's got long brown hair that falls in limp, messy waves to her waist. I'm not usually one to judge, but it could do with having a few inches cut off. It's her expressive eyes that stand out the most; they're large, round, and a stunning sharp blue colour. She looks so innocent, but also full of pain and sadness.

"Hi, I'm Lake," she greets softly and with kindness. "Joan sent me in to help you. What do you want me to do?"

"I'm Kayla," I greet back. "I guess you can help date everything with me. Is that okay or would you like something else to do?"

"No! No, that's fine. Do you need me to get some more labels?" she asks softly, and I turn to look at her to find her gaze studying me.

"Yeah, if you don't mind."

"Not at all," she promises, and walks off to the storage cupboard where Joan keeps all the supplies.

She walks back in at the same time everyone who helps out arrives. I haven't had a chance to meet everyone. I've mostly kept to myself since I'm used to it. But I know there are a few people around my age, and younger, who help volunteer. Which is why I'm not fazed when a few girls a year younger than me and a few in the same year at school walk in.

"Did you hear they had some deodorant go missing?" one girl tells her friend. Her friend giggles behind her hand, giving Lake a funny look. I glance at Lake to find her mindlessly minding her own business, but I can't help but notice the twitch in her jaw when her friend replies.

"Yeah, but I heard that the person who took it, needed it," her friend laughs back evilly.

The girls are trying to get at something, and I'm not sure whether it's to do with me or Lake. From Lake's reaction, this isn't the first time she's had to deal with their remarks. I know that look. I used to get them a lot.

"Can I help you?" I ask the first girl who spoke, hoping the firmness in my voice is convincing. She's not the normal type of girl I would usually talk to or even see here. I can tell by her body language and appearance that she doesn't want to be here. Most of the kids here volunteer as a punishment from their parents. I've heard them moan and groan about it a time or two.

"No, but you should keep an eye on this one," the girl snarls, curling her lip at me.

"And why is that?" I briefly glance at Lake, whose head is bowed.

"She steals things."

I don't know which one of the girls speaks up, but it gets my back up either way. I hate bullies like her. They always think they can intimidate whoever they want, say what they want, and to hell with the consequences.

"Well, she can't steal something that's free. Joan has already made that crystal clear," I remind them sweetly, which earns me a glare from both of them. I steel my spine and stare back, even though my body is shaking with nerves and fear on the inside.

"Whatever! She's a tramp. She doesn't belong here," the second girl announces, flicking her auburn hair over her shoulder.

"Listen up, bitches, I'm only going to say this one more fucking time: back the fuck off. I've listened to you go on and on about what you think of me, but there is something you've still failed to pick up on, which is I don't care. I don't care what you think of me, what you say, or what you think I've done. Its people like you who waste minutes, hours, weeks, *hell*, years picking on people and wormin' your way into people's lives just to gossip and be bitches who have no life. In the future, if you think I've stolen something then report me. It's only going to come back to bite you in the arse."

My mouth gapes open at her bravery. It's the most Lake has spoken since I've met her, or even been here. She doesn't speak to a lot of people; she mostly keeps to herself or goes to Joan. Now I can see why. These girls are ruthless. When they leave with a huff, I can't help but smile. Lake has got some bark. I envy her. She is someone I wish to be. I've never stood up for myself, but I have no problem doing it for other people.

"Thank you," she whispers after a few seconds. I turn my head away from the door and give her a big smile.

"I'm sorry. I wish I could have said more, I'm just not... Just not good with conflict," I admit ashamedly.

"I get that," she says softly, and reading my confusion, continues. "I heard one of the volunteer's mention who you were and a bit of your story. That's when I realised I'd read your story in the papers. I'm sorry... for what happened and for bringing it up."

"It's okay. I don't like talking about it," I tell her, ducking my head.

"I'm sorry," she replies, giving my hand a gentle squeeze.

I glance at the clock, uncomfortable with her kindness. "It's nearly lunch time; do you want to go and grab something to eat with me?" I ask, hoping she accepts. It beats sitting in the cafe or the chippy around the corner on my own for an hour and a half.

"No, I, um, I'm saving money at the moment. I'll eat later. I really should get these finished," she stresses, not meeting my gaze.

"We can do this later. There's no rush. And it's my treat. I honestly could use the company, and if you like, we can share a meal deal if you aren't that hungry. They have a large bag of chips either with sausages, fish, or donner meat for two people. It's no problem." She looks like she's about to decline again when I interrupt. "Please, I hate going on my own. You'll be doing me a favour, and I don't mind paying."

"Are you sure? I really don't have any money," she admits, chewing on her nail as one arm covers her stomach.

I can tell there's a story behind those broken, sad eyes, and seeing her reaction to my offer, it breaks my heart. She's clearly someone who doesn't get invitations like mine often.

"Yes, I'm sure. I wouldn't offer if I didn't mean it. Plus, I don't fancy sitting for an hour and a half looking outside a chippy window," I tease, and she laughs.

"Okay then. I'll just go get my coat," she tells me, and I move to the counter to grab my things.

CHAPTER
SEVEN

MYLES

A nother weekend of being bored out of my mind has passed, and I'd never thought I'd say this, but it's good to be back at school.

I make my way down the corridor to registration, feeling more relaxed than I have all weekend. And I know it's because I'll be seeing Kayla today.

All weekend I've had to listen to Max go on about some chick he met up with or some other crap. We were meant to be having a movie night at Denny's, but Hope got sick so we stayed away. And as the old Gunners' house is now burnt down, the parties have been getting less and less. The parties that are happening are in the park, and that's not my thing. Most kids my age go, but I'm not like most kids, and there is no way you'll get me hanging out in one either. Kids have to play in the place, and they all seem to forget that when they're smoking, drinking and doing drugs. It makes me sick. I don't even want to comment on the immature idiots who vandalise the playgrounds with shit kids don't need to read.

So, my Saturday consisted of watching bad movies, catching up with homework, and listening to Max whine about being bored, until he finally gave up and went to the park to get drunk and laid.

My Sunday wasn't much better. Max woke me up at the crack-arse of dawn to go watch him play footy. I don't usually go, but he said he was fed up of seeing me sulk all the time, so I went along to prove him wrong. I stood in the pouring rain for two hours watching him play. It was hell.

Walking into the classroom, my gaze immediately seeks out Kayla first. She's sitting in her usual seat, leaning back and gazing out the window, looking as beautiful as ever. However, today her eyes hold more sadness and pain in them than they usually do. She was like this last Monday too, and it burns my heart to see.

As I draw closer, I notice her body tense a little before relaxing, and I grin to myself, sensing she knows it's me. She's leaning her head in the palm of her hand while still gazing out the window, and I notice a purple bruise covering her wrist.

What the fuck?

"Hey," I call, sitting down in my seat. "What did you do?"

"What did I do? What?" she asks, shaking her head, which makes me grin. Her mouth opens and her tongue sneaks out, lightly running along her bottom lip. I have to clench my teeth and will my dick not to get hard.

Like it listens.

"Your wrist," I point out the offending bruise marking her silky cream flesh. "It's bruised."

She pulls her shirt sleeve down to cover it. "Oh, I fell down the attic stairs getting a box down for my mum on Friday. It's fine. It just caught between the box and the door."

She glances away, and I have a feeling she's not telling me the truth. I'm pretty good at reading people, but when I'm around Kayla, every brain cell I own turns to mush.

"Must have been some fall," I grumble when I notice her wince again for the third time since sitting down.

"Yeah, it was," she replies quietly.

"What did you get up to at the weekend?" I ask, changing the conversation so she can relax. It doesn't work, and I feel hopeless. I know if I push, she'll close up completely.

"I helped at the food bank Miss. Joan helps run."

"You did?" I ask, my brows rising at the news. Not that she spent her weekend doing something selfless, but that Joan didn't mention it.

"Yeah, it's actually pretty relaxing," she admits, and her smiles is genuine for the first time since I walked in. Her choice of words are worrying though. I've heard through Joan that it's busy and hectic, so what is happening in her life for her to find it relaxing?

"Yo! Yo! Yo!" Max's loud voice booms off the walls in the classroom. He high-fives, knuckle punches, and winks his way through other students like he's King of the school.

"God, he's something else," I mumble, and then hear a faint giggle to my side. My head snaps to the sound, my eyes raking over Kayla. Her hand is covering her mouth, but I still hear the faint giggle, and it only becomes louder when I send her a glare. "You think it's funny?"

She nods, laughing when Max comes barging past our seats to take his by the window.

"How's my future wife this morning?" he asks, swinging his arm around the back of her chair. Immediately, her giggling comes to a sudden stop, and it's my turn to burst into a fit of laughter at her wide-eyed expression.

"Don't think she likes the thought of being your wife, bro."

"Everyone wants to be my wife. Hey, Alisha, you'd be my wife, right?" he shouts across the classroom, and the girl in question, Alisha, looks back over to Max with *crazy eyes*, nodding furiously. She's practically panting.

"See; Alisha wants me." He grins.

"I'm pretty sure Alisha would have said yes to her pet dog," I joke. Alisha is one of those girls who, if you pay her an inch of attention, then she will stalk you for the rest of your life. She's creepy and obsessive.

"You're just jealous. Kayla, you'd be my wife, right?" he asks, giving her a light nudge. She glances from him to me with wide eyes. "Right?"

"He'll keep asking if you don't answer," I declare on a breath.

"Um, not to hurt your feelings or anything, but no," she replies, fiddling with the sleeve of her blazer nervously.

"Why not?" Max whisper-yells, outraged, actually looking genuinely hurt. *Does he have a thing for Kayla?* Just the thought of him liking her has every muscle in my body tensing up, and I want to actually punch my own brother in the face. It wouldn't be the first time I've hit him, but it would be the first time over a girl.

"Y-you're pretty high maintenance," she whispers unsteadily.

I burst into another fit of laughter, loving Max's crestfallen expression.

"I am not," he argues, his cheeks flaming red.

"You really are," I tell him condescendingly, which earns me a glare.

"What about Myles? Is he high maintenance too? We are twins after all."

Her cheeks turn pink. "Uh. I... He—"

"Don't answer him," I interrupt, not wanting to cause her any more embarrassment. Her speech is stuttered, and she looks seconds away from passing out. Her reaction is cute, because it means I get to her. I would have liked to know the answer, but not if it causes her stress.

"No! She has to. My ego is on the line here, bro," he whines, pointedly staring at Kayla with puppy dog eyes. As soon as her back is turned, he gives me a smug grin.

The bastard.

He knows exactly what he's doing.

I glare at my brother. "No, she doesn't," I warn, before addressing her. "Ignore him."

He knows how I feel about her, even though we've never actually spoken about it out loud. He knows and is playing a dangerous game.

"No, it's fine," she promises. "No, Myles isn't high maintenance. He's anything but."

She gives me a warm smile, and I melt at the sight. She's so goddamn beautiful when she smiles. It kills me that I can't touch her.

We're all silent for a few minutes, until Max breaks the silence.

"In all honesty, I think he's high maintenance. I'm easy." He grins, leaning back in his chair so it's resting on the two back legs, looking cocky.

"Too easy," she whispers, and I don't think she meant for me to hear.

My head tips back as I roar with laughter.

"Myles, Max, please keep it down back there," the teacher demands. Max groans, muttering about how unfair she's being with us.

"I swear she wants a piece of me," Max mutters. "She always singles us out. Have you noticed?"

Jesus, he has no filter. "Bro, we're the only ones making noise."

"And?" I swear, sometimes I worry about him and how we can even be twins. We're polar opposites. We have nothing in common like normal twins, and we act completely different.

"So," I start, grabbing Kayla's attention. "Do you want to work on the project tonight? We can meet at mine or yours again. It's up to you."

"Oh, I-I can't. Charlie and I arranged to meet up. She wants to come over to talk about something. I'm sorry."

"No. It's fine. I guess we can arrange for another night when you're free."

"Definitely! Is tomorrow good for you?"

"Yeah," I reply as the bell for first period rings. "I'll speak to you later then."

By fourth period, I'm missing her again. I haven't seen Kayla properly since Friday, and I enjoy spending time with her. It's not like we're a couple or anything. She drives me crazy, though, and the worst part is she doesn't even realise she does it. It kills me. She's all I can think about. It took me over two years to get over her. I don't want to go through that again.

I can still remember the first time I met her—well, saw her. She was walking down the hallway, her hair wild and falling in loose waves down her back. She was wearing her large black glasses that sat huge on her small, delicate face. She walked with her head down, clutching a pile of books in her arms. I had stopped to stare, my eyes taking in every inch of her. I couldn't believe someone so beautiful was walking down the halls of our shitty school. She looked so out of place. In a good way, of course.

She had pouty, full, red lips that were kissable. It took everything in me to move my gaze away, I was that overcome by her beauty. She didn't even wear makeup, or dress up for me to notice her. She was beautiful in every way that counts. She still is the most beautiful girl I've ever laid eyes on. No one else can even compare. She's beautiful inside and out.

"Dude, what the fuck is wrong with you today?" Toby, my friend, taunts next to me. We're in geography, another lesson I couldn't get with Kayla.

I'm sure he's been talking to me for the past twenty minutes, but my thoughts have been consumed with Kayla, her beauty, and those bruises I saw on her wrist this morning. I still don't buy that she got them from a fall. Does she really think I'm that stupid, or did she really believe her lie was good enough?

"Seriously, dude, you've spaced all lesson. What the fuck is up with you?"

"Sorry, I guess I'm just tired," I lie, shaking Kayla from my thoughts.

"Are you sure? You've been grunting all lesson, and every time I've asked you a question, you've completely ignored me."

I shrug, not knowing what else to say apart from 'I'm sorry'.

"Anyway, as I was saying, Dean is having a party later at his house. Do you want to come?"

I think about it for a minute and decide not to. It's not my thing anymore. The girls who throw themselves at you in the hopes they can cop a feel… It's all the same. Once you've been to one party, you've been to them all.

"I've got plans already, but ask Max. I'm sure he'll be up for it."

"Max is always up for it," Toby laughs.

I smile back at him, and my thoughts drift back to Kayla, wondering how I can get a girl as special as her to notice me. It's like she only sees me as a friend, and if that's all I ever get, then I'll live with it. I'll take anything she will give me. After everything she's been through, I know I can't push for anything more than friends until she's ready. If I try something now, she might push me away for good. And that is something I don't want to risk.

CHAPTER
EIGHT

KAYLA

Charlie arrives right on time. Her mum's horn honks outside, notifying me of her arrival. I rush down the stairs and make my way to the front door, peeking through the peephole. After a quick check to confirm it is in fact Charlie, I rush to open the door. I'm so excited. I feel like I haven't seen her at all since I got back, when in reality, it's only been three weeks.

"Hey," I greet her excitedly, but then my smile fades when I see how pale and tired she looks. "Are you okay?"

I step aside, letting her get inside.

"I'm okay. I've just had a rough couple of days. Can we just go crash upstairs for a bit and catch up?"

"Yeah, sure. Do you want something to drink?"

"Please," she replies. "I'll have water."

"Sure. Go on up and I'll meet you up there."

She walks away slowly, heading upstairs. She's usually bubbly, full of life, and chattering non-stop. This person reminds me of the girl she used to be, the one who was as quiet and shy as I am now.

Walking into my bedroom, she's lying down on my bed with her eyes closed, and for a few seconds, I actually believe she's fallen asleep, but then her head turns and her eyes open.

She sits up, taking the glass from my hands. "Come on, I want to know how things at school are going."

"It's going good. I've caught up on all the work I missed with the trial going on and only have a few assignments left. How's college?"

"Boring," she groans. "And I didn't mean your school work, I meant being there, after—you know…"

"Oh! O-okay I guess. It's been good. Myles is with me most of the time." I shrug, ignoring the tingles I get from mentioning his name.

"Myles Carter?" she asks, her voice suspicious. My back straightens, going on the defence already.

"Yeah, why?"

"Oh, no reason. So who else have you made friends with?"

I think about it for a few minutes and realise I haven't actually made any other friends apart from Max.

"Max?" I state, which comes out more like a question. I want to bury my head in the pillow, knowing what's about to come.

"Are you kidding me? You've made no other friends whatsoever?" she admonishes heatedly. "Kayla, we had a deal that when you came back, you would make friends, go out, and enjoy yourself. I've kept up my end of the bargain."

"Yeah, but you're so good at being bubbly, outgoing, and a people person. It's always been inside of you, Charlie. I'm lucky if I don't have a panic attack asking for no gherkins on my double cheeseburger. And technically, I still made friends with Myles and Max. Plus, if you include Harlow then that's three people I've made friends with since I got back. I'd say that's progress."

She looks at me like I've lost my mind and then sighs, thankfully giving in. "Okay, I'll let it go, but you need to at least make a few more outside of the Carter family," she tells me, and I smile, then remember the dinner I had with Lake on Saturday.

"Oh, and I made a friend at the church food bank. A girl called Lake who volunteers there. Some of the girls were being mean to her for no reason. We went out for lunch together."

"See, *that's* progress," she teases. I sit so that my back is against the bars of my bed, and cross my ankles. "Oh, and talking of the trial; how are you doing after all that?"

"I'm still in shock, I guess. I know he would have been sent to prison with or without my testimony, but I'm still glad I did it. I just thought getting closure, him being locked away, would change things. Change me. But it hasn't," I tell her honestly, my voice quietening.

"What do you mean? Has someone said something to you at school? If they have, I'll come kick their arses," she says vehemently.

I laugh. I can't help it. "No, Rocky. No one has said anything. I had people stare at me the first week or so, but it died down after that. I think the fact that whenever Max would catch someone staring, he'd walk right up to them and stare right in their face for a good five minutes, helped."

"He didn't?" She snorts, rolling to her side as she starts to laugh. "I can picture him doing that."

"He freaking did. One girl turned bright red and tried to get away from him, but he just followed her, getting in her face."

I laugh with her, remembering all the times the crazy boy did that for me.

"It seems like those Carter boys care about you," she points out, her laughter dying off.

I shrug. I try to come off unaffected, but I can feel the blush rise in my cheeks when I think about Myles and him caring about me. I know he must in some way, but I fantasise about him caring about me in other ways. I know it will never be more than just friends, though. Boys like him don't like girls like me, especially not broken ones.

"Maybe."

"Oh, come on! We both know Max doesn't associate with girls unless it's to do the nasty, and even then, he never sees the same girl twice. For him to be friends with a girl is a miracle all in itself."

"He's friends with Harlow and Denny," I remind her.

"That's different... Oh no, it's not. See, they're all dating his brothers, and Myles has a crush on you," she announces, looking giddy over it.

"Myles does not have a crush on me," I argue, even though the thought has my pulse beating rapidly.

"Pft, please. He so does."

"How would you know?" I question, arching a brow.

"Oh, come on. He was always making googly eyes at you. He could never keep his tongue from hanging out whenever you were around. I even heard he got into an altercation with Davis once, too, when, you know…" She doesn't finish. She doesn't need to. She means when he raped me, when he bullied me. The news that Myles would stick up for me against *him,* is surprising to hear. I didn't think anyone really believed me at the time. I remember the conversation I had once with Myles. I was sitting outside one of the school buildings, and he came and sat down next to me. He was the first person I really opened up to. Yeah, I told Charlie what happened, but not the same way I told Myles. It was like everything came pouring out when he was there.

"He doesn't make googly eyes. You're mistaken," I state, not wanting to talk about this or Davis.

"Keep telling yourself that, Kayla."

"Whatever."

"So, where is your dad?" she asks. I notice her fiddling with her fingers in her lap. She's nervous, which is worrying.

"At work," I admit, frowning. He said he wouldn't be working so many hours, but he lied. Again!

"I take it things haven't changed? How about your mum?" she asks softly.

"I don't want to talk about them. What about you? How are you? You said you had some news to tell me." I'm hoping she doesn't call me out on changing the subject, but I really don't want to talk about my parents just as much as I don't want to talk about Davis.

"About that…" she begins, and the tone doesn't sit well with me.

I sit up, worried about where this is going. "Go on."

"I had my check up a month ago. Things still haven't been going too well, and I didn't want to say anything until I knew for sure, but —" Her words break on a sob.

I immediately close the space between us and place my arm

around her. "Hey, it's okay. Take your time," I soothe. "I'm here."

"My body is rejecting my new heart," she chokes out, shoving her face into my shoulder.

Charlie has dilated cardiomyopathy, which weakens the heart muscle. Her father suffered the same diagnosis when he was younger. She had a transplant last year, so I know whatever else she is about to tell me is going to be bad.

"Shh, it's okay. Everything will be okay. They'll put you on the waiting list and you'll get a new heart, and everything will be fine," I promise, trying to sound convincing, but I don't know who I'm trying to convince... her or me.

"That's it though, Kayla. I don't think it will," she declares, pulling back to look at me. "I'm getting weaker and weaker by the day. I've already had a heart transplant. The chances of me getting another are slim."

"We can Google it. Find out what your options are," I tell her, feeling my own tears begin to fall.

I can't go to the worst-case scenario. She's my best friend, my saviour, and I can't imagine the world without her in it.

"I have. It's rare, Kayla. I read this one story, though; it was about a woman who suffered with the same condition as me. Five years after her first transplant, she got chronic organ failure that attacked her heart. She got put on the waiting list and received her second heart transplant. She died waiting for her third heart transplant."

"But it might not be the same results, Charlie. You can't worry like this, it won't do your heart any good," I plead.

"I know. I know it's different, but reading her story, the way she was, how inspiring she *is*, it made me see things a little differently. I may not pull through this; the chances are really slim at this stage. I guess she inspired me. She helped me understand certain things. I even found myself looking up all the articles Google had on her."

I quickly jump off my bed and grab my laptop before bringing it back over to the bed and sitting down next to her. I don't know all that much about Charlie's condition, but I know it's serious.

When I load up Google, I ask her to show me. It's then we read through all the articles on this woman. I can see why Charlie got fixated on her. She really is an inspiring woman. She went through so much treatment, surgeries and hospital stays. She married a few months before she died from what we can make out. She was beautiful. She didn't look like a person who had a heart problem; she looked radiant, glowing, and full of life. We talk about it for an hour, both of us soaking in what we can.

"Everything will be okay. You can fight this. You did it before," I remind her, closing the laptop down.

"I'm scared. I'm eighteen, nearly nineteen, and I've not even been kissed. I haven't had a boyfriend, had sex, or hell, I've never left the UK. Reading about this woman, Donna, made me realise just how much of my life I've wasted away. Look at everything she achieved in her life. She left this world knowing there was a man who loved her, and had a child she could influence even after she was gone. She was looked up to. She'll be remembered for all the greatness and help that she did. This website isn't just about her, it's about everything, and the support on there is out of this world. I've read so many other people's heart transplant stories on there, and for me, she started that. I want to do something so people will remember me."

"Even if you were going to die, which you're not," I choke out. "you'll always be remembered, Charlie. You're more special than you give yourself credit for. I'm lucky to have you in my life. If it hadn't been for you, I wouldn't have made it through the past few years. You've changed lives too. You changed mine."

"I'm just so scared," she admits, and we both lie down, crying into each other's arms. I want to be strong, to show her she has me, but each sob that shakes the bed, my heart breaks a little more for her. Charlie doesn't deserve this; she deserves a long, full, happy life. She deserves to have it all. And if I could trade places with her, I would.

I don't know how long we lie there holding each other, but it's not until Charlie's phone rings that I move for the first time. When I look over to Charlie, wondering why she isn't moving to answer her phone, I find her asleep. I gently shake her shoulder until she wakes up, looking disorientated and pale.

"Your phone. It was ringing," I whisper to her, just as her phone starts ringing again.

"Shit, I must have fallen asleep. Mum is going to kill me," she mutters before answering her phone. "Hey, Mum... Oh! Okay, yeah. I'm sorry. I fell asleep. I'll be down in a second." She ends the call and meets my gaze. "I have to go. She's downstairs waiting for me. When I didn't come home by curfew she started to get worried, hence the reason she's downstairs waiting for me."

"Come on. Let's go downstairs before she starts banging the door down," I tease, but there's no mirth behind it.

We both get up off the bed and stretch our taut muscles before heading off downstairs. Her mum is waiting outside in the car, and before heading down the path, Charlie turns around and embraces me in a tight hug.

"Thank you for being my friend. I love you," she whispers, before slowly turning around and heading to the car. Once she opens the door, she gives me one last teary goodbye with a wave, and then gets in the car.

I watch as the taillights disappear in the distance, my heart aching that much more the further away they get.

Shutting the door, I sink down to the floor, my head resting on my knees, and I let out the most blood-curdling sob I've ever heard. I choke on another sob, my chest heaving as I struggle to catch my breath.

Charlie could die.

Heart transplant.

I can't lose her. She's been here for me through everything, but it's more than that. Charlie has so much more to give in life. She doesn't deserve any of this.

With shaky hands, I grab my phone from my back pocket. I don't even think about what I'm doing, I just dial the number I've somehow memorised and put the phone to my ear.

"Hello?"

"I need you..." I choke out.

CHAPTER NINE

MYLES

The phone call from Kayla has me breaking in a sweat as I run through the streets to get to her house. Her sobs still echo in my ears. I hate knowing she's alone and hurt, and there's nothing I can do until I get there.

As soon as her words broke through the phone, I was out of bed and rushing for my shoes and jacket. I never even explained to Maverick where I was going when I rushed out either, but I know I'm going to have to give him a text when I find out what's wrong.

I rush up the pathway to her house and bang on the front door loud enough to wake up the neighbours. I hear a whimper on the other side, and my heart clenches.

"Kayla? Kayla, are you okay? Open up," I shout through the door. I sag with relief when I hear her start to unlock the door. As soon as it's open, I rush through the doorway, gently pushing her back and slamming the door shut behind me with my foot.

Kayla's eyes are red and swollen from crying. I take in every inch of her body for any signs of injury, but when I see none, I take a quick glance around the room, noticing nothing out of place.

"Hush, baby," I comfort her, taking her in my arms. "Can you tell me what happened?"

"I-it's Charlie... her heart," she chokes out, her breath hitching. "Her body's rejecting it and she may not survive."

Shit! I understand now why she's a mess. Charlie has been her rock. Kayla may not know this, but when she left before, I got updates from Charlie to see how she was. It ended though, about a year and a half ago, when Charlie stopped coming to school. I got mad that she ignored me, but now I understand she has been hiding her own secrets.

"I'm sorry," I tell her honestly, knowing how much Charlie means to her.

"She's scared, so scared she's going to die, and all I can say is 'everything will be okay.' How lame is that?"

"It's not lame. No one can predict what's going to happen, baby. Come on, let's go lie down. You look knackered."

She doesn't fight me when I lift her into my arms. She wraps her arm around my neck and cradles her head into my shoulder, seeking comfort. I'm not going to lie and say I don't feel anything with her in my arms because I feel everything. How her body fits perfectly against mine, and I love how her breath feels against my neck and how warm her hand feels palming my heart. It's heaven. No guy on this earth could resist feeling something for her.

"Did I disturb you?" she whispers once I lie us down on her bed.

"No, you didn't," I promise, pulling her back flush with my front. She stiffens at first, but soon relaxes when I run my fingers soothingly down her arm. I shouldn't be finding comfort in this, but I am. I get to hold her, and I have no regrets. "What did Charlie tell you about her condition?"

"I already know some about it. When she first starting showing symptoms, they thought it was due to stress from losing her grand-dad. But then when they did some further tests, they found out she had Dilated Cardiomyopathy. They did a heart transplant around five months later. She called me to tell me, and I wasn't here for her. My mother wouldn't let me come visit her, and to be honest, I wasn't in any fit state to leave on my own. I should have been there for her."

"You were there in the only way you could be. She knows that," I soothe. "If she's already had a transplant, then what will they do now?"

"Honestly? I don't know. She said they will be doing some more tests, and she'll be put back onto the transplant list. She's been getting short of breath easily, and has been getting severe chest pains. It's not looking good."

"There has to be something we can do," I mumble, feeling useless to her. She's called me because she needs me, and all I can do is hold her. There is nothing I can do to fix this for them.

"Nope, nothing but sit and wait to hear what the doctors have to say," she replies, wiping her tears away. "All I can think about is how scared she must be, and how scared she was when she told me. She's so young."

"Has she always had heart problems?"

"Yeah. She was born with it, I think, but with the right medication, she's been able to control it. When she came tonight, I knew something was wrong the second I saw her. She looked drawn, pale, and even though she had put on weight due to the tablets, she looks so freaking fragile."

"God, this sucks!"

"Yeah, it does. I just wish I knew how I could make it better for her."

"How about a girls' night out?" I offer.

"We can't. She can't do anything that will exhaust her." She sighs, rolling over so she's facing me. I move down the bed a little so that my face is level with hers, our bodies not far away from each other, but close enough so I can still reach out and touch her.

"Okay, so what about a girls' night in? I know Denny could use one; she's been bored with Harlow at college all the time. Harlow would love one, too. She's been moaning about college."

"Really? You think they'd be up for it? We could meet up here or something," she offers, and I feel like I've accomplished something big with the way she smiles at me.

"Denny will most likely have it at hers because of Hope. There is no way she will leave Hope," I point out, remembering the argument about leaving Hope with Grams while we all go away for the weekend. I'm hoping Kayla can come. I've mentioned it to Denny. She said she would ask her, that it's a good idea, so I'm hoping she does it soon so that Kayla doesn't use 'it's too short notice' as an excuse.

She smiles and my chest nearly bursts at the beauty of it. God, she's like sunshine on a cloudy day. "Yeah, okay; that sounds like a good idea. Let me text the girls."

She leans over me and I suck in a sharp breath, her scent surrounding me, making me feel intoxicated.

"O-oh, I'm s-sorry," she breathes out as she lies back down, her phone in her hand, but her eyes are fixated on me. She's so goddamn fucking beautiful.

"It's fine," I tell her, my voice low and husky.

She stares at me for a few seconds longer, her breathing heavy with the rise and fall of her chest. It's taking everything in me not to look down, knowing her plump, full breasts will be spilling out of her strapped top with every breath she takes.

Her eyes pull away, down to the light on her phone, and she starts clicking away at the buttons, a smile ghosting her lips.

"All...done," she announces.

"Good," I breathe out, as her phone pings with incoming messages.

"Denny is up for it," she laughs.

"What she say?"

"She said: Hell yes, baby. I need to socialise with someone other than Hope and Max."

I laugh at the reply, knowing how Max is getting on Denny's nerves. As much as she moans about him, I know she secretly loves the attention he pays Hope.

"That sounds like her," I retort as she pulls up the next message.

"Harlow is up for it too, and I think Charlie will be too. She's probably asleep right now. Hopefully, she can convince her mum to let her out of her sights. She was pretty obsessive with her the last time.

Charlie said she would fuss over her, baby her, and follow her every-where she went."

"Understandable," I answer. "Isn't Charlie an only child, too?"

"Yeah, she is. I think that's why we're so close. Neither of us grew up with siblings. Must be nice for you to have all your brothers around you."

"It is, but sometimes it can become too much. Max can be a handful if you haven't already noticed."

She laughs, and I've decided it's now my favourite sound. "Oh, I've noticed."

Looking at the clock next to her bed, it reads midnight. Shit! Maverick. Quickly grabbing my phone out of my back pocket, I unlock it and notice I've already received a few messages from Maverick.

Mav: Let me know you're okay. You ran pretty quickly out of the house. That can only mean two things. Either Max has done something stupid and needs bailing out, or Kayla called you.

Mav: Max is back with a black eye and you're not with him, so I'm taking it you're at Kayla's. Give us a text and let me know what you're doing tonight.

"Everything okay?" Kayla asks, watching me with her big green doe eyes.

"Yeah, it's just Mav. I left the house in a hurry and didn't get to tell him where I was going or what I was doing. I'm just going to text him back so he doesn't worry."

"Oh no, are you in trouble?"

"No, baby," I promise, loving it when a blush rushes to her cheeks. "Do you want me to stay? I can go if you need me to."

I don't want her to send me away. Her dad's car isn't out the front again, and from what Joan said the other day, he's been seen with another woman. Something tells me Kayla doesn't know this snippet of information, and I, for one, don't want to be the one to tell her. She has enough going on in her life without worrying about who her dad's banging.

Kayla looks over to the bedside clock before turning her attention back to me. "You can stay if you'd like," she offers hesitantly.

I nod, not wanting to look too eager, then fire off a quick text to Mav explaining Kayla was upset because she had some bad news. After letting him know I'll be back in the morning to get showered and changed for school, I put the phone down on the side.

"We should get some sleep. We have to be up in the morning for school."

"I'm just going to get changed," she tells me, and climbs off the bed, her body brushing against mine. I badly want to grab her hips and tug her down so she's straddling me. I want to kiss her and tell her she's mine, but I don't.

While she's gone, I quickly kick off my trainers, then grab my shirt at the back of my neck before pulling it off and chucking it over the desk chair. I leave my jogging bottoms on, knowing it will most likely scare her if I only wear my boxers. Plus, it's an extra barrier for when I get a hard-on. It's hard not to when I'm around the girl. She's a walking, talking goddess, and because she doesn't even see how beautiful she really is, it makes her that much more appealing.

She walks into the room after switching off the hallway lights. Just as she's about to turn off the main light to her room, she comes to a sudden halt, her body locking tight, and her eyes fixated on my stomach. I'm not like Max, who is a gym junky. I don't work out. However, it doesn't mean I don't have muscles where a lad should. But seeing her eyeing me, like she could eat me and lick every inch of me, is making my dick uncomfortably hard.

She visibly swallows, the movement making my dick jerk and throb, especially when her eyes slowly lift, running up my body until they meet my gaze. Her eyes are blazing with heat, and I can't look away. This is a side to Kayla that I've only seen twice. Once now, and the other is the last time I stayed and she woke up wrapped around me.

I clear my throat, breaking the spell between us before she can get scared. "You okay?" I croak, unable to hide the huskiness in my voice.

"Yes, I-I was just thinking." She blushes and I want to chuckle. Yep, whatever she is thinking about, I wish I had front row seats to it. I'd do anything to be able to hear what she is thinking right now. I'd give up my left ball. Why not my right? I have no fucking clue. It could be because I'm right-handed. And now I'm talking bollocks so I'm going to shut up.

"Come on," I gently order, lifting the bedsheets up before sliding in, moving as close to the wall as I can get, giving her room to fit. Her bed is a little bigger than a single bed, but I'm not a small lad. The last time I slept over, the blankets at the edge of the bed kept nearly falling off every time I tried to move.

Slowly but surely, she walks over to the bed, stopping for a second to switch off the lamp before getting in. Her body is locked up tight, and before I can give her a chance to freak out, I grab her hips and pull her against me.

"Relax," I demand softly, and I'm surprised she submits the second the word leaves my mouth. "Goodnight, Kayla."

"Thank you for being here for me tonight," she whispers into the dark. "I don't know what I would have done if you hadn't answered your phone."

"You're never going to have to find out because I'll always be here for you," I tell her honestly.

Her heart rate picks up. I can feel it against my chest, and I inwardly smile. She seriously has no clue how I feel about her.

"Thank you," she whispers, and for a second, I swear she sounds choked up.

"Goodnight, baby." I whisper the words against her ear, kissing her head once before lying back down on the pillow.

She snuggles up against me, her body completely flush against mine when she whispers her next words, the sound of her voice going straight to my dick. I'm just glad she hasn't said anything about my current wood sticking against her arse.

"Goodnight, Myles."

CHAPTER
TEN

KAYLA

The week passes pretty quickly, and soon enough the weekend arrives. I'm glad my dad talked to my mum about letting me stay home this weekend. Any other time, she would have refused, but then my dad told her about Charlie's condition, and she knew that if she argued after that, it would show her true colours to Dad. He still has no clue who she really is or what she's really capable of. I could tell him and get it over with, but I think a part of me doesn't because I feel like he should see it. He should see I'm not okay and that she's abusive.

I know there will be consequences for my absence, but the dread that normally cripples me is absent. My focus is on Charlie, and her only right now. My only fear is whether she'll wait until I'm next there or seek me out herself.

I've not been able to dwell much on it, since if I'm not thinking of ways to help Charlie, I'm thinking of Myles. He didn't hesitate to come to mine, even when he knew he worried his brother.

We seem to have gotten closer since that night, and I wake up each morning excited to see him. He makes me feel safe, seen, and I'm dreading the day it will end. I know my feelings for him go beyond friendship, but since moving back to Coldenshire, they've grown into something more, something I can't describe. There's a war going on inside of me because as much as I love this feeling, it's also a feeling I'm too scared to explore.

As I'm walking down the path towards Denny's house, my phone pings with a message. Pulling my phone out of my pocket, I'm surprised when I find the message is from Charlie.

Charlie: I'm so sorry, but I'm not going to make it tonight. I'm not feeling too good, and Mum wants me to stay in and get some rest.

Me: Is everything okay? Are you okay?

I pause to look up from my phone to knock on Denny's door. Her house is located at the back of the garden at the Carter house. Maverick and Mason—Denny's fiancé—built it for themselves, but when Denny found out she was pregnant, Maverick gave them his share of the house so they could move in. It's pretty sweet to be fair. The place isn't huge, but it is for them. I'm sure I heard them say it's a three bedroom. I've only seen downstairs and it's pretty spacious.

I startle when the door is tugged open, revealing Denny, who looks happy to see me. She's always been beautiful with her golden locks and flawless skin, but since she gave birth to baby Hope, she's radiant.

"Hey," she greets, scanning the garden behind me. Her brows pinch together. "Where's Charlie?" she asks, confused.

I hold my phone up, giving her a sad smile. "She just messaged me. She's not feeling too good so she's going to stay at home tonight."

"Why, what's wrong?"

"She's got the flu," I lie, knowing Charlie won't want anyone to know about her condition. She hasn't had time to process it all herself, so I know she won't be able to handle questions from everyone else. And I made sure Myles kept it to himself.

"Oh no." She pouts, pulling the door open wider. "Hopefully she can make it next time."

She heads inside, so she doesn't see my smile drop. My phone pings with another message, and I look down to read it.

Charlie: I'm good, just tired and short of breath. I'll talk to you tomorrow. I promise. Love you, and have fun

Me: I'll try. Wish you were here. LOVE YOU more, biatch. Xoxo

"Who's got you smiling?" Harlow asks as I walk into the front room.

My eyes widen at the sight that greets me. They've put tons of blankets on the floor, along with fluffy pillows; all I'm sure aren't part of the downstairs décor. The pile looks thick and inviting, like you could drop down without feeling the hard floor beneath.

I scan the areas not filled with blankets and pillows to find they've got bowls and plates filled with snacks and fingers foods, and another section filled with drinks.

"Oh my god, this looks amazing," I muse, soaking it in.

"Thank you," Denny gushes. "The minute you texted me on Monday, I began to plan everything. I may have gone overboard but I don't care."

"She even has wedding magazines to look at after the first movie," Harlow adds, grinning at her friend's enthusiasm.

"It looks amazing," I tell her, and start taking my coat off. Now I can see why she asked me to bring a spare set of pyjamas. It's like every teenage girl's sleepover fantasy, except we're adults. I've never had this, and looking around the room and at my friends, it makes me want to cry.

"So... who texted you?" Harlow demands, throwing a Skittle into her mouth. "And where's Charlie?"

"That's who messaged me. Charlie can't come. She's not feeling too good. She's going to be so bummed when she finds out what she missed out on."

"Is that why she hasn't been at college all week?" Harlow questions as I slide my shoes off.

I force a smile, not wanting to lie to them. "Probably, yeah."

"Well, send her our love. We can do this again for her, no problem," she suggests as Denny runs from the room.

"She'd love that," I reply.

This girl has shown me so much kindness when she has every

reason to hate me. She's sassy, beautiful, but can also be shy at times. I'm glad we became friends.

"You need to get changed," Denny demands, rushing back in the room with a clear box full of God knows what.

"Yes, Mum!" I laugh.

"Ha-ha, now go get changed," she tells me, arching her brow at me. "Hope is over at the brothers' house with Mason, so you don't need to be quiet going up. They'll be back in a bit, but Mason said he wouldn't disturb us."

I nod and give her a smile as I grab my bag. I rush upstairs before Denny decides I'm taking too long and dresses me herself. I change into the long-sleeved pyjamas with matching trousers I bought specially for today since I can't wear what I normally sleep in. My shorts don't cover the scars on the back of my legs, and I don't want to scare the girls by flashing them around. I also can't wear my T-shirt since I still have bruises from last weekend.

Once I'm changed and I've packed my bag with the clothes I already had on, I make my way out of the bathroom. A startled scream escapes my lips when I bump into a large, hard body.

"Hey, Kayla. It's me, Mason. I just came by to get some more nappies. It's okay," he soothes, holding onto my shoulders. Footsteps come rushing up the stairs, and Denny comes into view as I struggle to catch my breath.

"I told you to make yourself known, that Kayla was up here," she barks at him.

"Babe," is all he says, rolling his eyes.

The ease between them, and his reactions, helps calm me down. I take in a few more steady breaths to make sure I'm not about to pass out.

"It's fine. I just wasn't expecting anyone to be outside the door. I'm sorry. Bit of a good job you weren't putting a sleeping Hope to bed though, huh?"

"Yep, that scream would have definitely woken her up," Mason teases, and bends down to give Denny a quick kiss.

The look he gives her when they pull away has my cheeks heating. "Come on, Kayla, let's go downstairs."

———

We're all sitting on the blankets, leaning back with our heads resting on the sofa, wearing a face mask. After Denny dragged me back downstairs, she wasted no time in plastering us all with her face masks before doing her own. It was soothing at first, but now I'm wondering how much longer it needs to set.

"How has school been going?" Denny asks, breaking the silence.

"Okay." I shrug, and then silently curse myself when I remember they can't see with the cucumber they have over their eyes.

"What about you with college, Harlow?" Denny continues. "Everything going okay?"

She groans. "I thought college would be different than school. But it's worse. None of them are on time, and the teacher spends most of the lesson telling them to simmer down. I thought it would be different, and we'd finally get taught something. It pisses me off that none of them are taking it seriously."

"Jesus, you really aren't enjoying it then."

"I am; it's just the others who don't take it seriously and disturb those of us who actually want to be there. I really want to go to university, and I can't do that unless I pass college."

"Have you spoken with your tutor about it?" Denny asks.

"And look like a brownnose? Nope. I'm hoping in time they will either drop the course or grow up."

"What about you, Denny; how is it being a mummy and a fiancée?" I ask.

"Brilliant. I love it, but sometimes I miss you guys. I want to go to college, but with Hope being so young still, I don't want to leave her. Just the thought turns my stomach. I'm hoping to open my own business, but I never got to finish my evening business course, so I'm going to wait for Hope to sleep through the night before I start it up again."

"That sounds like a brilliant idea," I tell her. I know she wanted to go to college, but when she found out about Hope, she decided not to. The birth would have interfered with her timetable. There was no point in her starting college, only to miss so much time to look after Hope.

"How are things with Myles?" Harlow asks.

I know the question is directed at me, but I choose to ignore it since she didn't specify who she was asking.

"Kayla?" Denny pushes, giving me a nudge.

I feign innocence. "Oh, you're talking to me?" They laugh at my reply, and my heart sinks because I know I have to answer. But I can give it another try. "I don't know what you mean by the question."

"Oh, come on, Kayla. I heard Mav talking to Myles the other day about staying over at yours. What gives? What's going on?" Harlow demands, her tone teasing.

"Nothing. We're just friends. He came over and we ended up falling asleep. That's it," I tell them, only half lying. I think bringing up Charlie will only cause more questions, and I know Charlie won't want anyone to know just yet.

"Yeah, yeah," Denny jokes.

"Seriously though, if you ever need to talk, we're here," Harlow promises.

"I know you are. There's just nothing to tell."

"If you say so," Denny sings, and I can hear the smile in her voice. She shifts next to me before getting up. Come on, it's time to wash these off. Once we've done that, I'm ordering pizza—that is, if you don't mind pizza. I'm starving."

"I could eat pizza," I tell her, and Harlow agrees.

———

The pizza arrives as we begin the movie. Harlow and Denny decided on a horror film because the boys don't like them and get too scared. The declaration surprises me since I didn't think they were scared of anything. They're all a force to be reckoned with, especially Maverick, who is scary as hell. He's the only one with tattoos—that I've seen anyway. And something about them makes him seem less approachable.

It took us ages to choose a film because Denny originally picked up *The Hills Have Eyes*, but decided against it because of a rape scene, so instead, she went with an oldie called *Smiley*. The cover is chilling. If I woke up to that smiling down at me, I would die from a heart attack. I mentioned it to Denny and Harlow when they got it out, and they both agreed, laughing.

"These smell amazing," Denny moans, dropping down with the pizza boxes. The front door opens, and Mason walks in with Myles, Malik, Max and Maverick trailing behind him. Denny doesn't even look surprised. "Seriously, Mason?"

He grins sheepishly. "Sorry, we smelled pizza."

I feel the heat of Myles' gaze and feel my cheeks warm.

"Hey," he greets, and I give him a small smile in return, feeling flushed now that his brothers are all dominating the room. They're all big men, and in Denny's small front room, they look like giants.

"I got you each a pizza; they're in the kitchen. Now go away," she orders, before freezing. "Where the hell is Hope?" Her voice sounds calm, but her expression is anything but.

"Granddad has her. Joan went to bingo with a group of friends," he reassures her.

"Good," she breathes out, her shoulders dropping. "Now go get your pizza and fuck off."

"Jesus, who pissed on your cornflakes this morning," Max grumbles, walking away to get the pizza from kitchen with Mason.

"Hey, Kayla," Maverick greets, giving me a wave. I'm completely startled at first. We've never really spoken to each other, so for him to call me out by name is out of the blue.

"Hi." I shyly wave back, earning a grin from him and Myles. Unable to breathe with their attention on me, I glance away and tug the blanket further up my legs. It's gotten hot in the room, and with all the blankets it's getting worse, but there is no way I'm removing it with everyone in the room.

"Boys, she got us meat feast, hot and spicy, and even got Max his pussy margarita pizza," Mason shouts, walking back into the room with five pizza boxes, four boxes of chips, and another four boxes of chicken wings.

"It's not a pussy pizza," Max grumbles, carrying two bottles of pop.

"Yeah, bro, it is," Maverick laughs, along with Myles and the rest of us.

"Fuck's sake, it's not, okay? I just prefer to add my own toppings. At least then I won't get short changed with them."

"Max, you could have ham and pineapple, but you don't. You even moan over that," Myles laughs.

"I like cheese pizza, so sue me," he retorts, stomping out of the room, but not before adding, "They add extra cheese when I only order cheese."

"See you later, babe." Mason grins, bending over to give her another kiss on the lips.

Denny kisses him back, then steps away to put our pizzas on the floor when Myles speaks up. "What pizza did you three get?"

"Pepperoni and a meat feast."

"Are you going to eat all of that?" Maverick asks, licking his lips.

"Probably not. We have garlic bread, chips and barbecue wings, but I promise to call once we've consumed what we want," she promises.

Malik shakes his head. "I wouldn't promise anything just yet. Harlow could eat you out of house and home," he teases, earning himself a glare from Harlow.

"Are you calling me fat?" she asks with a deadly calm.

"No, babe. I love that you like your food. I'll see you later," he tells her, bending down to give her a kiss. My heart constricts at seeing Denny and Harlow both happy with their boyfriends. I wish I could have that. My eyes flick to Myles to find him watching me with a strange expression. It's like he can read my thoughts.

Before I can think any more about it, I hear Malik whisper to Harlow, "Make sure you call me first. These boys will demolish it otherwise."

Denny and I laugh as we're the only ones who heard what he said, and his brothers look at him suspiciously. He just shrugs, gives Harlow another kiss, before pushing his brothers out the door. Once they're gone, Denny turns to me with a sly grin on her face.

"Are you sure there is nothing going on between you and Myles?"

"What do you mean?" I ask, my brows pinching together.

"He couldn't keep his eyes off you," she answers.

I'm about to deny it when Harlow speaks up. "She's right. He couldn't keep his eyes off you. I think he likes you," she teases, and my face heats up further.

"Shut up and eat your food," I grumble, making them both laugh.

"Whatever you say," Denny sings, and hits play on the movie.

CHAPTER
ELEVEN

KAYLA

The pizza is gone long before the film ends. Now, Denny, Harlow and I are looking through bridal magazines, commenting on what we like or don't like. Denny has always been great with style, so I'm surprised when she asked for our opinions. And more, she seems to be appreciating the advice.

Harlow has a clipboard and is taking notes and ticking off her checklist as we go along. As maid of honour, she has the privilege of helping Denny organise the wedding. It's actually been pretty easy thanks to Denny's dad paying for it, with no expense spared. My dad would most likely give me a budget, and with the way Denny loves her clothes and shoes, you'd think her dad would have had some sense in doing that too. In all fairness though, Denny hasn't booked anything extravagant as of yet. She's kept everything elegant and simple.

"What colour are the bridesmaids going to be?" I ask, flicking through one of the wedding folders designated to bridesmaid dresses.

"I liked navy blue, but then I saw these coral dresses in one of the boutiques in town and have chosen them. You'll have to make sure you're free over the next few months for a dress fitting," Denny tells me before typing away on the keyboard. The pages of the book crinkle in my hands at the news, but she continues on like she didn't just rock my world. "Dammit, I'm going to have to pre-book the pick-and-mix stand and the photo booth separate. *Party Fusion* isn't open anymore. It's closed down."

She can't have meant it. Why would she ask me to bridesmaid? I must have heard her wrong.

Harlow, noticing my inner freak out, stops what she's doing. "Kayla, are you okay?"

Denny stops to look, and her brows draw in. "What's going on?"

"Why would I need to book time for a dress fitting? And why are you getting a photo booth?"

"Um, because you're going to be my bridesmaid," she explains, with that 'duh' expression. She continues to type, not explaining further. "Also, everyone needs a photo booth in their lives at least once. We had one once at one of the school's fundraisers, but the queues always took forever because of the lads jumping the line to go again. They were amazing though, and you'd be surprised how many bridal parties book them. And if you ask me why I'm getting the sweet stall, it's because I love sweets. Why wouldn't anyone want a pick-and-mix stand at their wedding?"

"It might as well be a party for Hope," Harlow retorts, laughing.

Tears gather in my eyes.

Bridesmaid.

She wants me to be bridesmaid.

That is so cool!

"You really want me to be a bridesmaid?" I verify, my throat closing up.

"Duh, of course I do," she replies, watching me like I've grown two heads.

I squeal before throwing myself at her, my arms reaching around her and bringing her into a tight hug. No one has ever asked me to do something so special. This is just... it's freaking amazing, and I'm so honoured she's asked me.

Denny laughs, knowing this is so out of character for me. Before I know it, Harlow is laughing along with us and throwing her arms around us both too. We all end up rolling to the side, Harlow and I rolling on top of Denny.

"Now *this* is what I like to see," a voice laced with laughter booms, making me screech.

Harlow and I jump off Denny. Harlow and Denny are laughing on the floor at Max, while my eyes are wide, and my hands are shaking. I never heard him come in. My breathing picks up, until my vision begins to blur and dark spots cloud my vision.

I should have heard him come in.

I should have sensed him, but I didn't.

"Hey, are you okay?" Myles rushes out, and I feel him drop down beside me.

I clench my eyes shut, panting as I try to control the panic attack. Nothing works, and with each breath, my chest feels tighter and tighter, and I begin to feel dizzy.

Strong arms wrap around me, before I'm pulled onto someone's lap. The second I smell his strong, spicy scent, I cling to him, breathing it in. I shove my face into the crook of his neck, my lips lightly brushing against his warm skin. His fingers begin to brush up and down my back, and the gesture is so sweet, I begin to relax in his arms.

The second I get my panic attack under control, I realise everyone in the room just witnessed it. I want to curl up under the covers and hide away, ashamed they had to see it. I whimper, clinging to Myles harder. *Why can't I act normal around these guys?*

"So, you don't like people-watching either, Kayla? It's okay. I get stage fright too," Max tells me, his voice not far away. I hear a hard slap against skin, and then Max howl in pain, and I can't stop the laughter that bursts free. "Seriously, brother, you have a child in your arms," Max hisses on a whisper to who I presume is Mason.

"I'm so sorry," I whisper against Myles when I stop laughing. He holds onto me tighter, and I'd be lying if I said this didn't feel good because it does.

"It's okay, babe."

I sit up, not moving from his lap as I peek out to see the others. Max and Mason are having a heated discussion over using violence in front of a minor, while Denny and Harlow are sending me worried glances.

"I'm so sorry. I didn't hear them come in and it took me off guard. I can't control it, but I understand if you want me to leave."

"You aren't going anywhere," Denny announces, like her word is final.

"You scared us is all," Harlow tells me, and then jumps when the front door is slammed open.

"Babe? Babe?" Malik shouts, walking into the house.

"Seriously, Malik! There is a *child* trying to sleep in here. Keep it the fuc—fudge down," Max hisses.

Mason rolls his eyes, and Malik just stares at him dryly before turning his attention to Harlow.

"Come on, we're going home," he declares, and from the look in his eyes, something tells me she's not going home to sleep.

"But we haven't finished the next film. We've got *A Little Bit of Heaven* left to watch." She pouts, folding her arms over her chest in a huff.

"Babe," he warns with a smirk on his lips, before stepping over the magazines, the leftover pizza box we forgot to call them about, and all the other bits and bobs lying around. Once he reaches Harlow, he picks her up. She squeals loudly as he throws her over his shoulder, and she shouts through laughter for him to stop. I can't stop the smile from spreading across my face at seeing the both of them so happy. I've known Malik a long time. He was in the same year as me at school when I first went there, and he was always so angry, getting into fights, and moody. Seeing him with Harlow though, it's like seeing a whole new person.

He slaps her arse. "Quiet, before Max has a hissy fit and calls the police on us for waking Hope up," Malik growls, amused, then walks out the door. Everyone starts laughing at her silence, and I end up shoving my face into Myles' neck.

"Angel, you ready for bed?" Mason asks Denny, a twinkle in his eye.

She turns to me. "Are you okay if I go to bed?"

"I'm fine," I tell her, and laugh when she jumps up, grabbing his free hand since the other is occupied with supporting Hope, who is sleeping soundly in his arms.

"Hey, don't you need your blanket?" I call out, ready to grab it for them, but then realise I don't know which one it is.

She waves me off with a smile. "I bought them especially for tonight, so it's fine. Don't worry about cleaning up either. I'll do it in the morning," she orders. "Goodnight."

"Goodnight." I wave back, still smiling.

I love how happy they all are. They deserve it after all they've been through. I just wish I could find that happiness.

"She bought all this *just* for tonight?" Max asks, eating some of the Jelly Tots we started to munch on earlier.

"It's Denny. Do you really need to ask?" Myles snorts, snatching the Jelly Tots off Max, who scowls back at him.

It's silent for a few minutes; the only noise in the room coming from the television. My hands start to become sweaty, and when I realise I'm still sat on Myles, I gently slide myself off, my face blushing red.

"God, this is more awkward than that time I looked for Narnia in my wardrobe," Max mutters, standing up. "I'm out." With that, he turns and struts out, whistling a tune that sounds a lot like *Happy Days*. I try hard to cover up my giggles, but it's hard to, and when I find Myles staring down at me, it only causes me to laugh harder. After a few seconds of watching me, he laughs too, his head falling back against the sofa just as a full belly laugh erupts from his mouth.

"I swear, sometimes I wonder if we're really twins," he declares.

"He's harmless," I reply.

"He's crazy is what he is," he tells me, then reaches over to the pile of magazines and starts to pile them together. When I realise he's packing it all away, I reach out and stop him.

"It's okay, I can clean this up," I tell him softly. "It's our mess."

"I know, baby, but I want to help. I knew you wouldn't leave it like she asked," he admits, and my stomach does a summersault at hearing him call me baby again.

I like it when he calls me babe, but when he says baby, I love it. My heart flutters, and I feel dizzy. The good kind of dizzy.

"Thank you," I reply, and begin to help him by clearing away all the rubbish and bowls. When I notice the washing up piling up, I make a mental note to do it before I leave tomorrow and head back into the living room.

Myles stands with the pile of magazines. "Jesus, there's so many of them," he announces.

"She wanted to make sure she had everything," I explain.

"Where can I put them?" he asks, looking around the small room loaded with blankets.

"Pop them on the sofa. I'm going to sleep on the floor," I tell him.

There's no point ruining the sofa when there's a perfectly comfortable bed already made up on the floor. It's soft enough and will probably be more comfortable.

"Alright. I'm going to grab a drink. Do you want anything?"

"Can you grab the bottle of Sprite from the fridge, please?"

He leaves, and I finish clearing up the other stuff before dropping down on the pile of blankets.

He walks back in with two bottles of pop and hands me a Sprite. "Do you want me to go, or would you like to watch another film?" he asks.

"As long as it's not another scary movie then I don't mind," I remark, feeling giddy over the fact he's going to stay. I love spending time with him. I love how I feel when he's around.

"God, no! I don't mind horror movies, but I prefer an action, thriller, comedy, or hell, even a romance," he boasts.

"Well, if it's okay with you, I brought *Ninja Turtles* if you want to watch that with me. Denny and Harlow don't seem like girls who would enjoy it, so I never mentioned it."

He drops down beside me, tugging a blanket over his legs. "You'd be surprised by what they like, baby. Denny surprised us all when we found out she's a huge fan of horror movies, and Harlow when we found out she listens to and watches anything that interests her. She doesn't have a specific taste. So, if you'd have asked them, you would have been surprised that they would have most likely liked to watch it with you."

I run over his words in my head. Listening to him say it like that, I feel like shit. I judged them unintentionally. Seeing how beautiful they are, how girly and well-dressed they always look, I immediately jumped to the conclusion that they wouldn't watch a superhero cartoon-type movie.

I force a smile, feeling ashamed of my choices. "I'll remember that for the next time we have a girls' night."

"Maybe you shouldn't," he mutters under his breath, but I hear him clear as day as he starts the DVD up.

"Why?" I blurt out, needing to know why he said that.

He smirks. "Because if you had watched this with the girls, then I wouldn't be sitting here watching it with you," he admits, his voice husky.

His gaze bores into mine, and I begin to feel hot all over. How can he look as good as he does, be a manly lad, a popular kid, and still be the kindest, sweetest, and most sensitive lad I know?

Most lads his age would say shit like that just to get into their girl's knickers, but I know when I hear things like that coming from Myles, he truly means them. It's not a line. It makes me like him that much more, and I'm starting to feel like I could quite easily fall for him and his charming ways.

Not knowing what to say, I keep quiet and concentrate on the movie. Or try to. It's hard when he's so close. My gaze flicks over to him every so often, only to find his attention is focused on the movie. Every so often though, he'll catch me looking, and his lips twitch as I quickly glance away.

I don't know how long into the movie we get before I start to feel my eyes droop. My head falls to the side, and in doing so, I fall onto Myles' shoulder. At one point, I feel his arm go around me, his fingers rubbing slow circles on my shoulder. It's seconds later when I fall into a deep slumber.

CHAPTER
TWELVE

KAYLA

s I wait for my bus to arrive at its destination, I can't help but think back to the weekend. I had so much fun, and didn't like waking up alone this morning. I wish I could rewind back to Sunday morning, when I woke up wrapped up in Myles' warm embrace.

Of course, I'd skip the part where Denny was standing in the doorway with a huge smirk on her face. *That* I didn't need to see first thing in the morning, especially when seconds later, Mason, Max and Maverick walked in, wearing only tracksuit bottoms, or in Max's case, boxers. They all took one look at me and Myles and pounced on us. Literally too. I'm sure I have new bruises to prove it. Their hard bodies took seconds to squash my small, delicate one, and Myles' hard one. I'm sure he took most of the brunt too, considering he had Maverick's weight and Mason's.

We all ate breakfast together, and that's when I reluctantly agreed to go to a theme park with them at the weekend. It's a seven-hour drive, but they assured me with a good playlist, it flies by. I couldn't say no with all the brothers looking at me with puppy dog eyes, and Myles' pleading glance.

I get off the bus at my stop, and I'm grateful to not be greeted by my mother. She called Dad last night and said she couldn't make today's session because she has an interview. I didn't believe it for a second, but I wasn't going to call her out on it. I hate it when she comes with us. She fills the therapist's head with shit and I end up set back in my recovery because of it.

My dad is waiting in the reception area when I step inside the therapist's office five minutes early.

"Darling, how was school?" he greets.

"Good. I did some mock exams today and I'm pretty sure I nailed them," I inform him. I revised like a mad woman and knew the answers confidently. There wasn't one I was unsure of.

"That's lovely," he tells me, gifting me with a smile. "Would you like to grab something for dinner once we're finished here?"

"Sure." I shrug, dropping my school bag to the floor by my feet. I won't hold my breath. Nearly every session he tells me the same thing, but as soon as I step out of the room, he has a phone call that has him stepping away for another meeting.

"Kayla Martin?" my therapist's receptionist calls.

I stand up just as my dad wishes me luck, and I make my way into the doomed room. It's not like the therapist rooms you see on the television. You know, the ones that have the comfy couches, or the lightly dimmed room that's filled with candles, that has soft music playing in the background? Yeah, that is so not like my therapist's office. It's a basic room. Walking inside, the desk is straight in front of you. Filing cabinets run along the wall behind it, and there's a large window with blinds half open on the next wall. To the left of the door are two sets of chairs which make school chairs look comfy, with a little round coffee table centred in the middle.

Mr Stanley gets up from his chair to greet me, holding his pudgy hand out to me. The man is overweight, balding, and the little hair he does have left is turning grey. His suit looks new and expensive, but he obviously hasn't looked after it considering he's still got crumbs on his tie, a coffee stain on his shirt, and I don't even want to imagine what the stain on the sleeve of his suit jacket is.

Vomit!

"Kayla, take a seat. Would you like something to drink?" he asks ever so politely. I'd love to say yes, because after travelling on the bus and being at school all day, I'm parched, but there is no way I'll accept a drink from him. The little made-up kitchenette he's made above one of the filing cabinets looks to have seen better days. I'm pretty sure I once saw a spider climbing all over his cup before he took a sip. I would have warned him, but my mum hates it when I interrupt him.

"No, thank you. I'm good."

"As you know from our last session, your mother was quite concerned about your behaviour. You seem to be distancing yourself from people and becoming confrontational towards her. Has that changed since we last spoke?"

For the first time, I can say what I really want to say. My mother isn't here to dig her fake, manicured nails into my arm.

"Since we finally have privacy, Mr Stanley, I'd like to point out that not once did you ever ask me about any of this when my mother was in the room. I never argued it, which proves I'm not confrontational. I also can't distance myself from people I hardly see, Mr Stanley. I've made huge progress since the first time you saw me, and I'll also add that I've made friends, and we're really close."

"I'm sorry you feel like you weren't heard. Your mother just seems to be very worried about you."

I want to laugh in his face, but although I've had this boost of confidence to finally speak my mind, I'm *not* that brave.

"Not to be rude, sir, but you don't know my mother. She isn't worried about me at all. If she was…" I stop myself short before I can say anything more, knowing he can report her.

"Go on," he orders, writing something down on his paper. I hate it when he does that because his eyes hardly move away from mine, and his gaze always has me feeling unsettled.

"It doesn't matter. What I'm trying to say is that I'm the one who was raped. I'm the one my mother made keep it quiet, making me feel ashamed about it, and I'm the one recovering from it. I'd like to say I'm completely healed, that I've finally come to terms with what happened to me, but I'd be lying. Who can really get over something like that? I'm never going to be able to, but what I can do is move on from it. Having these restrictions on me, especially at eighteen, is not helping, Mr Stanley, so I'm begging—no, pleading—for you to reconsider your last diagnosis."

"It's my job to look after your best interests, Kayla. You tried to kill yourself. Twice. We just need to make sure you're better." I go to speak, but he puts his hands up, stopping me. "That said, the last time I saw you, I did feel like you were doing much better. I spoke with your father about it and he agrees wholeheartedly that you have overcome so much since moving back to Coldenshire. Your parents were worried at first about how the move would affect you emotionally, but it seems you've been doing brilliantly. From now on, our sessions will be every six months. As for your restrictions, they've already been removed. I contacted your mother right after going over our last session. Did she not mention it?"

"No, she didn't," I grit out. His comment about me trying to take my own life also grates on my nerves. He knows nothing; no one does unless they've felt what I felt, suffered what I have. Every day was torture for me, and all I wanted was for the voices inside my head to stop, the images of what happened to stop playing over and over in my head. It didn't, and each day was a constant reminder of what happened to me.

For the first few months, I took the hottest showers possible, burning my skin and scrubbing it to the point it would be red raw by the time I walked out of the shower. My skin would be sore, and at one point, got infected.

My mother called me weak for what I did. Other's told me I didn't deserve to live, and reminded me that there are people out there fighting for their lives that would appreciate the chance I'd been given.

But none of them had to live a life where your nightmare is playing constantly in your mind, whether you're awake or asleep.

Hearing *his* voice around every corner and being too afraid to leave your room. Then there's the not feeling clean. Having to shower every chance you get, but still not feeling any cleaner and still feeling his hands all over you. But the worst part of it all was being powerless to stop it. In a way, I guess ending my life was my way of gaining power, and not just ending my living nightmare.

I never made the decision lightly either. Those thoughts played on my mind constantly. No matter how much I tried to fix those feelings, it all went back to ending my life. It was the only way I saw to make all of the pain, hurt, and memories go away.

It worked too. Until the very second I woke up in the hospital bed, and everything came flooding back. As soon as I had the chance, I did it again. I'm a stronger person now though; I'm learning to deal with more than just my nightmares, but with everyday living. I also don't have my mum breathing down my neck as much, being cruel with her sharp words.

"Right," he mutters, writing more down in that damn pad again, interrupting me from my thoughts.

"We've got half an hour left of today's session. Is there anything you would like to discuss?"

I shrug, hating this part. I never know what to say. And when I do finally talk, he listens, but he always stares, gauging every reaction, every movement I make. It's so unnerving. I hate it. I'd rather have a crowd of a million people watching me than have just that one-person stare at me.

"Okay, I'll go. You mentioned you made some friends. You want to tell me about them?"

And that's how I spend the last half an hour of my session. I tell him all about Myles, Max, Denny, and Harlow. I mention the other Carter brothers too, but mostly Myles and Max. I mention who Harlow is, what happened to her, and how it made me feel. I tell him about Denny, what happened to her and why, and he listens, gives me feedback, and asks me questions. I'm glad he doesn't think it's not a good idea for me mentally to speak with Harlow. He even said it was great that I had the courage to do what I did in meeting her, although he does believe I have nothing to be sorry for. He's wrong, though. If I had said something sooner, had the courage Harlow had, then he wouldn't have been able to hurt her, and his brother wouldn't have hurt Denny. And since he knows about Charlie, I talk about her, avoiding her new diagnosis.

"Carol, can you please send in Mr Martin, please," Mr Stanley calls through the phone.

A few seconds later, there's a knock on the door, before my dad walks in, carrying my school bag.

"Is something wrong?" he asks Mr Stanley before looking me over to check I'm okay.

"Yes. I just wanted to let you know that Kayla's restrictions were revoked at our last session. It seems Ms Martin forgot to pass on this information to you and Kayla. I'll also be stretching our appointments out. Our session will be every six months, but with the progress I've seen, and the confidence in Kayla in today's session, I can see us spreading them farther apart in the near future. Do you have questions?"

"So she won't need twenty-four-hour monitoring?" I turn to my dad when he speaks. I'm surprised by the tone in his voice. He almost sounds relieved, and my mind immediately goes to him abandoning me. Does he hate being burdened with me? His eyes begin to water, and mine widen at the sight. What. On. Earth?

"Thank you, Lord. I've been so worried she'd have another relapse. Honey, I'm so proud of you," he cheers, his tone filled with emotion.

"Dad," I whisper, tears pooling in my eyes.

He hugs me tightly before turning to Mr Stanley and shaking his hand. "Thank you for helping my daughter."

"Enjoy the rest of your day," Mr Stanley proclaims.

We leave him to his notes and make our way out of the building. The minute the fresh air hits my skin, he turns to me, a frown on his face.

"I know, I know, you've got another meeting," I grumble, waving him off, and his eyebrows rise to his hairline.

"What are you talking about?"

"You were about to tell me you needed to cancel our dinner date because you had a meeting, weren't you?"

"Um, no. I was going to say you can invite those friends of yours to dinner. We can wait until they get to the restaurant to order," he explains, and I'm completely taken aback, even more so when he turns to me, looking sheepish. "Do I really bail on you that much, sweetie?"

I decide not to sugar coat it. "Every darn session."

"God, I'm such a shit father. I promise, honey, no more. Actually, cancel on your friends. We can do that another time. Tonight, we need to celebrate. Plus, I have something I'd like to share with you. It's important."

I try to read his expression, but aside from looking unsure, he's masking his emotions. I want to ask him what it is but decide against it when he seems lost in thought. I follow him down the street to where he parked his car.

He takes us to one of the nicer restaurants in town, which shouldn't have surprised me, but I'm still wearing my school uniform, and I feel so out of place. The restaurant is somewhere you'd take a date, not your daughter.

After ordering our food, the waitress walks off and I turn to my dad, noticing him shifting in his seat.

"What did you want to tell me?" I ask since my thoughts have been running wild with what it is. I'm scared he'll force me to go to Mum's.

"Well, you know me and your mother have been separated for some time now?" he points out, then pauses for me to answer.

Please don't tell me you're getting back together with that witch. I gulp. "Yeah."

"Well, I've been lonely. Your mother and I haven't exactly had a great relationship. I think we were over before we were officially over—"

"Dad, just spit it out," I blurt out, placing a hand over my stomach.

"I'm seeing someone. She works for me. At first, it was just a fling, but I've come to really care about her."

He stops his nervous ramble and stares at me, trying to gauge my reaction. I should have seen it coming. He's a good-looking man for his age, and extremely wealthy. I'm just unsure how I feel about it.

"Is that all?" I ask, not knowing how I truly feel. I think I'm more worried she's going to be like my mother. I know I won't be able to handle another gold-digging witch, especially if it's as serious as Dad is making it out to be.

"Well, I'm also hoping—if it's okay with you—she could come over for dinner at the weekend?"

"Ah, Dad, that's what I needed to talk to you about. Now my restriction has been revoked, I was hoping you would give me your permission to go away for the weekend with my friends. They've planned a trip to a theme park, and they asked me to go with them. I said yes, but I wanted to check in with you first."

"That's okay, honey. We can reschedule for another time. I'm more worried about how upset your mother will be. She's expecting you this weekend, right? Or is it next weekend?"

"Actually, that's another thing I wanted to talk to you about. I'm not going to be staying over at Mum's again."

"What? Why? Don't you like it there?"

Shit. I said too much. "With all my homework and stuff, it's easier to work from home. The shelter I work at on a Saturday is closer to your house than it is Mum's. We still don't have the best relationship, and I'd really love it if you could support me on this, Dad. I'm a grown adult who has been through some bad stuff, but I know what I need. I just need you to support me." I hold my breath to stop the vomit from rising.

He looks at me with an appraising eye, and I start to panic that he knows more than he's letting on. If he finds out what Mum does to me, he'll end up in jail, or worse, she'll kill me and he'll be attending my funeral. I've never been brave enough to tell anyone anyway, just in case they never believed me. It would set me back years of work. It's easier to keep it to myself.

"I understand. I just don't understand *why*. Your mother will be really disappointed and upset."

Like hell she will. I just wish I could say that out loud.

"Please, she'll be fine."

"Okay, let me just give her a call—"

"No! Just... let's enjoy our meal first. Tell me all about this new woman," I demand, and like that, his attention is diverted and he tells me all about his new girlfriend, who now has a name: Katie.

———

D ad pulls up outside Charlie's an hour later, and I grab my bag off the floor. "Will you reconsider about calling your mum? She deserves to know, and it's unfair to cancel her plans with you on such short notice. She'll never see you if you stay home on weekends."

"She has a date tonight, Dad. It will ruin it if we call her, so please, just wait until the weekend," I lie. "Plus, she barely spends time with me. She wants to make a go of it with this new guy, and I feel like I'm just getting in the way."

"I don't like the sound of that," he mutters, glancing at his phone in the holder.

"Please, Dad, just leave it," I plead. "You heard Mr Stanley. I don't need to do this back and forth anymore."

"Alright," he relents, and I unclip my belt and get out. "Call me if you change your mind about being picked up."

"I will," I promise, and rush up the driveway to Charlie's.

I walk in, not bothering to knock on the door. I've never needed to. Charlie's mum greets me with a wide smile.

"Kayla, it's so good to see you. Charlie's upstairs in her room. She's feeling a little tired and sluggish today, so if you don't mind, you'll be sitting up in her room with her."

"I don't mind," I reply, and head toward the stairs.

"Would you take these up for me please, honey?"

I turn back around to see her mum pick up a tray of drinks, snacks, and a prescription bag.

"I don't mind," I tell her, taking the tray from her, thankful it's not too heavy.

"I'm so glad you're here for her, Kayla. You're a good girl," she tells me, her eyes glistening with tears before she turns and walks into the kitchen.

Charlie's house is big, but not as big as mine. And like mine, it's far too big for the three of them. They turned one of the spare bedrooms into a cinema. It's great in there, and Charlie's favourite room. I'm hoping I can get her transferred into there, so we can do what she loves and watch movies.

"Hey you," I greet, walking into her room and heading straight for her desk to drop the tray down.

"Hey," she greets back, and I'm startled by her appearance. Her complexion is yellow, yet pale, and she looks drained. She has dark circles under her eyes, and I know that the cinema next door is out of the question. She can barely lift her head, let alone get up to walk to the door.

"You don't look so good," I mumble, grabbing her prescription and her drink. "Your mum said to bring these up. I'm taking it that you have to take it now?"

"Yeah, sorry. I'm just so tired."

"It's fine," I promise, and pop the pill into her mouth after reading the label on the bottle. She's barely able to suck water up through the straw, and my heart aches.

"I'd ask how you are, but I can see you're not so good," I tell her, forcing a smile.

She chuckles, but it ends up turning into a cough, her face wincing in pain. Once it stops, she turns to me with tear-filled eyes.

"Please tell me about your weekend," she wheezes.

"It was really good. I wish you were there on Saturday. Denny pulled out all the stops at the sleepover, buying a ton of fluffy blankets and pillows for us to lie on. She said she's keeping them so we can do it again, so hopefully you'll be better by then."

"Sounds like a plan, Stan," she teases, gifting me with a strained smile. "How are things with Myles?"

"Good."

"Seriously, Kayla. Be honest. This is me."

"Gah, I swear he drives me crazy," I tell her, standing up to pace back and forth. "Every time he touches me, he sets my skin alight. Every time he looks at me, I get hot flushes, and don't even get me started on the tingles, or the way my belly does a summersault when he's near. Then there's his voice. God, his voice... It's so deep, so mesmerising, gentle and loving. I could listen to him all day. In fact, he'd be perfect to do one of those audiobooks you keep talking about."

"You love him," she states, and I glance at her, horrified.

"I do not."

"Do too," she argues. "Admit it, you love him. You deserve this, Kayla."

"I'm dirty, though," I choke out once I realise I do in fact have strong feelings for Myles. It may or may not be love; I don't know. What I do know is there isn't anyone other than him who I'd rather be with.

She glances at my clothes. "You look fine to me."

I glance down at my lap as I take a seat next to her. "Not that kind of unclean. Ever since my attack, I've felt dirty, tainted, ruined, and used. I'm all of those and more. He deserves someone pure. Someone clean and perfect. Not someone like me," I admit.

She reaches out with her cold hand and places it down on mine. She squeezes it gently, and I'm sure just that movement has taken up all of her strength.

"Kayla, you're far from any of those things. Myles would be lucky to have you. The way he looks at you is the same way you look at him, if not more star-struck. He's had a crush on you for years. Give yourself this, please. Promise me. I need you to promise me." She coughs once more, and I watch as more strength leaves her.

"You're not getting better, are you?"

"It'll be fine," she grumbles, unable to meet my gaze "I've just caught a chest infection or something." I can tell by her tone there is more to it, but she doesn't want to talk about it. I let it go, not wanting to work her up when she's feeling so down.

"I love you, Charlie, and I promise. I can't promise anything will happen, but I promise to start seeing myself differently when I'm with him. Just… promise me you'll fight. You'll fight whatever is happening, because I can't lose you," I choke out, tears falling from my eyes.

"I promise to fight, Kayla. With everything I have in me, I'll fight, but you need to also be prepared for the worst. I might not make it, and I need you to be okay if that happens."

She says it so confidently, so surely, and it breaks my heart. I lie down next to her and wrap my arm around her stomach.

"Nothing could ever prepare me, Charlie. You're one of a kind, and no amount of time will make any of this okay," I whisper, then hear her choke out a sob. We both lie there crying, clinging to each other.

Her mother walks in not long after, telling me it's time to go home. Her expression is full of pain and sadness, and I can see her eyes watering as she looks down at her sleeping daughter. Charlie exhausted herself from crying and talking to me about all her fears.

"Will you let her know I said goodbye and I'll be back soon?" I whisper, climbing over a sleeping Charlie.

"Of course, dear."

She waits until I grab my blazer before following me out of the room and down the stairs.

"Kayla," she calls as I reach the front door.

"Yes?"

"Thank you."

"For what?" I ask, my brows pinching together.

"For being a friend to Charlie, even when you moved away. She hasn't had a friend like you, one who will bring out the best in her."

"I didn't do anything, Mrs Young. Your daughter did it all by herself. She saved me. She's extraordinary, and I promise I'll be praying each and every night for her," I declare, before quietly leaving her to grieve. Her sobs open my own floodgates, but I know I need to be strong. She might be my friend, but she's her daughter.

CHAPTER
THIRTEEN

KAYLA

By the time I get home, I've worked myself up over Charlie. I'm scared for her, but I know I need to be strong. I hate that there is nothing I can do for her. I can't even ease her discomfort. I promised her everything will be fine, but now all I've done is promise the impossible.

I'm about to put my key in the door when my dad pulls it open, both of us startled to find the other.

"Hey," I breathe out, taking note of his work suit, his briefcase, and the phone in his hand. "Where's the fire?"

"Hey, honey. I was just about to call you. I've got to head into work for a bit, and after I'll be going round Katie's because she'll be finishing her second job by then."

Oh, so she's not a gold-digger like my mother then. She actually works for her money. Another interesting fact I need to add to the list of things I now know about her.

"Okay, I'll see you in the morning before school."

He bends down to kiss my forehead, shocking the shit out of me. He's never been this affectionate towards me, but then, ever since he left my mother, he's been acting differently. It's not even his actions, it's the way he moves. He's more at ease and there's no tension in his body. I almost asked him once if Mum hit him too, but I knew it would be wrong of me.

"Bye, honey," he calls, before racing off down the path. I watch him throw his briefcase over to the passenger side before he stops, calling back. "Oh, by the way, Myles is in your room waiting for you. He said it's about homework. I told him you wouldn't be long and he could wait."

"What?" I cry, but he's already shutting the door and driving off.

He let Myles into my room?

Embarrassment fills me. Not because he's in my room, or that Dad sent him there, but because there's no telling what he'll do unsupervised. I wish I had time to fix my face since I know it will show I've been crying. And I dread to think what my hair looks like. Most people call it ginger, but I prefer red since it's too dark to be ginger. But like anyone with red hair when it's humid, it needs taming.

Deciding it doesn't matter since he's seen me first thing in the morning, I make my way up the stairs. As soon as I hear music playing from my room, I know exactly what he's watching and move quicker. It's my year seven talent show, where I sang *My Heart Will Go On* by Celine Dion.

"What are you doing?" I squeak out, rushing over to the DVD player to turn it off when I enter.

"Oh, come on," Myles groans. "I was really getting into that. Before that, I watched you playing piano, and then another of you singing *Wannabe* by the Spice Girls. I was having fun."

"*That* is not having fun," I retort.

"Lighten up, Kayla. You were brilliant," he states, and I can hear the smile and pride in his voice.

"What are you doing here?" I ask once the disc is safely in its original case.

"I came by to see you, but also to show you the introduction to the project," he reveals, but stops when I turn around. "What's wrong?"

Dang it!

For once, I wish he wouldn't see me crying. He's going to think I'm a Debbie Downer.

"I went to see Charlie," I explain, knowing he'll understand.

The only other person to know is my dad, and that's because Charlie's mum filled him in.

"Is she okay?" he asks, tugging me into his arms. It's weird how easily I melt into him. If this was anyone else, there is no way I would have let them get close to me, let alone hold me tightly in their arms.

"She's not doing so well at the minute. She's been really tired and short of breath a lot. Her mum is really worried because Charlie has a chest infection," I tell him. "God, Myles, she doesn't look like she will last much longer."

"Shit! What have the doctors said? Do you know?"

"Nope," I sigh sadly, tipping my head back to look up at him. "Now, how the hell have you finished that introduction so fast? I've not even finished my research."

"Aw, poor Kayla," he teases, and I give him a playful glare. "I got bored the other day when I finished all my other homework, so I started on this. I'll need you to proofread it because there is no way I'm asking my brothers. They'd make me pay them or some shit, and won't even pick up on any mistakes. The whole process would just be useless."

The thought of Max helping Myles do homework is funny as hell. I could see Max pulling some prank, changing words to make a fool out of Myles.

"Point taken. Did you want to do this now, though? I just want to chill and relax." I hope I don't offend him. I'm just too tired to look over the introduction right now. Just the thought of it is giving me a headache.

"Nah, whenever you're free. Did you want me to go or do you want to watch a film?"

"You want to watch a film?" No matter how many times we've watched movies together, the thought of being alone with him, snuggled up on my bed, has my skin breaking out in goosebumps. Another part of me is afraid of the day he doesn't want to watch one.

"Yeah, I was hoping we could finish watching the one I just started," he teases with a mischievous grin.

It takes me a few seconds to catch on, and when I do, I send him another glare, wanting to wrap my fingers around his neck. "No way."

"Oh, come on," he pleads, picking me up. My body shivers with delight.

"No." I glare with no mirth, my lips twitching. He swings me around, and a smile lights up my face. "I'll let you pick any other film, but not that one. I've even got Netflix so you can watch *Castle*."

He chuckles as he lowers me down to the floor. "You play dirty, Kayla Martin. You know how much I love that show. Now go get dressed so we can get in two episodes before you start snoring."

"I do not snore," I growl. Yes, growl.

He laughs, throwing his head back. "No, you don't. You make these little cute noises that aren't quite a snore, yet it's like listening to a baby cub trying to roar."

"I. Do. Not," I argue, offended.

Myles steps closer to me. Bringing his hand up, he lightly runs his fingers across my frown lines and down my nose, before giving the tip a tap once with his index finger.

"Cute," is all he says, before turning and walking over to the bed to grab the TV remote.

I'm standing there, all heavy breathing, my whole body covered in goosebumps, while he looks calm and collected. It's not fair.

"Kayla. Dressed, now," he reminds me, and I jump from my position to quickly find some pyjamas to wear.

I leave to get dressed, which takes only minutes, before I'm back in my room. Myles' focus is glued to the television, his lips curled in an amused smirk.

"What's so funny?"

"Huh?" he asks, shaking his head.

"You. You're wearing a smirk. What gives?" I ask whilst climbing over him to get to my side of the bed.

"Oh, I was just remembering your dance moves to *Wannabe*," he jokes.

"You're such an arse," I scold, trying not to laugh.

"We're watching the frozen episode again. You know, the one where she's dumped and melting all over a construction site?"

"We've watched this one already. Why do you constantly watch all the old ones? You do realise there are, like, seven seasons or something that you haven't watched?"

"Because you fell asleep the last time we watched this, and I want you to get the full *Castle* experience."

"That sounds so wrong. I'll make a deal with you. If I watch this with you, then you have to watch an episode of *Veronica Mars*."

"You drive a hard bargain." He beams. I love his smile.

"So is that a deal?" I smirk, trying my hardest not to fist pump the air too soon. I've been trying to get him to watch *Veronica Mars* for a few weeks now, but each time he'll make me watch some other movie, so if he agrees, it will be a great achievement.

"Deal."

I fist pump the air, laughing. "Ha! You're going to be converted, I promise. Once you see how badass cool she is, you're going to want to be her."

When he doesn't retort with a witty remark, I glance over at him, only to find him watching me with so much depth, it scares me. "What?"

"I love your voice, but when you laugh like that, it's just…"

"What?" I whisper.

"Beautiful."

He's serious. He really does believe that.

And there goes those damn flutters in my stomach again.

My gaze is drawn to his full, plump lips, and I wonder what it would be like to be kissed by him. He makes a sound at the back of his throat that has my gaze snapping to meet his. His pupils dilate, and there's a longing there.

Surely he can't be attracted to me?

The thought of him wanting me has my gaze lowering to his lips again. It's times like this that I wish I wasn't so inexperienced.

I'm unsure of when it happened, but we've somehow moved closer. I can smell him, feel his breath on my cheek.

I tilt my head, trying to control the raging hormones going on inside of me. His pupils darken further, his gaze never wavering from mine.

This is really happening.

My eyelids flutter closed as I inhale gently. Seconds later, his lips meet mine, and they are as soft as they look. A gasp of air slips free when he kisses me again. With courage I didn't know I had, I mirror his movements, kissing him back.

Emotions run through my veins, and I feel like the world around me has stopped. My first kiss, and it's better than I ever imagined it would be.

His warm hand cups my jaw, sliding up until his fingers are gently pressing the sensitive part of flesh behind my ear, while his thumb is running lightly over my cheekbone.

He tilts my head a little and uses the move to flick his tongue along my bottom lip.

Every nerve is on fire as I grant him access. My heart races as I mirror his movements, hoping I'm doing it right as our tongues collide.

The kiss is slow, sensual, and it's like I'm floating on air.

The need to touch him comes out of nowhere, but I don't question it as I run my hand up his strong, muscular arm. I cup his jaw, before running my hand over the nape of his neck. My fingers easily run through his thick, unruly hair.

His hand slips away from my ear, and he runs it down my side until he grips my hip. I stiffen for a split second, but he deepens the kiss, distracting me. When he doesn't move his hand further, I relax, kissing him back.

I never want this to end.

When it does, my eyes flicker open to find him watching me. There are no words for the way he's watching me. I can only describe how I feel, and I feel like only he could ever make me feel this good.

I run my finger lightly across my lips. They feel buzzed and swollen.

"God, you're beautiful," he rasps, and he truly means it.

He isn't repulsed by me. He hasn't run away. I just hope I didn't mess it up and he enjoyed it as much as me.

Still feeling light-headed from the kiss, my words come out jumbled. "Did I... Was that..." I close my eyes. "God, I'm messing this up."

"It was perfect, Kayla," he promises, understanding my unspoken question. He presses his lips to mine once more, stealing my breath for a second, before he leans back to kiss the tip of my nose.

He runs the pad of his thumb over the creased flesh between my eyebrows. "Don't overthink it. It was perfect, or at least, for me it was," he demands, reading me once again. "Now, I think we should finish this episode so we can start watching this Ronnie chick who's meant to be a badass."

A dopey smile splits across my face. No matter what is happening, he always knows what to do or say to make me feel better.

"It's Veronica, and she is a badass," I reply teasingly.

He grins as he pulls me against his chest, pressing his lips to my forehead.

I get comfy, my smile still in place.

He kissed me.

And I loved every second of it.

———

Waking up in Myles' arms will never feel old, no matter how many times it happens. He makes me feel safe in a way no one has ever done before. But more, I love how he makes me feel. Like I can take on the world.

Saying goodbye, even for a short while, leaves an ache in my heart. He left to get changed and text me not long ago that he was on his way back.

It's non-uniform day today to help raise money for the library, and normally, I wouldn't put too much thought into it. But today, I found myself wanting to make an effort. I ended up with black leggings, a brown knit jumper that hangs off the one shoulder, and paired it with knee-length boots the same shade of brown as my jumper.

I grab my jacket from my chair and run downstairs. I time it perfectly since there's a knock on the door as I reach the bottom. A big, toothy grin spreads across my face. You would think I hadn't seen him in a week, when in fact, it's only been an hour.

I pull open the door. "What took you so…" I freeze when it's not Myles on the other side. "Mum! What are you doing here?"

I glance at the end of the path, shaking when I don't spot my dad's car or any sign of Myles.

"You little, conniving bitch," she snarls, shoving me back and following me inside. She slams the door closed behind her. "Did you think I wouldn't find out about your little plan? What have you been telling that psycho doctor of yours?"

"What? I don't… I… I need to go to school," I stammer, wishing she would move away from the door so I can escape.

"Like hell you are, Missy. We need to talk, and then we're going back to that office, and you're going to tell them that whatever you said was a lie," she demands, pinning me with her bloodshot eyes. I can smell the alcohol pouring off her.

"Mum, please, my friends, they—" I begin, but her hand lashes out, smacking me in the top of my arm. "Please, Mum, I haven't said anything."

She grabs my hair into her fist and pulls me close, her spit hitting me in the face when she states, "You're a liar. He called me, asking a lot of questions, then your father called me and asked why your doctor was asking questions about me."

She pulls tighter, and a whimper slips free as a knock on the door echoes in the house. We both freeze, and I clamp my lips closed.

"Kayla, come on. We're going to be late if you don't get your sweet ass into gear," Myles calls from the other side of the door. Panic sets in. Did he hear my mum yelling? I didn't want anyone to know, but mostly him. He already knows too much, and I'm worried that if he finds out my own mother hates me, he'll decide I've got too much baggage and leave.

"Mum, I need to go to school," I warn, and she lets go of my hair. I let out a breath, believing I've gotten out of it, but then she grabs my wrist, squeezing until I have to bite my lip to stop from crying out. I taste blood, which does nothing to ease the panic.

Her nails dig in as she drags me over to the door. "Get rid of him. You aren't going to school today," she announces, and her tone leaves no room to argue.

I nod in agreement, but the hold on my wrist only gets tighter. "Okay, please, just stop," I whisper, a small gasp slipping free.

I turn to the door, prepared to listen to her demands, but hearing him call my name once more, a strength I didn't know I had steels my spine.

I give her a quick glance as a plan forms in my mind. It's risky, but I can't let her keep hurting me. And she'll never do that in front of someone.

With shaky hands, I take a breath and pull the door open, smiling at Myles. "If we're late, it's because I was waiting for you," I tease, hoping my acting looks genuine.

"Are you okay?"

"Yes," I reply, and kick the door open more so Mum has no choice but to let go. "Mum was just here to tell me to have a good day."

Her expression doesn't say otherwise, so he doesn't question it as I grab the bag I dropped by the door and leave with him.

"Are you okay?" he asks when we're a good distance away from my house.

"What? Yeah, why wouldn't I be?" I ask, my mind still running over the consequences of leaving her like that. I should have stayed and taken her beating to get it over with.

I'm tired of being the person she uses as a punching bag. It never stops and it never ends. And as brave as I was back at the house, there's still a scared little girl inside of me, wondering what she did that was so wrong, that her own mother hated her.

"You're speed-walking like we're being chased by a serial killer.

And you seem a little shaken and pale. Is this about last night and our kiss?"

I slow down to answer. "Of course not. I told you when you asked this morning that I don't regret it." I stop and take his hands, leaning up to press a kiss to his lips. "It meant the world to me. I like that my first kiss wasn't stolen from me. You gave me back a first last night, and I'll never forget that."

His pupils darken as he tucks a strand of hair behind my ear. "Then something happened between me leaving and coming back. Did your mum say something?"

"It's nothing, I promise. Just excited to get to school," I lie, and start walking again.

"Did your dad come back this morning? I didn't hear him last night."

"Oh, he stayed the night at his new girlfriend's house—Katie," I reply, repeating everything my dad told me about her. "He's been seeing her for a while now, but he didn't want to tell me until it was serious. I'm meeting her next weekend."

"Oh, I know who she is. She's a really nice lady. She volunteers for a lot of things around town."

I change the subject. "Did your brother mind you staying last night?"

"No. I'm the last one he needs to worry about, so he trusts me. Speaking of though, I was wondering if you fancied another movie night Thursday?"

"I'd love to," I admit, and spend the rest of the trip to school listening to him tell me about his brothers.

He doesn't bring up my mum again, and for that, I'm grateful.

CHAPTER
FOURTEEN

KAYLA

The rest of the week passes by pretty quickly, and before I know it, it's Thursday morning.

I've been looking forward to this day all week, since not only do I get Myles for the night, but we get to spend the weekend together too. Thank God for teacher training days. We leave tomorrow morning for Exhilaration. I've never been to a theme park before and I'm beyond excited.

Even waking up from another nightmare at four this morning hasn't killed my buzz. I couldn't get back to sleep after, and not because of the nightmare, but because of the excitement for the day ahead.

I used the time to begin to pack my case, and Dad heard me shuffling around when he got up to leave for work. He popped in to give me some extra money to take, and gave me a run-down of what I can and can't do. He wasn't happy that no adults are going, even though technically, Maverick and Mason are. He left after he told me to have a good time and to call if I needed anything or more money.

The doorbell rings half an hour before I'm due to leave for school.

I should have expected Myles to decide to walk with me instead of going straight to the meeting he has with one of the teachers before school starts.

I head down, grateful I'm ready so I can get him there before he's late.

"Miss me alre—"

I'm dragged inside, and I faintly hear the door slamming closed. "Never, and I mean, *never*, dismiss me like you did on Tuesday," Mum spits out. "You're going to pay for it."

I should have checked the peephole.

I should have learned my lesson.

I should have done a lot of things.

Everything happens so fast. Her slaps turn into punches; her punches turn into kicks. The last thing I remember is curling up on the floor, blocking my head from the blows. Black dots blur my vision, and my cries for her to stop turn into broken rasps.

I beg for unconsciousness, but by the time it comes, the damage is done.

————

I'm accustomed to pain. I made it my friend. But it never makes waking up after an attack any easier. There's always a split second where I don't know what's happened, and it's blissful. It doesn't last. And neither does the adrenaline I get from the confusion. Once that leaves, every ache, bruise and cut throbs like a hammer is being whacked across my flesh.

I flicker my lids open, and for a moment, I listen to the sounds in the house. I don't move until I know the house is empty.

Bile rises in my throat, and I empty the contents of my stomach all over the laminate floor. My ribs scream in agony at the move, but I pant through it as I rise on all fours.

The room spins. There isn't a part of me that isn't hurting. I grab onto the banister and use it as leverage as I lift myself to my feet.

I glance up the stairs and whimper when the length feels like too much to handle. But if I don't, I risk someone coming in and finding me.

You've done this before. You'll be okay.

Each step has me crying out. Half way up, and I nearly lose my footing. My strength is slowly draining, but I breathe through it, taking another step. And another.

Until I'm at the top.

Spots of blood that are still weeping from the wounds on my arms leave a trail on the wall as I lean against it.

Each step has sharp, stabbing pains vibrating through me. I shove open the bathroom door and nearly sink to the floor in despair when I catch my reflection in the mirror. My face avoided most of the hits, but my lip didn't fare so well. Limping over to the mirror, I grimace as I turn my lip down, inspecting the damage inside. An angry thick cut runs from my gum to my lip, and is already swelling.

Tears sting as they begin to fall, but I keep going, removing all my clothes until I'm only in my underwear. I turn to the long mirror hanging behind the door and cry out at all the ugly, purple and blue bruises. My hip and left ribs have taken the worst of it, and I even have a cut on my groin where my zip must have cut into it.

I packed shorts for the weekend since my other injuries were barely visible, but now new ones are tattooed into my flesh, and there's no way I can use the excuse 'I fell down the stairs'. Stairs don't leave boot prints. All the injuries are ugly and swollen. I can't leave looking like this.

I hate her.

I seriously hate her.

More tears fall, but I angrily swipe them away. I'm angry at myself for letting this happen. I keep hiding her secret, and it began because I thought she would change. I know now that she won't, but I can't stop the scared little girl inside of me that stops me from speaking up.

I'm stronger than this.

Then why do you feel so alone?

I'm the girl who was bullied.

The girl who was raped.

I don't want to be the girl who was abused by her mum.

Davis took my power away the day he raped me, and I continue to let him each time I don't speak up. Because he warned me that no one would believe me. And they didn't. And now I'm scared that if I tell them about Mum, I'll be back to that time, where I'll be the girl who cried wolf.

Opening the cupboard, I grab a couple of painkillers and swallow them down dry before swilling my mouth out with some water from the tap.

My head bows because I know I won't be able to join my friends on the rides. It will jolt each injury and ruin the entire day if I'm in pain. I don't want to ruin their fun either, because I know they'll stay with me.

Tears blur my vision as I grab my dressing gown, and the stiffness in my arms and back has me turning back to the medicine cabinet. I grab another pill, wanting to make sure I sleep the day away. Then I grab my clothes from the floor, nearly passing out through the pain, before finally heading back to my room.

I grab my phone. I've got missed calls and a few messages from Myles and Max.

The fit twin: You playing hooky without me? It's not fair. I know all the best places to hide out at and Myles didn't have to know.

After registration one day, I found out Max had programmed his number into my phone without me knowing. He thought it would be funny to set his ring tone as '*Let's talk about sex, baby*' and then call me in the middle of class with 'The fit twin' as the caller. Luckily, the teacher found it as amusing as everyone else and let it play out. But this is the first time he's used my number to message me.

I scroll down to the next message, which is Myles. More tears fall again, since the one person I want here, can't be. He'll see how unlovable I am if he knew my own mother hurt me.

He'll see me as weak.

The only twin: I'm outside school. Where are you?

The only twin: I got you a hot chocolate, and it's gonna go cold soon if you don't come and claim it.

The only twin: And I got you a bagel from the shop you love in town.

The only twin: Is everything okay? I'm really worried. You aren't answering, so message me as soon as you get this. If I haven't heard from you by lunchtime, I'll come round.

Looking at the time on my phone, I'm thankful to find out I wasn't out very long. So, I quickly type back my lie, and hate every second of it.

Me: I'm spending the day with my dad. He feels bad that he's been spending so much time at work, and because I'm gone the whole weekend, he said I may as well call in sick. I'm going to have to cancel tonight too, but don't worry about collecting me; I'll meet you at yours. X

I dump my phone down on my bed and head back out to clean up the sick downstairs. I don't want Dad coming back and having to explain to him why sick and blood are on the floor.

Sweat breaks out as I reach the kitchen to grab the cleaning supplies. I do the best I can in the pain I'm in to clean it away, and just as I prepare myself for the pain of getting back up, the bag by the door catches my attention.

It's my mum's. My breathing picks up. A hot flush works its way over my body as I grab it, wanting it out of here, but my hands shake. I drop the bag, and the contents scatter across the floor.

Whimpering because she could be coming back at any minute, I rush to get it all back inside. An envelope grabs my attention, so I pull the letter out and scan it.

I don't understand most of it, but the basics of it is that she owes money. A lot of money. But I'm confused as to why. Dad pays her bills, and the solicitor's fees were covered in the settlement.

I don't dwell on it and throw the letter back inside the envelope. I make a mental note to ask Dad about it when he's back.

This time when I go to the door, I peek out of the peephole, checking the coast is clear. It is, but it doesn't mean she won't be back, and I don't want to give her a reason to knock on the door again. I leave it out by the door and pray like hell it isn't stolen before she misses it and comes back. She'll only blame me, and I don't think I can deal with another hit right now.

My chest heaves with a sob as I slam the door closed. I should have looked first. I'm so angry I let her do this again.

———

My eyes are sore when I wake up, and everything around me blurs in a kaleidoscope of colour. I'm not sure if it's from the pain or if it's the two other painkillers I took when I woke up briefly the first time. It was then that I threw on a tank top that wouldn't rub against my sores, and a pair of shorts.

Finally gathering my composure, my senses come to life, and they're telling me I'm not alone. I jerk up and roll over to face the room. Myles is sitting on my desk chair, his head bowed, and from this angle, I can see his jaw is clenched.

"Myles?" I rasp, and he startles, meeting my gaze.

Sadness seeps out of him. "Who?" he asks, his voice hoarse.

"What?" I whisper. I'm too scared to move because I know I won't be able to hide the pain.

"Don't play me, Kayla. Who did that to you? I've seen the bruises. Your shirt rode up whilst you were asleep. So did Max. We were worried when we saw your dad in town with Katie, and he said he hadn't seen you since this morning, so we came to check on you," he explains, his jaw clenching. "So tell me, Kayla, who the fuck did that to you?"

Ashamed that he and Max saw me like this, I avert my gaze. "I can't talk about it, Myles. Please don't make me," I whisper, my words breaking.

"I'd never make you do anything," he retorts softly, getting to his feet.

I tense, not strong enough for him to get close. I will break, and I don't want to break like that in front of him.

"Where is Max?"

"He's gone to get some food. We didn't want to leave you like this."

"You can go," I assure him, my heart breaking at the devastation in his gaze.

This is bothering him, and not in the way I thought it would. He doesn't like that I'm hurt or keeping things from him. I want to hold him, to tell him I'm okay, but I don't want to keep lying to him.

"I'm not going anywhere, Kayla. I need you to tell me who it is. Is it your dad?"

Tears gather in my eyes at his plea, but his accusation causes me to let out a dry laugh. He immediately jumped to my dad doing this, which is what I've always been afraid of happening. No one ever questions my mum.

"My dad has never laid a finger on me. No one did. I'm just clumsy. I fell in the shower," I lie, and I know he knows I'm lying because I can't look him in the eye when I tell him. My inner thoughts are screaming at me to tell him, to finally let go of all this pain my mum has made me carry around for years. She blamed me for having to move house after I was attacked, she blamed me for her divorce, and for everything that happened after.

"You're lying, goddamn it," he growls, and I startle at his outburst. "Who did this, Kayla? Why won't you tell me? Why are you protecting them?"

"Yo, bro, chill," Max orders. I didn't hear him enter. He lowers the food on the desk and gives me a brief look before he concentrates on his brother. I love their bond, and knowing they have each other's backs, no matter what. They fight for each other.

"Not now, Max," Myles grits out, his eyes watering as he kneels down beside me.

I'm angry at my mum for putting me in this situation, and frustrated at myself for doing this to him.

I need to let him go.

"I fell in the shower. Please, don't make me talk about it," I snap, but my words are a broken rasp. "Why won't you just believe me?

Why? If you don't want to be here, then just go. I never asked you to come."

Tears slip down my cheeks as I meet his gaze. Max moves, kneeling down next to us. His huge frame makes my room look tiny.

"Why don't you want to talk about it?" Max asks, showing a side to him I've never seen before.

"*Please*. Stop asking me," I plead, looking away from Myles to Max. He nods, and a look of understanding passes over his face as he rests his hand next to mine on the bed.

"We'll stop asking and leave you be. But I do think you should tell *someone*," he declares. "We can protect you. I know we didn't do a good job with the other two, but with Harlow and Denny, we were like training GI Joe's. We've got skills now, so you don't have to worry that we can't."

I think his attempt to lighten the mood is more for his brother, who looks ready to burst. It saddens me that he believes I think they can't take care of me. I know they would. They just shouldn't have to. My issue is fearing people not believing me or treating me differently.

"We have to know who to protect her from," Myles argues, his voice filled with emotion. "How can you dismiss this? You saw her bruises."

I don't want them to argue, so I reach out, placing my hand over his. "Myles, I'm fine. It's nothing, I promise."

"It's not nothing," he snaps heatedly, his gaze lingering on the bruises on my arm.

"Myles, you aren't helping," Max warns, before addressing me. "You aren't alone. You can tell us when you're ready, but you can bet your sweet arse that we aren't leaving your side until you do. And if it's us you don't trust, we can call Maverick. Malik and Mason will come too, but since they are all loved up, they'll tell their girlfriends and—"

I reach out, grabbing his wrist with wide eyes. "You can't tell anyone about this. No one. I mean it, Max. It was an accident, nothing more, but you can't tell anyone."

"Yeah, we know all about accidents," he replies evasively.

Myles glares into space.

"Please, don't be mad at me. I didn't want you to see me like this. I didn't want you to know."

He snaps out of his daze. "Kayla, someone is hurting you. I know this isn't the first time it's happened. I've seen bruises on you before, but I believed your excuses or let you distract me. I'll let it go until we're back from the weekend, but after that, all bets are off. I won't stop until I get answers and stop the person doing this," he warns.

This is a side to him I've never seen before. I always knew he was the type to protect, but I never saw the side where he'd go to war for someone.

Max tilts his head, humming sharply. "That sounds way better than my idea."

My brows pinch together. "You said you'd leave it be."

"No, I said I'd stop asking you. I didn't promise not to beat the shit out of your dad and get the answers from him," he amends.

Sly little dog. "You wouldn't."

He shrugs. "Don't worry, Daddy is safe… For now."

"He hasn't done anything," I argue, narrowing my gaze on him. He holds his hands up in surrender, and I wish I could wipe that smirk off his face.

They think it's my dad, and they aren't afraid to hurt him, but what will they do if they find out who it really is? Because I don't think they'll harm another woman. I know it won't stop them from doing something crazy, like gluing her to the bed, or planting something on her and reporting it to the police.

My stomach growls with hunger, and my cheeks heat with embarrassment.

"Luckily, I got us a Chinese," Max teases, then stands. "Myles, go grab the painkillers."

"Where are they?" he asks.

"In the bathroom," I reply, and he leaves to go find them.

Max takes my hands when he sees me struggling to sit up. "You can trust him, you know," he whispers.

"I know," I reply.

He keeps his hands in mine as he gets me to my feet. "If you think he won't understand, you're wrong. He'll understand more than you know."

"What?" I ask, but he doesn't add anything further.

"What's going on?" Myles asks, rushing to my side.

"She's sore, and needs those painkillers," Max replies, and together, they both fuss.

I finally glance away from Max, hoping one day, he'll explain that comment to me. I don't have a right to ask now since I won't talk about my own issues.

One day, I will.

CHAPTER
FIFTEEN

MYLES

I've tossed and turned all night long, unable to sleep. My mind has been going over who could have hurt the girl who has come to mean everything to me. She doesn't have a lot of people in her life, and since I know it isn't one of us, my money is on the dad or someone else related. What has me so confused is she seemed like she was telling the truth when she said her dad didn't hurt her. But I can't see who else it could be. Her dad was here yesterday and the last one to see her. He lives with her, for god's sake.

But then I think on it, and I question others who also protect their abusers. Something is stopping her from telling us, and I need to know what. I need her to know she can trust me, and I'll protect her.

And if it's not her dad, my money is on her mum. She's a raving lunatic. And after what she put Kayla through after her assault, I wouldn't put it past her.

Kayla's body is cocooned tightly around me, and it's the only thing that has brought me comfort. My alarm blares, and I inwardly groan that our time snuggling is up.

Her lashes flutter open, and she tilts her head back, smiling up at me. "Morning."

I need to kiss her. "Morning," I rasp, leaning in.

Then Max breaks the spell, reminding me we aren't alone.

"Please don't have a boner while I'm in the bed with you. This just feels so fucking wrong," Max grumbles, rubbing the sleep from his gaze. I fell asleep before the movie finished, and I didn't realise he was still here during the times I was awake.

"Please tell me that's not Max," Kayla whispers.

"All me, baby," he teases.

She shoves her face into the crook of my neck. "Oh God."

"What the fuck are you still doing in here?" I snap.

"Jesus, I forgot how grumpy you are in the morning."

"That doesn't answer my question."

"You both fell asleep." He shrugs. "I was comfy."

"You were comfy?" I demand.

"Plus, I didn't want to get caught sneaking out. I mean, I could pass off as you, but then she'd still have to explain to her dad why she let you stay. If he had found you in her bed, well, I guess that beating would have happened sooner. Forget about his daughter explaining why she had twin boys in her bed."

"We need to get ready," Kayla mumbles. "And you don't need to worry about my dad. He's at his girlfriend's."

"That's my cue to get to the loo before you," Max announces, jumping over the both of us with ease. He didn't even jar us. "Fuck, that rhymed."

I gently roll Kayla off me until we're on our sides, facing each other. Her smile is soft, unsure, and my chest tightens at how beautiful she looks.

"Did you sleep okay?" I ask, and briefly press a kiss to the tip of her nose.

"Pretty good considering," she replies, still watching me with those big green doe eyes. I lean down, needing to taste her. She kisses me back, her fingers running through my hair. I love it when she does that. It's so comforting.

Shit, for someone who admitted she had never kissed before, she sure knows how to.

Suddenly, she pulls back, her eyes wide. "I have morning breath."

"And yet, you still taste fresh," I admit, and lean in again.

This time, she places her fingers over my lips. "Nope. No more kissing until my teeth are brushed."

"Alright, I'll stop," I chuckle. "How are you feeling?"

"Okay, I guess. Those tablets worked, but my skin still feels tender when I move," she admits, before running the pad of her thumb over the flesh between my brows. "Relax, otherwise your face will stick like it with all those frown lines."

"I'm just worried about you," I explain. "Are you sure you slept okay? You didn't have any nightmares?"

I've been worried she's keeping them from me since I've not woken up to her screaming or gasping for breath.

"No, I didn't have a nightmare," she promises, her words drifting off.

"What's running through your mind? If you've had one, you can tell me. You can wake me up too. I don't mind. I know the last few times I've stayed, you've not had one."

Her hands rest over my chest. "Myles, I never get them when I'm with you."

"Huh?"

"I've had them..." She stops for a second before her eyes go wide.

"What?" I ask worriedly. "Are you sure?"

"I'm positive. Now you've pointed it out, I only remember having nightmares on the nights you aren't here."

"Maverick will be leaving in fifteen minutes, so I'd get a move on if I was you," Max interrupts. "I'm going to make something to eat. Is that okay, Kayla?"

"That's fine," she replies, but he's already out of the room. She looks at me, her eyes shining with excitement. "We're going on a trip."

"That we are," I chuckle.

"Let me take a quick shower. I've packed everything already, but I need to put last-minute things in."

I cross my hands behind my head and lean back. "Take your time."

———

"**M**ax, will you just pick one fucking song and let it play?" Maverick barks, and Kayla's body shakes with laughter.

We decided to sit in the far back of the people carrier we borrowed from one of the volunteers at the church with Harlow.

Malik, who is currently sulking after being separated from her, is sitting in front of us with Denny and Mason. Poor Maverick got the short straw and has Max up front with him, though I'm pretty sure at the next stop, that will change.

"How long have we got left till we get there?" Max whines again for the fiftieth time since we left Kayla's two hours ago. "I'm hungry and I'm bored."

"You ate twenty minutes ago, Max. Plus, you had breakfast at Kayla's, made us take you to McDonalds before we left, and when we stopped off at the garage to get petrol, you bought a shit ton of crap to eat. We'd get there sooner if you'd stop making us fucking stop every ten minutes."

"You just said I ate twenty minutes ago, not ten," Max argues. "Don't be so dramatic. I'm a growing lad."

Kayla's laughter starts again, and I'm enjoying every minute. I love to see her happy. And I'm glad they didn't separate us, since now, I get to have her pressed up against me for seven hours.

When she first snuggled up to me, everyone just stared with open mouths. Kayla took it in stride, giving them a smile in return and a wave, like it was no big deal. Max being Max, boasted that he knew first and found us kissing.

I thought for sure it would turn her away, but if anything, she seemed proud that everyone knew. And because of that, I've had a permanent smile on my face.

"Pass me that," Maverick orders, and I look up in time to see him snatch the phone from Max's hand.

"No, don't," Max protests, and Maverick glares, chucking the phone behind him to Mason.

"Pick some music," he demands. The car radio doesn't work, and none of us thought to bring CDs with us. Thankfully, Maverick thought to bring the cable that connects a phone to the car's stereo system, but so far, Max hasn't let a damn song play all the way through.

Mason bursts out laughing. "What the fuck is this?"

Max stops fighting to get his phone back and turns back in his seat, slumping down in a huff. "Classics," he mutters.

"Oh my god, he has different lists," Mason jests.

"So fucking play one already," Maverick snaps, clearly getting annoyed with his younger siblings.

"You sure?" Mason asks, unable to control his amusement.

I lean forward to see what he finds so amusing, and begin to laugh when I see the list. Denny leans in and starts laughing too.

"What's so funny?" Kayla asks.

The answer begins to play as *Cotton Eye Joe* starts playing through the speakers. The only person not laughing is Max.

"Seriously, Max?" Maverick teases. "What else does he have?"

A Disney song starts to play, and there's more snorts of laughter. "*Frozen*, Max? Fucking, *Frozen*?" I holler.

"It's catchy, so fuck off," he grunts.

"Sing it then," Mason taunts, and the girls start singing along with it, huge smiles on their faces.

When Max finally joins in, his voice overpowers theirs. That's when I notice Malik has finally snapped out of his sulk and is recording Max singing wildly to *Love Is An Open Door* with an evil smirk on his face.

A car horn honks from the side of us, and I've never laughed so hard in all my life when I spot a group of girls in a mini convertible with the hood down driving next to us.

I didn't even notice we had hit slow moving traffic and were gaining an audience.

When the girls start laughing, Max turns around in his seat and glares at all of us. "I'll get you back, you bunch of pricks."

One of the girls shouts something to him and he rolls down his window, sticking his head out.

"What did ya say, babe?" She says something back, but since we aren't near the window, we don't hear. "My brother has kids," he replies.

But then Mason changes the song again, and my sides hurt from laughing when Max screeches like a girl at the sound of *Vengaboys* playing.

"Seriously, Mason?" Max hisses.

"Will the wire stretch so I can have a look?" I ask.

Mason passes it back, and sure enough, it does reach. "Have at it."

I scroll through the phone at his lists. When I see a 'do not play' list, I click on it. On it is every love song and break up song that you can think of.

"Max? Why do you have a 'do not play' list with a bunch of love songs and shit in it?"

"Because I do, okay? Look on someone else's phone."

"If you don't like them, why have them on your phone?" Malik asks.

"Because chicks love that crap, that's why," he growls, and we all snicker.

"Here, give me the wire," Kayla gently demands, and connects it to her phone.

She clicks on the album with various artists and lets it play.

Looking down at Max's phone, it vibrates with a text message.

Poppy: I thought we had something special. Why are you ignoring my calls and texts? We shared a magical night together.

I snicker and double check Max isn't looking before deciding to mess with him.

Kayla looks down at the phone, clucking her tongue. "He shouldn't mess with girls' emotions like that," she whispers.

I nod in agreement and start typing out a reply.

Max: We did have something special, Poppy bear. I'm not

ignoring you; I'm just trying to let you down easy because I'm not good enough for you. No one will ever be good enough for you in my eyes.

Poppy: Oh Max, you are good enough. What we shared was the best night of my life. Do you want to be my boyfriend?

Ash: Want to meet up later?

"Here, I'll text Poppy back, and you can text Ash. I can't believe he has this many girls on the go," she scolds, glaring at the phone.

Max: Poppy, I need you to know something... I'm not good enough because I like boys. What we shared was me getting my frustration out on a boy that I'm in love with. I'm sorry if I've hurt you. I'm a complete asshole who doesn't deserve friendship from you. Please forgive me.

I smother my laughter as I watch her type, loving this fiery side to her. She passes me the phone, looking unsure, so I chuckle and bump her under the chin with my knuckles. "It's fine. He deserves it." She smiles, her eyes soft, and I bend down to kiss her softly before focusing on the message to Ash. I re-read the message and try to think of any Ash's that we know. I can't think of any, but then again, most of the girls he meets don't go to our school. I decide to go with the same storyline as Kayla did with Poppy.

Max: I'd love to meet up, but I'm hanging with my boyfriend tonight.

Just as I hit send, another message comes through.

Poppy: Oh Max, why didn't you tell me? I would have totally understood! If you ever need to get that frustration out again, just give me a call.

"What a hussy," Kayla whispers, making me chuckle, just as another message comes through.

Ash: What the fuck?

I decide to reply to Ash first.

Max: I know you wanted something special with me, and I dig that you're into me, but I'm spoken for.

Ash: Max, dude, are you gay?

I re-read the message, then chuckle. "Do you think Ash is a girl or a boy?" I ask Kayla, and she shrugs, grinning. Her eyes dart to Max, before she takes the phone out of my hands.

Max: Want to find out?

Ash: Excuse me?

Max: There's only one way to find out if I'm gay. Care to have a night with the Maxter?

I snort when she types 'Maxter' because it sounds just like him. She's been watching too much *American Pie.* I take the phone from her, wanting to send the next text.

Ash: Fuck off. I 'ent gay, you prick.

Max: Don't knock it till you try it. Every hole's a goal, right?

A couple of minutes pass with no reply, and we end up laughing quietly to ourselves in the back.

"Hey, where's my phone?" Max calls.

I quickly delete the messages we sent and hold it up. "Here."

We all fall into a comfortable silence, listening to the music playing as we pick up speed on the motorway now that the traffic has disappeared.

It's another hour in when I begin to doze off, but then Max yelling snaps me out of it. "What the fuck, dude? Who is Adam?" he asks, pressing the phone to his ear. "Why would I want your cousin's number? A date? Please tell me this is some prank right now. What has Ash got to do with anything?" Max's head whips around in his seat, and he sends an evil glare our way. Kayla lowers herself down, struggling to hold back laughter. "No, I'm not fucking gay. I love pussy. Love the taste, love sticking my dick in it, and I love tits, so you can put that in ya pipe and smoke it. Now tell Ash my brother's sense of humour isn't what it used to be. It's years of being dropped on his head."

He throws the phone on the dashboard, and Maverick briefly pulls his gaze away from the road.

"Not gay?" Maverick asks, his voice filled with amusement.

"This Adam… is he not your type, Max?" Kayla teases, and it shocks me that she spoke up and made a joke.

Max glares again, but his phone beeping cuts off whatever retort he was about to say.

"Now fucking Poppy Little is texting me. Oh my god, she's asking me to practice in her arse," he mutters. "That bitch is crazy. I spoke to her one night and now she thinks we're a couple. Apparently, I was drunk enough to kiss her. What the fuck did you do, Myles?" He furiously smacks the screen as he types his reply.

"Let her down gently?" I question.

"I'll get you back for this, asshole."

Like he could. "Yeah, yeah."

"I need something to eat," he snaps, still typing away on the phone.

"We're not stopping again," everyone yells simultaneously.

CHAPTER
SIXTEEN

KAYLA

It's taken longer than the seven hours it should have taken to get to Glensaugh because of Max and his ever-empty stomach.

I'm just glad the drive is over because my legs and back have started to ache a bit.

We've just booked into a Travelodge close to the theme park. It's still a fifteen-minute drive to the park, but it's the closest we could get, and staying on the actual park would have cost us all a fortune.

"Did you hear me?" Myles calls, clicking his fingers in front of me. I'd zoned out, staring at the beautiful landscape outside whilst waiting for them.

I shake the daze away. "I'm sorry, what?"

He chuckles and pulls me against his chest. "We're going to have to share a room. Is that okay? I don't fancy sharing one with Max or Maverick, and they don't have any rooms left."

"That's fine. We sleep together most nights anyway." I shrug.

"Well, get you two love birds, sleeping together," Denny teases, and my cheeks heat.

"Myles and Kayla, sitting in the tree, K.I.S.S.I.N.G..." Harlow sings.

The boys waggle their eyebrows, and it's then I realise they think we had sex.

"I didn't mean it like that," I rush out, and my face grows hotter.

Maverick snorts, and I send him my best scowl. Now I've gotten to know him, I'm not as scared of him as I once was. He's the quietest of the bunch of brothers, which is saying something since Malik mostly communicates with grunts. The most I ever hear him speak is when he talks to Harlow. Maverick is a different kind of silent, and I feel like there's a lot about him that we don't know. And I'm not the only one who thinks that. Harlow and Denny have both expressed that they'd like to get to know him better. He only lets us see what he wants us to see.

"Come on, let's go find our room," Myles suggests.

We make our way inside and head up to our floor. Everyone starts to break off to go inside their room.

Myles and I have a basic room. There's a double bed, a dresser with a mirror above, and a ton of plug sockets beneath. There's a table with a kettle, mugs, and two glasses in the corner, and a TV hung up on the wall opposite the end of the bed.

The bathroom is in the small hallway that has a wardrobe on one side that's big enough to hang five outfits.

"This is great," I muse, running my finger along the sheet. It's perfect, and I can't help but smile. I turn to see what Myles thinks, but he's staring at me with an amused smirk. "What?"

"You look like I've walked you into a fairyland and not a basic Travelodge," he teases.

"I'm just happy to be here," I answer truthfully. I can't wait to explore the town and the park tomorrow. It says on their website they have an Enchanted Forest, and I love Disney, so I'm hoping I can check that out. I'm also excited for the firework display, and the light up boat parade they have on the night.

"Good," he replies, and glances at the bed. "Now, which side do you want?"

"I'll take the right."

"The right? That's specific."

I shrug. "I like the right side."

He steps toward me. "I need to know why. You answered it quickly, like you already knew which side you'd pick."

I laugh when his arms wrap around me. "I'm not telling you. You'll think I'm evil or something."

"I'd never think that of you," he replies, losing the smile.

"Okay, but remember you asked for this," I tell him, giving him a pointed look. "I don't like being the closest to the door."

His brows pinch together. "Why?"

I exhale, ready for the judgement. "Because if a murderer with a chainsaw or something comes barging in, they'll get you first, and I'll have time to escape."

He throws his head back, laughing. "You'd seriously run out of this room and leave me to get murdered?"

"Yeah, but I'd set the fire alarm off and call the police. I certainly wouldn't run and hide until they came to find me," I promise, which makes him laugh more.

"You, sweet Kayla, are something else," he muses. "Come on, the rest will be waiting downstairs for us. Max is hungry."

"Have you not got him tested for worms?"

"Multiple times," he answers, taking my hand.

I grab my handbag on the way out, and we head downstairs to meet the others.

———

Dinner goes down a treat. I slouch back in my chair with a groan. *Stick a fork in me, I'm done.* The table falls into silence before I'm startled by laughter. That's when I look up to find everyone staring at me.

"I said that out loud, didn't I?" I moan, pressing my cool hands to my cheeks.

"Aw, she's going red," Mason teases.

"She's going redder now," Maverick adds, and he isn't lying. I can feel the heat.

222222

22222

"Well, if you stopped pointing it out, I wouldn't be so red," I scold, pouting.

"So cute," Myles announces.

"You finished then?" Max asks. He doesn't wait for me to answer before sliding my plate in front of him and polishing off what's left.

"Myles says you've never been to *Exhilaration* before, is that right?" Maverick asks, watching me.

I glance away, a little embarrassed to admit it. "No. I've never been to a theme park at all."

"What are you excited to try out?" he continues, whilst the others begin to mention rides they like that I've never heard of.

"I want to see the Enchanted Forest. The fireworks and boat parade sound awesome too. I'm not keen on that ghost ride. It looks scary as hell. But Myles said there's a boat one that takes you around the park or something. That sounds good too."

"Such a girl," Max remarks around a mouthful of food. "Don't think I'm walking through a prissy Enchanted Forest."

"Shut up, Max. We're all going together. If she wants to go, she'll go," Myles warns, giving his brother a pointed look. I go to say that it's fine so they don't argue, but Maverick speaks up.

"Myles is right. If she wants to go to the Enchanted Forest, she can."

"I want to see that too," Harlow admits. "It says on the leaflet that the best time to go is seven pm. It's not as magical in the day apparently."

"I read that somewhere too. From the pictures I've seen, the whole forest lights up," I inform her, excited someone else wants to see it.

"We should go there before the parade starts at eight-thirty then," Denny interrupts, typing away on her phone.

"Babe, she's fine," Mason groans, looking adoringly at his fiancée.

"I can't get freaking signal, and I want to Facetime Hope."

"I've tried too, and I can't get hold of her," Max speaks up, finishing his food.

"Seriously, you two are as bad as each other. Hope is a baby," Harlow points out. "She doesn't have a phone, and even if she did, she can't talk yet. I'm sure Gram's is fine with her. She has Mark and your nan there, Denny."

"She's my niece. I should be able to talk to her when I like," Max growls, putting his phone in his pocket. "I swear, Joan has turned her phone off or some shit, because ever since I called an hour ago, she seems to be avoiding my calls."

"That's because between you, Denny, and Mason, her phone hasn't stopped ringing all day," Malik reveals.

"What do you know about it?" Denny asks, accusation in her tone. "Is she okay?"

"Jesus, she's fine, Denny," Malik promises. "Joan is fine, but you're driving her and Granddad mad. Between you three, her phone has been ringing every ten minutes. Now, stop worrying. Joan said to tell you she will ring you at half ten when Hope's last bottle is due."

"Jesus, Malik. You make us sound like stalkers," Mason grumbles.

"How about we go to the bar down the road? Max and Myles never get asked for I.D and the girls are all old enough," Maverick offers.

Everyone agrees, but I feel apprehensive and wish I had the courage to speak up so I could politely decline. I've never drunk alcohol before, and I don't really want to start now. I never want to lose any sense of control over my body, and I know alcohol does that to you. I've seen it enough with my mum over the years. I also don't like crowded places. They terrify me, and with drunken lads around, I'll most likely black out from a panic attack.

"Kayla and I brought a film with us to watch. Why don't you guys head on out and we'll see you in the morning? The park doesn't open till half ten so we can grab breakfast first. There's a Little Chef next door," Myles observes.

My shoulders sag with shame. I know he's doing that for me, which means I'll be ruining his night. He's young, and he should be doing fun stuff, but I'm here, holding him back. And hearing him make that excuse, it makes me realise just how much I'm holding him back from.

I feel gazes on me, but I don't bother looking up from the table napkin. When everyone tells us they'll see us tomorrow, we start to gather our things to go and pay the bill. When I reach into my bag to grab some money, a hand touches my arm, stopping me.

"I'll pay," he offers.

"No, I'll pay. I have money," I assure him, going to reach into my bag for my purse.

"I've got it," he promises and hands Maverick our share of the bill.

Once everyone leaves, we make our way back to the Travelodge, both of us walking in silence. I open my mouth a few times, then close it, never knowing how to start. Then Myles speaks, breaking the silence.

"Are you okay? You've seemed really quiet since we finished eating. Is it 'cause I paid for our food?"

His voice sounds so sad, it makes me look up at him. He seems hurt by my silence, so I decide to be honest. "I don't like that you had to come back with me when you should be having fun with your brothers. I feel like I'm ruining your fun."

He pulls me to a stop outside the Travelodge. "You aren't ruining anything. I want to watch a movie with you."

"Yeah, but if I wasn't here, you would have gone."

"Do *you* want to go?"

"No, but that's not the point. I don't like that you feel the need to babysit me."

He wraps his arms around my waist. "I'm not babysitting. I want to spend time with you. This is what I want to do. Going out was never on their agenda until Maverick mentioned it."

"So you wouldn't have gone if I wasn't here?"

"Honestly? Probably not. We've been in the car most of the day and we've got a long day tomorrow. I just want to relax," he admits, kissing me on the lips. "I'm just lucky I get to do it with you."

"Okay, but you better have brought the Adam Sandler movie with you," I warn, and he bursts out laughing.

"The one with Jennifer Aniston in it?"

"The one and only," I cheer as we make our way inside.

"Then it's a good job I did."

He is perfect.

———

"That was so good. How funny was the part where he kicks the wrong woman under the table?" I'm still laughing over it.

This had to be one of the funniest films I've ever seen. I love romance and comedy, and this movie had both. Every single time the kids were on the screen, I was laughing so hard, tears were drawn. When the little girl tried to impersonate a British accent, it was comedy gold. Not many people here sound that posh, but every time, they do the same accent, like we all sound like it.

"Want to watch another?" he suggests. "It's only half nine."

"Did you bring a video store?" I tease, leaning over to see a bag half filled with DVD's.

"Are you teasing me?" he asks, arching a brow.

I bite my lip to stop from laughing, but then he moves, and I know what he's going to do. I slide out of bed. "Don't you dare tickle me. You'll hurt my injuries," I laugh.

"I'm not going to tickle you," he promises, and gently wraps his arm around my waist, pulling me back onto the bed.

I laugh as he crawls over me, settling between my legs. The way he watches me stops time, and Charlie's words echo in my mind.

Promise me you'll try.

So, I do. Reaching up, I grip the back of his neck and bring him down. I'll never get tired of kissing him. His lips are so full, so ripe, and so *mine*.

He growls into the kiss, and a shiver runs down to my core. The sensations of him pressed against me, and the touch of his tongue, it becomes too much.

His tongue reaches mine, and I moan, unashamed and loud. Myles reacts by tightening his hold on my neck and where his hand lays on my hip.

Tingles shoot down my spine and butterflies flutter in my stomach as the kiss deepens, and I know I'll never feel anything as good as this. When my body moves on its own accord and rubs against his hardness, I gasp in horror. Myles doesn't give me time to freeze, or to panic; he just moves his leg over until he's straddling one of mine, and in that moment, I know I'm definitely in love with Myles Carter.

The hand on my hip slowly glides over my ribs, above my shirt, until he cups my boob through the thick material. I'm wearing a bra, but his touch makes me feel like I'm not. I moan, startled by how good it feels when his thumb rubs over where my nipple is erect.

I never thought I could feel this good, or crave a touch as much as I do right now. I roll my hips again, loving the pulse of desire that vibrates through me. He smirks at the sound I make, and I pull back to see if I've done something wrong.

"You're so fucking beautiful it hurts," he rasps, his eyes boring into mine.

"So are you," I whisper, wanting more.

A deep chuckle vibrates against my chest, and I tilt my head to the side, wondering what I said that was funny.

"Babe, I'm not beautiful. Never call me beautiful, especially in front of people, and definitely not with Max around," he teases.

He doesn't get it. I don't mean beautiful in the sense people would call a flower or a painting beautiful. "But you are. The way you look at me, the way you treat me, and the way you touch me; I can't think of a better word to use," I tell him, my voice choking up with emotion. "But since I know you mean appearance wise, I promise to call you handsome, sexy or hot. We could have cute little nick—"

He cuts off my words by kissing me, and I get lost in him. He deepens it, but I still want more, and I find myself grinding down on his thigh.

I'm on the brink of something wonderful, and each time he drives a new sensation through me, or explores my body, I want to cry out in pleasure.

His hand glides under my T-shirt, but he pulls back. "Can I touch you?" he requests softly.

I nod, my words trapped in my throat. He kisses me again, making me forget what he's about to do. I pant against his lips as he runs his finger gently over my flesh. There's a hunger in his eyes that makes this all the more special.

I'm nervous, and honestly, a little scared. But then Myles reaches back down, his mouth pressing against mine, and I lose all coherent thoughts, my mind dizzy with lust.

Slowly, and showing me respect, he pulls back again. "Can I take your T-shirt off?"

"Yes," I whisper, and lean up to help him remove it from me. I meet his gaze, and although I'm a little scared, I've never wanted anything more. "Please touch me."

He unclips my bra and pulls the cups down before removing it completely. I shiver as the cool air hits my flesh, but I soon heat up when he touches me.

Skin on skin, he drives me wild. He leans down, kissing me once more as he cups my boob in his hand. His thumb rubs over my nipple, and I moan into his mouth.

"Oh God," I softly gasp.

He shoves his thigh between my legs when I begin to thrust against him. The motion has my back arching, rubbing harder and harder, chasing that feeling. My body craves it, and although I don't want to go past what we're doing now, I know I don't regret it.

He tugs and plays with my nipple whilst pressing his leg in the spot that has me flushing all over.

"Fuck, you are incredible," he growls, and the vibration of it has me exploding in pleasure. I clench my eyes shut, arching my back, as wave after wave of pleasure flows over me.

My lips part when it's over and only a tingle is left pulsing between my thighs. "What was that?" I ask, overwhelmed by the sensations still tingling all over my body.

He leans up before looking down at me, his eyes glassy and dark. He gives me a soft look before leaning down to give me a peck on the lips.

"That, Kayla, was an orgasm."

"But... but we..." I pause, looking away. "We didn't—you know, *do it.*"

He smiles down at me, and it's then that I feel his erection pressing against my thigh. I wonder if it's hurting him.

"You can have an orgasm without having sex. Are you feeling okay? I didn't hurt your bruises, did I?" he asks softly.

"No. No, you didn't hurt me," I tell him truthfully. I haven't really thought about them. They've ached all day, especially after sitting in the car for so long, but other than that, they've surprisingly been okay. I think it's helped that I've had Myles and the others to keep my mind off it.

"Good," he replies, and as though he can't help himself, he leans down for another kiss.

When he pulls back, he has my bra and T-shirt in his hands. He helps me back into them. "Thank you."

"I'll put the film on," he offers.

I watch him jump out of the bed and move to put the film on. This one I've already seen: *Red Riding Hood.* After putting the disc in, he's just about to jump back into bed, when a commotion from outside stops him in his tracks.

He glances at me with a wide grin on his face, like he knows something I don't. I'm feeling mellow and relaxed, so I don't have the same enthusiasm as him.

I just had my first orgasm. And it was mind-blowing.

Max ruins the buzz by bellowing down the hallway. Myles moves back into bed since we can hear them clearly in here.

"She wanted me, I'm telling you," Max argues, sounding confident in his comment.

"Bro, she threw a drink in your face," Malik retorts, or it might be Maverick. I'm unsure.

"She wanted me," Max hollers.

"Bro, get over it. She made it clear how she really felt about you once she found out your real age."

That was definitely Mason.

"I wasn't going to lie to her, man. She was all over my junk. She was just scared she couldn't handle me. She threw that drink so she could *accidentally* cop a feel."

"Bro, like Malik said, she threw a drink in your face on purpose," Maverick states, letting me know it was Malik earlier. "It wasn't an accident to cop a feel."

"Girls?" Max whines, obviously needing back up. I cover my mouth to smother my giggle when neither Denny nor Harlow answer. "Great, now Kayla is going to think I got a drink thrown in my face."

"Night, Max," Denny calls, sounding like she's right outside our door. Denny and Mason are in the room next to us, and Max is on our other side. Maverick is in the room next to him, and Malik and Harlow are a room down from Denny and Mason.

"Kayla, she wanted me," Max shouts through the door, and Myles and I burst out laughing.

"Is he drunk?" I ask, thinking I'm being quiet.

Clearly, I'm not, because Maverick answers. "Yeah, Kay, he is. Idiot thought he was cool doing shots of sambuca with a bunch of college chicks," he taunts. "Night, guys."

"Night," we call back, snuggling down into the blanket.

"Night, twinny, may you have a shit night's sleep," Max yells. "Love you, brothers, and ladies. But you, Myles... you, my twinny, are my bestest. You starved so I didn't have to." I hear flesh meeting flesh, followed by a grunt, and I know someone just smacked him. "Okay, okay, damn it, I'm going."

"Twinny?" I repeat, laughing.

Myles rolls his eyes. "Don't ask. He gets affectionate when he's had a drink. He's all hands on."

"What was he on about when he mentioned you starving?"

"Oh, I was the smallest when I came out. Max had taken all the nutrients," he explains. "He was 7lbs new-born, while I was only 4lbs. He thinks I did it to be kind, when medically, he was stealing them."

"So nothing has really changed," I tease, and a shiver runs over my body.

"You cold?"

"A little."

"Come on. Let's get you into bed," he tells me. We both jump up off the bed and pull the blanket back, but end up struggling. We look at each other in horror, before tugging at it with more vigour.

"Shit, did they super glue the thing down to the mattress or something?" Myles groans, then steps back a foot when his side of the blanket comes loose. I watch in amazement since the sheet is wound in tight to the bed. He made it look easy, whereas I'm using all my strength and getting nothing.

Myles, seeing my dilemma, comes to help, and doesn't prepare for his own strength when he pulls too hard and lands on the floor. His eyes widen. "Jesus. Who makes these beds? They should come with a warning label."

"Some of us are trying to get to sleep," Max shouts through the wall, and I grimace. "Fuck, someone stuck my blanket to the bed."

We both fall to the bed, laughing when we hear a thud on the floor. He definitely did what Myles just did.

He presses play on the movie after lifting the blanket up. I yawn, snuggling against him, and I know I won't last five minutes into the film. My eyelids are drooping, and I'm ready for sleep, when banging against the wall behind our heads rocks the room.

Myles groans and sits up, banging his fist against the wall. "Max, shut up," he snaps. "What the hell are you doing?"

"Breaking the bed in," Max states, like we should already know.

"You went to bed alone, Max," Myles grumbles.

"Not that kind of breaking in," Max hollers through laughter. There's another thud before he continues. "The fucking bed is rock solid, man. You could get more softness out of a cardboard box."

I bury my face into the pillow, laughing at his antics.

"Max, just go to sleep, for fuck's sake."

"Kayla, laugh all you want, because if I don't get my eight hours of sleep, I'm an unhappy Max, and nobody likes an unhappy Max. Everyone loves a happy Max."

"How much has he had to drink?" I question.

"Kayla, baby, you should have come with us. I'd have rocked your world," Max declares, before we hear another voice boom at him to shut up.

"Maverick, I'm going to sleep now. Did you break your bed in?" Max pauses. "Fuck, yeah, goodnight. Night, Twinny. Night, Kayla."

The last thing we hear before there's silence, is another thud. Myles lets out a breath and tugs me to his side. He presses his lips to my head. "Goodnight, baby."

"Goodnight, handsome."

CHAPTER
SEVENTEEN

KAYLA

W
e arrived at the park a few hours ago, and the place is rammed. I'm not sure how I feel about being around this many people yet, but with Myles at my side, I've not stressed about it too much. Everyone has picked up on it, which is why I think Myles and Maverick have been hovering close. Even on the rides I did join in on, they made sure one or both were next to me. I know it's intentional because I overheard Myles and Maverick talking about it.

I'm glad when they decide to stop for lunch because I'm starting to ache. Max slouches over the bench in front of me, looking a little green.

I feel bad for him, even though I know it's self-inflicted. "How are you holding up, Max?" I ask, poking him in the arm so he knows I'm asking him.

His bloodshot eyes meet mine. "Starting to wish I didn't do that last shot of sambuca last night," he admits.

"Well, *Twinny*," I tease. "You've certainly learnt your lesson."

"Oh God, I called him Twinny again, didn't I?" he asks, mortified. Myles and Maverick, who also witnessed it, chuckle.

"Yep," I tell him, amused when he groans.

Mason and Malik arrive with trays of food and begin to share the boxes of food between everyone.

"Get some more food in ya," Mason demands. "It will do you some good."

Max grunts, and immediately tucks into his burger. Everyone does the same, and once finished, no one rushes to leave the table, happy to let it go down. It's only Max who leaves, heading for the toilets.

Denny starts asking where they want to go next, and Swap is mentioned. It's not a ride I particularly want to go on, but with Max looking so green, it seems like our best option. I really don't want to be on one of the big rides and have him throw up, especially if I'm sitting behind him.

"Isn't that the haunted boat ride? It's meant to be good," Maverick offers.

"Yeah, sounds ace," Myles pipes in. "Plus, don't we need to do that ride in order to get the ticket to do the graveyard?"

His arm goes around my waist, sliding me along the bench closer to him. "We're doing *Dead End,* the graveyard maze?" I squeak.

That is definitely something I didn't want to do. Walking around in a maze, with no way out—and dead people chasing you—is my worst nightmare come to life.

I already know what will happen. I'll be running around in circles screaming for my life when someone will jump scare me and I'll have a panic attack.

Stop being a party pooper, Kayla, and have some fun, I hear Charlie telling me in my head. She's always telling me to let go, to have fun, and to hell with the consequences. I turn to question Myles, but he's sharing a look with Maverick, a mischievous look in his eyes. They're excited for it, and I don't want him to feel like he has to stay back with me. I'll brave it, for him.

He notices me watching, and leans in to kiss me. "We don't have to do the maze if you don't want to. We can sit at a concession stand and get something to drink."

"No. I'll be fine. Just don't leave me in there," I plead, not realising just how much being trapped with no way out bothers me. With Myles, though, I know he won't leave me. He makes me feel safe, safe enough to go into a graveyard maze in the dark with dead people chasing you. Hell, last night I let him touch me in a way I never thought I'd be touched. With him, I feel like I can do anything.

"I won't, babe. I promise," he swears.

"I'll be there too," Maverick adds. "If it gets too much, we can run to the exit and leave."

Max walks back to the table with more colour to his face, and it makes me wonder if he just spent the last ten minutes in the loos throwing up. I'm about to ask him when Denny grabs my attention.

"Kayla, are you free in a few weeks to look at some bridesmaid dresses with us?"

"I should be; depends on the time. I'm at school, remember," I remind her.

Although I'd be happy to skip for that. I'm honoured she asked me to be bridesmaid. I've always wanted to wear a bridesmaid dress, or even a wedding gown to see how it will look.

"Oh, I've booked it for a Saturday. I got us an appointment at that *Flora's Boutique*, near London. I know it's a long drive and all, but..."

She doesn't need to finish. Even someone like me, who knows nothing about fashion, knows how big Flora's dresses are. She's one of the top wedding gown designers in the UK. It takes celebrities months to even get a consultation with her, let alone a fitting. So for Denny to get a consultation at one of her new stores says something big.

"Will she be there?" I breathe out, giddy with excitement.

I've never met anyone famous. The closest I got was when I went to the big shopping centre where they had some meet and greet with the cast of some TV programme called *TOWNIE*, or *TWOOIE*... No, *TOWIE*... It was definitely TOWIE. But I have no clue who any of them are.

Denny gives me a big, toothy grin. "Yes! My nan—if you can

believe it—knows her. I mean *knows* her. The minute I told my nan I wanted a dress made by her, she told me to leave it with her. I thought she was going to find someone to replicate the style, but she didn't. She explained to Flora about my situation and what my mum did, and she was more than happy to help. Flora has even offered to pay for all the bridesmaid dresses. I couldn't believe it when Nan told me."

"Wow! How? I mean, I know your nan is one tough cookie to say 'no' to, but this… this is huge. I heard Flora turned down an actress who just wanted an appointment. She even offered to pay millions to get her to change her mind and make time to see her. I forgot her name; I was too busy staring at the dresses they had on the page," I gush, when I notice the table has gone quiet. Everyone else looks like a deer caught in headlights, except for Myles, who is watching me with a smile. "What?"

"Cute," he mutters.

Denny, ignoring their behaviour, continues. "She is expensive, but luckily, she's opened up a discount shop that's open to the public. There's still a waiting list, but it's not as hard. I looked at some of the designs, and as soon as I saw a certain one, it took my breath away. It's everything I ever wanted," she breathes out.

I glance at Mason to get his reaction, but he looks happy to see her so enthused. He really does love her, and it's clear to see. They were made for each other, and I'm glad they found their way back together.

"I'm so happy for you. I can't wait to see the dress."

"We also need to talk about the bachelorette—" Harlow begins.

"Can we please go? As much as I love you as a sister, I don't want to hear about Flora dresses and shit," Max interrupts. "Can we go on *Turn* now?"

"We're going on—" I go to correct, but Myles jumps in.

"Let's go."

He shrugs with a smirk when I give him a questioning look. I have a feeling the look he shared with Maverick earlier has something to do with it.

We begin to head in the direction of *Swamp*, and Myles takes my hand. Butterflies flutter in my stomach at the touch, and I can't help the smile that breaks over my face. I feel like the luckiest girl in the world when he does this.

We reach our destination, and Max stops, booming, "What the fuck!" Max turns furious as he glares at everyone around him. "Is this some sort of sick joke?"

I step closer to Myles. "What is he going on about?"

"You'll see," Myles promises, amused.

Max jabs his finger at Myles. "You!" he growls, and begins to stomp over to us. A shiver slivers up my spine, and I step back. Max notices and stops short. His glower is still present though. "Why would you bring us here?"

Why is he so angry at Myles? I stand in front of Myles, not liking Max's behaviour towards him. "It was my idea," I blurt out. "Stop yelling at him."

Myles pulls me back against his chest. "Calm down, wild cat."

Max's shoulders drop, and pride replaces his scowl. "Look at you standing up for Myles, sweet Kayla."

"Why are you mad, Max?" I ask, and scan the others, seeing they aren't as confused or as startled as me.

It makes me feel like an outsider, like they are all in on this but me. Even Max seems to know what is happening.

"Mad Max?" he sings, seeming fond of the comment. "I'm not mad. I just don't want to go on this ride."

Ah, now I get it. I tilt my head, unable to stop the twitch in the corner of my mouth. "Are you scared?"

I notice others are stopping to watch, and I feel unnerved under the scrutiny.

"Why would I be scared?" he retorts defensively. "It's a ride. It's not real, Kayla."

I throw my hands up before slapping them down at my sides. "So why are you getting so worked up over it?" I argue, arching a brow.

He rears back at how harsh I sounded. "I'm not; I would have just liked to be informed is all."

"Well, now you know, so pull on your big girl pants and move it," I order. "The line says it's a half hour wait."

"Alright," he answers, staring at me intensely. "There's no need to be mean about it."

I step closer, pulling Myles with me. "And don't be mean to Myles again," I finish, before walking off.

Everyone begins to tease Max as we join the queue. It doesn't take half an hour, but Max still uses the time to work himself up. And I'm the one who pays for it.

I get now why Myles and Maverick had their silent communication about it, and seemed amused. The ride attendant has me sit next to Max, even after I pleaded to sit next to Myles. He wasn't having any of it, and because I was holding up the queue, others started to moan, so I went along with it. I thought it wouldn't be bad considering I was with Max.

I was wrong.

So very wrong.

I'll never make the same mistake again.

I have nail marks imprinted into my hands and arms from the death grip he had on me. There's a ringing in my ears from his screams, and I'll never get over the trauma of listening to it.

"You sounded like you were being murdered," I snap when we exit the ride.

"I wasn't that bad," he argues.

I stop and kick him in the shin. He howls in pain, rubbing the spot I hit. "You cried and blamed it on me." Myles laughs as I remind them all of what he told the group of girls close to us when we got off. He blamed the cries on me. I spin on Myles. "And don't you laugh."

He holds his hands up in surrender, smirking. "What did I do?"

"You knew," I accuse, and point to the others. "You all knew. I'm going to be hearing his screams for months. Months! Why would you put me through that kind of trauma?"

"We did try to get him next to Maverick or Malik, if you remember," Myles replies, trying to make me feel better.

"He screamed in my ear," I whisper, still not over Max's reaction. My gaze runs over our group, not finding him. "Where did he go?"

"Bathroom," Harlow answers.

"I'm sorry, baby," Myles states. "I promise not to let him near you for the rest of the trip."

"He tried getting in my lap at one point. In *my lap*. In the middle of a ride, Myles. It was horrific. The only good thing about it, is that I never saw anything because he was all over me like a bad rash."

Not even Denny or Harlow screamed that much. I rub my ear again, trying to get rid of the buzzing noise, but it doesn't work.

"*Now* can we go on Ride?" Max announces out of nowhere. I startle, gripping Myles like my life depends on it.

Max laughs, arching a brow. "Jesus, Kayla, don't be such a baby. It's not like I snuck up on you."

I'm not a violent person. I'm not. But I take a step towards him, knowing it will be worth it.

Myles pulls me back, laughing against my neck. "Okay, wild cat; let's go on Ride."

CHAPTER
EIGHTEEN

KAYLA

The sun has set, and the moon and stars are finally out. I've wanted to go to the Enchanted Forest all day, but then Malik said to do the Graveyard stint first. Which is probably for the best, since I want all the scary stuff out of the way.

We've been queuing for an hour and a half. In that time, we've watched the sun go down, the stars and moon come out, and Max and Malik eat their own body weight in junk food. I've never known anyone to eat as much as the Carter brothers do. But Max, he's so aggressive with his food. He doesn't share, but he demands people share with him. He doesn't do small portions, but can still complain large portions aren't big enough.

We're getting closer to the start, and I begin to fidget. Myles notices and leans in close. "Are you going to be okay doing this?" he whispers so the others can't hear him. I meet his gaze, melting at his protective behaviour. He's been attentive to my needs and feelings all day, and I love him for it. He's put me at ease when I've felt out of place, and made sure I kept up with painkillers, so I don't pay for it later.

And like I predicted, he stayed with me whenever a ride looked too much for me. The last one was Twist, and the name said it all. It twisted, turned, and spun so fast, people were still spinning walking off. I knew going on it would have done more damage to my already bruised side, so Myles told the others he wanted to sit this one out and actually *asked* me if I would keep him company, like I was doing him a favour.

The only person other than Myles who knows about the bruises is Max, so the others had no idea that Myles was only doing it for me. He got teased the rest of the day about it.

"Kayla," he calls, nudging me.

"Sorry, yeah, I'm good," I reply, still worried about what awaits us. "Just don't run off and leave me."

"My name is Myles, not Max," he retorts. "He'll be the first one to ditch."

I run my hands over my thighs. "We're moving."

Malik high-fiving Mason behind Harlow and Denny's backs catches my attention. The girls don't notice, nor do they see the devilish smirks on their faces.

I know that look. I became accustomed to it during the day, and I know they are up to something.

"Come on, Kayla; we're next," Harlow calls, reaching back to take my hand.

I pull my hand away. "I'll take my chances with Myles," I vow. I don't have the courage to tell them I think their boyfriends are up to something. For one, I think they'll find enjoyment out of it. Me, I don't like being scared. I live in fear every day. I don't want to look for it.

"Come on, us girls have to stick together. Don't we, Max?" Denny teases.

"Fuck off," Max mutters, his feet shifting from one foot to the other.

I'm pretty sure there's sweat beading at his forehead.

That's when the line starts moving quicker, and we make our way through the first set of gates. We follow the rest of the group in front of us and stop in front of five sets of doors, where a man dressed in white overalls covered in blood splatter, stops us.

"I need you to get into groups of six and stand in front of a door. If you've come today in a large group, split up," he calls over the noise, and a woman wearing a similar outfit joins him, guiding people to a door.

I cling to Myles when I notice Denny and Mason being separated. I don't want that to happen to us. Denny sends him wide eyes, but he just grins, winking back at her.

"Door number three, please," the woman orders, and I jump when I realise she's addressing us. I hadn't even seen her move.

Myles laughs and walks us over to door three. I gulp when I see we've been paired with Max, but I'm grateful Denny is with us. Another two girls are added to our door, and then haunted music starts playing, a creepy, deep voice booming from the speakers.

"Enter at your own risk."

Like I have a choice, I think to myself.

We huddle through the door, the place pitched in darkness. I hear Max squeal, which makes me squeal. The doors slam shut behind us, and one by one, the sound of locks clicking shut echoes through the speakers.

I whimper, and cling to Myles tighter.

The lights start to flicker on and off, and it's eerie. I'm waiting for them to flicker on, only to find someone standing in front of me. My heart races as I wait for it to happen, but it's only mirrors we find.

Max screams, causing Denny to scream too, and I laugh when they do, feeling adrenaline pump through me.

"Find your way out and you shall live," the ghostly voice warns.

Max and Denny start touching the glass, making sure they're not walking into any mirrors.

"Oh my god, is that Maverick?" I ask, looking to my right. Maverick and a group of people are struggling the same as us, trying to find their way out, and I realise it's not only mirrors.

"Yeah." Max waves, thrusting his hips at them. When that doesn't get their attention, he moves closer, shoving his face against the glass.

The lights choose that moment to dim, and when they light up again, a face is pressed up against Max's on the other side.

He screams, falling back. I laugh, even though I'm scared shitless. Denny helps him to his feet, and we move quicker through the maze.

Denny's hand touches a glass panel when the lights turn off. A voice sounds through the speaker. We freeze, listening to their words.

"Do not move. Keep very, *very* still," the ghostly voice warns.

"Is it bad that I'm going to pee my pants, I'm that freaking scared?" Denny whisper-yells. I silently agree with her, my body frozen and rooted to the spot.

All of a sudden, a crack of thunder fills the room, and the room is bathed in light. We all scream loudly, Max the loudest. Up against the clear glass where Max is standing, is now a scary-looking dead woman. Her face is deformed, the makeup artist making her look like something from *The Walking Dead* T.V. programme. We all turn to run, but Max runs smack-bang into another panel, causing everyone to laugh. The girls who have joined us, run ahead of us, screaming at us to hurry.

"Time is running out," the voice booms above the speakers, and my heart rate speeds up when I hear the distinct sound of a chainsaw behind us.

"Oh my god, we need to go," I squeak, pulling on Myles' arm to move forward. We catch up to the girls and notice why they've stopped.

"Are those real people?" Myles whispers to me, his hand clutching mine tightly. On the floor, lying down, are a bunch of dead bodies. Obviously not real, but the effect feels it.

"Maybe this is the wrong way?" one of the girls in our group states.

"Nah, look, it says exit over there, babe," Max promises, rubbing the egg-shaped lump on his forehead. "Why don't you go first?" He doesn't wait for her to answer. He pushes her in front of him, and she laughs, pushing back.

"What if they're real people? I'm not stepping on them," she argues through her laughter.

Myles steps forward when we hear the chainsaw coming closer. He nudges the body with his foot and laughs.

"It's a dummy. Just don't step on them," he orders as he steps over the first one.

I follow, having no choice in the matter. Denny clutches my spare hand and follows. When we're halfway to the exit, the floorboards beneath us move, and we all scream, which turns louder when sprays of water hit us from above. We all move faster, and I can't believe how fast my heart is racing. Adrenaline is pumping through my veins, and I can't help but laugh as I hear everyone effin' and blinding behind me.

Reaching the exit door, a body jumps out from the side of us, and we all scream in fear, pushing each other forward to get away. Once we're all through the door, we take a minute to catch our breath, laughing our heads off. The two girls start eyeing up Max and Myles, and I feel myself stepping closer to him, not wanting them to get his attention.

One of the girl's notices and gives me a small, shy smile, which makes me relax. When I scan our surroundings, I shiver at the grave-yard. It's not a real one, but it has the same creepy feel to it. The gravestones are bigger, the grass is more like wheat, and the place is full of fake cobwebs. We hear a squeal to the left, and I swear it's Harlow we heard.

"Reminder," an announcement calls from a speaker at the entrance to the graveyard. "The rules from the beginning apply. No actor will touch or harm you in any way. They may come close, but they will not make contact. Please keep the journey safe for both you and our actors and enjoy the ride."

We all look at Max and give him a warning look. He acts offended and huffs out an annoyed breath. "I know the rules."

"The chainsaw man has escaped," a woman wearing a ripped dress says, scaring the shit out of me. Where the hell did she come from? Everyone else must be thinking the same thing when I see them looking in the direction her voice first came from. "You need to go," she orders frantically, looking around, her eyes wide with fear. "He's coming. He's coming!"

Her screams die off as she runs away, and my heart races more.

Then little twinkle lights shine on the ground when we enter the maze. The gravestones look real, and my hand reaches out to touch one, but it's just decorated poly blocks. They look so real. I'm just about to take my phone out to take a picture, when we hear the chainsaw again. We all turn around to the sound and scream. A man dressed as Leather Face from the Chainsaw Massacre is standing at the entrance. We all turn and run when he takes a step toward us.

Denny is in front of us, Max and the girls behind, all of us screaming our heads off. We end up in a bigger field, and it's obviously joined with the others because I can hear other people screaming around us.

I'm between laughing and peeing my pants when Max comes shoving past us, nearly sending Myles and I to the floor. He just gets ahead of Denny when a zombie walks out of the open grave ahead of him. He screams, pushing Denny in front of him and running off in another direction, leaving us all behind.

"Are you okay?" I laugh, rushing over to Denny, who is quick to get back on her feet.

"I'm going to kill that fucker. Did you see his face, though?" she snorts.

We glance around to find it's just us, since the girls have gone too, and when we turn in the direction we came from, I can see why. Getting closer is the man with the chainsaw, the noise of the engine making me quake with fear. That's when we hear an "Argh" coming from behind us, and we remember the zombie. We all scream, laughter following, and run in the direction where the smoke is still lingering from how fast Max hightailed it out of here.

"This way," Myles shouts, grabbing my hand. I grab Denny's, and together we rush through the pathways built on what I think is supposed to be a cornfield. Rounding another corner, we all come to a sudden stop, then burst out laughing when we come face to face with Maverick and Harlow.

"Where's Mason and Malik?" Denny asks.

"Mason legged it before this creepy bloke came out to warn us to run," Maverick says dryly.

"And we lost Malik when I pushed him out the way and legged it," Harlow admits, not even sorry for it.

"Max did that to me, but literally pushed me over before he legged it," Denny explains, then her eyes widen. "We need to go."

Maverick points up ahead. "That has to be the way out because we've been back there and all the other paths are blocked by either zombies, or a bloke with a hatchet."

We follow behind Maverick and Myles, us girls linking arms and squealing every time we pass a grave that has a zombie trying to escape. It's not long before we come to another building. One says exit, the other says Enchanted Forest. We take the Enchanted Forest option, and walk in to find Max, Malik, and Mason all sat on the ground, howling with laughter.

"Seriously, Max, you'd leave the mother of your niece to be murdered?" Denny snaps, walking over to Mason.

"She'd be in good hands with me," he promises.

"Yeah, until another zombie walks into your life and you leave her to fend for herself."

"I wouldn't do that to her. She's my princess."

"Liar," Denny snaps, and Mason cuddles her to his chest, kissing her neck.

"Cheers, babe, nice of you to leave me to get here by myself. I nearly got taken out by a group of girls and this one," Malik growls, looking pissed at Max.

"I needed to scope out the place before I let any of you walk in," Max snaps, defending himself.

"Whatever, bro."

"Sorry, I thought you were behind me," Harlow lies, her cheeks turning pink.

"Babe, you ran out of there so fast, I'm surprised your feet didn't set on fire."

We all laugh, and then join the queue, still talking about the ride and what a chicken Max had been. We're all so lost in our own little world that we don't feel the outside air until we're standing in an archway.

Just like on the water ride we went on earlier, they have a platform moving clockwise with mini boats waiting to be loaded.

"It's four to a boat," the man tells us when we are closer to the front of the line.

"Max is not with me," I shout quickly, and then blush when Max turns to me, glaring.

"We'll come with you," Malik and Harlow offer, and I smile.

Myles takes my hand when it's our turn to load the boat. We quickly get in, leaving the rest to get in the boat behind us.

"Are we on the right ride? I thought we walked through the forest?" I ask Myles. I didn't see anything about boats in the leaflet.

"Yeah, I heard one of the groups in front of us mention it takes us through the back way. When it's the end of the ride, we can walk through to the main park area. That way we don't have to walk all the way through and miss the boat carnival."

"Okay," I tell him, and snuggle into side when a cold chill runs over me. It doesn't help that I'm wet from being sprayed in the graveyard.

"Do you reckon there are crocodiles in this water?" Max asks from the other boat, which sets off alarms for others also enjoying the ride.

I lean my head on Myles' shoulder, and his arm wraps around me as we take in the lanterns, fairy lights and sparkly decorations surrounding the beautiful wildlife. I can see why this attraction isn't open all the time. It must take a lot of work to keep the decorations in good condition, not to mention lighting all the lantern candles.

They change the theme every once in a while, but the fairy lights have always been there, according to their website.

The atmosphere on the boat is smooth and relaxing. With all the dull lighting, and the glow from the moon, it gives off a romantic feel.

Malik and Harlow are making out in the front of the boat, and I blush before looking away. That's when Myles turns my head, his lips moving towards mine before giving me a tender, loving kiss. It's soft and gentle, and I feel it with every fibre in my body. Every time he kisses me, it just gets better and better.

When we pull away, we're both out of breath, my heart beating at a rapid pace. He gives me a small smile then pulls me into his arms. I sigh, feeling content, and rest my head on his shoulder. The ride continues for another five minutes before we come to the end.

Myles steps out first before helping me out, then we stand off to the side to wait for the others, this part of the day becoming one of the best parts. Hell, it's become one of my best memories.

CHAPTER
NINETEEN

MYLES

Although I've enjoyed our day together with everyone, there's a dark cloud looming above us. It hit me when she packed up her things ready to leave in the morning. I'm going to have to say goodbye to her, all the while knowing someone in her life is hurting her. I want to be with her every day and night, but I know it isn't possible, considering she lives with her dad, and I have Granddad and Maverick wanting me home.

Knowing it is out of my control, and that if I could, I would be there, doesn't make this feeling go away. I don't like feeling powerless to help those I love.

The others split off to their own rooms once we ate, but I know they were feeling just as sad to leave, only for other reasons. The only one still on cloud nine is Kayla.

"Today has been the best day ever. I thought for sure I would be on the side-lines looking in because of my injuries, but I wasn't," Kayla gushes from the bedroom. "I wish Charlie didn't have to miss it. She would have loved today. She would have spent the day taking photos. She's obsessed with photography."

I stick my head around the bathroom door, my mouth full of toothpaste. "I know it's not the same, but between us, we took some pretty good photos. Maybe we could get them printed for her." I head back into the bathroom to finish up.

"Oh my god, she would love that. I'm gutted I didn't think of it. Maybe we can get one of the firework photos printed on a canvas for her. She loves fireworks too. Always has," she rambles, and I find it adorable. "When we moved, she came to visit me in the six weeks holiday and dragged me to this firework display that was happening where we lived. She gushed over it for months, and I remember her telling me that if she could, she would paint her room to look just like that firework display."

I step out of the bathroom, wiping my mouth whilst she's bent over, searching through her bag. "I love seeing you like this," I exclaim.

Since we got back, she has ranted about the events of today like I wasn't there with her for them. Her excitement and energy has been contagious.

It's freaking cute.

"Like what?" she begins, turning to face me with her pyjamas in hand. Her cheeks flush, and she rushes from the room.

I glance down, forgetting I'm still in my Calvin Klein boxers. Not wanting to make a big deal out of it, I answer. "Happy, carefree, excited."

I sit on the edge of the bed, shoving today's clothes into my ruck-sack, listening to Kayla ramble about the walk through the Enchanted Forest. I'm not usually into all that girly shit, but I have to admit, the place looked fucking amazing.

I hear clothes rustling and glance at the mirror hanging on the mini wardrobe. It reflects inside the bathroom, where Kayla has forgotten to close the door.

I freeze, my jaw locking as my hands close into tight fists. Her bruises are worse than I first anticipated. I knew they were bad, but not like that, spread all over her creamy, soft flesh. There isn't much skin that isn't covered with angry bruises and marks. There is so much damage to her side. I memorise every mark, hoping that one day, I'll get to make the same ones on the person who hurt her.

I can't understand for the life of me why someone would want to hurt someone so kind, innocent, and caring.

I'm so busy trying to rein in my anger, not wanting to scare Kayla, that I don't hear her walk in. She must have taken one look at me, and known something was up.

"Is everything okay? I know I've talked a lot…" She pauses, taking a breath. "And I'm rambling again. I'm sorry."

"I love hearing your excitement," I promise. "I guess today has knackered me out."

I force a smile, which she returns as she gets into bed. I shove the last of my shit into my bag, making sure to take out the clothes for tomorrow before joining Kayla on the bed.

"Did *you* have a good day?" she asks.

"I had the best day," I reply honestly.

She loves my answer. "You did?"

"Bet your ass I did."

I lean over, and as always, my lips reach hers and my whole body lights the fuck up. No one has ever set my body on fire the way she does. God, it's like it burns only for her. She only has to touch me, and I'm fighting back a hard-on.

She pulls back, letting out a soft puff of air. "Goodnight, Myles."

I pull her close, kissing the top of her head. "Night, babe."

"Thank you for today," she declares, snuggling up to me.

———

My mind has been on Kayla since we dropped her off three hours ago. She's going out for dinner with her dad, and there was nothing I could do to get her to change her mind. I tried to talk her into coming to mine to stay for dinner, anything to get her away from that house. I'm still not sure who's hurting her, but with my past experience, my guess is it's her dad. He was the only one there that morning who could have done that to her.

She's not been having any problems at school; I would know if she was. That only leaves two other people I know who are present in her life. Her mum or her dad.

I glance at my phone, wondering when she'll call so I can hear for myself if she's okay, but there's nothing.

"Fuck it!" I grumble, getting to my feet. I could go by and see if she's okay.

Granddad walks into the room with a plate of food in his hand. "Joan wanted me to bring you over a plate." I take the plate and sit back down, placing it next to me. "Is everything okay, son?"

"Yeah, why wouldn't it be?" I lie.

"Don't lie to me, boy. Talk to me," he demands, dropping down in the recliner.

I groan, scrubbing my hands down my face before addressing him. "Granddad, if you knew someone was being hurt, but you couldn't prove who was hurting them, what would you do?" I ask, meeting his gaze.

It's been killing me not knowing how to help Kayla, or how to keep her safe. She's been avoiding my calls and texts since we dropped her off, and she promised we would talk about it when we got back. I know what she's doing, but she can't avoid me forever.

His eyebrows rise. "Someone is hurting Kayla?"

"What? I didn't…"

"Your face says it all. Plus, she's the only one aside from your brothers and their partners who you would look murderous for."

I sigh, knowing I need to tell him. I have to, for my own peace of mind. "Max and I went to hers on Thursday when she didn't show up for school. She texted me saying some bullshit about being with her dad, but then we saw him in town with his new missus," I begin. "Me and Max went to her house and found her asleep in bed. We were going to leave, since she was okay, but the blanket had moved down, revealing some bruises on her side. Granddad, it was fucked up. She's had bruises before, finger marks and shit, but I've just pushed my worries aside, hoping she'd come to me. But she never did. Then last night, I saw them all. I'm ashamed that I looked when she didn't know, but Granddad, it looks like someone took a fucking hammer to her stomach and ribs. I don't know what to do. I've left her alone with her dad tonight, and he could be the one hurting her." My voice breaks at the shame of leaving her.

"What the fuck?" Maverick thunders, and I turn with wide eyes, finding him glowering at me.

"Please, you can't say anything. She can't know that you know. She made us promise we wouldn't," I plead. "She seemed really panicky about it."

"I can't promise you that," he retorts tightly. "Who the fuck would hurt her? She's like a freaking fairy."

"Sit down, the both of you," Granddad orders, looking at us both with a determined expression. "Maverick, calm down before you set him off even more. Let him explain why he thinks it's her dad."

I shrug, because I don't have proof. "Who else would it be? She's with me every day at school; I would have heard if someone was hurting her there. The only other place she could be hurt is at home. She goes to her mum's, but that morning, the only person she could have seen is her dad, since she has to go to her mum's house to see her. It makes sense that it's him. I left her that night, and he was home. She messaged me late morning with that lie."

Granddad rubs the scruff on his jaw. "I dunno, kid. I've known her father awhile, and although he let a lot of shit slide before, he loves that girl."

"What has Kayla said?" Maverick grits out.

I feel helpless when I look at him. "She won't tell me anything. She said she would talk about it today, but now she's ignoring me."

"Maybe she's out or she's asleep," he offers, which could be true. It is nearly ten at night.

"What do I do?" I plead. "Please, help me."

"Son, I've only had the privilege of meeting the girl a few times now, but she's strong. Yes, she's beyond fragile on the inside, but I believe with you by her side, she will talk to you. Don't go pushing her for answers, or suffocating her. It won't work," he states, and his gaze flicks to Maverick. "Her will has been taken from her, her whole life; she doesn't need that from you too."

"But what—"

"But nothing, son. I know what you boys are like. You're loyal to the bone and when you love, you do it strong and you do it fighting. Kayla doesn't need that. She needs you; just you," he promises, forcing a smile.

Tears fill my eyes, and I don't care how weak it makes me look. She's everything to me. I couldn't protect her the first time, and I don't want to make the same mistake twice. Knowing I could be doing something to help, but doing nothing, doesn't sit well with me. I want her to know I'm here, and I'll fight for her. She could be at home now, wishing someone would save her from her dad.

"He's right, Myles. I saw the way you looked at each other over the weekend, and that girl worships the ground you walk on. I'm not saying I agree with Granddad about waiting until she tells us who is hurting her, but I do agree she needs to make the decision for herself. She'll feel stronger for it. More empowered. All you can do until then is stand by her, and be there for her," Maverick offers, coming to sit down next to me, patting my back.

"When did you become so sentimental?" I tease, glancing up at him through glistening tears.

"The day I had to raise you guys and watch you grow into men," he admits, before getting up and walking over to Granddad. He pats him on the back before leaving us with one more thing. "And the men you've become is thanks to this man, so take his advice." He parts with that last statement, heading upstairs.

"So what are you going to do?" Granddad asks.

"I'm not going to run over there, guns blazing, and threaten the fucker, if that's what you're worried about. I'm going to wait until she replies. If she hasn't called me by tomorrow morning before I leave to meet her for school, then I'll make sure to go see her."

"Good lad. I'm really proud of who you boys have become. You never had a great upbringing, and a part of that was due to my negligence."

"No, Granddad, it wasn't. It was because we had two fucked up parents who didn't deserve to produce kids. You were the best thing that ever happened to any of us. Without you, we would probably get into trouble more, rob shops for our next meal, and probably wouldn't have made it through high school. Don't ever blame yourself."

He chokes up, his eyes watering. I know that must be hard for him to show his emotions like that. He's not one to sit and have a heart to heart. He usually tells us to 'shake it off and carry on' or 'build a bridge and get over it'.

He nods twice before standing up and walking over to the sofa. "I'll be next door if you need me, son; day or night, for whatever you need."

I wait for him to close the front door before getting up and locking up after him. Max is out at some party. Some chick texted him when we were twenty minutes away from home, inviting him to go, and he said yes. Knowing he has taken the backdoor key, I push the chain across the front door before heading upstairs to bed.

Lying in bed, I stare up at the ceiling, watching the reflections that the moon and streetlamps are causing. I've been in bed for a good half an hour to an hour, mindlessly thinking about everything Kayla. She's consuming my mind more and more, especially since we first kissed. I crave the taste of her cherry lips, and the smell of the vanilla scented body lotion she must wear.

I'm just about to give up on her texting me back when the light from my phone lights up the bedroom, the screen flashing.

In a rush to hear from her, I fall from the bed, my knees banging on the carpeted floor with a thud.

"Fuck!" I yelp, getting back up. Slowly this time, I grab my phone.

Kayla: Sorry, I went to Charlie's after my dinner with Dad. I was too excited to wait and tell her about our trip tomorrow. My phone died, and I only just got back to charge it. Is everything okay?

Me: Yeah, baby. Did you show her the pictures? And are you okay? Your dad home?

I wait for what feels like hours after sending her a message back. I hate the thought of her being alone with him in that house, especially when her neighbours would never hear her screaming for help. Just the thought has tremors raking through my body. I have to bite my lips to calm myself down.

Kayla: She begged me to show them to her, but I said I wanted it to be a surprise ;) When do you want to go get them printed? And he's in bed asleep already. He was snoring away when I walked past. I'm good. Why wouldn't I be?

Me: We can go Tuesday, after school, if you like? That way, we can get some more of our presentation finished. Just asking—I miss you xx

Kayla: Aww, aren't you sweet. Tuesday's cool. I miss you too <3 x

Me: Really?

Kayla: Really, really. I thought you'd be asleep by now.

Me: Nah, I miss you sleeping next to me.

Kayla: You can sleep Tuesday. Dad will be away for the night again. If it's okay with Maverick that you sleep. I think I heard him telling someone on the phone that he was going away for a weekend in a few weeks. Maybe we can get everyone together around mine to watch a movie?

Me: It's a date. You looking forward to him being gone for the weekend?

When she doesn't answer right away, and when the three flashing dots don't appear to show me she's writing back, I start to panic. It's just confirmation that it is her dad hurting her. Otherwise she'd answer simply instead of taking so long. I'm about to dial her number after a few more minutes of silence, until my message alert goes off.

Kayla: Not really. I hate it when he's away. I don't like being on my own in the house.

Another reason I'm so confused. If her dad is hurting her, wouldn't she prefer him being away? But she doesn't, and it confuses me. Then there's the fact she could legally move out whenever she likes. If it is him, she wouldn't need to stay there to endure it. It's not like she has siblings keeping her there.

Me: Well, now you never have to be.

Kayla: Promise?

Me: Pinky promise.

Kayla: LOL. Pinky promise... I'm off to bed. Are you still meeting me at the corner shop in the morning to walk to school?

Me: Yes, I'll meet you there at 8.15. Night, baby. Make sure you dream of me ;)

Kayla: Always ;) Night xx

I set my alarm with a grin on my face. Knowing she's going to be dreaming about me makes me hard as fuck. God, the girl is beyond fucking sexy. My mind drifts to our night at the hotel, and I still can't believe it happened. I'll never forget it.

Although I'll see her tomorrow, I plan on waiting until Tuesday to get her to talk to me. I need her to know she can trust me no matter what, and trust that I'll do everything in my power to help her. She shouldn't have to live with this. She shouldn't have to suffer any more than she already has.

I just hope my girl is strong enough to withhold the interrogation she's going to get on Tuesday, because there is no way I'm going to take 'no' for an answer.

CHAPTER
TWENTY

KAYLA

I sit at the kitchen counter, chewing my nails over Myles' behaviour. He seemed so off yesterday, and I put it down to the busy weekend. But then he was like it again today. My mind has run wild with what it could be, and I'm thinking the worst. I'm beginning to wonder if he regrets what we shared over the weekend, and wishes he didn't do it.

It breaks my heart to think of it, because the memory of it is something I'll cherish forever.

I don't want him to regret me, or for him to leave me. Our friendship means more to me than my own freedom from my mother. I'm not going to be able to cope with losing him.

He was so quiet, so withdrawn and distant yesterday, it took everything in me not to get to my knees and beg him to forgive me for whatever it is I've done.

I love him.

I love him so much that yesterday has scared me more than anything I've ever experienced. I've been going over and over the possibilities of what I could have possibly done, but keep coming up short.

There's a knock on the door, startling me from my thoughts. After a quick glance at the clock, I see he's early. We cancelled getting the pictures done today because he got them done yesterday during his free period as a surprise. I didn't even notice that he took my phone at lunch to download them onto a memory card. It was only at the end of school today, when he said he was collecting the prints, that I knew about it.

Reaching the door, I lean up on my tip-toes and peek through the peephole, surprised to find Maverick standing there.

I pull open the door, my heart racing. "Has something happened to Myles?" I greet. "Is he okay?"

Or more—has Myles sent him here to end things with me?

"Myles is fine," he promises, glancing over my shoulder. "Are you alone?"

"Um, yeah, my dad is out," I reply. "Is everything okay?"

"Can I come in and talk?"

Maybe he wants to set some ground rules between Myles and I. He does spend a lot of time here, and Maverick probably doesn't like it.

I don't hesitate to open the door further, knowing Maverick would never hurt me. I head into the living room and gesture for him to sit down on the beige sofa. "Is everything okay?"

"I was hoping you could tell me," he answers evasively, his gaze downcast.

"I'm sorry. I'm confused," I admit, running my palms down my leggings.

"Has Myles ever spoken to you about our past?"

"Some of it, but I know it's not everything," I admit, hoping I won't get Myles into trouble. My hands begin to shake, so I shove them under my thighs.

"Our dad was a mean man. He was sick in the head. He didn't care what happened to us, or whether we were fed or clothed. He didn't care when he hurt us or if other people hurt us. He found joy in it.

"Our mum was just as bad. The boys were too young to remember, and I think Mason just blocked it out. I'm not sure. But I remember everything. I remember my skin burning from the fags she'd stump out on me. I remember the bite of her nails digging into my skin, and the feel of high heels kicking into my ribs. I remember it all," he explains, his words calm, but his pupils are dilated, like he's back living that memory.

His words hit close to home. I think back to the way my mum would burn me on purpose with an iron when I didn't get all the creases out of her clothes, or when she'd kick me after coming home drunk from a night out with her friends. It was never ending, and I don't think I'll ever forget the pain in those memories.

"I... I don't know what to say," I confess as a tear rolls down my cheek. I brush it away. "I'm so sorry that happened to you."

"You don't need to say anything. I just need you to know that I know what it's like. I know what it feels like to have the one person who should protect you, love you unconditionally, and be your hero, hurt you."

"He told you," I whisper, feeling betrayed.

I thought I could trust him.

"Don't be mad at him. I overheard him talking to our granddad. He's worried sick about you, and he hated to break your trust by telling our granddad," he assures me. "I didn't hear everything, but I heard his concern and heartbreak over it. I know it's killing him not being able to protect you, and even worse not knowing who is actually hurting you."

"No one's—"

"Don't lie," he roughly remarks. "Please, don't lie."

"I'm sorry."

"Don't be. When Myles comes around in a bit, you need to talk to him. Don't protect the person who is hurting you, because trust me when I tell you, if the roles were reversed, they'd kick you in front of a bus," he starts, and my chest begins to tighten.

"You don't understand," I tell him, breathing heavily.

"I do. You don't owe your dad anything, so please talk to Myles. You're old enough to move out, and you don't have to be afraid of not having anywhere to go. You are welcome to come and move in with us. Whatever you need for us to help, we will do it. You need to know you have choices."

Oh God. They all think it's my dad.

"My dad isn't the one hurting me," I heave out, panic in my voice.

What if they go to the police and accuse him of it? He'd never forgive me for keeping it from him.

This is such a mess.

He places a comforting hand on my shoulder and meets my gaze. "I know. I just needed to confirm that it's your crazy bitch of a mum," he states, his voice calm. Whereas I'm a mess inside. How? How did he know? "Tell him. And don't go near her again. If she tries to bother you, or if she shows up, call me or Myles. We won't let her hurt you. But I do think Myles needs to know. This is affecting him. Not in the same way it is you, but it is."

I brush my hair away from my face, trying to gather myself and control my breathing. "But you said... How did you know? I don't understand," I ramble, lost for words.

No one ever suspected her.

And he believes me. He doesn't think I'm making it up for attention.

"I knew your dad wouldn't hurt you. He has come into the bar a few times with business associates, and he has praised you non-stop. But Myles thinks he has it figured out because of you living with your dad. You need to put him straight, and out of his misery. You also need to let us help you so that she can't hurt you anymore. If you ever decide that you want to go to the police, then we'll be here to support you."

Tears fall down my cheeks at his kindness. I was so scared people would leave if they knew. "Why are you doing this for me?" I rasp.

"Because we're your family now. And family sticks together," he announces, blowing my mind. A sob breaks free, and he gets down on his knees in front of me, resting his hands on my knees. "Please don't cry. You're not alone. We understand more than anyone about what you're going through. Trust us."

"Telling someone will make it real," I admit, my words breaking. "It will make years of pain and suffering feel that much worse."

"It could also set you free; make you stronger," he adds, his words gentle.

I glance away. "When I was raped, I needed her more than I ever needed her. I thought she would comfort me. I broke as I rehashed all the awful things he did to me, and instead of holding me, she pushed me away like I was filth. I still continued to cry, begging her to help me, and she forced me into the shower and told me to stop being dramatic." I cry for the broken girl who had so much stolen from her in the cruellest way. "All I ever wanted was for her to love me, but I knew in that moment, she never would. I hated myself so much, I tried to end my life. She slapped me for being an attention seeker, and beat me. I tried again, because all I felt was self-loathing inside. It was a cancer spreading through my veins, threatening to kill me slowly. Then I came back, and Myles made me feel everything but those things. He saved me, and he doesn't even know it. I feel clean, worthy and loved for the first time. Telling him what she does could change that. He could look at me differently."

Maverick's jaw clenches, his fingertips applying pressure to my thighs, but not enough to hurt. "He'd never do that to you," he promises. "Do you see him differently because of his upbringing?"

"What? No! I'd never."

"Exactly. Have more faith in him, Kayla. You'd be surprised at the lengths he'll go to in order to protect you."

"I can't lose him," I choke out, and he moves, sitting beside me to wrap his arms around me.

"You're not going to lose him, but if you keep crying, you might lose your brother-in-law. He's due any minute now, isn't he? If he finds us like this, he's going to string up my balls for making you cry. Or worse, he'll get Max and gang up on me, and the two of them together is something I can't handle."

I chuckle at his attempt to lighten the mood. I can only imagine what they have put him through.

I pull back, wiping under my eyes. "Thank you."

I wish I had the words to tell him how much. He didn't come here hoping to help me with my problems. He came to help Myles, and because of it, he helped me too.

"I didn't do anything, Kayla. You just needed someone who understood everything you're going through, and to tell you everything will be okay."

"You did more than you'll ever know," I whisper, forcing a smile. He smiles back, but it doesn't reach his eyes.

"I'd best be going before he arrives. I wasn't joking about what he might do. And if he thinks I'm hitting on his girl, he'll skin me alive."

His girl!

"He wouldn't... I'm not..." I stutter, and my cheeks heat as I fall over my words.

"You're his *beginning, middle,* and *end,* Kayla. Don't ever doubt that," he tells me. He taps me under the chin before getting up.

I follow him to the door. "Thank you for coming to talk to me."

"Thank you for hearing me out," he tells me. "Everything will work out. You'll see."

"I hope so."

He nods. "I'll see you later."

"Later," I reply, and close the door behind him.

I head back to the living room, collapsing on the sofa. I never expected that today, or for anyone to see what's really going on. I think about the words he said, and those he didn't. I think about it until there's a knock on the door once again.

This time, I know it's not another surprise guest, but I check through the peephole to be sure. It's Myles. Today he's wearing a pair of ratted jeans, a white T-shirt, and his Vans. He wears the simplest of things yet looks good every time.

I pull open the door. "Hey," I greet.

"Hey, babe," he greets back, stepping inside. He glances into the empty living room. "Is your dad here?" He doesn't bother to hide his distaste, and now I know why.

"No, he's out for the night, remember? You said you were staying over," I remind him. "You are still staying over?"

Even after Maverick's talk, I'm still worried he's ready to break up with me. It's consuming, and has me on edge.

"Oh shit, yeah. Sorry, I forgot," he quips. "And yeah, I'm still sleeping over."

His smile doesn't reach his eyes, and I'm more paranoid that he's ready to break it off with me.

When he reaches for my hands, I pull them away at the last second. "What is going on? Are you okay with me? Have I done something? You've been really off with me and I'm worried."

His brows pull together. "Woah! Slow down. Nothing is going on, I promise. I just need to talk to you about something and I've been struggling with how to address it."

"What is it?" I ask, my knees locking together so I don't fall.

This is it. This is where it ends.

"It's about Thursday and the marks on your body," he answers, and I relax a little.

I'm still not ready to talk about it, but Maverick's words come back to me. "It is? I thought you were going to break up with me."

His forehead creases. "Never," he says, a frown lining his face.

"Good," I breathe out. "Do you want to go upstairs and talk? I'd feel more comfortable there."

My bedroom is my safe haven. It's the one place I feel safe in, no matter the situation. My therapist said it's because it's surrounded with my own personal things, but I feel like it's more than that. It's my comfort. And for months, it was where I'd always be. My dad tried for months to get me to go out more, or to sit downstairs, but then we moved and he stopped trying when he had to work so much. Not that I'd have listened to him. I love my room.

We walk up the stairs after I grab us each a can of Coke and take a seat on my bed, pulling the pillows behind us.

He doesn't speak at first, so I nudge his foot with mine. "You said you wanted to talk."

"I know it's your dad," he blurts out. "I don't want to push you into talking, and I don't want you to feel forced. But I want you to know

I'm here, and I'll do anything for you. I also think you should consider going to the police or even calling social services."

"I'm eighteen, Myles. What can social services really do for me?" I point out, since I already thought about that.

He links his fingers through mine. "He's been hurting you for a while, Kayla. Did it start when he got custody of you?"

"It's not my dad, Myles." I pause, meeting his gaze so he knows I'm telling the truth. "It's my mum."

He lets go of my hand, jumping from the bed. "It's your fucking mother?" he growls. "How could she hurt you?" Tears well up in my eyes when he says how, and not why. I got asked a lot why I thought I was raped, like I'm the one who committed the offence. "How did I not fucking see this? My god, I should have known and done something."

He begins to pace back and forth, and I see the very thing Maverick was worried about. Myles has been stewing over this for days, and it's gotten to him.

"Please, don't blame yourself," I plead.

"I should have known that bitch had something to do with this. When you were attacked, Joan and my granddad could never understand why your mother went to such lengths to stop you from testifying. Or why she never stepped in afterwards when all those people bullied you," he rants.

"Please stop talking," I whisper, shaking uncontrollably.

I never want to go back to that place. It was bad enough having to deal with the trauma of being sexually assaulted, but it was much worse dealing with the constant torment and torture from everyone around me. It never stopped, and neither did the cruel pranks they played on me. My chest heaves with silent cries.

"Did you know I beat up a couple of kids from your year? Yeah." He nods, his temper rising as he continues to ramble. "My granddad thought they mixed Max and I up, believing it couldn't have been me. It was me. I hated watching you walk down those halls enduring everything they did to you. And all along, your fucking mother was one of those people. She'd been hurting you long before then, hadn't she?" When he finally stops to look at me, the blood drains from his face. He rushes over, sitting down on the edge of the bed. "I'm so fucking sorry. Shit, I... I didn't mean to react like that. Fuck!"

When I don't stop crying, he moves further onto the bed, pulling me onto his lap. I cling to him, sobbing years' worth of grief into his chest.

His breathing is hard and ragged, and I know he's trying to rein his temper in for me.

"I'm sorry," he whispers. "I made this about me, and it's not. Please, talk to me. When did it start?"

"She started hurting me when my dad took me out of the all girls' boarding school. Katherine, who looked after me the majority of my life, died when I was thirteen. She was everything to me and showed me love that my parents never did. When my father told me I'd be moving home, and attending a public school, I was so thrilled. I loved my parents. Well, I guess I loved the idea of them.

"My dad and I had a good relationship. He'd come see me every weekend and a few times in the week when he was passing through. Most of the time though, our visits were scheduled during the holidays. My mother was always distant. I'd never really had a relationship with her, but at thirteen years old, I guess I wanted one. Then I came home and she was just so formal all the time."

I pause as I remember sitting down at the large oak table, where the scent of the food the cooks were cooking in the kitchen bathed the room. Mum joined us as it was being served, and I remember feeling so out of place. It was nothing like the meals I shared with Katherine before she died. She'd always make me laugh, talk about our days, and make fun of stupid commercials. I even tried to make one up at the table with my parents to break the ice, but my mum looked at me with a horrified expression, telling my father they didn't pay thousands of pounds a month for me to be raised like that.

"You okay?" Myles asks when I get too lost in thought.

"Yeah," I croak, before clearing my throat. "Anyway, the weekend after I came back, my dad had to leave again for work. I guess that's when it all started."

I don't want to go into detail, at least, not tonight.

"Does your dad know? He must have seen the bruises," he declares, running the tips of his fingers through my hair.

"If he does, he acts well at hiding it. It's laughable how you and Maverick guessed so quickly about what I'm going through, but my own father, who I live with, doesn't know a thing."

"Maverick?" he asks, a hint of hurt lacing his voice.

"Oh, um… Well, he came over before you turned up. He wanted to talk to me. He told me some things, and opened up my eyes to some stuff. Please don't be mad at him. He was worried because he loves you. That's not a bad thing," I admit softly. "I guess with my situation hitting so close to home with you all, he was worried about how much it would affect you."

"He didn't say anything," he acknowledges. "Did he upset you?"

"No! God, no. He honestly just wanted to talk to me before you did. He wanted me to know how much this was worrying you. I'm not ready to tell you everything—I don't know if I'll ever be—but I don't want you to worry over me anymore."

"I'll always worry about you," he declares, before pressing his lips to my head. "Haven't you realised yet? No matter what is going on, I'll always worry about you. Because you, Kayla Martin, are everything to me."

CHAPTER
TWENTY-ONE

KAYLA

Another week at school has flown by and I can't believe how quickly it's gone. I'm excited for the next chapter in my life, whether it be college, work, or straight to university. It's a time I've been looking forward to for a while because it means I'm one more step closer to leaving *her* behind.

Today is the first Saturday I've arrived at the Salvation food bank feeling happy. After Tuesday and confiding in Myles and Maverick, I feel lighter than I have in years.

"Morning, Joan," I sing cheerfully when I walk in carrying one of the food boxes from outside.

"Well, aren't you a sight, child. If I wasn't mistaken, I'd say you were in love," she teases, with a wink.

I laugh. I love how easy-going Joan is. Even the volunteers who are half her age aren't as laid back as she is. She makes volunteering here fun.

When I don't argue with her statement, she stops what she's doing with her chart. She gives me a once over.

"If only we could get our Max all loved up," she alludes. "I knew my Myles would, and he picked good. I couldn't wish for anyone better. But my Max… he will need a push or two. I can't wait to have some fun."

"I don't think Max is the settling down type," I point out, sad to crush her hopes for him.

"Oh, Kayla, you have a lot to learn," she cackles. "That boy is going to get what's coming to him sooner or later. We had to drive down to the station last night because he got caught trespassing and vandalising someone's barn."

My jaw drops. Myles never said anything. "Oh my goodness; why would he do that?"

She shakes her head, clucking her tongue. "That boy will never learn. Even with a firm talking to from his Gramps and I, he still sat there with that cocky smirk of his. I knew then what his punishment would be. I'm going to make him fall in love."

"I don't think that's going to work, Joan. He loves a lot of girls," I conclude, feeling uncomfortable with this topic.

"Sit back and watch, dear. All will be revealed real soon," she announces, then leaves, cackling loudly. I stare at the empty space, wondering if I should worry for Max or warn him.

"Hi, lady," a sweet voice greets, tugging on my top.

I turn to investigate and find a cute little girl around four or five with big, blue eyes staring up at me. Her clothes have stains on, and they seem to hang off her small frame. Her wavy blonde hair is feathered along her chubby cheeks.

"Hello, pretty girl," I greet, kneeling down.

She removes her thumb from her mouth. "My mummy is getting us some food. Do you need food too?"

"Everyone needs food, sweetie. Want to go see what toys and girly clothes we can find, if your mummy says it's okay?" I ask, not wanting to overstep my bounds.

She nods excitedly, grabbing hold of my hand. She drags me out of the side door and into the main hall, clearly knowing her way around. The main hall is where we ask the people who come in to wait and have a cup of tea and biscuits, while we get their bags ready.

"Mummy, dis wady says I can get some new toys and cwose. Can I?" she pleads, addressing a middle-aged woman. She's dressed in trousers that are torn at the bottom from being too long for her, and is wearing a faded T-shirt. And she's beautiful, just like her daughter.

"Oh, Pippa, I don't think—"

"If it's okay with you, I can get her some bags of clothes sorted while she picks out a few toys she likes. We had someone bring in a big order of donations, so it's fine."

The mother's smile is warm, and I know this means something to her. No one who seeks help here is judged. I don't know this lady's situation, but she must be struggling to accept our help. I've seen so many families come and go, and all of them have different stories to tell. Our job is to make sure they leave here with everything they need.

"If you're sure? Dean, do you want to go with your sister?" she asks a boy around eight or nine years old. He's sitting on one of the chairs, chewing a cookie and looking like he'd rather be anywhere than here. He shakes his head, and his mother turns back to her little girl. "Be good, and listen to this nice lady when she tells you what to do, okay?"

"Okay, Mummy," she agrees, before grabbing my hand again.

I take her through to the back—where we don't usually let anyone other than staff come in—and show her the toys. She squeals loudly, talking about Santa Claus coming early. Her gaze moves from one toy to the next, and she picks them up, like she's struggling to choose.

I smile at her enthusiasm and joy, before leaving her to pick whilst I sort her clothes out. I grab the box of girl's dresses, and guessing her age and size, I start rummaging through, picking a few dresses and folding them up on the table. I do the same with the trousers and tops. I get lucky and find a nice warm coat that's the right size for her. Once I'm happy she has enough, I move over to the boys and start picking out a few sizes I think will fit her brother.

When I'm done, I fold them all into the big shopping bags that we have especially for the clothes and walk over to Pippa to find her playing with a soft rag doll. It's a pretty little thing, and even I had to admire it when I saw it a few weeks ago. Apparently, one of the ladies who volunteers for the church makes them. They are beautiful.

"Do you like her?" I ask, sitting down next to her, quietly putting the toys she's thrown out back in the box.

"I wove it. I want it, pwease?"

"You may. Would you like some books and jigsaw puzzles too?"

She nods, but her attention is focused on her doll. Not wanting the boy to be left out, I get up and head to the boy section, where I notice an old Nintendo Game Boy. I snatch it up, along with the games brought in with it, and bag them up for the boy. I'm just praying he doesn't already have one.

When we're done, we head back out. I have a few bags with various items, and I made sure the mum got some stuff too. I know some people are apprehensive about wearing second-hand clothes, but these ones still have tags on. I'm just hoping I don't offend her with the sizes I picked out.

The mother's eyes pop out when she sees how much I'm carrying. "Oh my god, we can't possibly take all this."

I lower the bags to the floor. "It's fine. We need to get it cleared before our new donation boxes come through. I hope you don't mind, but I picked up some outfits for both the kids. I guessed their sizes, so if they don't fit, just bring them back and I'll swap them out. We also had some women's clothes donated a few weeks back. They've all still got their tags on. I was hoping they might be of some use to you, if that's okay?"

This is the part I always hate. We have to go by assumptions. Not all people who come in have the courage to ask for things. They take what they are given and are grateful. So, we have to use our initiative to get them what we think they need.

The woman's eyes well up. "Thank you. Thank you so much," she chokes out, picking up the bags. I quickly grab the Game Boy I left on the top and hand it to the boy.

"Hi, I'm Kayla. I got you this. I wasn't sure if you already had one, but it seems a shame to have it sitting on a shelf," I tell him.

His face lights up like Christmas as he takes it from me, and my heart feels full. "No way! Mum, look at this!" he hollers, lifting it up for her to see.

"What do you say?" she scolds softly.

"Thank you," he cries, still overjoyed with his new toy.

"You're welcome," I assure him, and turn to the mum. "If you need anything else, don't hesitate to come back."

I turn to leave, needing to finish unpacking the food orders, when the little girl runs into my legs.

"Thank you." She smiles real big.

"My pleasure, sweetie." Giving her a hug, she wraps her tiny arms around my neck and squeezes.

She gives me a peck on the cheek before running back off to her mum, who is waiting by the door, holding her hand out for her. I watch them leave with a smile before turning around to find Lake watching me.

"Oh hey," I greet, happy to see her. "I didn't know you were in today. Have you been hiding?"

She lowers her gaze. "I was in the back stacking some shelves. That was real sweet what you did for that family."

"It's what we do."

I shrug her words away, knowing any one of us today would have done the same. Well, maybe not everyone. There are a bunch of girls who volunteer who do nothing but take the piss out of people coming in needing help. It's people like them who stop us from helping more people. It's the same with charity shops. People turn their noses up at the idea of going in and selecting items, but then they have no problem buying second-hand items off Facebook.

"Not everyone here would do what you just did, Kayla. Take a compliment," she teases, walking with me towards the storage room. "Joan wants me in here with you. One of the girls is getting on my nerves and I think Joan knows I'm seconds away from snapping."

This is the most conversation I've ever had out of her. Even during our lunch, she barely said anything. I don't mind it since I'm the same. I never know what to say or how to keep a conversation going. By the time I think of something, the topic has changed or the moment has passed.

"What have they done this time?" I ask, not needing to ask what bunch of girls has said stuff. It's the same group of girls I mentioned who make people feel uncomfortable. I don't know why they let them volunteer.

She starts emptying a box. "The same as normal. Not knowing when to keep their mouths shut."

"I don't know why no one is saying something to them. They've been like this for as long as I've known them."

"It's because some of their parents donate big to the church. I already made a complaint about them. I can't afford to get into trouble."

"Is that why you haven't said anything to them yourself?" I question. "Sorry, that sounded rude."

"No, it wasn't. But yeah, that's why. If it was a few years ago, I'd be all up in their faces, yelling to demand what their problem was."

"Then why don't you? It's not like they'll kick you out. You work the hardest here."

She glances behind her and turns away. "It's my punishment," she whispers, thinking I won't hear her. But I do.

Opening my mouth to question her further, I'm stopped short when Myles walks in, looking handsome as ever.

"Hi," I cheer, rushing over to him. I lean up to give him a quick kiss. "What are you doing here?"

"I came to see if I could steal you away," he replies.

I turn to Lake, who is watching us. "Go. I've got this covered."

"Well, that saves me asking," Myles chuckles.

"Are you sure?" I press, knowing there's a bit to be done.

"Go, I've got this," she promises.

"Where are you taking me?"

"It's a surprise," Myles answers. "You can't say no. If you do, Mason will want me to go clean out the storage unit at work, and I don't want to. I want to spend the day with you."

My stomach flutters. "All right, but let me check it's okay with Joan first."

"Already asked her. She didn't even let me get my words out before she said to make sure I spoil you."

I grin because that sounds like Joan. I think about telling him what she said about Max but decide against it. It will be better to see what she does.

———

"**W**here are we going?" I ask once we slide out of the taxi. He points to the leisure centre behind us. "We are going to a roller disco. They have an over eighteen one here."

Oh my god. He has to be joking. *Please tell me he's joking.*

"Please tell me you're joking?" I stress, fearing for the lives of people I'm about to take out. I'm awful at skating.

He smirks, and I melt on the spot. He could get me to do anything with that smirk. "Nope."

"Do we have it rented out for ourselves? Do people know you're going to let me loose in there?"

His eyes widen when he sees I'm serious. "Surely you can't be that bad."

"Oh no, I'm worse. I'm terrible, Myles. Picture Bambi learning to walk. That's me on skates," I inform him, letting him know what he's in for. "The last time I went, I knocked two front teeth out of a girl's mouth, broke a little boy's arm, and then while trying to get help from the DJ, I skated into his booth and smashed his sound system. I'm a disaster."

Instead of taking me seriously, he laughs. He laughs so hard that his face turns bright red, to the point he looks like he got his face painted.

"Don't laugh," I hiss, stomping my foot, but it just causes him to laugh harder.

"This is just... I wish I brought Max now," he shares through laughter, moving to take out his phone.

"Don't you dare! I'm not going in there if you call him," I warn, then groan when I realise I just said I'll be going in there. I should be talking him out of it.

Shit!

I really wasn't joking about the destruction I caused when I came to one of these the last time. I missed out the part where a fire started.

"I won't," he promises, unable to keep a straight face. "Come on, let's go pay for our tickets. I've booked us some skate hire too."

"You should have got life Insurance while you were at it," I mutter, and he laughs in return, guiding me to the small line waiting to enter.

By the time we've paid and got our skates on, I'm shaking like a leaf and ready to bolt. *I can't do this!* I tell myself everything will be okay, but then we enter, and I freak out.

"Oh my god, they are professionals. Look at him skating back-wards, and I'm not going to go there with that bloke over there. I can't do this. This must be an advanced session or something. We're in the wrong place," I ramble. I get so lost trying to talk him out of taking me that I don't feel him sliding me across the wide-open hall. The place is where they must play ball games and stuff. It's like a huge school gym.

Music is blaring through the speakers around the hall, so I can barely hear what Myles is saying.

"What?" I shout.

"Just hold on to me and you'll be fine," he assures me, believing that will save everyone in here.

Does he seriously believe I'll be vertical at any point during our time here? I should have made it clear I'll be on the floor, horizontal, the whole time.

I wobble when he moves me forward, his arm no longer around my waist to keep me up, and I end up failing to keep upright. I try to let go of Myles so we don't fall at the same time, but he clings to me tighter. The move snaps me forward, and my head smacks into his mouth before we fall to the floor.

I clench my eyes shut as he groans in pain beneath me. We haven't even made it to the group of skaters, skating clockwise in a circle.

"Shit, girl. As much as I love the position we are in right now, now isn't the time," he teases, sounding pained. I roll off him, letting him get to his feet first to help me up. I notice people laughing at our inexperience, but they'll soon lose that once I'm done in here.

They haven't seen anything yet.

"Why don't I just walk while you skate?" I offer hopefully.

"Not allowed, babe, unless you're a member of staff," he replies, sounding smug about it as he helps me up.

He's totally freaking lying. I just saw a group of girls wearing ten-inch high heels. I playfully go to punch him but end up wobbling and falling on my arse again. Thankfully, he doesn't fall with me. Only one of us needs to suffer.

Jesus, my arse is going to be bruised.

He holds his hand out to help me up and I gratefully take it. When I'm up, I shove my hair out of my face and blow out a breath.

Right, we can do this. Just one time around the circle, and we can go, I chant to myself, hoping one circle will be enough to make Myles happy.

"Don't move a second," he shouts near my ear over the music. I listen to what he says, I really do, but I'm on freaking skates, for Christ's sake. They have round wheels. I end up rolling a little, but thankfully, he's ready for it, and places his hands around my waist. I silently thank him, not caring that he can't hear me.

When he's behind me, he presses his body against my back, his hands firmly on my waist. He kicks my feet together gently, not enough to make me topple, then leans in again.

"Keep your feet still, don't lift them or try to move. I'm going to skate and you're going to... roll with it," he jokes, and his chuckle vibrates across my flesh.

He starts to move, and I squeal. With a mind of their own, my feet start to separate, sliding away from each other.

Like I said, Bambi!

"I can't do this," I whine, then curse myself for becoming that girl. You know, the type that whines over the stupidest things.

"Come on, you can do it," he cheers, before skating effortlessly in front of me. He skids to a halt and takes my hands. "Let's try it this way. Keep your feet together." He begins to skate backwards, but I don't watch for long, since I need to concentrate on keeping my feet together.

We finally make it to the circle, and I squeal with happiness. It was the wrong move. I let the success get to my head, and before I know it, I'm flying forward. Myles steps in to help, but then my feet slide out in front of me.

Everything happens so fast.

I knock into a person behind me, and I turn to apologise, when my hand hits another person. Before I know it, we're falling, and it's not just us. I don't even get the chance to gather my bearings before there's a pile up of people on the floor behind us.

Myles, the only person safe from the catastrophe, skates over to where I'm lying, grinning from ear to ear. "You really do cause chaos."

I tilt my head. I want to cry when I see blood spurting through a woman's hand, where she's covering her nose. The lad next to her is crying out, clutching his leg, and the one next to him has a lump the size of an egg on his forehead.

I glance at Myles, holding my hand up. "We need to go," I demand, and slip when he tries to lift me.

My chin smacks off the floor, and I groan in pain as Myles helps me to my feet. Staff members come rushing over to help the injured, and my face flames in embarrassment. When one asks what happened, the one with what I think is a broken arm turns to me with a thunderous expression and points.

Oh, shit.

I rip my skates off, not bothering to pick them up before running out of the hall. I'm so freaking embarrassed.

Myles rushes out behind me on his skates, his face full of amusement. He's carrying my skates, and I'm glad he picked them up when I remember that I can't get my shoes back without them.

He hands the guy behind the counter our skates, and we wait for him to bring back our shoes.

"So... do you want to talk about it?" Myles starts, but I hold my hand up to stop him.

"Not now. Not now," I warn.

It's quiet for a couple of seconds, until I hear him laughing all over again. I glare at him bent over, gasping for air.

"Oh my god, that was... that was..." He stops short to catch his breath. "How could you be that bad at skating?"

"I just am, okay? Can we not talk about it? I want to forget the whole ordeal," I declare. A couple walks out, clutching their injuries. I cower into myself when they glare at me. "Oh God, they're cancelling the rest of the session, aren't they?"

When more people come walking out with grumpy faces, I can tell I must have caused some serious injuries in there. I look to Myles with wide eyes, but he just laughs and hands me my shoes. Before anyone can jump me or start spouting nasty words off at me, I slide them on and rush out of the building. I inhale when the cool air hits my face.

"Come on. It was funny. You should have seen your face," Myles teases. "I have a fat lip, a guy has a broken arm, and I'm not even sure what the other injuries were. I had tears blocking my vision."

"Funny," I snap, then I notice a cinema over the road, and an idea forms in my head. My favourite author has just released another film this week, and I'm just betting it's not something Myles usually watches. "Come on, we're going in there."

He looks over to the cinema and frowns. "Babe, there isn't anything good on. There's only some crappy chick flick and some cartoon crap."

"But, *babe*, we're seeing that chick flick," I tell him sweetly.

He stares at me for a moment, before bending to lift me up over his shoulder. I half squeal, half laugh when he rushes over the road with me still over his shoulder.

"It's like a hideout while the skater crews calm their skates down," he jokes.

Even with nearly killing a room full of people on skates, he still makes me laugh. Only Myles could do that to me, and I'm thankful every day that I have him in my life.

It wouldn't be the same without him.

CHAPTER
TWENTY-TWO

MYLES

Kayla and I walk out of the cinema hand in hand, both comfortable with our own thoughts. When she said she couldn't skate, I didn't believe her. I just thought she wasn't a fan of it.

When Charlie called me this morning, telling me to get her out of her comfort zone, I jumped at the chance and asked what I should do. She told me that skating is one thing Kayla has always wanted to do. And since Charlie is the only other person to know Kayla like I do, I know she did this on purpose. She knew exactly what she was doing when she put that idea into my head.

I didn't mention it to Kayla because I don't want her to think I was being forced to take her out. I've gotten a good read on her reactions, so I know her negative thoughts come from years of abuse. Her mum made her feel like that, which makes me hate her more. She doesn't see what a fantastic daughter she has.

We walk over to the deserted taxi rank to wait for a taxi, and I'm surprised Kayla hasn't started to relay the movie. It's something she does after everything we do that she enjoys. I find it adorable and cute, because I know I'm a part of that reason.

Lately, she's come out of her shell, and I've noticed small changes in her. She's more confident when she speaks, and she is more outgoing with those around her. She still has her moments where she is shy and anxious, but her bravery overrides all of that. She's one of the strongest people I know. Not many who have endured a fraction what she has can go on and live like she has. It makes me envy her more.

"So, shall I address the elephant in the room, or street rather?" Kayla mentions.

I glance at her, my brows pinched together. "Huh?"

Did I miss something?

I know I space out a lot when I'm thinking of her, but I normally still hear what she says.

"Oh, come on," she teases, nudging me with her shoulder. "I saw, Myles. I'm not blind."

Now I'm really baffled.

"Um, I didn't say you were blind," I assure her. "I have no idea what the hell you're going on about."

"The tears—you totally cried."

Fuck! Fuck! Fuck!

I thought I hid that well. That movie would have made someone who doesn't feel emotions, cry.

"I had dust in my eye," I lie, unable to look at her.

She laughs. "Are you really going with that?"

I groan. "Okay, okay, I cried," I admit, then point at her accusingly. "But so did you, so you can't tease me."

"I totally can," she argues. "You said before it started that films like this are so unreal it would make an Essex girl look authentic."

I glower down at her. "Let's not get into that right now, okay? Let's just take you home and enjoy the rest of our Saturday with pizza and another movie."

My phone begins to ring, and I pull it out of my pocket when Kayla's starts ringing too. "Hello?"

"Hi, Denny…" she answers, but her conversation is drowned out by the annoying twit in my ear.

"Dude, you have to come right now. Hope said 'Mama'," Max yells, squealing like a girl.

I grin big; though I feel sad I missed it. That girl is just something else, and cute doesn't even begin to describe her. She's looking more like her dad every day, the poor sod; but thankfully still holds a strong resemblance to her mum.

Kayla must have got the same call, because she's smiling and giving me those eyes. I know what she's going to ask before she even speaks.

"We'll be there in ten," I tell Max, before cutting him off. A taxi pulls up at the same time Kayla says her goodbyes. We give him Denny's address and sit back.

"I can't believe she said mama," Kayla coos.

"She probably just had wind," I joke.

"No, she's seven months now. She'll be talking more and more from now on," she supplies.

"True," I agree. "When she first walks, they'll be throwing a party. Max threw a movie night when she first smiled and made us sit and watch cartoons with her. None of us saw her smile either, and Max didn't let us hear the end of it. Luckily, she didn't make us wait too long and smiled again the next day."

"He really loves her, doesn't he?"

"Yeah. We've always wanted a sister, but instead, we got blessed with the next best thing," I explain. "A niece. She's going to be spoiled rotten."

We pull up outside mine. I haven't even got out before Max is running down the path with Hope in his arms.

"Say Mama," he coos, talking like an idiot as we get out of the car.

Hope giggles, smacking his mouth with her tiny chubby fist before repeating his words.

"Mamaaaa."

"Oh my god, aren't you a clever girl. Yes, you are!" Kayla gushes, and I chuckle at how high her voice has gone. I'm just as bad, but hearing other people talk like that to a baby amuses me. Plus, Hope loves it when we talk to her like it.

Hope repeats it again, making it into a game and loving the attention she's getting.

"You're going to be the cleverest girl in the world. Aren't you, Hope? 'Cause you're a Carter, aren't you? Yes, you are. Yes, you are," Max starts and leads us back to Denny's.

"We're ordering pizza for dinner. You want in?" Mason asks as soon as we walk in. "We thought we'd wait for you before we ordered anything."

"Yeah, I'm in. We were having pizza anyway," I admit, as I take a seat.

I go to pull Kayla down into my lap, but I notice she has stolen Hope from Max. She notices and gently lowers herself onto my lap, still gushing over Hope.

"Who's your favourite uncle, kid?" I ask, lightly running my finger down her soft cheek.

She rambles some 'goo, goo, ga, ga' back, and I smile. "I know, kid. I love you too."

Kayla chuckles and brings her lips to Hope's neck and blows raspberries. Hope laughs loudly, her fist clinging to Kayla's hair. I try to untangle them, but it causes Hope to hold on tighter.

"Hey, princess, can you let go of my girl's hair?" I ask, still trying to pry her hands away.

I hear Kayla's breath deepen for a second before she lets it out. Every time I've called her my girl, she's had the same reaction. It's like she doesn't believe it, and whenever she hears it, it's like a shock to her. I'm just going to have to work harder to make her believe she's mine and always will be.

Hope finally lets go of Kayla's hair, but only so she can reach her arms out to me, her body flying towards me. I reach for her before she can fall and sit her on the other side of me.

"So, what have you two done today?" Denny asks, and before I can think of the consequences, I open my big mouth.

"Kayla took out a whole hall full of skaters by just being there," I announce, but it's only Mason who looks like he believes me.

"What happened?" he asks.

"She literally caused a huge pile up like the ones you'd see on the news, but with skaters," I reveal, getting into it. "I'm pretty sure one dude had a broken arm. The rest weren't faring well either, and there was a lot of blood."

"Stop!" Kayla squeals, trying to place her hand over my mouth.

I push it away, continuing. "She said she couldn't skate, but I thought she was being cute when she said she'd caused accidents before."

"Really?" Max asks doubtfully.

"Yeah, look at this video I got before she stormed out," I order, throwing him my phone.

Kayla glowers at me. "You did not record it," she hisses.

"Oh, come on, babe, they have to see this. This shit belongs on YouTube."

She tries to escape my lap to grab the phone, but I'm quicker, locking my arm around her waist.

The phone is ripped away by Max, and Maverick holds it up, laughing when it begins to play. "Shit. How the hell did you manage all that?"

Mason and Max glance over his shoulder and order him to replay it. They all crack up laughing and Kayla sighs, sulking in my lap. I pull her to me, smiling.

"Babe, it was funny," I exclaim.

"Tell that to all the injured," she mutters.

"Come on, how did this happen, and why didn't you record it from the beginning?" Maverick asks and begins to type into the phone. "I'm sending it to Malik."

"I can't skate. It took us ten minutes to even get me into the actual room because I was so off balance. Then when Myles finally got me to move without falling over, I got excited, and you know the rest," she pouts, not looking happy. "Just please don't post it on anything. I mean it. I can handle you guys seeing it, but please, no one else."

She gulps, and I notice her hands shaking. "Hey," I call, nudging her until she meets my gaze. "I promise it won't go further than this room."

She watches me for a moment, before relief has the tension leaving her body. "Thank you."

I know her anxiety is from having her bullies record their pranks and assaults. She had to live with people watching them and making fun.

Her phone rings, vibrating against my lap. She scrunches her nose up in a way I've always found cute before she grabs it out of her bag.

"It's my dad," she murmurs. "Hello? I'm with Myles at Denny's, why? Oh no! I'm so sorry, Dad. No, I've not eaten. Okay. See you in a sec." She grimaces as she ends the call. "It's my dad. I forgot I have that meal tonight to meet Katie."

"Oh crap," I hiss, forgetting all about it. I know she's been worrying over it, not knowing what to expect. She's got nothing to worry about, though. I've met Katie and she's lovely.

"Yeah," she sighs. "He's going to pick me up in a second, but I feel bad for forgetting. Well, I knew, but with everything that's happened this afternoon, I forgot."

"That's what happens when you take a whole hall of people out," I tease, trying to ease her anxiety about meeting Katie. She lightly smacks my arm, and I grunt, pretending it hurt. She sees through it and rolls her eyes.

Her phone beeps, and Kayla sighs, standing up. "I'll see you all another day. I've got to go. I forgot I had a meal planned with my dad," she announces before bending down to kiss Hope on the head. "Bye, clever pants."

I stand up ready to hand Hope over to Maverick, since he's the closest, but Max is there, prying her from my arms. I give him a 'what the fuck' look, but he just shrugs and starts talking to Hope.

I walk Kayla out, but before we get to the road, I grab her arm and pull her to a stop.

"Do you want me to come round after your meal?" I ask, wrapping my arms around her waist.

"Can I text you and let you know?"

I nod, agreeing. "Sure, baby. Now kiss me," I whisper, but don't bother waiting for her to lean up and kiss me. Instead, I kiss her softly, my lips against hers.

A car horn beeps, and I grin against her mouth. Kayla looks hesitant to go, but I give her an encouraging smile. "You'll be fine. Call me. Anytime."

"Okay," she agrees. "I'll text you later."

She smiles but it doesn't reach her eyes, before she leaves. I wish I had remembered the meal so I could have helped prepare her.

Turning around, I head back to the house. The others stop talking when I walk in, looking at me like I've grown two heads.

"What?" I ask defensively.

Max arches a brow at me. "You are so p-whipped, my twin."

"Says the person who can't go ten minutes without seeing his niece. It's unhealthy, and I don't just mean for you," I tell him, but just like his comment, there's no heat behind my words.

"One day, you're going to meet a girl, fall head over heels, and wonder why you didn't do it sooner. It's going to knock you over so goddamn hard, you'll need time to recover," Denny sings, daring him to argue.

"Yeah, until I get my sanity back and realise what a freaking pussy-whipped mistake it was. Don't you guys get bored? Not asking you, Myles, before you go kung fu on me. I'm asking the others. You know, having one pussy each night, every night."

"Not in the slightest," Mason retorts.

"Not done the whole girlfriend thing, but it must be better than random hook-ups," Maverick mutters, glaring at Max distastefully. "Can we not talk about it, please? They're like my sisters."

I grunt in agreement, and Denny leans over, smacking Max upside his head, making Hope giggle.

"Ever refer to me like that again, and I'll never let you eat here again," she threatens.

"Whatever. I'm just saying, falling in love and having one girl just isn't for me. Whatever floats your boat and all, but I'm into the whole sharing is caring motto," he replies.

"That's how STDs are spread," Mason interrupts. "Maybe sharing is caring shouldn't be the motto you follow?"

"And I thought you didn't do the sharing thing," Maverick points out.

"With food," he snaps.

"I'm actually looking forward to him falling in love now," Mason declares. "If he can find someone to put up with him, he'll be eating those words."

"Jesus, when is this pizza coming?" Max snaps, not fooling anyone. I grin at his discomfort at the conversation turning on him. "Wipe that grin off your face, Myles. It doesn't suit you."

"Grouchy," I tease, laughing. He chucks one of Hope's building blocks at me, but I manage to catch it before it reaches my head.

I can't wait for the day he finds his person. Because Denny is right, it will knock him off his feet when it happens. He acts so cool about it now, but when it happens, he won't know what's hit him.

And I'll be there for it.

CHAPTER
TWENTY-THREE

KAYLA

We're nearing home, and my stomach is in knots. My dad hasn't noticed because he's been too busy scolding me for being so inconsiderate since they rearranged plans to find a day that suits me. I tried to explain that I didn't do it on purpose, that I didn't intentionally set out to hurt anyone, but he's letting his own nerves about us meeting get in the way.

Even after he finally let me explain what happened, he still wasn't happy about it. I know he wants to comment on Myles and me, but the conversation is above him. He doesn't know how to speak to me about boys, and I'd probably end up in tears of embarrassment if he tried.

He parks up outside, switching the engine off before letting out a breath. "Are you sure you're okay with me seeing Katie? I know you love your mother, but we're separated now."

It takes everything in me not to react.

He has no idea that the only emotion I feel towards my mother is hatred. I want there to be a day when I feel nothing for her, because she doesn't deserve anything. Which is why I plan to never step foot inside her house again.

I don't like that his thoughts have gone to that place or that I've hurt him this much. "Dad, it's fine that you're with Katie. I'm really glad you've found someone. You deserve to be happy," I promise, and my words are genuine.

I never understood why he stayed with my mum for so long, or why he continues to provide for her long after they got divorced. They were never happy, and it made everyone miserable. We might not be perfect now, but at least no one walks around on eggshells.

"Are you sure?"

"I promise. I know I let you down today, but I was being truthful about it slipping my mind. It wasn't because it isn't important to me, or because I don't want to be here. It is important and I do want to meet her."

"Good," he breathes out. "But if there is ever a time when it's not okay, tell me."

"I will," I swear.

"Alright, we should go in. She's due to arrive any second," he announces, as a red car pulls in behind us. "She's here."

We step out of the car, and I shove my hands into my coat as a tiny brunette with wild, curly hair gets out of her vehicle.

Dad wastes no time in moving over to her, and I take a step closer, enthralled by his expression. He really is happy. "Hey, darling," Dad greets, pulling her in for a hug.

I smile at how soft her expression goes when she hugs him back. She likes him too. I've never seen him act like this with anyone, and I wish I had seen it before.

Lost in thought, I don't realise they've pulled away and are watching me.

Why are they looking at me like that?

Dad jerks his head down to Katie, narrowing his eyes a little. She stands closer to him, giving me a wave.

She seems kind and sweet, but I've seen my mother put on a

performance in front of people. It's why she gets away with everything she does.

"This is my daughter," Dad introduces, puffing his chest out.

"It's nice to meet you," I greet. "I'm Kayla."

"I'm Katie, but you already know that," she teases, a faint blush coating her cheeks as she reaches out to shake my hand.

Oh God.

I reach out to take her hand, unable to hide my trembling. Her hand is warm and soft, and I quickly drop it before shoving my hands back in my pockets.

"We should head inside out of the cold," Dad announces, placing his hand at the small of her back. "Kayla is making her special seasoning steak. You're going to love it."

They fall in front of me, missing my jaw hanging open. *Since when was I meant to be cooking?*

What if I mess up and she reacts like Mum?

God, what if she doesn't like it and demands I make something else?

If I knew I'd be cooking, I would have ignored the call and stayed at Denny's to eat pizza. At least then I wouldn't have had to cook, and I would have got to spend time with my favourite person.

Knowing I'll need to start prepping now, I head right to the kitchen, leaving them to chatter to each other. I grab some ingredients out of the fridge and cupboards and lower them down onto the counter. Slapping the steak down on the cutting board, I go to reach for the mallet in the drawer, when I notice Katie standing in the doorway. I scream, placing my hand over my chest.

"Oh my god," I cry, breathing heavily.

She rushes over. "I'm so sorry," she stresses, and reaches out. I flinch at her hand on my shoulder, and she quickly drops it. "I didn't mean to scare you."

I inhale and exhale slowly, catching my breath. "It's okay. I didn't expect you to come in. I overreacted. I'm sorry."

"I wanted to come in and help, if that's okay?" she offers, tucking her hair behind her ear.

"No, no," I refuse. "You're our guest. I can handle this."

And I can. I've probably cooked more meals than I've eaten.

"I don't mind, sweetie," she promises, grabbing a peeler out of the drawer. "Your dad has just gone to answer a call, so he'll be a few minutes. I like to cook and keep busy."

I force a smile as she begins to peel the potatoes, working with ease in the kitchen. Not used to a shadow in the kitchen, I try to hide my discomfort and carry on preparing dinner.

"Do you like peas?" I ask, my voice low as I grab a pot out of the cupboard.

"Yes," she replies, and watches me as I pour some into the pot. "So… your father says you want to become a social worker. Is that right?"

My eyes widen a fraction. I didn't know he talked that much about me. "Kind of. I'm more interested in the therapist side of it, but my goal is to help kids get through certain obstacles in their life."

"It's not the easiest of jobs to do, but I can imagine it's the most rewarding if you can help at least one child. Or at least, that's how my mum explained it. She was a foster parent," she reveals, and I stop to listen to her, interested in what she has to say. "She mostly looked after troubled teens since they were the hardest to home. She helped them through so much, and never gave up. I admire you for wanting to do the same."

I tilt my head, curious to know more. "How many teens did she foster?"

"I think she is currently on her twenty-ninth. She has a teenage boy called Daniel right now, who was abandoned by his parents when he was eight. He moved in with some relatives shortly after, but sadly, they passed away. There was no one left after their death, and because of his age, it's hard to find someone to adopt him. Then she has Sally-Ann, who arrived not long after Daniel. She suffered years of abuse from her parents, and sadly, she's now in the same position as Daniel."

My heart aches for those kids. "What your mother is doing is incredible," I whisper. "All a child wants is someone to understand, who loves them regardless, and she's giving them that. I bet they find it hard to convey it to her, so you should make sure she knows."

I could have been one of those kids if my dad wasn't here. A lump forms in my throat. I'm glad he never gave up on me or thought my mental health was too much for him to cope with. He could have left me with Mum and led his life forgetting I was ever born.

She watches me intensely. "She's an incredible mother. You should talk to her about doing a placement when you start your degree," she offers.

Why would she help me?

I'm not sure what to trust, and I don't want to be in a position where I owe her.

Still, I don't want to be rude. "I'll think about it," I promise, glancing away.

"Is it okay to make some tea?"

"I can do it," I offer, feeling ashamed that I didn't ask before.

"No, I've got it," she promises, and begins to search the cupboards.

I stare down into the boiling water where the potatoes are cooking. I want desperately for her to be different to my mum. I don't want her to take my dad away, to be left in a position where I'm not important anymore.

Or worse, what if I'm not a part of their plan and he tries to send me to Mum's? I'll never go, but the rejection would sting all the same.

A cool hand touches my arm, and I flinch, lifting my arms up to guard my face.

"I did it again," Katie cries. "I'm so sorry."

I lower my hands, shaking uncontrollably. Her eyes are wide, horrified by my reaction. I force a laugh, but there's no mirth to it. "God, I'm jumpy today."

She doesn't look like she believes me. "The potatoes are boiling over," she states, and leans over slowly, turning it down.

I step back, still shaking. She glances at me, her eyebrows drawn down. "I'll finish off the dinner," she assures me. "Why don't you go and lay the table and take a seat when you're done."

"I should finish this," I decline, flipping the steaks over.

She gently places her hand over mine. "Kayla, I've got this, honey. I promise."

I nod and grab the placemats from the cupboard before leaving. I inhale and exhale heavily as I lay the table. If she didn't already think I was crazy, she does now.

My dad walks out of his office at the same time I walk out of the kitchen. He gives me a look of concern.

"Where's Katie? Is she okay?" he asks.

I sigh, dropping my gaze to the floor. "She offered to finish dinner. Can you lay the table? I forgot I need to email my teacher about the assignment I have to hand in," I lie, passing him the plates.

I rush out of the room as tears gather in my eyes. One day, I want to be his priority. I want him to see me and care enough to know something is wrong.

Laughter fills the kitchen, and I begin to wonder if this is how it will always be. Will I always be the broken girl who isn't good enough? I know he loves me, but sometimes, I don't know who is worse. My mum for beating me or my dad for looking through me.

———

Twenty-minutes later, I take my seat at the table, still trying to calm my nerves. I don't know what has me so on edge because Katie seems like a nice person. The pressure to get everything right, to make a good impression, is too much.

I glance up when Katie walks in, struggling to carry the sauces. I stand, knocking the chair back to help her. I take the sauces and place them in the centre of the table before heading to the kitchen to grab the plates of food.

Katie follows, and whilst I pick up the two closest to me, Katie grabs the one left along with a plate of garlic bread.

"Whose is who?" I ask when we reach the table.

"That one is yours, and that one is mine," she points out, and flashes of my past come in droves.

I can hear my mother screaming. It was the first time I had to stay alone with her, and she had just sat down to eat. She told me I didn't get to sit with her.

I can remember her punishing me by not letting me eat.

I was frozen and didn't know what to do.

"Kayla, are you going to give her the plate?" Dad asks, his brows pulled together.

I push the memories aside and lower my plate to the table before doing the same for Katie. But my hands shake so badly, the plate slides from my fingers and falls into her lap.

She cries out, brushing off the hot food as she jumps to her feet.

"Oh my god, oh my god, oh my god." I chant the words over and over, loud enough to hear over the ringing in my ears. I grab a tea-towel from the side and wipe the hot food from off her tight fitted, knee-length skirt. "I'm so sorry," I swear, and notice her hand by her side begin to rise.

My vision blurs with black spots, and I launch myself away, knocking my head into the table. I cover my face, whimpering.

My pulse races as I wait for pain, but nothing comes. I peek out, my lashes wet from tears, and see Dad and Katie watching me. Dad looks seconds away from cussing at me, but when I look at Katie, all I see is sorrow.

"I didn't mean to. I just… It slipped from my hand. I didn't mean to. I'm sorry," I choke out, ducking my head in shame.

Katie drops to her knees, reaching for me. She gives an unhappy glance to my dad. "It's okay. It was only an accident," she assures me softly. "Why don't you go upstairs and clean up? I'll clean this up so by the time you come back down, we can finish our dinner together."

"No!" I blurt out. "I'm fine. You can have my plate. I ate a big dinner before I came." I glance away at my lie and face Dad. "I'm sorry for ruining your evening, Dad. Why don't you eat with Katie, and I'll clean everything up in the morning?"

"Kayla," he begins, and I can hear the disappointment in his tone.

"I'm sorry," I rush out, before running off, taking the stairs two at a time. Once I make it to my room, I slam the door closed behind me and fling myself onto my bed, burying my head in the pillow.

I cry over everything I did wrong. He wanted one meal, and I ruined it. I wouldn't be surprised if he hasn't already called for an appointment with my therapist.

I cry for the girl inside of me who just wants to be normal. Katie was being nice, and all I did was act like a spoilt brat. My door opens, and I glance up, preparing for my dad, but it's Katie.

She quietly closes it behind her, and I inhale sharply.

"I really am sorry," I promise, holding my hands up. "I will make it up to you. I promise."

"I know you are sorry," she promises. "And you have nothing to make up for."

"Please, I want privacy," I plead when she steps further into the room.

She drops down on the bed next to me and drops her hand to my knee. "Remember I told you about my mother?" she questions, and I try not to flinch at her touch.

"Yes," I whisper, unable to look away from where her hand is. I'm so scared she'll lash out. I know I'm overthinking it, but there's a voice in my head telling me to prepare for her nails to dig into my skin.

"Well, I never told you why she started it. You see, she had a friend who lived down the road from us. Tracey had a daughter a few years older than me, who would come around our house and play. Lindy loved being at ours and would find excuses to come over. I never understood it until we went to her house. She didn't smile or laugh there. She didn't behave the same and was always on edge," she reveals, and my gut knows where this is going. Before I can beg her to stop, she continues. "She never invited me to her room to play, no matter how much I begged. I asked every time I went, which was every other week. And back then, I was too curious for my own good. When their downstairs toilet broke, I was finally allowed upstairs to use the main bathroom." She pauses for a minute to take a breath. "I didn't go to the bathroom. Instead, I searched the two bedrooms to find hers. And do you know what I found?"

Riveted by her story, I find myself replying. "What did you find?"

"Her parents' room had a huge bed covered in the fluffiest blanket

I had ever seen. Half of it was filled with throw pillows and the rest of the room was just as warm. It had personality and it was theirs," she replies, and her gaze drops for a moment. "Lindy had a sponge mattress and a bucket in her room."

Tears gather in my eyes. "She had no toys?"

"Nothing. Not even a teddy bear," she admits. "Later that evening, I told my parents. They thought I was joking and scolded me for being nosey. My mum called Tracey to tell her, and I heard them laughing about it. I didn't understand what was so funny."

"What happened?"

"The next day, our street was filled with police cars and ambulances. Her parents had killed her."

Tears slip free. "I'm so sorry."

"I blamed myself for years afterwards. I should have been a better friend," she admits. "I should have seen that she was being beaten. She was nine when she died, and do you know what they said in the news?"

"What?"

"That she was lucky to survive as long as she did with all the trauma they found during her autopsy."

I feel sad for what she went through, but... "Why are you telling me this?"

She meets my gaze. "Because I know how it feels to not know who to trust. For a long time after her death, I was scared to tell my parents anything. It wasn't just them either. I couldn't open up to any adult because I was scared it would happen again. A part of me felt like she would still be alive if I had kept quiet, but it's not true. I'm not responsible for her parents' actions or for what happened to Lindy. Just like you aren't."

"What?" I breathe.

How? How does she know?

"I know something is going on," she replies unflinchingly. "I won't run to the police or downstairs to your father and repeat anything you tell me. But I want you to know I am here. I see you, and I'm listening. I will help you."

Tears stream down my cheeks and I grip my sheets like an anchor. For years, I've silently screamed at my dad to just look. To see what she's doing and stop it. I dreamed of him saving me, and when it never happened, I lost a part of my soul.

I want to tell her so desperately, but those words don't come. "I don't understand. Nothing is going on."

She meets my gaze. "Does your father hit you, Kayla?"

I want to laugh at her accusation but not because it's funny. But because in the past few weeks, everyone has immediately jumped to my abuser being my dad.

"No, my dad doesn't hurt me. He'd never lay a finger on me," I assure her.

"I need you to tell me if he is," she pushes.

And that is why she wants to know. I laugh, and the sound is disturbing. "He'd have to be around to hurt me, and he's not."

"Hey, I'm sorry if I've hurt your feelings but I want to help," she promises softly.

"No, you want to know if you're dating a child abuser, but rest assured, you aren't. You couldn't be more wrong," I snap, and my words cut through the air. "I'm sorry. I didn't mean it like that."

Her gaze softens. "No child, no matter who or their age, should suffer with abuse, Kayla. I'm asking because you show signs of it, and I don't believe it's in my head," she reveals. "Yes, your father has come to mean a lot to me, but it won't stop me from walking out of that door if he is the one hurting you. I know we don't know each other, but I will fight to protect you."

Relaxing at her words, I reply. "He's not abusing me. I promise. If he was, I would have warned you whilst we were alone." I glance away so she doesn't see the lie in my eyes when I say, "I've just been jumpy lately because of my past trauma and I let it get to me. I'm really sorry for worrying you."

"I believe you when you say it's not your father, but I will let it slide until you are ready to come to me. I won't make the same mistake I did all those years ago."

"Please, can we start over and forget about this?" I plead.

She stands and leans down to kiss my forehead. It's such a sweet gesture, my throat tightens. "I'll keep our conversation private, but I'm here whenever you are ready to talk."

She leaves, and I struggle to come to terms with everything she said. How is it that the one person who has known me my whole life is blind to everything, yet the people I've only just gotten to know can see the truth?

I drop down on the bed, sobbing into the pillow. Life is unfair and cruel, and if I continue down this path, I'm going to lose everyone. My dad probably hates me, and I don't know how to explain tonight to him without risking him sending me back to the therapist.

I don't know how long I'm crying for, but when the hallway light shines through the room, blinding me, I'm pulled back from my thoughts. A large silhouette is barricading the doorway, and I gasp in fright, until I see him.

"Myles," I choke out. He wastes no time in rushing over and climbing into bed with me. He pulls me into his arms, and I sob harder. With broken words, I explain everything that happened, from the beginning until the moment Katie left my room.

Myles remains silent, content in listening and comforting me.

CHAPTER
TWENTY-FOUR

KAYLA

A few more weeks have passed since the disastrous dinner. I made it up to both of them the day after and cooked them a Sunday roast. Myles stayed to eat, so it went a lot smoother.

She could have left Saturday or told my dad what we talked about, but she didn't. She stayed and asked him if there was anyone they could call for me. Which is why Myles came over.

Dad set some rules that night, which Myles told me about the next morning. He basically told Myles he wasn't allowed to sleep in my room if he wasn't in the house, and he didn't want me sleeping at Myles'. Myles appeased him, but straight up told me he was never going to do it.

I've not told Dad about us being a couple, but I think deep down, he knows.

I'm not completely out of the woods with Dad, and all isn't forgiven. Since the dinner, he has wanted to be involved with every aspect of my life. He's asked questions about school, my future, and about Myles and my friends. I've told him everything, and even let him know how Charlie has been doing. He was even surprised to find out I'm going to be a bridesmaid for Denny.

But it feels strange and almost suffocating because there are times it doesn't feel like a conversation between us. I feel like I'm being interrogated. But I won't complain since this is all I ever wanted.

My phone rings, and I excuse myself from the table. It's the weekend of Denny's bridal fittings, and we're all grabbing something to eat at the restaurant before we head back to the hotel. Originally, the plan was to travel up and spend the night, but then Denny decided we should all go up together and stay for two nights. As soon as the lads heard the plans, they decided to tag along. Which meant Denny arranged for Mason to go with the lads to get their suits.

"Dad," I whine. "You promised you wouldn't call to check in on me every hour."

Again, it's not the calls I mind, it's that sometimes I feel like he doesn't trust me.

He chuckles through the phone. "I know, and I hate to interrupt what you're doing, but I promise, it's not that kind of call."

"I left some meals in the fridge for you. You just need to heat them up," I remind him, since I know he isn't the best cook.

"It's not that either," he replies, and I can hear his amusement. "Bob from Leeds has called me. He needs me to go down and sort out his accounts before they shut him down. I'll be back by Monday night, but your mother has offered to stay the weekend with you."

Dread fills my stomach. I don't want her tainting our house any more than she already has. "Dad, I'm not going to be there, so she doesn't need to do that. Plus, even if I was, you've let me sleep at home by myself before."

"Well, that was before you had a major freak out and scared me half to death," he argues, and I hear a rustle over the phone. He groans, and I can picture him pinching the bridge of his nose. "Sorry. I'm just stressed."

"It's okay," I reply quietly. He's never snapped at me like that before.

"It's not. I've been a shit dad to you for years, Kayla. I know nothing I do now will make up for all those years I missed, but I want to try. I've not been doing a good job of that, and I want to do better. I want to be the dad you deserve."

I glance through the window of the restaurant to where all my friends are sitting. They are all laughing and joking, so I step out of view so they don't see my downcast expression.

"Dad, we're good, I promise. But please, don't bother Mum. Call her back and cancel. It seems pointless her staying at ours when I'm not there. I'm here until Sunday, and then I'm sleeping at Denny's."

I'm not technically going to be sleeping at Denny's. We'll probably go there, but I'm actually spending the night at Myles' home. We have the week off, so we want to spend as much time as we can together.

"I'll give her a call now and let her know," he gives in. "Be safe, and I'll call you when I get to Leeds. I'll see you Monday. If it changes, I'll message you."

"Alright. Love you, and hope you get everything sorted."

"I need to go," he announces, distracted. "I've got a call, but I'll speak to you later."

He abruptly ends the call. I sigh and go to head back in, when I bump into Myles. "Everything okay?" he asks.

"It was my dad. He has to go away for a few days and called to say he had Mum coming over to stay with me. I think he arranged it because of the reasons I gave him for why I don't want to go there."

"Your mum will be there?" he grits out.

"No, because I reminded him I'm not going to be there," I reply, and he relaxes, pulling me into his arms.

We haven't spoken much about what my mum does, and I'm grateful he doesn't pressure me about it. Knowing he is there if I need to talk about it makes me feel better.

"Does he know you'll be sleeping at mine?"

"No. He thinks I'll be at Denny's," I sheepishly admit. "I mean, she technically lives on the same property, so it's not like I'm completely lying."

"I love it when you're naughty," he teases, and bends down, capturing my lips in a kiss.

God, I'll never get tired of kissing him. Ever!

I pull back breathless. I notice my faint red lipstick has smudged across his lips, but before I can warn him or wipe it away, Joan's voice echoes through the open doors.

"That's it! You tell him," she yells, before chanting, "Dump that sad loser."

The sweet little lady doesn't look so sweet as guests watch on, shocked. Myles grabs my hand and pulls me back into the restaurant. I thought for sure she was shouting at the couple leaving the restaurant, but her attention is actually focussed on the diners a few tables over.

"Grams," Harlow hisses, before forcing a smile to the couple. "I'm sorry."

The girl at the table, however, stands, nodding to the chant Joan is still bellowing.

"You're right, old lady," the woman calls out, grabbing her bright pink blazer from the chair. "I'm dumping this loser's arse. He slept with my mother, and my sister, you know."

Myles and I take our seats as she spills red wine all over her bloke's head. My eyes widen whilst the others laugh.

The boyfriend stands, ready to argue, but a dollop of green sauce hits him between the eyes. And it wasn't the girlfriend who threw it.

"Grams, don't throw food," Harlow scolds. "You're going to get us kicked out."

"No one is going to throw us out. Us sisters have to stick together, you hear me? Oi, you, the one who needs to make sure he washed his dick after fucking your mum and sister... I ain't no old lady. I've got more stamina in me than most of you young folk," Joan announces. Whilst our table erupts in groans and protests, other guests laugh.

"Oh my god," the girl protests, looking a little green. She slaps her boyfriend around the face. "You better have washed. I don't want their DNA inside of me."

Myles groans. "She already shares it."

Her boyfriend holds up his hands, his expression pleading. "It didn't mean anything. I thought she was you."

The girlfriend's blonde hair whips over her shoulder as she glances at the door. "Oi, Mum, Sandra, come 'ere."

Oh no!

The two newcomers still when they notice everyone is watching them, but then slowly make their way over.

Two waiters come to intervene, but the manager we met earlier pulls them back by their shirts and shakes his head. He grins, leaning against the bar to watch the entertainment.

"Old lady, do you think she could be mistaken for me?" the girl-friend asks, pointing to the younger of the two. Neither look alike. One has blonde hair, and the other dyed red hair. Both are scrawny looking, but the blonde has more depth to her features. She reminds me of a chav version of Elle Woods. The other looks more like the stepsister from Cinderella—the one with Chad Michael Murray.

Joan curls her lip up at being called old again. "I hope you get diseases," she confesses.

"What's this about, Casey?" the older lady demands.

"I'll get to you next," Casey snaps, and notices her boyfriend is about to bolt. "Dave, don't even think about it."

"What is going on?" the younger girl asks, smacking her lips around some gum.

"Do we look different?" Casey asks, and again, her question is directed at Joan.

"Don't get involved," Harlow warns.

"God yes. Stop letting him distract you," Joan snaps, before glaring at Dave. "What excuse do you have for fucking the mum? Wanted to keep it in the family?"

"Oh God," the young girl gulps.

"You're not *Jeremy Kyle*," Harlow hisses, but Joan shrugs it off.

I would feel bad for watching it play out, but when I look around, I see everyone else is too. I go to see what they are doing, when suddenly, her mum and sister have soup dripping down their faces. Casey slams the two bowls back down on the table, where she stole them from.

"Girl, you should think about getting your nan her own TV show,"

Casey suggests, before making her way out with her head held high. A man dining on his own stands and whispers something to her that makes her laugh. She takes his hand, and together, they leave.

The second the door shuts, I swear I hear every head turn to watch the three who are left standing.

"So... I guess now isn't the time to tell you I'm pregnant?" the mother announces.

My jaw drops as they slowly exit, leaving Dave standing there, utterly confused. It's seconds later that he races after them and the restaurant erupts with laughter and chatter.

"What the hell was that?" I whisper, still not really understanding.

"That, my dear, is London. Full of drama," Joan cackles before taking a sip of her martini.

Myles nudges me with his shoulder. "I've got a surprise for you after. You up for it, or are you tired?"

"As long as it's not skating," I tease.

"Bro, why the fuck are you wearing lipstick?" Max shouts across the table.

I freeze for a second before laughing. I forgot to tell Myles about the lipstick, and it's stained his lips. He holds up his phone, scrubbing his lips with the back of his hand. When it doesn't wipe away, he begins to panic.

As the table begins to tease him and make commentary on what just happened, I feel undeniably happy. So much so, I could burst from it. I love each and every one of them, and I'm proud they made me a part of their family.

Maverick meets my gaze, and he gives me a subtle nod. He knows where my thoughts are, and I feel so grateful. Because he gave me this too. I smile briefly before Myles pulls my attention away, and I enjoy the rest of the meal.

CHAPTER
TWENTY-FIVE

KAYLA

When I see the surprise, I jump up and down with glee. I thought for sure we were going to the theatre, or maybe to even do some sight-seeing. I never expected that he'd join the queue to go up on the London Eye.

"Oh my god, I can't believe we're going on the London Eye," I gush.

I don't care if people are watching. I have wanted to go on this for years but never found the courage or chance to go.

"You're excited then?" he teases, and I throw myself into his arms, squeezing him tight.

"More than. This is amazing," I declare.

He brushes my red locks away from my face and palms my cheeks. "I'm glad," he replies, then leans in, capturing my lips with his.

I'm breathless when I pull back, and the look in his eye leaves me wanting more. All of this is new to me. Him, us, and this happiness I want to scream to the world about.

"Thank you," I whisper against his lips, kissing him once more before we move forward in the queue.

The place is lit up with so many lights. They change colour from blue to red to pink and so on. It's magical.

It's not long before we're directed into a room, where they stand us in front of a green screen. "What's going on?"

"It will show one of the capsules in the print," the photographer explains.

Myles pulls me flush against his chest and folds his hands over my stomach. I smile wide when I feel his lips on my cheek.

The flash of the camera blinds us, and the worker points us to the exit. I thought we'd have to wait in the queue until the ride, but they direct us into a room where there's a 4D cinema.

Myles gets a few calls and text messages when we're in there, but he presses ignore before clicking his phone on silent.

"That was amazing," I laugh, touching the wet strands that have curled my hair.

"You look beautiful," he promises, tugging my hand away.

Then we notice people queuing at a booth. We make our way over and notice our photo up on the screen.

My lips part at the sight of it. We look so happy and in love. I'm not sure if he feels the same way, but I know with all my heart that I will never love anyone as much as I love him. And I do love him. I love the way he makes me feel when we're together, but more, I love us. I love our friendship, I love our bond, and I love how strong it feels.

But that isn't what has me choking up. It's me. Every time I look in the mirror, I'm revolted by the girl who stares back at me. But seeing me up there, smiling in the arms of the only person I've ever loved like this, I don't feel like I did before. I feel vibrant, alive, and free of all the evil in the world.

I want to keep that moment with me for the rest of my life. I step forward, wanting a copy, but Myles beats me to it.

"I'll take two of number one-zero-nine please," he orders, handing over a twenty.

"I could have gotten them," I point out. "You got the tickets and dinner."

"This is my treat. I love seeing you happy, so it's worth it to me," he declares. "Let me do this."

I lean up on my toes and kiss the corner of his mouth. I pull back a little, meeting his gaze. "You really know how to sweet talk me."

"And only you," he admits, before taking the photos. He keeps the bag as we walk up to the gates, the queue getting smaller and smaller by the minute.

We walk onto a passenger capsule, and I feel giddy with excitement. I also feel nervous about going up so high. When I see the view, I rush to the far end of the capsule and look out at the water. The doors close, and we're left in a capsule with six or seven other people. The ride ascends and everyone begins to take photos. I only spare them another glance before my gaze reverts to the view.

"It's beautiful," I whisper.

Myles crowds in behind me, resting his chin on my shoulder. "So are you."

It's not long before we're at the top, and the ride stops to give us all time to appreciate the view. The Houses of Parliament lights up gold, and I take in all the streetlights and sigh. It's more beautiful than I ever imagined. It's perfect.

"This view is incredible. It's bizarre to think all those lights belong to people. There are people living a life that we aren't a part of. It reminds me of how big the world is and how much we're yet to see."

"As long as I see it with you, I don't care," he admits, rubbing slow circles on my hip bone.

I turn in his arms until my back is against the bar running around the glass. I run my arms up his shoulders until I lock them around his neck. I meet his gaze, and unable to keep what I'm feeling inside, I blurt out, "I love you."

I don't expect to hear it back, but when I do, tears well up in my eyes. "I love you too."

"Y-you do?" I stammer out.

His lips brush along mine, but he doesn't move to kiss me. "Yes. I never knew you could love someone this much, but I do. You are the first thing I think about when I wake up, and the last thing before I go to bed. You consume me in the best possible way," he whispers. "I love you, Kayla. I love you so much."

The tips of my fingers press into the nape of his neck, and he leans down, kissing me. His grip at my waist tightens as he pulls me against him. I can feel his arousal against my stomach, but instead of being freaked out by it, it makes me feel wanted.

He loves me.

And there's no doubt in my mind that he does.

I never thought anyone would love me, not after what happened to me, but it was my own trauma telling me that.

I kiss him until I lose sense of time and coherent thought.

A cough interrupts us, and I notice the capsule has stopped moving. I pull back and see a staff member waiting by the door.

"It's time to get off," he orders, then groans when Myles arches an eyebrow at him. "Not that kind."

I duck my head as we pass him, never once letting go of Myles' hand. I'm not even disappointed we didn't get to take photos or enjoy more of the view, because hearing him tell me he loves me was worth it.

Myles swings me around once we've exited. "Do you want to get some snacks before we head back?"

"Yes," I agree, but right now, I'd agree to anything.

Because I feel deliriously happy.

———

Back at the hotel, we're lying down on the double bed, watching a movie on the laptop in front of us. The TV in the room doesn't have an HDMI lead, or even a DVD player built in, so it's a good thing Myles thought to bring his laptop.

We're halfway through watching Bridesmaids—the irony of it isn't lost on me—when I move for the millionth time.

There's an ache between my legs, and nothing I do eases it. It got worse when Myles stripped down before getting into bed. But now, it's getting uncomfortable.

"Are you sure you're okay?" Myles rumbles, and his voice hits straight to my core.

"Yeah," I reply, but the ache begins to pulse. I clench my thighs together, but it doesn't help.

"Kayla?" he calls softly, gaining my attention. He's watching me with half-mast eyes and a soft expression. "Are you turned on?"

He flips the laptop closed, moving it to the side table. He lies on his side, glancing down at me.

"Hey! It was getting to a good bit," I lie, not wanting him to know that I think I am.

He flicks his tongue out to wet his bottom lip. "Can I touch you?"

My chest rises and falls heavily. "Yes," I rasp.

His finger lightly runs down my cheek, and I close my eyes, enjoying the sensation. His breath tickles my lips for a second before he presses his mouth against mine. My hand automatically reaches for him, landing on his strong, hard chest.

His touch trails down my side, and I begin to burn all over when he reaches under my shirt. I giggle when he gets to my side. "That tickles," I whisper.

"It does?" he questions, then kisses below my ear, and my laughter dies away.

I'm taken off guard by the sensations gliding through my body. It's overwhelming as much as it is exhilarating.

His fingertips run along the pull string of my shorts, and he glances up. "What do you want?"

"I want you to touch me," I reply, and my body shakes with vulnerability.

I want him so badly, it hurts. But I don't know how to describe what I need.

"You're killing me," he growls.

I sit up and pull my T-shirt off, shaking the entire time. I took off my bra when I got changed, and never put it back on.

My lip trembles as I lie back down, watching him. His pupils darken. "I don't know what to do. I'm worried it might be too much."

I feel so innocent when I take his hand and place it over my boob.

"I'm not ready to have sex, but I'm ready for more. I want to do this, but I don't know what to do."

He is the only person I'm comfortable talking about this to. I can feel the heat in my cheeks, but it's the topic and the thought of him rejecting me.

"We can wait," he promises. "We don't have to do anything."

And that's when a thought occurs to me. "If you're not ready, we can wait," I state, grabbing my T-shirt.

He pulls it away, looking pained. "I'm always ready," he admits. "I just want to make sure this feels good for you."

"Everything you do feels good," I promise.

"If at any point, you want me to stop or slow down, just tell me. We won't have sex, but I'm going to make you feel so good," he declares, lifting up on his elbows.

His fingers run along the seam of my shorts, and my cleavage bounces when I shudder. His touch is torture, but he keeps it light, teasing, before bringing his lips down to mine. I moan into his mouth as he lightly runs his fingers into my shorts.

He rubs me over my knickers, and I pull back breathlessly, "I want to make you feel good too."

He growls low in his throat. "In a minute."

Everything after feels like a dream when he continues to rub my clit in small circles. My chest bows out and he leans down, capturing my nipple into his mouth. He sucks, licks, and nips, driving me wild.

He sits up and moves between my legs. His gaze never leaves mine. "Can I remove them?"

"Yes," I answer breathlessly.

Not once averting his gaze, he pulls my shorts from my body. I focus on him and nothing else, wanting to enjoy every minute. He discards the shorts and is gentle when he begins to explore my sex.

I stiffen at his touch, but when he presses his thumb over my clit, I relax, loving the sensation it causes. He's gentle, loving, and he makes me feel at ease every time he changes his movements.

Panting and wanting more, I say, "Please, let me make you feel good too."

I don't know whether it's the pleasure or just us, but I reach over, touching the outline of his erection through his boxers. I can't help but admire his six pack when he flexes.

He groans, dropping his head back. "Fuck!"

I snap my hand away. "Did I do it wrong?"

"Touch me," he demands, and takes my wrist, guiding my hand to his dick.

I do, gently squeezing it in my hand. "Take your boxers off," I rasp.

He moves, taking them off, before kneeling between my legs. I'm so nervous, but at the same time, want to do this so badly. He's large, thick, and the tip is bulging red when I touch him. I swallow thickly, scared at the thought of that one day being inside me.

"Remember, any time you want to stop, just say the word and we'll stop," he reminds me, his voice deep.

He places his hand over mine, guiding me on what to do. "Now move up and down like this," he orders, and I grow wetter when I see how much he's enjoying it.

After a few seconds of getting into a rhythm, and Myles showing me how he likes it, he moves his hands from over mine.

"I'm not going to penetrate you, but I want to try something. Is that okay?" he asks.

"Yes," I agree, trusting he'd never hurt me.

He holds his dick in his hand, mirroring the movement he just taught me, but this time, he presses the tip against my clit.

The warmth, and the feel of his pre-cum mixing with my own desire, has me falling back against the pillows, moaning in pleasure.

"Is that okay?" he whispers.

"God, yes!" I breathe out, thrusting up to meet his erection. It feels so good.

He doesn't move to go further, but he does massage the tip against my clit whilst jacking off. "Fuck!" he growls, pumping his fist fast.

My tits bounce with each move, and I grip the bedsheets on either side of me, tilting my head.

Faster and faster, he sets my body alight. I clench my eyes shut, crying out when my orgasm hits me.

Seconds later, warm liquid spurts all over my sex, where I'm still sensitive.

I pant through the aftermath of my orgasm, feeling sated now that the dull ache has gone. I meet his gaze, an overwhelming sensation taking over.

"Did I go too far?" he panics.

"No," I rush to explain. "You touched me. I touched you. And I didn't freak out."

"You shouldn't be sad after that," he teases, trying to lighten the mood.

I meet his gaze. "I never thought I would have that."

"Baby," he rasps, and lifts me into his arms until I'm straddling him, not caring that he's getting cum all over him. He brushes my hair back. "I love you."

I meet his gaze, melting at the love he is showing me. "I love you too. Thank you for giving me something so beautiful."

He runs a finger along my cheek. "You're beautiful."

I hold him, not wanting to let go. I've spent countless nights awake because of nightmares, but in this moment, he gave me so much to dream about.

CHAPTER
TWENTY-SIX

KAYLA

I've had a permanent smile on my face all morning because of last night. Myles loves me, and nothing will ever feel as good as I do right now. I just wish he wasn't leaving to go for his suit fitting appointment.

We make our way to the entrance of Flora's Boutique, and Denny stops at the doors, letting out a dreamy sigh. "How is it I feel this much joy and excitement, but feel so nervous too?"

"Because the dress makes it real," Mary, her nan, explains, and pushes her through the door.

This place is huge, and not what I had in mind when she said boutique. There are racks of dresses everywhere, but it still has that intimate, warm feeling.

I gape at the lady not much younger than Mary, who steps out from behind a curtain with a measuring tape hung around her neck like a piece of jewellery.

This is Flora. And to match her name, she has on a white floral suit, with the skirt falling to her knees. Her white hair is perfectly styled in a low bun at the nape of her neck.

"Mary, darling," Flora coos, wrapping Mary up in her arms.

"It's so good to see you, Flora. You're looking fab-oh-lous," Mary gushes, kissing each of Flora's cheeks.

"So do you," Flora compliments, before diverting her attention to the rest of us. "Now, which one of you beautiful ladies is Denny?"

When Denny doesn't move, awestruck by the designer, Harlow shoves her forward. "This is Denny."

Flora beams and begins to size Denny up. I can see her mind already designing. "My god, aren't you a walking beauty. I have just the dress." She glances to the other side of the room, ordering, "Charlotte, can you take Miss Denny here to section five, and get refreshments for her guests?"

The girl in question looks overworked and stressed but doesn't complain as she does as she's asked. She's wearing a similar suit to Flora's but in a dark shade of blue.

"Yes, Flora."

We follow Denny up the stairs that are decorated with bridal flowers. The place is beautifully decorated. The gowns look expensive, but after seeing a few, I can tell they're worth it.

When we get to the top of the stairs, I gaze around the room. In front of us is a half-circle love seat that faces a row of cubicles covered in white and blush curtains.

"Please, take a seat," Charlotte orders, before escaping into a room in the corner.

"What is that for?" Harlow asks, pointing to the stand in the centre of the room.

"That's where the brides stand when they're showing their dresses off," I explain, keeping my voice low like hers.

I don't know why, but I feel like we need to be quiet, like we're in a library. The place is so quiet; the only noise is the light music playing in the background. This is a setting I could become too relaxed in, and easily fall asleep. Which I hope I don't do.

A clanging noise to my right startles me, and I follow the direction the sound came from. Flora walks out of a lift with a rack full of bridal dresses.

"That damn lift is going to be the death of me," she mutters before addressing Mary. "I had workers come in to take a look at it. They told me it was normal and just rusty. Did that sound fine to you?"

Mary snorts. "You haven't changed. You still stress over everything," Mary teases. "Why don't I introduce you to everyone. This is Joan."

"I've heard a lot about you," Flora teases.

"Whatever she said is most likely all true too," Joan cackles back.

"Me and you are going to be best friends then," Flora remarks with a mischievous grin.

Mary rolls her eyes and continues. "This is Harlow, Denny's maid of honour. And this tiny one here is Kayla, her other bridesmaid."

"Hey," Harlow greets with a wave.

"It's so nice to meet you," I breathe out, still star struck.

Flora taps her chin, frowning. "Good lord, your dresses are going to be a pain to pick."

"Why?" Mary demands, her gaze snapping to us. "What's wrong?"

"Have you seen their chests?" Flora asks, and I quickly cover mine with my jacket. "They'll either have cleavage that will have everyone's attention on them and not the bride, or a dress that they'll never breathe in to cover them up."

My voice shakes as I reply. "I don't want people staring at me or my cleavage," I declare, uncaring about the attention it's bringing me. I will wear a lot of things, but I can't do that.

I can't.

The thought of people watching me with desire...

Oh God, I'm going to be sick.

Joan places her hand on my back. "Baby girl, don't worry about it. We will sort it."

"I'm sorry. I don't mean to make this difficult," I announce, and notice Mary giving Flora a look. Flora, clearly knowing what it means, nods.

"I'm rich for a reason. I'll make you look beautiful," Flora promises, and gazes at Denny. "You, my girl, need a glass of champagne."

As if it was magically conjured, Charlotte walks out carrying a

silver serving tray. On top is a bucket with two bottles of champagne
and a bowl of strawberries. On another tray are some champagne
glasses.

"If you don't want to drink alcohol, then please, help yourselves to
something else or ask Charlotte. It's all in the kitchenette room where
Charlotte just came from."

Harlow and I are both old enough to drink, so when we're handed
our glasses, we take them. Although, I don't plan to drink mine.

Mary stands, holding up her glass. "To Denny. May she find the
wedding dress of her dreams, and lingerie that will have Mason
bursting in his pants," she toasts.

Without thinking, I take a sip of the champagne, the sweet, bubbly
taste filling my tastebuds. I cough at the taste and put the glass down
on the table in front of me.

"Now, you, let's try this dress on. We'll save the one your nan said
you liked until last," Flora orders, and grabs one of the dresses hidden
in the protective bags. She ushers Denny into the biggest cubicle,
which is centre in the row. "Strip down to your knickers and then call
me when you're done."

And that's how it goes for the next few hours. Denny tries on a
dress, and then comes out and stands on the podium, getting our
opinion.

By the time she is on the last one, the dress she liked in the
pictures, we've only all agreed on one other dress.

"I'm ready," Denny whispers, and knowing this is the last one,
we're all off our seats.

Denny steps out, and we all inhale sharply. This is the dress for
sure. The princess-cut, sweetheart neckline, strapless dress is tight
around her bust, enhancing her cleavage. The natural fitting waist has
crystal and diamond beading, and to finish it, she has a greyish/silver
ribbon tied snug around her waist. The dress flares down in layers to
the floor. I've never seen anything so elegant or fairy-tale-like. It has a
beautiful cathedral train.

Mary, who has cried at each reveal, cries harder. Denny's eyes
water at our reaction as she stands on the podium.

"You look so beautiful," Mary cries, dabbing her cheeks.

Joan clears her throat, her expression soft. "Utterly breath-taking."

Harlow, though, she drinks. "You look seriously hot."

"You look prettier than a fairy princess," I add, overwhelmed by her beauty.

"This is the one," Denny whispers, and turns to look in the floor-length mirror. Mason is going to be knocked off his feet over the dress, never mind the matching lingerie I saw Flora telling her about.

Mary asks her to do a twirl, and from the back, it's just as beautiful. The ribbon around her waist has been tied up in a bow, but the back of her dress is laced up like a corset.

"I love it," Denny gushes.

"We have to make a few alterations, but nothing that will take much time. You will need to come back for one more fitting, but that's it," Flora advises. "Now, what colour bridesmaid dresses are you going for? I'd recommend the dark grey unless you want to change out the ribbon around your waist."

"Can we see them?" Denny asks.

"Yes, let me go grab them. Is it just one maid of honour and one bridesmaid?"

"Yes, and then a flower dress for my daughter, Hope."

"Denny, you look beautiful," Mary gushes, wiping her eyes as she goes to stand next to her granddaughter.

"You really do look like a princess," I point out, taking a sip of the water I grabbed earlier. Harlow agrees, before continuing to type on her phone.

"I hope you're not texting that boy of yours?" Mary scolds Harlow.

Harlow's face turns red. She glances up from her phone like she's being caught red-handed. "Why?"

"Because it's bad luck."

"To text my boyfriend to see how the suit shopping is going?" she asks, frowning.

Joan cackles, and I slyly take the nearly empty bottle of champagne away from her. Harlow took a sip of her drink then left it the same as me, but it didn't stop Mary and Joan from finishing our glasses, and then the bottle, stating 'waste not, want not.'

"Oh, I thought you were spying for Mason. I know he's desperate to see this one in her dress," Mary explains, three sheets to the wind. "Just don't take pictures."

"Here we are," Flora calls out, and I swear, she isn't wrong about the lift. It's been getting louder with each use. "Before we get you changed, just check out the colour for these dresses."

"I love it," Denny promises.

"This one is for Kayla. The strap goes over one shoulder and ruffles a little over the chest. It's elegant, but not too much, and it won't show off any cleavage. Because of how much is going on with the dress, I would wear your hair up, away from your face," Flora states, before holding up another. "This one is a darker tone, which will make you stand out as maid of honour. It shows off your cleavage, but with a necklace and your hair up, it will look stunning. Or, I have this picture and you could both wear your hair like this."

We lean in to see the picture, and it's of a girl wearing a dress like the one she picked for Harlow. Her hair is plaited in a loose braid, before falling into a messy bun behind her ear. It has strands of curls coming from the bun and they've added some accessories.

"It's beautiful," I comment.

"This is everything I wanted for them," Denny breathes. "Thank you, Flora. Thank you so much."

"It's my job, dear. Now go with Charlotte and get out of the dress whilst we help the girls into their dresses," she orders, before turning to Charlotte. "When you're done, come back in and help Harlow into her dress."

"Okay," Charlotte agrees.

I follow Flora to another cubicle, where she hangs the dress up on the hanger. "Call me when you're done, and I'll come in and tie the dress up."

She closes the curtain, and I begin to undress. I'm in my underwear with the dress over my head, when I get it stuck in my hair.

Worried I'll rip the dress, but more concerned about what they'll see if I ask for help, I want to cry. And the more I fail to get it off, the closer I am to passing out.

"Are you okay? Do you need help?" Flora calls through the curtain.

"No," I cry out, panting heavily. "I just need a minute."

"I can get one of your friends if you prefer," she offers.

But that's even worse. They'll never look at me the same when they see the scars.

Knowing what I need to do, I take a breath. "I'm stuck. Can you please help me, but make sure no one else sees or comes in?" I whisper.

Seconds later, the curtain is pulled open, but only enough for her to slip inside. My back is to the mirror behind me, and I know she can see my scars in the reflection.

Her eyes widen a fraction, but she brushes it aside and quickly helps me untangle the dress from my hair. It rolls down my body effortlessly but is gaping open at the back.

She inhales sharply, and I clench my eyes closed, unable to see her expression.

Her cold fingers touch the small of my back as she tugs the zipper up. Once she's done, she turns me to face her, and sadness looks back at me. "I don't know your story, and I won't ask, but never be ashamed. You should carry those scars with strength, because whatever happened to you to get them, you survived it. Not many people can move on from that kind of pain," she reveals, and a tear runs down my cheek. She swipes it away, smiling at me. "You wipe those tears, hold your shoulders back, and enjoy today."

"Thank you. No one has seen them, so please don't mention it," I plead quietly.

"Kayla, come on; what's taking you so long?" Denny calls.

Flora's eyes crinkle in the corners. "Impatient bride," she teases, before raising her voice. "Just a minute."

She begins to mess with the sides, pinning it in places, before working on the front. She works for a few minutes, adding pins here and there, before finally stepping back with a nod of approval.

"Come on, let's not keep her waiting," she orders, and pulls back the curtain.

Everyone stands at my entrance, but it's Denny I'm watching. She takes one look at me and cries.

"Do I look that bad?" I tease, rubbing a hand over the smooth dress.

She shakes her head and snatches the tissue Joan offers. "You look so freaking beautiful, it hurts," she assures me. "I'm so blissfully happy. I get to spend the rest of my life with the man of my dreams, and I get to share our special day with all of my family and friends. I'm glad I let Mason talk me into doing all this properly because I would have missed doing all of this."

"Let me guess, you thought if you didn't hurry up and get married, he'd change his mind," Mary guesses.

"Partly," she confirms. "But really, I just didn't want to waste time doing all of this. I just want him. I don't care how we do it as long as we do."

"That boy isn't going anywhere," Joan promises.

Harlow steps out from behind the curtain and twirls. Joan whistles, and I understand. Harlow looks like a Greek goddess in her dress.

"If you say no to this dress, I might just buy it anyway," Harlow announces, then notices me. Her eyes widen as a slow grin spreads across her face. "Myles is going die when he sees you. You look beautiful."

"And she's blushing," Denny jokes.

"Stop," I scold through laughter.

"I don't usually do this, but for you, girl, I will," Flora announces, addressing me. "Where's your phone?"

I point to the table where I left it after Dad messaged to check up on me. She takes a few photos, glancing at me with a smile.

When she doesn't immediately hand it over, I bite my lip, wondering what she is doing. "What did you just do?"

"Love is good for the soul. And to keep it going, you have to tease a little," she declares. "I sent your boyfriend a picture but only revealed a little bit of the dress."

I step down off the podium and take my phone, when suddenly, everyone's phones begin to ping.

Denny snorts. "Mason texted me. He would love a photo too, but only if it's what I'm wearing under my dress."

Harlow reads hers next. "Malik put, 'Why the fuck is Myles getting pictures but I'm getting left in the dark? Take a selfie for me; I want to see you in a dress again. And the dress better not show your tits off. There's only so many times I can hit Max before he's brain damaged for life.'"

"Oh, he won't have to worry about Max much longer. Soon, the roles will be reversed and the others can get their payback," Joan declares.

Denny looks at me. "What did Myles say?"

I glance down at the screen, my heart melting at his words. "He said…" I clear my throat, which is choked up with emotion. "He said: 'I can't wait for the day I get to watch you walk down the aisle in a white dress. You take my breath away. You look absolutely beautiful.'"

He can't even see all of me and he said all those things to me. The others awe at his sweetness, and Joan remarks about needing to save for another wedding.

I'm still stuck on him wanting to marry me.

We aren't there yet, but it isn't a far-fetched notion. I can't imagine marrying anyone else or growing old with them. It's him. And it will always be him.

"Right, girls, get back in the changing rooms and get those dresses off," Flora orders. "We have one more to try on."

"Last dress?" Joan asks, but no one answers since Denny has moved closer to her nan.

"Nan, I know the traditional arrangement is to have a mother of the bride, but I don't have that or want it."

"I should hope not," Mary retorts.

"No, because I have something better. I have you, and I want you to be there at the front, watching me share my vows. You raised me to be the woman I am today, and without you, I would have felt so alone.

You have loved me for all of my life, and I want you to be my nan of the bride," she declares.

Mary, finally understanding, takes Denny in her arms and weeps. She pulls back, dabbing at her eyes with the tissue Joan throws at her. I can see how much the gesture means to her. "But I've already bought a dress."

"You can save it for Harlow's or Kayla's wedding, since Myles is already picturing it," she teases. "Or Hope's christening."

"Well then; how can I say no to that?" she replies, before turning to Flora, smacking her hands over her boobs. "I need to get me a young man, so push these beasts up."

Laughter echoes off the walls, but Denny groans. "Nan!"

"What?" Mary remarks, sniffing. "I need me a man who can go all night, and I can't get me one of those unless my beauties are standing upright and not hanging around down south."

We all crack up, and Flora agrees, amused with the comment.

Before we head into the cubicles, Denny walks over to us, taking our hands. "This has been the perfect weekend. Thank you so much for sharing this day with me," she blubbers.

"Stop before you make me cry," Harlow scolds, but it's too late. Tears are pooling in her eyes.

I lean into Denny. "Thank you for letting me be a part of this."

I want to describe what it means to me, but there are no words to express that without sounding weird.

Only one other person has ever made me feel included like this, and she couldn't be here today.

And that's Charlie.

CHAPTER
TWENTY-SEVEN

KAYLA

M yles walks me to my door, our long weekend unfortunately over. I've had such a blast with them all, but nothing beats the time Myles and I shared.

We didn't do anything intimate like we did our first night there, and I think for the most part, that was because of me. I don't want to run before I can walk, and Myles respects me enough to keep things slow.

I can't wait to see Charlie and tell her all about it. I've missed seeing her this weekend, but I will fix that once her mum gives me the okay to go over again.

The house is filled with darkness, which means my dad isn't back yet. My battery died last night, and since Myles and I don't share the same phone, I've not managed to charge it.

"Will I see you tomorrow?" I ask, wishing we didn't have to part.

"I can't tomorrow. I have to go to that college interview, and then my granddad wants to take us out for lunch. I can't cancel because he made a point to arrange it so none of us would. We've not spent much time together recently."

"I understand. We have the week off so we can arrange something for Wednesday."

"It's a date," he promises, then leans in to capture my lips. "I'm going to miss you so much."

I wrap my arms around him, not wanting to let him go. "I'll miss you too," I promise. "I love you."

He kisses me breathless, and I'm about to beg him to stay when Maverick honks the horn. I laugh at the put-out look Myles gives me. "I love you too and wish I didn't have to go."

"I hear distance makes the heart grow fonder," I soothe, running the tip of my finger along his collarbone.

"Let's not test that theory," he quips. "I won't be able to handle being away from you."

"I'll message you all the time," I promise.

"You'd better," he orders, kissing me once more.

Maverick honks the horn again, letting it bellow longer. "You'd better go before he drags you away."

"I don't know why I can't move," he whispers against my lips. "I just have this feeling that I should be with you."

"That's the testosterone speaking," I tease. "Go. Maverick is unclipping his belt."

"I'll see you Wednesday," he declares.

"Wednesday," I repeat, then watch him leave.

"Love you," he yells when he reaches the door.

"Love you too," Maverick replies.

I laugh when Myles begins to argue with him. It's only when they pull away that I reach for my keys and let myself in.

It feels weird being alone, since I've had so much company over the weekend. And they're all out-going people, but in a good way.

I flip the light on, and a pan swings in my direction. I never expected it. I didn't see it until it was too late. My scream is cut off as I fall to the ground, bathed in darkness.

———

y head drops to the frame of the bed, where my hands are tied. I fought back, and I fought hard to escape when I woke up from being knocked out. But it was no use. She was stronger, faster, and didn't care that she was hurting me. I cared. I don't find pleasure in hurting someone else.

The first time I tried to escape, she beat me with the trophy I won in year four at a talent show, then tied me to my bed.

I have no idea how long I have been here. It could be days or hours, even though it feels like weeks. It's all been a blur.

I'm not only physically weak, but mentally too. She has screamed, yelled, and called me everything under the sun whilst she hurt me. They are words that will stay with me forever.

My head stopped bleeding not long ago, but my lip hasn't. My hands lay limp beside me, which is why I haven't attempted to escape again. It hurts too much, just like the other injuries to my body. My only reprieve from her torture is when I pass out. I'm not sure if it's from the pain or from not being given food or water. But each time she hurts me, I pray I pass out.

I hear the front door open then close, and my heart races at hearing she's back. I gave up on my dad coming to help, and I want to try and get her to talk again, which hasn't been easy. Every time I've opened my mouth, she has hit me again, her anger fuelled by some unknown force.

My bedroom door slams into the wall as she enters. It's still weird to see her so unkept and dishevelled. "Dad is going to be home," I announce, pained.

She kneels down in front of me. "He isn't back until Friday," she spits out. "If you answered your phone, you would have known that."

"Why? Why are you doing this?" I plead.

"Because I can."

"I'm your daughter," I cry. "What did I ever do to you?"

"You were born," she screeches, and spit lands on my face. "I planned to get an abortion as soon as we were married, but then things happened, and I knew that if it wasn't for you, he would leave. I would have lost my home, my money, and my life if he did that. So I had you, and you know what he did? He left me to raise you until you went off to school. He worked all the damn time, and I got stuck with a baby who whined."

Evil stares back at me. "I didn't ask for this."

Not hearing me, she continues to rant. "He owes me," she barks. "He thinks because you've stopped coming on the weekends that he can stop my money? I don't think so. If he doesn't give it to me, then you will."

"This is about money?"

Her hand snaps back before she swings, smacking me around the cheek. I cry out, the binds tying my hands cutting into my skin.

"It's always been about money," she snaps. "The only enjoyment I get out of you is when I hit you. It makes putting up with you for years, worth it. You are weak."

"Then take everything. Take it and leave, and let me go free."

She stands, pulling out a ring. I remember the ring from the photos that used to hang in the living room. It's her wedding ring. "He thought he could take this from me in the divorce. It's been in his family for generations and is worth a pretty penny. I knew I couldn't fight him since he put it in our prenup, but I've been waiting for this moment to get it back."

"You have what you want, so please, leave," I beg, not sure how much longer I can take this.

She kicks her leg out, before booting me in the side, the tip of her boot digging into my armpit. "I'm not going anywhere until I'm sure you've learnt your lesson. Things are going to change, and you will do as you're told."

"What do you want?" I cry, as she kicks me over and over, laughing whilst she does.

"I want everything he gives you. I know you have an inheritance coming, and you will be giving it to me. You'll come on weekends again, and during the times you aren't with me, you will get your dad to send me money. I don't care if he has a new girlfriend who thinks her shit doesn't stink. He owes me."

I clench my jaw as she grips my broken wrist. I meet her gaze unwaveringly. "I'm not doing anything for you. Someone will find me. They will come, and I will tell them everything."

She grips my cheeks, squeezing until I meet her gaze. "Who will you tell? Your dad? Because I'll make him believe your pretty little boyfriend did this to you," she warns. My eyes widen at the mention of Myles. She grins at my discomfort. "Yes, I know about the boyfriend. I'm surprised you haven't cried rape."

"Leave him out of it," I demand, swallowing down bile when she grins.

"I will if you follow the rules," she replies, curling her lip up. "If you don't, I will make sure everyone thinks you cried rape a second time, and take him down with you. I will have everyone believing he rapes and beats you. By the time I'm done, he won't even be able to look at you."

"No one would ever believe that," I spit out. "And he loves me."

She throws her head back, laughing maniacally. "Then where is he?" she goads maliciously. "'Cause he isn't here."

"He will come," I declare.

She leans into me, meeting my gaze. "No one is coming for you. Don't you get it? No one loves you. You are a weak little girl who everyone feels sorry for. It's not love. It's pity."

"You don't know what we feel."

"I'm your mother, and I can't stand the sight of you," she spits out.

"And how do you plan to explain my injuries to Dad when he sees me?"

She snorts. "You think he'll care? He's too busy fucking his stuck-up girlfriend to deal with you. You tell him you fell down the stairs and he'll believe it. Because if you haven't noticed, your dad doesn't make much of an effort."

Her words sting. "And if he doesn't believe it?"

"Then I guess you'd better come up with a good excuse and hope he believes you."

"You won't get away with this!"

"You tell anyone, and I will hurt the people you love," she warns, and jerks when banging on the front door echoes inside the house.

I meet her gaze. "I told you someone would come for me."

She grips my face so tightly, I whimper. "And if you call for him, I will hurt him," she threatens, and walks over to the door. She grabs a bag from the floor, lifting it up over her shoulder. "I have things to pawn."

"Kayla," Myles booms, his voice distant. I hear the letterbox close.

Mum looks at me, smiling. "It's sweet, but calling for him won't save you from me. I've proved over and over that I can get to you whenever I like. Nothing will stop me," she promises, taking a step to leave. She doesn't get far before she leans around the door. "Remember, keep it shut, and maybe then I'll untie you when I'm back."

She leaves as Myles calls my name again, and I have to wonder how she expects to leave without being seen.

Once she's gone, a little bit of strength fills me. I don't want to live like this anymore. I don't want to be scared to open a door, or have to watch my back wherever I go.

I know the consequences and what she will do, but it doesn't stop me from calling out. "Myles, help me! Myles!" I cry.

I keep crying until I hear wood splintering. "Kayla, where are you?" he booms.

"Myles," I choke out, tears streaming down my face. "Myles, I'm up here. I'm in my room."

His footsteps charge up the stairs, and seconds later, he's stumbling into my room. His eyes widen at the sight of me, and he freezes for a moment, before his body is jerked forward.

"Holy fucking Christ," Mason breathes when he sees me.

I duck my head as Myles comes unglued and races over to me. He drops to his knees beside me and begins to untie me. "Who did this to you?"

I meet his gaze. "I couldn't stop her," I rasp. "I tried. I tried so hard."

"What is going on?" Mason asks, helping me to my feet.

I cry out at being moved, and I hear Myles growl. "Let's just get her to the hospital."

"What day is it?" I ask as we exit my room.

"Fuck!" Mason grits out. "You don't know what day it is?"

"What did she do to you?" Myles growls. "It's Thursday. I've been trying to get hold of you since yesterday, but… it's a long story."

"Would someone care to fill me in?" Mason snaps.

"Not right now," Myles replies. "Go start the car. I've got her."

Every step down is torture. My ribs are on fire, and there are sharp stabbing pains all over my body.

"God, I can't do this. It hurts too much," I cry.

"You can do this. It's not much further," he promises, his voice cracking. "I'm so sorry, Kayla. I'm so fucking sorry."

"You didn't do this," I heave out as the cool air hits me first. The rain hits me next, and it soothes my burning marks.

Freedom.

"I shouldn't have left you."

"You weren't to know."

"You need to file a report," he commands, as I step into the road.

Mason is parked across the street, in the only available spot. "She said she'll make you pay if I do."

"Then let her. I don't care as long as it's not you," he decides. "You want to work with abused children, Kayla. If one of them came to you with this, would you suggest they tell someone or force them to keep it to themselves?"

"No," I whisper, feeling ashamed when he puts it like that.

My legs shake as I take another step, focusing on the car where Mason stands, holding the door open. His eyes widen as a car engine revs. "Myles," he roars.

My body flies forward to the ground, and I cry out in pain. There's a loud thud, and I turn, seeing Myles get thrown away from the car that hit him.

"No!" I scream, crawling over to his unconscious body. "Myles, wake up. Wake up!"

The car speeds away, the lights disappearing into the distance as Mason drops down beside us, a phone to his ear. He tells the person on the other line what happened, before focusing on his brother, who is yet to move.

"Come on, bro. Shake it off. Get up and shake it off," he pleads.

He doesn't move to touch him, and I can see why when I see Myles' leg at a weird angle. His head is bleeding, and there's a lot of blood.

I did this.

I'm the reason he's lying on the ground unconscious.

"Please don't leave me. Please," I beg.

"It was your mother," Mason spits out. "Why would she hit Myles? Why were you tied to your bed? I deserve to know what is fucking happening."

I roll my head away from Myles and vomit all over the ground. I sob for the pain I've caused and pray they will forgive me.

"This is all my fault," I cry.

"What is? What is happening?" he yells, slamming his hand into the tarmac. "Goddammit, explain it to me."

I meet his gaze. "My mother beats me. She's done it for as long as I can remember. Myles saw the marks she left, and he wanted me to report it. But I was so scared to. It was stupid, and if I had listened to him and Maverick, we wouldn't be here right now. This is my fault."

"Your mum did that to you?"

"It's not the first time, but I was scared. I was so scared of going through what I did after Davis hurt me. This is my fault, and I'm so sorry."

I can hear sirens in the distance, and I silently pray for them to get here and save him.

"Kayla, this isn't your fault."

"It is," I argue.

"No, it's not. It's your fucking mum's, and I don't want to hear you say otherwise," he snaps. "We are conditioned to not speak up, thinking we're doing it to make it better. But all we're doing is protecting them. I get why you did, but you don't need to anymore."

"I didn't mean for him to get hurt," I break, taking Myles' hand.

"I know, and so does he," he tells me.

In minutes, the paramedics are on scene and have Myles on a stretcher. They are loading him into the ambulance when the female paramedic looks me over. "Do you need us to call another ambulance?"

"No, but can she go with you. We were about to take her to hospital when my brother was hit."

"Come on," she orders, and helps me into the back.

Mason promises to meet us at the hospital, but I can't find the words to reply.

Myles still hasn't woken up, but they assure me he's stable, but unconscious. They tell me they won't know more until he's assessed, but I can already tell it's bad.

His head wound is still bleeding, and there's no telling what kind of damage it's done internally.

He is hurt because of me.

Because I couldn't speak up.

If he doesn't make it through this, I won't survive.

I know I won't.

Because without him, life isn't worth living.

CHAPTER
TWENTY-EIGHT

KAYLA

My leg bounces up and down. I'm anxious to get to the others and see how Myles is doing. The nurse wouldn't let me leave until I had my X-ray, and when they confirmed my wrist was broken in two places, I had to wait longer for someone to come down and plaster it. Normally, you are sent to the fracture clinic, but knowing I would never make it there, the nurse asked for them to be called down to my cubicle.

I have no idea how Myles is because the nurse wouldn't give me an update. I don't have my phone to call one of the others, but even if I did, I'm too scared they won't answer.

Thankfully, I won't need to give a formal statement until later. The police got what they needed to start, and I told them everything. I told them what she did to me and how she ran Myles over, and that she stole from my dad. They left, telling me they'll go to her house and see if she's there.

The nurse finishes up with my arm. "Are you sure you don't want any stronger painkillers?"

"My boyfriend is somewhere in this hospital, and I need to see him. If I take anything stronger, I won't be able to stay awake."

"I'm done, but I still think you should stay until your dad arrives. He said he is on his way."

I slide off the bed, grabbing the bag filled with the clothes I had to remove. I'm grateful for the scrubs they gave me since I don't know how long I'll be here. Since I had peed myself, and got blood over my clothes, I didn't really want to sit any longer than I had to wearing them.

"Do you know where they took the boy I came in with?" I ask, wiping my tears.

"If you go to the waiting area on level three, his family and friends are there waiting. I went up to hand over some notes."

"Thank you," I whisper, and head straight for the elevator.

My balance is still unsteady from going without food or water, but I make it to the lift without falling. I had been hooked up to fluids, but I made them remove the line after they said I was okay.

The lift takes forever to get to the third floor, but when it does, I step out, finding my way down to the waiting area.

In my need to get to Myles, I never stopped to prepare what I will say to the others to get them to let me stay.

Their heads turn at my arrival, and their expressions drop at the sight of me. I hold my hands up, choking over my next words. "P-please, don't make m-me leave. I just need to know he's okay. He has to be okay."

"We haven't had any news yet," Harlow announces, her demeanour mournful.

"Please, let me wait to see if he's okay, and then I'll leave you."

Maverick is the first to reach me. I expect him to berate me and give me a lecture on how he told me so. But he doesn't do that. He wraps his arms around me with a gentleness he has shown me before. "Myles will want to see you, but you should be downstairs in A&E. I was going to update you the first chance I got."

I meet his gaze. "It's my fault. She told me she would do something if I yelled for help. But I didn't want to live like that anymore. I couldn't," I heave out, unable to catch my breath. "Myles has shown me what it's like to really live and be loved, and he gave me hope for the future."

"This isn't your fault, it's your mum's," he promises, ducking his head until our eyes meet.

"Yes, it is. If it wasn't for me, he wouldn't have been there," I cry.

Denny stands, her expression crestfallen. Her body trembles as she approaches, and an uneasy feeling has me stepping back.

She gulps. "Kayla, there's something you need to know, and I don't know how to tell you."

Harlow, who is now cuddled up to Malik, looks away. Mason ducks his head, and Maverick can't meet my eyes. Max is the only other person who hasn't reacted, and that's because he's sitting on the floor, his back to the wall, with his head bowed to his knees.

"W-what? You said you didn't know anything about Myles."

She takes my hand, tears spilling down her cheeks. "It isn't about Myles."

"Then what?" I ask, my gut sinking. "Tell me!"

"The reason Myles waited until today to visit you is because he thought you was already here."

My brows pinch together. "I don't understand."

"I had a phone call from Hannah about Charlie. She couldn't reach you and thought you might be with us. Myles went by yours but saw the lights were off, so thought maybe you had already headed to the hospital. He didn't want to disturb you here, but when she called again this morning, he knew something was wrong," she explains. "I'm so sorry, Kayla. Charlie was rushed here yesterday, and it's... it's not good."

My knees give out, but Maverick is there, guiding me over to the table. I gasp for breath, unable to believe that the two people I love the most are fighting for their lives.

"Breathe," Maverick demands, but I can't catch my breath.

Harlow rushes over, kneeling in front of me. She places her hand over my chest, applying pressure. "Breathe, Kayla. We've got you."

"Is she..." I begin, but the words don't fall easily.

"She's on the floor below us if you want to go and see her," Harlow offers.

I meet her gaze, conflicted. "But Myles..."

"It's what Myles would want you to do," Maverick promises. "It's the reason he came to you. He knew you would never miss coming to her side."

"I'll come down with you," Denny offers, and glances across the room to Mason. He's deep in thought, his gaze on Max, who is yet to speak. "Mason, will you message me if you get any news?"

"Yeah, I will," he agrees.

Denny helps me to my feet, and we leave the others in the waiting room. We're in the lift when she clears her throat. "I'm so sorry for what you have been going through," she declares, wrapping her arms around her stomach. "My mother abused me emotionally for years, and I know it's not the same, but you could have come to me. You didn't need to be alone."

"I was ashamed," I admit on a broken whisper. "And my stupidity got Myles hurt. I never meant for this to happen, and if I could, I would change places with him in a second. It's me who deserves to be here, not him. You have to believe me."

"Myles loves you. He jumped in front of a car to save you," she points out. "That's how much you mean to him. Do you think he'd be doing any better knowing it was you in that hospital bed? Because he wouldn't be. He would be a shell of person."

"I should have listened to him when he told me to tell someone," I admit, ashamed I didn't.

"It's not too late," she shares. "You can tell someone now and put an end to this. I hate that you felt like you couldn't come to us, but we aren't going anywhere. We've got your back."

"I already informed the police. I told them everything," I whisper.

The lift opens and we step out together. Before we go search for her room, she stops, gently pulling me into her arms. "I love you. You are one of the strongest women I know."

We continue down the hall, and she stops at a door. "I'll be here if you need me."

I nod and push open the door. I hardly recognise the girl lying in the hospital bed. She's so pale, yet there's a yellow tinge to her flesh. My body is screaming to hug her, but I don't think either of us are strong enough for that.

"Kayla?" Charlie wheezes, sounding weak as hell. With each breath she struggles to take, a wheeze echoes around the room. Her eyes widen at the sight of my injuries. "What happened to you?"

I break, crying uncontrollably as I reach her. "I'm sorry it took me this long to get to you."

"What happened to you?"

"I'll tell you after. It's a long story," I avoid. "What have the doctors said? Where are your parents? You don't look so good."

"I've been better. Tell me. What happened?"

Each breath sounds pained. I take her hand, bringing it up to my lips. "Charlie, what have they said?"

She opens her mouth to reply, but then stops, rethinking her next words. "I'm scared," she responds. "If I don't get a transplant soon…"

I lean forward, my breath hitching. "No. You will get through this. You will," I declare with so much conviction, it almost sounds like the truth.

"I don't think I will this time."

My heart breaks for her. "Charlie," I rasp.

Her lower lip trembles. "I know in time, everyone will heal, but I'm so scared about what this will do to my mum and dad. They are barely hanging on," she reveals, her chest wheezing with her breaths. "I know in time everyone will move on, and I shouldn't worry. But what happens to me? Where will I go? Will I still remember my life? If Heaven is real, will my grandparents be there waiting? Will I get to see any of you again? Every time my mum or dad leave the room, I'm petrified it will be the last time we ever see each other. I'm afraid this will be our last conversation, and I'm tired of trying to be strong."

I press my lips against her hand, failing to keep it together. "Then don't. Let us be strong for you because you need to get through this. You have to. You're my best friend, Charlie. We are meant to grow old together. We're going to have kids the same age, and they'll grow up to be best friends too."

"We could move in next door to each other," she teases, her breath catching. "But we both know it won't happen."

"You don't need to be scared," I promise her. "I'll visit your mum and dad all the time. And I believe there is life after death. Not like this, but I believe our souls are reincarnated. We will meet again; I'm sure of it."

"You are the bestest friend I have ever had," she declares, and I lean up, wiping her tears away.

"I love you, Charlie. Regardless of what you believe, you changed my life. You gave me a reason to keep on living. You made a difference in this world."

"Promise me," she gasps. "Promise me that when I die, you will keep going. You were born to help people, Kayla. Live for the both of us. Live, Kayla. Don't waste your time on what ifs. For me, please, will you do that?"

"I promise."

"Now, tell me why you look like you've been hit by a car."

I slide onto the bed next to her, minding the tubes and wires she's connected to. Tears fall, splashing against my hand.

"I messed up," I admit.

She places her hand over my cast. "What happened?"

I run over the events, and her expressions falls. "I should have told someone. And now he's here, and I don't know if he's okay."

"She can't get away with this."

I take her hand. "She won't. I'm going to stand up to her."

I stay by her side for the next half an hour. She asks me to talk about something to distract her, so I go over the weekend's events before the nightmare began.

Just as I'm finished telling her that, her mum walks in. Denny is by her side, and I sit up. "Is everything okay?"

"Charlie's doctor is here to check her over."

I slide off the bed, still holding Charlie's hand. "Can I stay?"

Charlie weakly shakes her head. "Go and check on Myles. Come and see me later and tell me about the rest of your trip."

"I don't want to leave you," I admit.

"I've got her," Hannah promises. "Go and check on your boyfriend. I heard about your ordeal and I'm really sorry, Kayla."

"Are you sure?" I ask, wanting to stay.

Charlie musters up a smile. "I'm positive. Mum will get a message to you if anything changes."

A doctor in a white coat steps into the room. "Is now a good time?" he asks.

"Yes, we're just leaving," Denny assures him.

I lean down, pressing my lips to Charlie's cheek. "I love you. I'll be back as soon as I can."

"Love you too," she replies.

Her mum gives my good hand a squeeze when I pass her. "Thank you for coming to see her."

"I wish I could have been here sooner."

"Go check on your boy."

Denny takes my hand as we leave. "I'm so sorry this is happening to you."

I squeeze her hand back, letting her know I heard. It's not happening to me though. It's happening to the two people who mean the world to me.

And I'm not sure I'll have either by the end of the day.

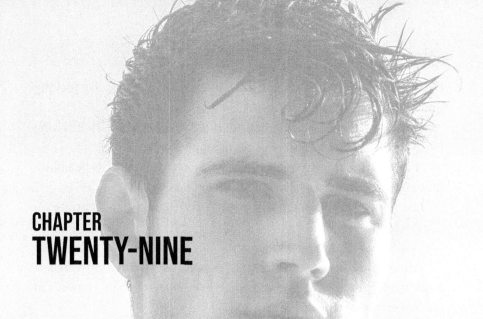

CHAPTER
TWENTY-NINE

KAYLA

The atmosphere in the waiting area is still tense. Denny and I arrived back forty minutes ago, but only five words had been exchanged between everyone. I want to remain invisible, so I stay in the corner, my mind going back to happier times with both Charlie and Myles.

Malik snaps, throwing the can Joan gave him across the room. "What the fuck is taking them so long?"

"Calm down," Mark demands.

"No. I won't calm down. They said someone would be out shortly, but it's been forty fucking minutes."

Mason grunts in agreement. "He could be dead, and those fuckers have us in here like sitting birds."

"Sitting ducks," Denny corrects, but there's no teasing there. He meets her gaze and pulls her against his chest.

"He's fine," Max croaks, and I think it's the first time he's spoken. Everyone looks surprised to hear him.

"Max?" Maverick calls, his brows pinching down.

"He's not dead," Max states, sounding stronger. "I'd know, right? I'd know if the other half of me had copped it. I'd know. I'd fucking know."

Joan leans down, placing her hand on his shoulder. "He's strong like the rest of you boys. He will get through this."

"I know. He's the strongest," Max whispers, dropping his head into his hands. His shoulders shake with silent tears.

Everyone glances away to give him privacy, and I concentrate on the clock on the wall.

Tick, tock. Tick, tock.

I'm not sure how much time passes with me staring into space. It must have been a while because when everyone suddenly stands, I'm the last one to get up, my joints sore.

I glance at the entrance, and I meet his eyes.

"No," I whisper.

I feel everyone's gazes on me, but it's Denny, knowing who he is, who makes a noise.

"I'm sorry," the doctor I met earlier announces.

"No, no, no. Not now," I cry.

I don't see who touches me, but they break my fall as I collapse by lowering me to the floor.

"She's been running on fumes for hours," Joan scolds from somewhere close by.

I place my palms on the ground, gasping for breath.

This cannot be happening.

"Kayla, breathe. Breathe!" Maverick snaps.

"Take deep, slow breaths," the doctor orders, and I lift my head, my hair whipping back.

"She's dead, isn't she?" I ask. The pain in my chest is like a thousand knives slicing through me. It burns. "Oh God."

"Mrs Roberts asked me to come and inform you of Charlie's passing. She doesn't want to leave her alone," he explains.

There's a ringing in my ears as Maverick comes into view, cupping my cheeks. "Kayla, you need to snap out of it."

I've never felt anything like this. I've been bullied, raped and beaten, and I thought it broke me. I attempted to end my life more than once because of it, but never once during that time did I ever feel like this.

I don't feel empty or void, but something else. Something that has me getting to my feet. "He's wrong," I tell Maverick, before addressing the doctor. "You are wrong. She's okay."

"Kayla," Denny whispers.

I shake my head vehemently. "No. It's not true. It can't be."

"I think you need to sit back down," Maverick commands, his hands on my shoulder.

I brush him off. "No, I need to see her. She can correct all of this."

"Wait," he calls out, but I leave, racing down the corridor.

I don't know how I found the strength to move. My joints are stiff and aching. I brush it aside, concentrating on where I need to go to get to Charlie.

I hear footsteps behind me, so I skip the lift and head right for the stairs. I keep going, even when they call for me to stop.

Reaching the corridor where Charlie's room is located, I find her dad sitting on a chair outside her room. His head is bowed, his shoulders shaking.

If he isn't in there with her, that has to mean she's okay.

My heart is pumping hard as I pass him. He doesn't even flinch or look up. I push open the door, and immediately look to her bed.

I relax, my world feeling right once more.

She's sleeping.

That's all. She's sleeping.

Tears spill down my cheeks, and I inhale sharply. Hannah's expression falls and she cries harder.

"She's okay. She's just sleeping," I repeat, breathing out.

Red rimmed, swollen eyes stare back at me. "Honey, she's gone. Her heart couldn't take it anymore," Hannah explains, as more tears fall.

"No, she can't be," I deny. "She always looks peaceful when she sleeps."

"Please, she's gone," she chokes out, her breath hitching.

"No, she's not!" I cry, taking Charlie's hand. "Please, Charlie, wake up."

"Oh, sweet girl," Hannah breaks.

"Please, Charlie. You need to wake up," I plead.

Denny moves to my side. "Kayla, she's gone. Don't do this. Not here. Not now."

"No!" I scream. "She can't be gone. Please. Please wake up."

"Maverick, do something," Denny pleads.

I reach down, pressing my head against Charlie's as I clutch our hands between us. "Please, please wake up. Don't leave me. Please, don't leave me. I lied when I said I would be okay. I won't be okay without you."

Hands run down my back, and I stand to find Hannah there, her expression crumpled with pain. "Feel her chest, Kayla. Feel it."

I slowly reach down, placing my hand over her chest. There are no breaths, no pulse of her beating heart. I crumble, and Maverick is there, pulling me against his chest.

I bend down, heaving with cries. "We needed more time. We had so much more to do and to say to each other. She can't be gone."

Her mum sobs, clutching her husband. "She held on for as long as she could. Once you came, she declined even more. She held on for you."

I brush Charlie's hair away from her face. "I'm so sorry. So, so sorry."

She did so much for me when I was raped. She was there for me through the good, the bad, and the ugly. And I couldn't even be here in her final moments.

I let her down, and I'll never be able to tell her how sorry I am.

Hannah reaches across, lowering a white envelope onto the bed, but it's her dad who speaks. "Charlie wrote this letter to you. She made us promise to give it to you once she had passed. She loved you like a sister." He pauses, unable to find the words. His next ones are broken, barely audible though his pain. "We are so grateful she had you. You made her life full, and she died knowing she was loved."

"We will give you a minute," Hannah sobs. "We need to sit outside for a minute."

"You don't need to leave," I weep.

"We won't be far. Take your time," she assures me, and gives my hand a gentle squeeze.

"Do you want us to stay?" Denny asks.

"No, I'd like to say goodbye."

She presses her lips to my cheek. "I'm so sorry for your loss," Denny whispers, her voice filled with emotion.

I lower myself onto the chair and watch Charlie for a moment. The blanket has been tucked under her armpits, and someone has folded her hands over her stomach. The tubes and wires have now been removed, and now that I'm really seeing her, I notice how unnaturally pale she looks.

This shouldn't have happened to her.

The letter in my hand crinkles. I glance down, my tears dropping onto the envelope, and I pull it away, not wanting to smudge any ink.

It takes everything in me to open it, pulling out the two pieces of paper neatly folded inside.

Kayla,

I've held this pen for a while, unable to find the words I need to say. It's not easy to say goodbye to your best friend, and I hate that this goodbye will be harder for you. It's unfair, and cruel, but you've faced worse, so I'll know you'll be okay.

When we met, I was in such a bad place. I was being bullied and had no friends to turn to, and I felt so alone. Then you came into my life, and you made me feel like I was the popular girl at school. I think I knew we'd be best friends for life before you did. You drew me in with your kindness, something no one else had shown me before you came along. I truly believe you'll change the world simply by being you because you changed mine.

I wish I had more time, but I know I got my miracle the day I met you. I wished for you, or the idea of you, for so long, and I don't regret a minute of it. I believe we were supposed to meet each other and help each other through our pain.

I know I've asked a lot from you recently, but I need you to do a little more. *I need you to live, Kayla. I need you to take one step in front of the other and live because life can be beautiful. It can be. As sad as you'll be, as dark as your world will get, there is always something good around the corner, and the light will shine once more. I don't want you to go back to that place. Just because my life was cut short, it doesn't mean yours has to be as well. So please, live, and die old, telling your grandkids about me.*

There are three more things I need from you. I know you're in pain, and grieving for me, but keep reading. I need you to do them.

Please sing at my funeral. I don't want some church hymn to be sang in my memory. I want words. I want your voice. Your singing has always made me feel free, like I was floating through the air. Brush off the crowd attending my funeral, and sing for me because I promise, wherever I may be, I will be listening.

And be there for my mum. I know that's a lot to ask, but she's going to feel this much more than my dad. Being a mum is all she ever wanted to be and all she has been aside from a wife and daughter. She sacrificed her life and career to raise me, and I don't want her to spend the rest of her days grieving for me. I have letters for her and Dad in my knicker drawer at home. I hid them because I knew I couldn't handle her heartache.

On the next page is a bucket list. Complete it. Not just for me, but for you. I never got to experience what I wanted, so I hope you'll do it for me.

I'll love you forever, Kayla.

Please don't grieve for me forever. It's not what I want. When you think of me, think of how I used to be and not this version. And take comfort in knowing I'll no longer be in pain. I'll be free from it, and I need you to find peace in that.

Be brave.

Live.

Love.

But most of all, be you.

I love you, Kayla.

Charlie.

The words are a blur on the page. Even in her last moments, she thought of me, and was being my friend.

I swipe the tears away and bring the next page forward.

KAYLA'S & CHARLIE'S BUCKLET LIST!

(I don't expect you to tick them all off, but I'm hoping you know which ones I'm most serious about. I love you whether or not you choose to do them.)

1. *Fall in love. (I added this to give you an easier start because I know you're already there.)*
2. *Make love. Experience sex the way it's supposed be had. (And make sure you come visit my grave to tell me about it when you do.)*
3. *Tell someone about your bitch of a mum. I know you think you hid it well, but you didn't. I wanted to do more, but then my condition declined, and I never got the chance. If I'm wrong, you should still remove yourself from her life. She has never deserved you.*
4. *Make friends. You're worth being friends with. There will be someone out there feeling lonely, like we were, who needs you.*
5. *Get drunk. (And yes, I mean it) I think you're in a safe place where you can have a drink. Throw up, be hungover, but experience the things you've missed. And because I know you need a safe space to do it, I roped in Denny with this one.*
6. *Do something reckless. (Personally, I'd have loved to witness you do this one because if there is something you aren't, it's reckless).*
7. *Get a tattoo (You know you want to. I saw you eyeing those angel wings; don't deny it).*
8. *Pull a prank on someone who bullied you back in the day. I have the perfect candidate. Bruce Lockwood. He was such an asshole to you and should be held accountable.*

This next one will be hard, but I have no doubt in my mind you can do it. I've never met anyone as strong as you.

1. *Tell someone about what happened to you. People should know just how much you suffered. People should see the strength that you have inside you.*

I can't read the next one without weeping. She thought of every-thing. She ends the page with:

Never forget me. Every time you think of me, I want you to smile and look up into the sky and know I am there.

Until we meet again...

I take her cold hand in mine, sobbing silently as I think of her. I already miss her voice, her laugh, and her sassy remarks. I miss her, and I know for as long as I live, that will never change.

The hinges on the door screech, alerting me of someone's arrival. Thinking it could be Maverick, or her parents wanting one last good-bye, I turn to the door, surprised to find my dad.

His eyes widen as he assesses my injuries, then water when he sees Charlie lying on the bed. He rushes over, kneeling in front of me as pain engulfs me.

He pulls me against his chest, and I cling to him. "It's not fair."

"I'm sorry, Kayla. I really am sorry," he tells me softly. "But the police are outside and they have more questions. They said they have your mother. I don't understand what is going on. I thought you were involved in a hit and run."

I get to my feet, brushing my tears aside. I feel numb inside, and I blame it all on my mum. She took precious moments away from me and Charlie. She ran over my boyfriend. I blame her, and I'm not leaving until I know she will pay for everything she has done. "Then we should go and talk to them."

His brows pinch together. "Sweetheart, I think they'll understand if you need more time."

"No, we should go now and get it sorted."

"If this is about your mum, you don't need to worry. I can get her out as soon as we're done here."

I meet his gaze, disgusted that he still can't see it. "I wouldn't do that if I were you," I warn.

"Kayla, what is going on?" he demands.

I move back, giving Charlie one last kiss before leaving the room. Maverick, Denny and Katie are in the hall with Charlie's parents. "Is Myles okay?" I ask when they step away from the door.

Maverick nods. "He's awake and asking for you."

Katie reaches out to tuck my hair over my shoulder. "How are you doing? Are you ready to talk?"

"I don't understand," Dad groans. "Why do I feel like I'm the only one missing something?"

Maverick's jaw clenches. "Two parents are standing there after losing the light of their life. I bet if I asked, both would volunteer to take her place. But you..." he accuses. "You are so blind to what is going on you still don't see it."

"W-what? You can't speak to me like that," Dad growls.

"Dad, I will explain everything when we talk to the police. Until then, please, back off."

Katie takes my dad's arm and pulls his stunned frame back. "Let's give them a minute."

I walk over to Charlie's parents. I owe them an apology. "I'm so sorry for my behaviour. It was cruel to act like I was the only one grieving."

"We understand," she assures me. "Are you okay?"

I nod, but deep down, I'm falling apart, and I need some space to get myself together. I want to fulfil the promise I made to her, but to do it, I need time.

"She wanted me to tell you that she has letters written for each of you back in her room. They are in her knicker drawer."

Hannah grips onto her husband, tears filling her eyes. She's conflicted on what to do. She wants to go to her daughter, but she also wants to rush to read her last and final words to them both.

"Thank you, Kayla. Thank you for being her friend."

"She was more than my best friend. She was my sister, and I'll never forget her. Your daughter is the hero in my story, and she changed my life. I want to thank you for raising her, and I'm terribly sorry for your loss."

Charlie's dad runs a hand over his face, covering the tears that fall. "Thank you."

"We want you to be included in the funeral arrangements. She would want that," Hannah reveals. "If you are up for it."

"She asked me to sing," I admit.

Her mum smiles. "I'm not surprised by that. She told me you had the voice of an angel and couldn't wait for the day you showed the world."

I force a smile, trying not to cry at her statement. "I'm so sorry for your loss."

Dad clears his throat. "The police are here."

I glance down the hallway to where they are standing, before turning to Hannah. "I will see you soon. I promise."

"You go do what you need to do. She would be proud of you, you know."

"I hope so."

As they head back into the room, Dad reaches out to take my hand, but Maverick blocks his path, giving him his back. He looks down at me. "Do you want me to come?"

"I can do this," I rasp. "But will you tell Myles I'll be there soon?"

"I will."

With that, I lean into Katie as we make our way down the hall. I let my grief for my friend and relief for my boyfriend fuel me.

I know what I have to do.

And my dad isn't going to like it.

CHAPTER
THIRTY

KAYLA

The hospital was kind enough to let us use one of their private rooms, where staff go to take five minutes. It's not a big room, and with the four of us filling the space, it feels smaller.

Along the wall opposite the door is a kitchenette and countertop. It has a kettle, microwave, and three cupboards lining the wall. In the centre of the room is a square table with two chairs on either side. The sides of the room have boxes stacked up that look like they might be stock.

Katie, having an idea of what this is about, chose to stay outside. The policeman wanted Dad to stay with her, but I asked for him to sit in on the interview with us. He has questions, lots of them, and I don't have the energy to explain everything twice. I want to get to Myles, to see for myself that he is okay.

The older gentleman, who I swear I've seen before, takes the chair opposite me. "I'm PC Howard, and this is my partner, PC Smith. Earlier today, a report against Jessica Martin was filed by you. We made an arrest earlier this evening and now need a statement from you. Are you okay with that?"

I still hate that I share her last name. After the divorce, she never changed it back.

"Why on earth have you arrested Jessica?" Dad interrupts, before facing me. "Why would you make a statement against your mother?"

The other policeman, who isn't much younger than PC Howard, speaks up. "I understand your frustration, Mr Martin, but it is best if Kayla is the one to talk."

PC Howard addresses me. "Do you want to walk us through the events of the incident that occurred earlier today?"

"On Monday, I got back from a weekend away with my friends. My boyfriend walked me to the door before leaving," I begin. "I had just closed the door behind me when my mother assaulted me with a frying pan."

"What?" Dad yells, slamming the palm of his hand down on the table. "Why would you say that?"

I meet his gaze. There is no concern for me, only anger at my accusation. "Look at me, Dad. Does this look like an accident? She hurt me, and it's not the first time."

"Mr Martin, please abstain yourself from interrupting. We will remove you if you continue to talk," PC Howard informs him. "Please, continue. You said your mother hit you with a frying pan."

"Did you see it?"

"Yes, but before I could react, it was too late. I lost consciousness."

"What happened next?"

I tell him about the abuse she inflicted, and the things she did. I tell them about the threats she made, and what she took. All the while, my dad sits there fuming. The tension coming off him is suffocating, but I don't have it in me to address his concerns.

"Myles found me tied to my bed. He's the reason I got free. We just reached the car when she came out of nowhere in her vehicle. Myles threw me out of the way and took the impact of the hit, and here we are."

"We need to ask this, but have you sought medical attention, and if so, are you willing for the hospital to share their notes?"

I nod and list the injuries that occurred in her presence.

"Has your mother hurt you or shown signs of this behaviour in the past?" PC Smith asks.

"Of course she hasn't," my dad snaps.

I ignore his outburst and gulp. "Yes. Every time I was in her care," I answer honestly.

"Kayla," Dad breathes, and for the first time, he looks guilty. "How? When? Why?"

"Mr Martin," PC Howard snaps, before addressing me. "What made this time worse or different?"

What he isn't asking is: what made her go too far. Before today, I would have answered that she didn't need a reason. And although I know that to be a fact, I also know this was fuelled by money and hatred.

"Money. It's always been about money," I reply. "My dad recently cut her off, and she was desperate."

"This is my fault?" Dad breathes.

"No, because I think even if money wasn't involved, she would have still hurt me. She found reason after reason to hurt me and found joy in it."

"Why haven't you come forward before?" PC Howard asks.

"Because I was scared no one would believe me. She made me believe things that weren't true and got in my head."

"And is there anyone who can collaborate your accusation?"

"There is. My boyfriend and his two brothers. They both saw previous marks, and then Mason, Myles' other brother, was there today."

"We may need to question you further, but we have all we need right now."

"I'll have to talk about this again?" I ask.

"Yes. But we can record the next one, so we don't need to come back."

"And what will happen to my mum?"

"She can rot for all I care," Dad bites out. "I'm so stupid. I should have seen this."

My throat closes with emotion as I focus on the policemen. "She has been arrested, and when we go back, we will charge her on the abuse and the hit and run."

I hope she rots in prison for the rest of her life.

"Can I go?" I question. "I haven't seen my boyfriend yet, and I don't know how he is."

He holds his finger up to me but addresses my dad. "We need to ask Kayla some questions alone. She won't be long."

"Kayla?" Dad asks, seeking permission to stay.

"It's okay, Dad. You can wait outside," I reply.

He nods, ducking his head as he leaves the room. He reminds me of a scolded child, but I don't have it in me to console him. I don't blame him for her actions, but I am angry he didn't see it. Even after seeing me, he kept his head in the clouds, not believing my mum was capable of something so horrific.

The door clicks shut behind him, and I turn to the two men.

"Kayla, I know this has been a difficult day for you, but your safety is important to us," PC Howard begins.

My nose twitches. I'm unsure of where this is going. "Thank you."

"We have to ask this," PC Smith explains. "But would you like for us to arrange for somewhere safe for you to sleep tonight or do you believe you will be okay leaving with your dad?"

"My dad has never touched me, if that's what you're wondering. I promise."

He closes the folder in front of him. "We will contact you shortly. You can leave to visit your boyfriend."

I leave the room, and Dad pulls away from Katie. I can see the questions on his face, but I'm in charge now, and I don't want to answer them.

"I'm going to go see Myles; there's something I need to do," I tell him. "I'll answer your questions later."

He doesn't argue as we leave the hallway and make our way upstairs to where Myles is getting treated.

The silence is deafening as we approach their floor. I don't mind it as it gives me time to plan my next steps, knowing what I want to do.

Mark is outside, his ear to the mobile in his hand when we arrive. He spots me and ends the call. "He's okay. He'll be released in a few days."

"Is it okay if I go in and talk to him?"

"He keeps asking for you," he reveals.

Dad clears his throat. "Don't be long, Kayla. We have things to discuss," he warns.

I nod to let him know I heard, and step into the room. The others lift their heads at my entrance.

"Let's give them some space," Maverick orders, grabbing his jacket.

But my gaze is on Myles. The air gets trapped in my lungs at the sight of him. His leg is elevated in the air, covered in a cast, and he has a bandage wrapped around his head. He has road rash, which is already starting to swell and bruise.

"I'm not going anywhere," Max argues.

Myles gives him a droll look. "Leave before I make you."

"You can't even walk."

"Don't make me hurt you," Myles warns.

Max grins, getting to his feet. "Alright. I'm going."

I wait for them to leave before moving closer to the bed. "I'm so sorry, Myles."

He winces as he sits up. "This isn't your fault."

"We both know that isn't true. I'm partly to blame," I rasp. "Are you okay? What did the doctors say? What took them so long?"

"I'm fine. Just a broken leg, a few bruised ribs, and a concussion from my head injury," he claims, although it looks like much more. "I heard about Charlie, baby. I'm so sorry."

"I'll be okay," I promise. Something feels different between us, like there's a barrier between us now. "I'm worried about you."

He forces a smile. "I'll be fine."

"Are we okay?"

His brows pinch together. "Always," he states. "The drugs they have me on are making me drowsy, but other than that, I'm wondering why you're still all the way over there."

A breath I had been holding goes free, and I move until I'm at the side of his bed. Tears stream down my cheeks as I take his hand. "I'm so sorry this happened to you. I don't know how to fix this."

"You have nothing to be sorry for," he retorts heatedly. "But I need to know what you want me to do with my statement. The police will be by soon, and I won't lie to protect your mother."

Horrified, I lean in. "Myles, I'd never ask you to do that," I assure him. "I've told them everything. I won't let her get away with this, I promise."

He relaxes back against the pillow, relief pouring off him. "Thank fuck!"

"There's something I need to do, and whilst I know this isn't the best time, I hope you understand why I need to leave."

He takes my hand. "Don't you dare break up with me," he demands, his voice cracking. "She won't hurt me again."

I lightly touch his cheek, soothing him. "It's not that, I promise."

He places his hand over mine on his cheek. "Then what?"

"I realised tonight that I rely on people too much, and I can't do that anymore. I nearly got you killed today because I was too afraid to speak up. I need to find my own strength, and to do that, there is something I need to do."

"Baby, you didn't do anything to me."

"No, but my actions did. Please, this is important for me. For us."

"And you promise you aren't leaving me?"

I lean down until my lips touch his. "I promise. I could never leave you," I declare. "I love you too much."

"I love you too," he replies, and kisses me.

I groan when we pull apart. "I have to go. My dad only got parts of the story today, and he has questions. I don't want to leave you, but I have to."

His eyes water. "When will I see you again?"

"Soon," I promise. "In fact, come to the school next week. I will text you the time and date closer to the time, and all of this will be revealed. Just know that I don't want to leave you, but if I stay, I'll never change. I'll never grow into the woman you deserve me to be."

"You are perfect to me," he huskily remarks.

"Will you be there?"

"I'll be there," he assures me. As I lean down to give him one last kiss, my tears drop onto his cheeks. He wipes them away, smiling sadly. "It won't be forever."

"I know. I love you," I choke. "Please get better soon."

With another painful goodbye, I exit the room. The guys approach me, giving me their condolences, and Katie rushes to my side to support me. My dad still doesn't know what to do.

Everyone goes back inside the room to visit Myles, but I pull Maverick aside, informing him of my plan. He thinks it's a good idea and promises to keep me updated on Myles in the meantime.

In a week, the whole school will know my story.

They'll know my pain.

And they'll know my strength.

CHAPTER
THIRTY-ONE

KAYLA

My hands shake as I pace back and forth behind the curtain that is blocking me from view. I can hear the bustle of students arriving in the school hall where assemblies are given, and it only causes me more anxiety. When this idea came to my head, I had the courage to do it, but now that I'm here, I'm nervous. I must stink by now because I haven't stopped sweating since I arrived.

Today is the day I leave my past behind me and start living. I've spent years believing that what I feel and think doesn't matter. Charlie taught me it is does. People matter, and if there is anything I have learnt during all that has happened, it's that it only takes one person.

It only takes one person to change your life, or in my case, it's a team of them.

But today, I'll stand up there alone and make them proud.

The last person I expected to see here was Maverick. I freeze, my gut bottoming out. "He's not coming, is he?"

I've only messaged Myles once since I left the hospital. I've been so consumed by what I need and want, I forgot about what he needs. He has been my rock through everything, and the one time he truly needed me, I bailed. And it was my fault he was in the hospital anyway.

I have kept in touch with Maverick throughout his recovery, so I wasn't completely in the dark. I just hope he realises today why I couldn't talk to him. I knew if I did, I would tell him what I was doing. He would have talked me up and offered to be by my side, and I would have let him. I would have let him hold my hand through it all, which would have made all of this pointless. I need him to see I can be strong for him, that he doesn't need to worry about me anymore.

"He's in the hall waiting for you," he assures me. "He misses you."

"I miss him too," I admit.

"Then make sure you go to him after your speech. He wants to be there for you tomorrow."

My expression falls. I don't want to think about tomorrow. It hurts too much to know it will be my last goodbye to Charlie. "How did you know I would be here?"

"I asked the principle. She sent me here," he explains. "How are you feeling?"

I wring my fingers together. "Nervous."

"You can do this," he brags, his voice strong.

"I hope so. Otherwise, all of this will be for nothing."

"It's not for nothing," he swears. "How are things at home?"

I shrug. "Okay. Dad has taken it hard, but I'm just glad he's not denying it anymore."

"He's a fool," he states, gritting his teeth.

"He's something," I agree, before exhaling. "I know he'll never be the dad I need him to be, but I'm at peace with it. I know he loves me, but sometimes, I think he just finds it hard to express it. He had strict parents, so he was never taught to show affection. He's getting there, but…"

"But?"

"He's driving me crazy. I need space, but he refuses to give it. He thinks I'm saying it to make him feel better, but I'm not. I know he feels guilty for what happened to me, but he shouldn't. If it weren't for

Katie being a mediator, I think I would have walked out and rented a room somewhere."

"This is where we differ a little bit," he declares. "He should feel guilty. He might not have raised his hand to you, but neglecting to see it is just as abusive." He pauses to let those words sink in. "Me and my brothers are all completely different people, but we've never been blind to what the other person is feeling or thinking. I don't get to spend as much time as I'd like with them, but I do know I'd never be too busy if one of them ever really needed me. Your father is just realising that and is reflecting his own personal misgivings onto you. Let him make it up to you, because he owes you, Kayla. He owes you years of neglect."

My eyes fill with unshed tears, and I'm angry at myself for letting them form.

"Kayla, we're ready for you," Principal Collins interrupts. "Hello again, Maverick. It's been good seeing you."

"You too, Miss. Collins," he returns, before tapping me under the chin. "Good luck, kid. You're gonna smash it."

He leaves, and I move to the side of the stage, listening to Miss. Colins introduce me. Hearing my cue, I step out onto the stage.

The crowd applauds my entrance, and I swallow back bile as I look out at the sea of faces staring back at me.

Being centre of attention is my weakness. I don't like it, care for it, or want it.

Miss Collins gently squeezes my wrist before moving off to the side. I scan the crowd of faces, stopping at the back, where Myles is sitting in a wheelchair. Maverick has left him in the centre of the aisle, so he has a better view.

My lips pull up at the corners, giving him a smile when his prideful gaze meets mine. He isn't alone either. Beside Maverick are the rest of his brothers. Harlow and Denny are standing there too, giving me a thumbs up.

My throat closes, and I have to look down at the podium to gather myself. When I glance back up, I straighten my spine.

"Good morning," I begin. "For those who don't me, I'm Kayla

Martin. I'm supposed to be doing a presentation on child abuse and bullying for my Health and Social class, and I asked Miss Collins to let me do it here today. I promise not to take up too much of your time, and in return, I'd like you to promise to listen. Because what I'm about to share isn't pretty.

"Over fifty-thousand children are identified as needing child protection in the UK. But what about the other large number who suffer in silence? The ones not added into statistics?

"I'm one of those numbers."

I take a breath and scan the room, making sure I have their attention. And I do.

"My mother has been physically hurting me for as long as I can remember. The one person who is supposed to protect me, hurt me. She didn't just use objects or her fists, but cruel words. You can't see the scars they left because they are on the inside. Those words still echo in my mind, but I hope in time, new words will replace them.

"I lived through this feeling like I had no one to talk to. I was too afraid of the consequences to ever really learn that it wasn't me who'd be facing them. It was her. I believed keeping silent would help me, but all it did was get the person I love the most, hurt.

"Until recently, no one knew what was going on behind closed doors. They didn't see the injuries or witness the abuse, and it was lonely. I felt invisible, and the one person who did see me, used me as a punching bag," I reveal.

"My abuse didn't stop there. The one place I went to for escape, turned into another personal hell. I enrolled in this school excited for the possibilities and change. I wanted to be just like you. I wanted to fit in and make friends. I wanted to enjoy life and not fear it. I wanted to date, to go out with my friends. I wanted to be accepted. I thought escaping my old life and starting new would change everything, and I'd have all of those things.

"It didn't change anything," I admit, holding my head up high.

"When I was thirteen years old, one of my bullies raped me. He stripped me of my dignity, my power, and my innocence. And after all that was done to me, my torture still continued.

"I was trapped in a bubble, where I wasn't safe here or at home. My rape had been broadcasted to the world, and my world came tumbling down around me.

"I felt worthless and unloved, and in my worst moments, people recorded me for their sick entertainment. I was an outcast and felt like I had no one to share my pain with. I hated that I gave everyone that power of me. I became a shell of a person and let self-loathing take over. I wanted my nightmare to stop. I wanted the constant reminder I was attacked to be over. I wanted the cruel words and torment to end. And the only way out that I saw, was to end my own life," I choke out, noticing a few people near the front have tears in their eyes.

"I attempted to end my own suffering twice."

Gasps can be heard from the crowd. My story is ugly, but it's also honest and real, and they need to hear it all.

"I'm not telling you this to make you feel sorry for me. I'm telling you because I don't want to be a statistic anymore. I don't want to be the girl known for being raped, or the girl who was abused by her mum. I don't want to be the girl who is laughed at when people remember the things they did to me.

"Because I can assure you, there will be a time in their life when they'll regret the things they did to me. They'll have children of their own one day, and if a time comes when they have the same problems I did, they won't want their own child to face what I did.

"Bullying isn't funny. It isn't cool. You don't get to make someone else's life worse, so you can feel better. It's not a cool trend, or something you need to take part in to feel accepted. It doesn't make you popular. It's cruel, demeaning, and irreversible. You can't take it back. You can't fix what has already been done. And one day, it could be your words that pushes a person into ending their own life. It could be your actions that make a person feel like it's their only way out.

"You can tell yourself it's not your fault, or it's not your problem, if someone does it. You can tell yourself you only did this or that, but it matters. Your words and actions matter.

"I spent most of my childhood alone, and all I ever wanted was to be seen. I wanted people to stop and hear my cries for help. But mostly, I needed someone to see what was happening to me and speak up, instead of turning a blind eye to it. They thought by not being involved or participating, it gave them a get out of jail free card. But their silence made it worse."

I pause for a moment, giving them time to soak up my words and hear them. My presentation is coming to an end, and I thought for sure people would have lost interest by now.

A lone tear slips down my cheek as I continue. "If you or someone you know is being bullied, I want you to fight back. I want you to stand up and scream about it from the rooftops. Because if there is one thing I have learned from my trauma, it's that silence only makes it worse.

"Your bullies, whether it's here or at home, don't want you to speak up. They may threaten you into silence, but that's only because they are afraid. They want to keep control over you so they have the power to keep doing it.

"Don't suffer in silence. Don't do what I did. Take back your control and speak up. Turn the cameras to the bullies. I know first-hand how hard it can be, but you can do it. You just need to believe.

"And to those who are the bully: if you're listening, think about your actions. Is being a bully who you really want to be known as for the rest of your life? Because I can assure you, that is only how people will ever see you. School may feel forever, but it's not. So ask yourself: what you are really achieving by bringing down another person? If control and power is what you want, join a club. Lead it. Control it. But don't risk the lives of others so you can feel better about yourself.

"I hope you all think about my words with an open mind and leave this room feeling just a little bit better. Because I learned recently that it only takes one person to make a difference," I finish, and Miss Collins steps up next me, her eyes watering with unshed tears.

The students stand, surprising with me with a round of applause. Tears blur my vision as I meet Myles' gaze. He beams, cheering for me.

My gaze moves through the rest, and I'm startled to find Dad and Katie standing there. I didn't even know they were coming.

"Before you leave," Miss Collins begins. "I want to announce that thanks to the courageous actions and determination of Kayla Martins, she has managed to find funding for the school to have a councillor on staff. She is here for you to confide in and give you the right support you need. You are not alone here." She pauses. "Now, let's hear it for Kayla one more time."

I don't wait for the applause. What I need is Myles. I race down the stairs leading off the stage and make my way towards him. I drop to my knees in front of him, placing my hands in his.

"Thank you for being here and believing in me," I rasp.

He tucks a strand of my red hair behind my ear. "How did it feel?" he whispers, love shining back at me.

"Freeing," I admit.

He smiles wide. "And how do *you* feel?"

"Lighter," I answer.

He reaches down as I lift up, our lips meeting. It's dizzying, and exhilarating, and this week has been too long without him. I never want to let him go.

He pulls back, resting his forehead against mine, still holding me. "So, now that this is all done, what do you plan on doing?" he whispers.

I brush my lips against his before pulling back. "I'm going to live."

CHAPTER
THIRTY-TWO

KAYLA

W e're following the hearse carrying Charlie at a slow speed. It's almost comforting as we approach the church.

Hannah weeps into her tissue as the crowd makes their way up to the church. "There are so many people."

"She was loved," I answer.

"Thank you for riding with us today. I know you had plans to drive with your boyfriend. It just didn't feel right you not being here with us. You were like a sister to our daughter."

"I'm happy to be here," I declare, my words breaking.

The car pulls to a stop, and Hannah reaches out to stop me from reaching for the door. "Charlie would have been so proud of what you did yesterday. It took courage to stand up and talk about what happened to you. We're sorry we couldn't be there to support you."

"I understand. I wish she could have been there." I sniff. "She's one of the reasons I found the courage to do it."

We spoke about my abuse during one of my visits to help with the funeral arrangements. She confided in me that she knew something was going on, which is why she phoned anonymously to social services. Her complaint went ignored, but she didn't know that until I said they never visited. She had been looking out for me the entire time because Charlie shared her fears. I didn't see it, but knowing now that they were, it means everything to me.

Mr Roberts clears his throat. "It looks like a lot of her friends have turned up."

I glance out the window, spotting people from when Charlie and I attended school together. I narrow my gaze, knowing some of them watched her get bullied. Not all were directly involved, but still, doing nothing about it makes them just as bad.

Hannah's breath hitches. "She would have loved to know this was her turnout."

At her words, I know I can't say anything. I can't tell her these people didn't know Charlie the way I did. None of them loved her the way I did or tried to help her when she was being bullied.

She deserves to give Charlie the best send off, and I think deep down, Charlie would be amused that they are here. Charlie used to joke about making it because she had haters.

The funeral director who I met a few days ago, opens the door for us. Myles is beside him, and I step out, taking his outreached hand.

"How are you doing?" he asks.

"I'm good," I whisper, and we step away as Hannah and Mr Roberts talk to the vicar and director. "There are so many people here."

"Denny sent out a message to everyone. Some are just here to be here, but some wanted to show their support. I think it's their way of making up for everything they did wrong."

Tears slip down my cheeks when I fail to keep them at bay. I told myself to wait until after, but hearing what they did for Charlie, I can't hold it in.

"She would have appreciated this more than you know. Even if their presence isn't sincere, the thought was there. They didn't get to know her when she was alive, so hopefully, after today, they'll get to know who she was."

"I feel useless that I can't do more than this," he grouches, glancing down at the cast. Today, he opted for the crutches, but I know Maverick will have the wheelchair at hand.

He's referring to carrying the coffin. To Hannah, using the pallbearers to carry Charlie's coffin down the aisle felt impersonal. She wanted people who cared for Charlie. I mentioned Hannah's troubles to Myles at a family dinner last night, and all of them jumped at the chance. Malik, Max, Mason and Maverick will all take a stand and help carry her down with Mr Roberts and his brother.

"But the fact that you would means everything," I assure him.

Hannah walks over to me. "It's time," she declares.

Myles leans down, capturing my lips with his. "You can do this."

"I'll see you in there," I shakily reply, and as he begins to make his way inside, I turn to Hannah. "I don't want to mess this up."

"You could never do that," she promises. "Are you ready?"

"Yes," I agree, and together, we make our way into the church. People openly stare as we make our way to the front of the church. We split up; Hannah leaves to take her pew, and I head up to the podium, where the vicar and a woman are waiting.

A woman working for the church gives me the nod, letting me know she's about to play the sweet melody of, *In the Arms of Angel* by Sarah McLachlan.

Mr Roberts and his brother come into view, and my words flow softly around the room. I sing about a second chance for a break, about memories seeping from my veins and about finding peace tonight. The words hit me to the core, and I hope after today, I do find peace knowing she is no longer is pain.

My voice breaks during the line about finding some comfort, and I hope with all of might, she has comfort up in Heaven.

The coffin is getting closer, and my voice breaks more. My best friend is lying in there, her soul now at rest.

Hannah weeps for her daughter and can be heard over the sweet melody. There isn't a dry eye in the house. And I know, another minute and I will crumble. Myles catches my gaze, and he's gives me that look. The one that tells me I've got this. I can do it.

They lower the coffin onto the stand as the last of the words flow from my lips. Her dad weeps as he joins his wife in the front pew.

The vicar stands beside me, and I know it's my cue to leave. I take the step down, and unable to stop myself, I lower my hand onto the coffin, where her head is resting inside.

"I will love you forever too," I whisper, answering her letter.

My knees are weak as I join Myles at the front. Her mum is beside me, clinging to her husband as the vicar begins his service.

I can't take my gaze away from the coffin. I hate that this is the end. My hope for her is that wherever she is, she gets to keep her memories. I wish for her to know we will be okay, and that she no longer needs to worry about her parents. But more, wherever she may be now, I want her to be happy and well.

I don't know what comes after death. But if there is life, I hope she gets everything she's ever dreamed of, and knows that we'd do anything to be able to share it with her.

Myles places his hand on my knee, gently applying pressure. Wrinkles form between his eyebrows when I glance up at him. "Baby, you need to do your speech," he whispers.

My stomach bottoms out as I slowly rise from the pew. When Hannah asked me to give a eulogy, I wanted to refuse. But she knew before this day came that she would never be giving one. Charlie had asked her not to, and instead asked that she give her eulogy whilst she was alive, and she could hear it. Her mum explained that Charlie didn't want anything left unsaid. She didn't want Hannah to regret the things she didn't say. So, in the privacy of their own home, they gave Charlie her wish and both read her their eulogies. She couldn't stand up there and do it herself. She said it was too painful, and not what Charlie would have wanted.

I reach the podium, my hands shaking as I unfold the piece of paper with the speech I prepared. But as I search the crowd of faces, seeing the people I love, and the people who loved Charlie, I can't bring myself to read the words I wrote. They don't celebrate the life she had or convey just what she means to me. I guess until now, I had been scared to really write down what I wanted.

"I've made two speeches in the past two days, and this one is by far the hardest," I begin. "You've heard the vicar talking about Charlie's life and the accomplishments she achieved, but they are just pieces of her. I could stand here today and tell you how great Charlie was, that she was beautiful inside and out, but for those who knew her, we already know that. We know how lucky we were to have her in our lives.

"So instead, I'm going to tell you what she meant to me. Because Charlie wasn't just my best friend; she was my sister, my confidant, my rock. She was the rainbow on a rainy day, stars on a dark night, and the breeze on a warm summer's day.

"She wrote me a letter that I received the day she died. She knew I would find it hard to say goodbye, and she was right. It's the hardest thing I've ever had to do.

"She told me I changed her life, and that we were supposed to meet when we did. But she changed mine. She made me realise how beautiful this world can be. Even in her darkest moment, she found light and shared it with those around her, to make them feel better," I choke out, the ache in my heart growing. I meet her parents' gaze, breaking when I see their anguish.

"You raised an incredible daughter. She had so much to give, and so much love to share. My world will be dimmer without her in it, but I promise to keep her last wish for me, and live life for the both of us," I confide, before turning back to the room.

"Charlie maybe gone, but she'll never be forgotten," I breathe out, struggling to find the next words. I glance down at the coffin, my tears falling in streams. "You will never be replaced. I will carry the memory of you for the rest of my days. You can rest easy now, my sweet Charlie. I love you. I miss you. For always."

I step back, needing five minutes as her mum wails over her loss. I cry harder, wishing I could go back and give her one last hug.

The vicar uses my breather to inform everyone that their donations made today will be going to the British Heart Foundation in Charlie's memory. He also lets them know organ donation forms are located at the entrance.

He finishes his speech with, "Charlie requested a special song to be sung by Kayla, one close to her heart. Please remain seated until she leads the procession out."

Thankfully, Myles could alter the music since I won't be able to sing all of the song and walk down the aisle. The plan is to sing half before leading the casket out, where we will then head to the burial plot.

Charlie picked Jessie J's *Flashlight*. The words are fitting, since I'm frightened of the things I don't know. I don't know what tomorrow will bring, or if this pain will ever ease. But it was Charlie's favourite song, and she would get me to sing it when she couldn't sleep.

The words are broken as I begin. The words hit me, their meaning different now she's gone, and I struggle to catch my breath.

I'm reaching my last verse when I hit the lyrics about being stuck in the dark. I rasp the word, flashlight, knowing that is what she was for me. She was the person who got me through my darkest days, shining her light so I didn't feel scared or alone.

Myles, ignoring the protocol, hops up onto the platform to meet me. I throw myself into his arms, sobbing uncontrollably.

He grips my face, resting his forehead against mine. "She would be so proud of you."

Jessie J still blares through the system, and Mark pushes the wheelchair over when the boys lift up the coffin. Myles drops down into the chair but doesn't let go of my hand as we follow her parents out. Mr Roberts is consoling his wife as she finally lets her grief out.

I only know a fraction of how they are feeling.

As they load her back into the hearse, I know in my heart that this isn't the end for us. We'll meet again.

Until then, I'm going to be brave.

I'm going to love.

I'm going to live.

EPILOGUE

KAYLA

It's been just over a month since Charlie's funeral, and every day has been hard without her. I've found myself reaching for my phone to call her, and it hits me all over again.

Tonight hasn't been any different. She would know exactly what to do and say to me.

I'm freaking out, and I don't know what to do. I drop down on the pile of clothes, feeling defeated.

When Myles invited me to our end of school prom, I assumed it was just a school party. I went to one back in year six, and everyone wore normal clothes. But then Harlow and Denny mentioned it was formal, but I've left it too late. There are no dresses in town, and now it's too late to do anything.

I don't want to let Myles down. He seemed so happy and excited. But I don't want to embarrass him by turning up in a summer dress that I outgrew years ago.

There's a knock on my bedroom door, and I panic, glancing at the time. Seeing it's too early for him to arrive, I call out, "Who is it?"

"It's me," Katie calls out.

I get up to unlock the door. Although my mum is no longer around to hurt me, my dad wanted to give me back some power and installed a bedroom lock on my door. He's spending more and more time with me, but tonight, they're sleeping over at Katie's. She knows I want Myles to sleep round without my dad checking in on us every two minutes. I'm glad for her interreference.

"Hey," I greet. "I thought you were sleeping at yours tonight?"

"We are," she promises, then holds up a white garment bag, and a smaller black one. "I bought you something."

"W-what? How?" I ask in awe.

Can she read minds?

She grins. "Myles called saying Denny told him you didn't have a dress. He knew you would be stressing, so he called me and asked if I could help."

I melt at her words. "He did?"

God, I love him. I really do.

"You have it bad, sweetie," she teases, and I don't bother to deny it. "Anyway, I have a friend who runs a shop making dresses. Myles said it was a 'Far Away' theme. The dress is more fairy-tale-like, but it will work. She promised other girls who ordered theirs had something similar."

"I don't know what to say," I reply. "Thank you."

My mum would never have done anything like that for me. Katie hasn't known me long, but she has proved over and over that she can be trusted. We actually get on better than me and my dad.

"It's no bother," she promises, and hangs the dress up on the back of the door. She unhooks the zip, revealing the stunning ballgown. "What do you think?"

"I love it," I breathe, running my finger along the waist.

The top half is a tight-fitted, forest green bodice that gives off a fairy vibe. It has petals and a floral pattern that disappears into the waist. It flares out, dropping elegantly to the floor.

"It's beautiful," I whisper, my throat tightening. I give it one more last glance, before pulling her in for a hug, surprising her. "Thank you so much."

"It was my pleasure," she promises, squeezing me a little.

I pull back and twiddle a strand of wet hair around my finger. "Now I just need to do something with this and learn how to do makeup."

She smiles wide. "That is where I come in," she declares, holding up a carrier I didn't see before. "By the time I'm done with you, Myles won't recognise you."

Tears gather in my eyes as she steers me over to the chair. This is everything I ever wanted. For someone to guide me, to love me, to support me.

After she sits me down, it's a whirlwind. She does magic with my hair, pulling it back into a neat but loose bun. A thick braid drops from my parting before reaching back to fall over the bun. She even blow-dried a sweeping fringe for the same side, making it look more stunning. It's beautiful, and something I would never have attempted to do.

I stand, glancing in the mirror when she finishes my makeup. She kept it light on my face, only adding a little blush and shimmer. My eyes, however, she went all out on. She gave them a smoky look with a shimmer of green, and added some black charcoal eyeliner that has my green eyes popping. I've never looked like this before, and I can't look away from the mirror.

She helps me out of the dressing gown she used to protect my dress, and I marvel once again at how beautiful it is. Not even my cleavage showing could make me take this off.

"You look absolutely beautiful," she gushes.

"Thank you. I feel it," I admit, my voice barely a whisper as I run my hands down the gown.

I hear a rustle behind me and turn to find Katie going through the black bag she brought with her. She turns back to me, finding what she needs.

"Hold your hand out," she gently orders.

I do, and she clips a bangle around my wrist. The black band has diamonds inside, and it sparkles in the light.

"Oh God," I gush, holding it up.

The doorbell echoes into the house and my stomach flutters. "Turn around," she orders, more in a rush now. I do, and she clasps a necklace around my neck.

I glance in the mirror at the beautiful black diamond chain holding a beautiful emerald green diamond. It fits snugly over my breastbone, and I reach up, touching the stunning piece.

"It's perfect," I whisper. "Thank you so much, Katie. I don't know what I would have done without you."

The doorbell goes again, and she laughs, passing me my clutch, which already has my phone, keys and money inside.

Banging echoes on the door, and she groans. "One last thing," she demands, and sprays my neck and wrists with perfume. "Now, let's go before your dad needs to buy a new door."

I laugh and follow her out. Dad didn't seem bothered about the door being broken when we arrived back from the hospital, but he did get stressed when it took them weeks to fit a new one.

We reach the door and pull it open. Myles is about to knock again but stops mid-swing and gapes at the sight of me. "Holy fucking Christ."

"And my job here is done," Katie teases. She leans up, kissing my cheek. "Have fun, and call me if you need anything. If we don't speak to you before, we'll see you tomorrow."

"Thank you for all of this," I tell her.

"My pleasure."

She brushes past Myles, who is still gaping. I lamely wave. "Hey."

"You are breath-taking," he replies earnestly. "You look absolutely stunning."

I run my hand along the flare of my dress and duck my head. "Thank you," I whisper. "You look handsome."

"Ruggedly handsome?" he teases, bringing up our conversation from weeks ago.

I laugh and take his outstretched hand. "Yes. You look ruggedly handsome."

And he does. He's wearing his black tuxedo, and he even has a green handkerchief sticking out of his breast pocket that matches my dress.

He growls as his arms go around my waist. "I wish we didn't need to leave. It's selfish of me, but I want to keep you to myself."

I grin and kiss the tip of his nose. "It would be wrong to let this dress go to waste. Plus, Katie made me look pretty."

"You always look pretty," he declares.

"Come on!" Max yells. "Dude, the party's waiting for me to arrive."

I peek out behind Myles and laugh at Max leaning out of the sunroof of the black, sleek limo.

"Remind me again why we decided to limo share with him," Myles groans.

"Because he has detachment issues," I tease.

I'm only half lying. Since Myles got hit by the car, Max has been insufferable. So much so, he refused to book another limo. I understand his anxiety over Myles; it took me weeks to stop having nightmares that he died.

"Thankfully, he has his date to distract him," he retorts as I close the door behind me.

"You mean three," I amend.

Max didn't want one date. He wanted three. How he managed to get three girls to agree is beyond me, but he did. Fortunately for us, we only have to deal with the one in the limo. Because whilst Max likes variety, he isn't picky; much like he is with his food.

"Hot fucking damn." Max whistles, eyeing me up and down as we approach. "I'll ditch my dates and take you to prom if you ditch yours. I am the better looking one."

I roll my eyes. "Max, you have no chance," I mumble as Myles open the door. I take his hand and he helps me inside, careful not to ruin my dress. I'm just about to shuffle over when Myles replies.

"Stare at my girlfriend again, and I'll leave you here," he warns.

"Shit, sorry. I get horny when I've had a drink," he admits, and Myles slides in next to me as Max drops back down into the limo.

His date is at the other end of the limo, taking selfies and ignoring the rest of us. She looks stunning in her ruby red, tight-fitting dress. She wears it with confidence, unlike me. Glitter has been sprayed on her chest, which she has managed to get shots of. Her makeup is flawlessly done, and it doesn't look like it will move.

I fiddle with the material of my dress, not feeling as confident as I did a minute ago.

"You look beautiful. Stop fussing," Myles demands, his lips brushing the lobe of my ear.

I shiver, my eyelids drooping. "I'll try. I'm nervous." When he pulls back, he meets my gaze, his pupils dilated. "What?"

"I can't stop looking at you. You've always been beautiful to me, but tonight, you are glowing," he reveals. "You look happy."

I lean into him. "That's because I am."

He kisses me, and I get lost in the kiss. I know that no matter where life takes me now, I'll do it with Myles by my side. We're forever.

MYLES

I never thought I could love Kayla more than I already did, but each day, I love her more. She took my breath away tonight in her green dress. I'd never seen anyone more beautiful or radiant in that moment, so I captured the moment, wanting to hold on to it forever.

Seeing her tonight, laughing and dancing, she looked free. When I snapped a photo as Max swung her around, I knew I'd spend the rest of my life making sure she stayed that happy.

The night is over, and we're back in Kayla's bedroom. She excused herself to get out of her dress, and I used the time to strip out of my suit. As much as I want to look good for Kayla, I'm not a fan of wearing it.

I want to remember tonight forever.

The door slowly creaks open, and I glance up, about to ask what took her so long, but the words get trapped in my throat.

I sit up, my jaw dropping at the strapless bra and lace knickers she has on.

Fuck me!

"W-what?" I stutter, too lost for words.

Seeming pleased, she walks over to the bed and stands between my legs. "I'm ready Myles. I know prom night is a cliché, but I can't imagine a more perfect night to do this."

"Are you sure?"

"Yes. I want to wake up tomorrow and be able to say you were my first and my last. I love you, Myles. I loved you yesterday, and I'll love you more tomorrow. You taught me a touch can be gentle. You gave me the courage to explore. I want you. And I want to give you this."

"Baby, whether we have sex today or next year, it doesn't matter. You'll always be my one and only."

"And you'll always be mine," she whispers as she climbs onto my lap, straddling my thighs.

I grip her hips and groan as her lips touch the side of my neck.

Holy fucking shit.

I run my hand up the curve of her back and pull back to meet her gaze. "Same rules as last time. If at any point you want to stop, you tell me. You need me to go slow, tell me."

"And if I want you to go fast?" she brazenly remarks.

I groan, slamming my lips down on hers. She rolls her hips as I deepen the kiss, and I struggle not to combust in my pants.

I meant what I said when I told her it didn't matter when we had sex, but I won't deny I haven't imagined it a thousand times over.

And it's better than I could ever conjure up.

"You're so fucking beautiful, it hurts."

"So are you," she rasps.

I reach around, unclipping her bra with a slip of my fingers. She inhales as it falls to her waist. I lean in, unable to look away, as I close my mouth around her nipple.

She moans, her sex rubbing against my dick. My body trembles with anticipation, but also from the pressure. I want this to be good for her. I want her to dream about it, to think about it, and use it to chase away all her demons.

I'm also scared I'll do it wrong. Contrary to popular belief, I've actually only slept with one girl, and I was too drunk to remember it. I regretted it almost immediately, and even more so now since I never thought Kayla would come back into my life. It happened not long after she moved out of town.

I love her.

And I'll love her until my dying breath. Some people may say we're too young, but I beg to differ. We're never too young. Kayla and I are just blessed we found each other now, instead of finding love later in life. I know what I want, and I know how I feel.

She's my forever. My always. My only.

Her wetness seeps through the thin materials separating us, and I growl low in my throat. In a haze of lust-filled pleasure, I pick her up effortlessly at the waist and stand.

I'm glad I took my boot off when I did. I'm not supposed to since it needs a few more weeks to heal, but I didn't want to risk kicking her with it in our sleep. I wouldn't have been able to lay her down on the bed and climb up between her thighs with it on.

For minutes, we both explore each other with our mouths, and remove the last of our clothing. I lick, nip, and bathe every inch of her body with attention.

Our kiss turns hungry, and neither of us let up for air. She clings to my hair, pulling at it, and my dick twitches against her flesh, almost making me come undone.

"Are you sure?" I rasp.

Vulnerable want, need and desire stares back at me in her big, green, doe eyes.

God, I love her.

She nods, unable to find her words as I kiss the corner of her mouth. "I need to hear you say the words, babe."

"Yes," she shivers, gripping my hips with her thighs. "I'm sure."

I rise to my knees and run my hands down her stomach, my

tanned skin a contrast against her pale flesh. My hands feel rough against her soft skin, but my touch seems to be lighting a fire inside her. Her breathing is heavy, and she watches me through heavy-lidded eyes.

I rub my tip over her clit, loving the mewling sound that slips through her lips. When I position my dick at her entrance though, it's me who hesitates. I'm afraid I'll mess it up.

"Please, Myles. Don't treat me like I'm made of glass," she pleads, her words shaky.

"I've only done this once, and I'm ashamed to admit, I don't remember it," I rasp, bowing my head.

She exhales, reaching up to cup my jaw. I meet her gaze, and I melt into her touch. "I'm nervous too. We can learn together," she promises. "If it feels this good now, it's only going to be mind-blowing when we have sex."

I groan at her choice of words. "Don't use that word right now."

"We can do this," she assures me.

I don't want her to be surprised by my size, so I gently coat my fingers in her desire and slowly thrust them inside her.

Her back arches, her moan echoing off the walls. I push her further, scissoring them inside her until I can feel she is ready.

I slide them out of her and bring them to my mouth, sucking off her taste. Her eyes widen, but I can tell it's turned her on.

Reaching down between us, I line my erection up at her entrance, but then I remember. "Shit, I don't have a condom."

She reaches under the pillow, presenting me with one. She smirks sheepishly. "It was just in case."

"Liar. You were planning to seduce me all along," I tease.

"Maybe."

She loses the smile once I line up at her entrance. Her forehead creases, and I lean down, kissing the corner of her mouth. "Relax."

"I'm nervous," she admits.

I gently push the tip inside her, and she inhales sharply, her walls clamping around my dick. I know from the sensation that I'm not going to last. I'm going to embarrass myself.

"Is that okay?"

"More," she whispers. I push in more, and she whimpers. "It stings a little, but it doesn't hurt."

"Then you need to relax."

"I don't know how to."

And I love her even more. Only we could be talking about this. I capture her lips, and once I feel her body relax against me, I push in more.

She cries out in pleasure. "Oh God."

She rocks her hips to meet each thrust, and I let her, wanting her to set the pace. She squirms more the faster I go, and my balls tighten each time.

I reach down, pressing my thumb over her clit, and rub in slow, circular moments. Her chest rises and falls, her tits bouncing with each thrust, and it's more than I can take.

"Keep your eyes on me, baby," I demand. My words spur her on, and she clenches around my dick like a vice. "I love you."

"Oh God," she cries, her core tightening around me.

My throat clogs with emotion at the sight of her orgasming. Her eyes are wild with desire, her cheeks flushed, but it's her expression, one filled with pleasure, that undoes me. Her lips part in bewilderment, and I can feel her love for me in my soul.

I come undone, my release tearing through me, and wave after wave of pleasure rolls over me like I've never experienced before.

And I know I'll never forget this moment.

After a few seconds of catching my breath, I drop down beside her. I discard the condom, throwing it in the bin.

It's only when I lie back down beside her that I notice tears rolling down her temples.

"Talk to me. Did I hurt you?" I stress, my gut bottoming out. I was careful not to lose control.

She cups my cheeks. "Never. For once, these are happy tears," she reveals, and I relax against her touch. "You gave me back control, Myles. I never knew love like this existed until you. You showed me what it was like to be loved. I was scared to be touched before you. I never thought I'd ever be intimate with anyone. But you made me feel safe. You took my worst nightmare and turned it into something special. Because when I think of my first time, it won't be what happened to me. It will be this. It will be this moment. It will be you. I love you, Myles. I love you more than you could ever imagine."

I brush her hair away from her face and kiss her. "I promise to never tarnish the gift you gave me tonight. I promise to love you until my last breath. I'm yours, Kayla. And I'll always be yours. I love you."

She rests her hand over my chest and lays her head on my shoulder as I rest back against the pillows. "I don't want this night to end."

"We have forever," I promise as I run my fingers through her hair.

Neither of us speak again, both content to hold each other. It's Kayla who falls asleep first, and I drift off listening to her breathing.

I feel like I've only had a few hours' sleep when the ringing of my phone stirs me awake. Kayla's naked body is pressed against me, and for a minute, I marvel in her beauty.

My phone stops ringing, only to start up again seconds later.

Kayla moans, pressing further into the cushions. "Make it stop," she grumbles.

I reach over to the windowsill and grab my phone. I glance down at the screen, and my nose twitches when I see it's Maverick.

"This better be good. It's," I pause for a minute to look at the clock before continuing, "four in the morning."

"Myles, I need you to come outside…" Maverick begins, and I sit up, hearing the news.

Shit.

Kayla's is on alert as I end the call to grab my trousers from the floor. She flips the light on, her face a mask of concern.

"What's going on? Is everything okay?"

I pause with my shirt in my hand. "I have to go."

"I'll come with you," she declares, and sits up, keeping the blanket close to her chest.

I press my lips against hers. "I'm sorry, but I don't know how long I'll be. I'll be back as soon as I can," I inform her, hating that I need to go. I don't want her to feel abandoned after our night together, but I have no choice.

"What's going on? What's happened?"

"It's Max," I reveal, pausing to meet her wide-eyed gaze. "He's been arrested."

THE END

ACKNOWLEDGMENTS

I love and hate writing these. This hasn't changed during the time I've been writing, and I don't think it ever will.

I never know quite what to say to express how I'm feeling. The gratitude I have for those who continue to read this series never fails to amaze me. You opened up your hearts to these characters and have shown them so much love. It's inspiring.

Re-writing these books was nostalgic as much as it was eye opening. There are things I never got to say, and things that never got published due to formatting errors. But I feel like this is everything the book should have been from the beginning. There are new scenes, new content, and fresh works to enjoy, and I hope I haven't disappointed anyone by doing this.

There's a long road ahead of me to get these done, but I can finally start to see the light at the end of the tunnel.

Myles' was the second book I wrote that had true events in. But it was the first book I wrote where I expressed my own grief and feelings.

Donna Mansell is still an inspiration to me thirteen years later. She fought until her last dying breath, and I'll never forget her strength. I will never forget her.

I want to take a minute to relay my original acknowledgement and thank all of those people who helped me. Charlotte Perry, my sister from another mister, and my long-time best friend: Thank you. You cheered me on and supported me throughout this entire series, and I'll always be forever grateful for you.

Thank you to Rachel, who became my online assistant. She helped me with release parties, blog posts and everything else in between. I couldn't have done it without her. Literally. I sucked at doing it.

To Cassy Roop, who has designed my covers for years now: thank you. You take a simple picture and bring my books to life, each and every time. It hasn't changed over the years, and there is no replacing you. I love you, and I'm sad our time working together will be nearing the end soon enough.

But these new editions wouldn't have been possible if it wasn't for Stephanie Farrant. When she offered to do these for me, I was blown away by her kindness and generosity. She believed in me even when I didn't believe in myself. Without her support, this wouldn't have been possible.

And thank you to Michelle Carder, who has become such a great friend. My books brought us together, but it's our friendship that keeps us together. I am forever grateful for your kindness, your help, and for everything that you do. You are a remarkable woman, and I am so glad I get to call you a friend.

Thank you to all the readers, whether you are original or new. I'll never stop being grateful for your support and kind words. I have the best readers, and I will argue with anyone who says otherwise.

Please think about leaving a review on Amazon or the appropriate platform. The book is nearly eight years old and could really benefit from some love.

Until the next one…

ALSO BY LISA HELEN GRAY

Carter Brother Series

Malik ~ Book One

Mason ~ Book Two

Myles ~ Book Three

Evan ~ Book 3.5

Max ~ Book Four

Maverick ~ Book Five

Forgiven Series

Better Left Forgotten ~ Book One

Obsession ~ Book Two

Forgiven ~ Book Three

Whithall Series

Foul Play ~ Book One (Willow and Cole's Book)

Wish It Series

If I could I'd Wish It All Away ~ Book One (Standalone)

ABOUT THE AUTHOR

Lisa Helen Gray is Amazon's bestselling author of the Forgotten Series and Carter Brother series.

She loves hanging out, but most of all, curling up with a good book or watching movies. When she's not being a mom, she's been a writer and a blogger.

She loves writing romance novels, ones with a HEA and has a thing for alpha males.

I mean, who doesn't!

Just an ordinary girl surrounded by extraordinary books.

Printed in Great Britain
by Amazon

45123632R00199